The Night They Came For Til

*A battle scarred midwife fights
to protect an innocent child.*

Rebekah Lee Jenkins

This book is dedicated to Azelin, with all my love.

Chapter One

I woke up on a ship sailing west with a note from Malcolm, money, clothes, and my doctor's bag. That was it. The list of what I didn't have was longer. My eyes slid shut as I tried to block out the thought.

A week and a half at sea and I still couldn't bring myself to open the note. I was afraid of what it said. My hands shook with terror thinking that Til may be dead. There was no way to manage that thought. The fragile grip holding my sanity would slip; I would be lost. Wincing with pain, I went to my doctor's bag and pulled out the laudanum and the note. A slow, long sip of laudanum, much more than the suggested fifteen drops, swirled through my veins and unlocked the pain, taking the sharp edges away from my thoughts.

I ran my fingers over Malcolm's handwriting, anything to be close to him. I picked up the note to see if I could smell his aftershave.

A knock on the door interrupted my thoughts.

"Your supper, Miss Stone," the steward shouted through the door.

I put the laudanum bottle on top of the note and went to the door to retrieve my tray. I wondered how much Malcolm had paid this little man to serve me my meals so I could stay alone in my berth.

"Thank you." I gave him a tip. I tipped him every day because he was the only thing preventing me from starving to death. Most days I couldn't stand the thought of facing anyone.

I alternated between worrying about where the ship was taking me and not caring. Some were speaking about Canada—I shut their voices out. I was so sick I wanted to die, then I wanted to fight something, and in the end, I lay there day after day, as my body slowly healed. The bruises were fading; the cuts were healing. Before long, I could sit without wincing in pain. My body was young and resilient; inexorably it healed and left my mind far behind, still broken.

Fragments of the past came back to me, often when I was sleeping. The memories would make me wake screaming. If I thought of the attack, it made me sick to my stomach. After calculating dates to figure out how long I had been at sea, my mind stubbornly refused to acknowledge the fact that my time of menstruation had not occurred yet. My hands shook as I carefully went through the numbers again. Cold sweat of sheer terror soaked through my bodice as the realization sunk in that I was pregnant. My mind raced back to the attack; I couldn't stop it.

***

The night they came for Til, Malcolm found me half in the gutter and half on the street. He closed his eyes and turned away so I couldn't see the horror on his face. Then he pulled off his coat, bundled me up, and carried me to a hospital where he knew a doctor.

"Where's Til?" he asked through clenched teeth before placing me on a gurney.

"She told me to run. I shouldn't have," I wept.

His eyes met the doctor's.

"I trust you, Joshua, take extra care," Malcolm said

in a voice so low the doctor leaned in to hear him.

I drifted in and out of consciousness. I wanted to scream and never stop.

"No expense spared. Do you understand what I'm saying?" Malcolm demanded.

Joshua must have nodded because I didn't hear him say anything at all to that except, "I'll look after it."

**

Can I prove that The Society for the Suppression of Vice ordered this attack? No, I cannot. My body doesn't care; my mind can't comprehend it.

Pregnant with my attacker's baby, my mind was fragmented with disbelief. The dates did not lie. Finally, I took another deep swig of laudanum and opened the letter.

September 30th, 1904

Dear Shannon,

It is with a heavy heart that I send this letter to you. Putting you on that ship with no one to assist you is one of the hardest things I've ever done. I wish we were right there with you. Someday we will all be together again. It's a promise.

In July, Til received a letter from a close friend, Lady Madeline Harper. She had asked Til to send a midwife to Oakland, Manitoba, Canada. At the time Til was going to say no, as you were already enrolled for the school year. In light of recent events, I have sent instruction that you are to be that midwife. I have already sent your qualifications, including your two years of training at the

London School of Medicine for Women and date of arrival. Lord Harper has assured me the town constable has been retained to ensure you are protected at every step of this journey. You will have your own home, so you will have privacy to study and heal in the months ahead.

Til has been incarcerated on charges of the promotion of vice. The pamphlets detailing the proper use of birth control were traced to her clinic. I suspect the printer we switched to handed her name to the Society. Her trial date has not yet been set. I have established a legal team, and she will be exonerated in due time and with due process. Do not worry yourself for her. She has the finest legal minds at her disposal.

It is Til's wish that you are not here for this "circus" as she calls it. It is her sincere desire that you have a long and prestigious medical career. She is concerned that your reputation as a doctor would be muddied by this attack. It is her wish that you remain in Canada until we have this settled.

The clinic was burned to the ground at the time of attack, so there is no need to worry about who will care for the premises.

I know that you have been through a horrendous ordeal and I am so sorry, Shannon. I am hoping that Lady Harper will take care of you as you take care of her in her time of need. I will find the men who did this and I will deal with them to the fullest extent of the law.

Know that we love you and care for you. I will keep you apprised of all matters relating to your aunt. If you want for anything, do not hesitate to ask. I understand Lady Harper's husband is most reasonable and generous. I trust they will care for you, as you are so easy to love.

I'm so sorry about the interruption of your education. We will arrange for you to continue your studies next year after Lady Harper's baby is born.

I hope your travel has been as pleasant as possible. A letter will be ready for you when you arrive.

With Love,
Malcolm

Pain sliced through my heart. Right then, in that moment, I needed Malcolm. He was the only father I knew. I understood his whole life would revolve around Til's trial, and I couldn't help with that. A staunch supporter of the Malthusian league, Til faced two years in prison for educating women on how to use diaphragms and various other means of birth control. She had worried about the new printer but had no choice. The women we helped couldn't read and needed diagrams. The Society for the Suppression of Vice believed the diagrams were obscene. Her trial would be a long, bloody battle. Grudgingly, I saw the wisdom in getting me out of England to preserve my professional reputation.

I reread the letter, the part about how my attackers would be prosecuted to the fullest extent of the law.

I wished that promise healed my heart.

***

I arrived in Brandon after traveling across Canada. I was weary and so thin my clothes didn't fit. Two long weeks ago, I had run out of nux vomica and I couldn't keep anything down. During the day, I refused to think about it. Only at night, when I had no control over my thoughts, the images came back. I desperately tried to push it out of my mind.

I sat, freezing to death in a train station, in what looked like the middle of a frozen wilderness. How could it be this cold? It was only the middle of November! I put my head between my legs since I worried I would throw up again. My throat was raw from the frequent vomiting. When my stomach finally settled, I got up and wandered to the window.

As I did so, a man approached. He was wearing a uniform and stood over six feet tall with broad shoulders. I hoped this wasn't the constable. The sheer size of him terrified me, until he smiled; his hazel eyes crinkled at the corners. He came closer, that smile genuine and warm. I tried to smile back, but instead I vomited. All over his shoes. I groaned with mortification and wished for the ground to open up and swallow me.

It didn't.

Chapter Two

"Miss Shannon Stone?" He handed me a handkerchief to clean my mouth. "I'm Cole McDougall, the constable from Oakland. It is so nice to meet you."

"Nice to meet you, too," I replied, still hunched over. If I stood up too soon I would be sick again, so I stayed this way until I felt the nausea subside. I wanted to die, and he took the whole thing in stride as if people vomited on his shoes every day of the week.

"Are you sick, Miss Stone?" His voice was deep, sincere, and concerned. He handed me another clean handkerchief, which I took gratefully. It had been a long, dirty journey.

"Please, call me Shannon." I couldn't look at him. Instead I dropped to my knees to clean his shoes with the handkerchief. He crouched down and took the vomit-stained cloth from my hands.

"It's alright. There is no need." He helped me back up, adjusting my coat so I would be warmer. "Since your train was late and the stage coach driver had to leave an hour ago, I am going to take you to a hotel. I hope that will be alright?"

"Sure," I said. Terror made my throat clench. "I think I should lie down before I fall down."

He smiled at me and my sad attempt at being casual.

"Of course. You just have a seat on the bench. I'll

load up your bags, and we'll get you settled right away," he said cheerfully.

I tried to smile because he was trying hard to put me at ease. Somehow he had his shoes cleaned and my bags loaded in record time and then we were on our way to the hotel.

"Hotel" was hardly the word I would have used for my accommodations. He escorted me through a lobby and up some stairs to a room with a sheet for a wall. I looked at him in alarm.

"This was all that was available, but I'll be staying in the next room," he said in a hurry.

"Oh." I forced a smile.

My "room" was against the side of the building, and the wall glistened with something. Upon further inspection, I realized it was ice.

Mercy... ice on the walls! I'm not going to survive the night.

The room had a bed, a tiny coal stove heater, along with the sheet that was supposed to be the other wall. I didn't want to think about what was on that sheet. Since the attack, men made me nervous to the point of terror.

A sheet will not stop a man from coming in here.

I felt the cold tendrils of panic creep up and close my throat as I took in my surroundings. Cole's size concerned me— he was so tall and broad, he filled the room. He put my trunk down on the floor and then straightened up. I thought of asking him to step back, outside the room until the panic subsided. Instead, I moved to the corner and created as much space be-tween us as I could. He could tell I was afraid of him and moved away from the door so I wouldn't feel trapped. I could easily bolt if I needed to. Seeing a clear path out of this abomination of a room helped me calm down.

"I need to apologize." He set my doctor's bag down beside the trunk. "This is not a hotel I would pick, but when the train was late, this was the only place I could find. I'm sorry. I know it's terrible, and when Lady Harper finds out you spent the night here, she will have me flogged before Lord Harper fires me. Can I get you anything, though? A bath perhaps?"

Mortification made my face flush red. Not only had I vomited on him, I clearly smelled so strong he was suggesting a bath.

"Is it that bad?"

"I can tell it's been a long journey," he said tactfully. He moved to put coal in the little stove and turned his back to me, giving me time to stop blushing. I appreciated his attempts to allow me to retain some semblance of dignity.

"Is it possible?" My spirit soared at the suggestion.

"Let me see what I can do." He left to see about my bath.

My hair didn't move when I took the pins out. I grimaced at my reflection. My stomach was fine for the moment, and I wanted to scrub myself clean in a real bath. I felt dirty in ways a bath wouldn't help, but there was no use thinking about that.

Cole knocked on the door.

"Please, come in," I said timidly.

"I spoke to the proprietor. If you get your things together and follow me, I'll take you to the bath area."

"Oh, thank you! I didn't want to meet Lady Harper looking like this. I really appreciate this."

"Of course, I'm going to stay outside to be sure no

one comes in. They aren't used to ladies in this, uh, establishment. They screened off a section for you, and I'll guard it. It's the best I can do, and I promise, no one will bother you on my watch." His wide smile crinkled his eyes again. His smile was so genuine, so sincere. I could tell he was trying to put me at ease, and it was working.

I didn't have much choice but to believe he would take care of things, so I gathered my bath things and a fresh dress. He led me down a narrow, dark hallway.

When we arrived, it was clear the screened-off area was not secure. There were men on the other side of the screen! I stopped walking forward as nausea filled my stomach. Cole mistook my hesitation as embarrassment.

"I don't think I can do this," I said and wiped the cold sweat off my forehead. "There has to be fifteen men in here. What if they... how would you..."

"I can say with certainty that you will be fine. No need to fear."

I hesitated but saw the steaming bath and couldn't stand the thought of going to bed dirty again.

"I promise you, you're safe." He straightened his shoulders. "No one is coming through this screen. I guarantee it. Including me."

"You're sure?"

"Don't rush. Take all the time you want."

I sank into the bath and soaked my hair, soaped it three times, and left the soap on to cut through the grime. I scrubbed and scrubbed until every inch of my skin was pink and then soaked some more. Despite my surroundings, this felt like heaven. For the first time since the attack, I felt tension leave my shoulders. I became self-conscious that I'd made him wait too long. I pulled a bucket of fresh water off the floor and poured it over my head.

As soon as I poured the last bucket of clean water over my head, I felt nauseated. I quickly pulled a towel around me and sat on a pail. I didn't move for a few minutes and then felt like I was going to throw up again. *There is nothing to throw up! How is this possible?*

I grabbed the empty water bucket and felt my stomach heave.

"Miss Stone, are you alright?" I heard the concern in his voice.

"No," I moaned and started vomiting again. Nothing came up despite my body's efforts. I waited for the feeling to subside and then rinsed my mouth. Of course, that started it all over again. The men on the other side of the screen were quiet for a minute. *He said my name. They know I am in here.* Fear pooled in my stomach, causing me to dry heave even more.

Slowly, I crept to the window and breathed in the cool drafts of air. Then, for the first time in my life, I fainted dead away.

When I came to, Cole was standing over me. He covered me in a towel and with great care, he moved the towel with me as I curled to my side.

"I'm taking you to a doctor," he said with finality.

"I don't need a doctor. I am almost a doctor," I protested in exhaustion.

"You don't have a choice," he said so firmly I squinted up at him. "Almost doctors can't write prescriptions. You're going to a doctor, and that's final. I tried to find a woman to help you dress, but there isn't one. You're stuck with me."

Bossy.

I groaned again and pressed my face into the icy cold floorboards.

"I have never been so embarrassed in my entire life," I whined, not caring that I sounded like a spoiled child.

"Me neither," he countered as he produced another towel to make sure my chest and shoulders were covered. "A night like tonight, I'd be playing cards and having a whiskey with the guys. Here I am in a bath house with a girl who can't keep any food down."

As I tried to get off the floor, he quickly rendered assistance by taking me by the upper arms and carefully pulling me up onto my feet.

"We're all in this together. You're going to a doctor and you can come with me of your own volition or I'll drag you. No one terrifies me more than Lady Madeline Harper. If you die on me, I'll have to answer to her, and already I'm in trouble when she hears about this hotel. I'd like to keep my list of offenses to a minimum."

He helped me dress as he talked; part of me knew it was to calm me down and distract me from what was happening. His hands were as impersonal as a doctor's. He knew his way around the labyrinth of woman's clothing, which disturbed me a bit.

It shouldn't matter if he knows his way around a corset, for heaven's sake! I chastised myself. He was being professional; I should be, too.

Finally, he took a towel and gently squeezed all the water out of my hair and then wiped my face.

"If I had a bit of bread, that might help settle my stomach," I suggested timidly, feeling like a burden.

"I can't leave you here." He glanced anxiously at

the screen separating us from the men, the *many* men, on the other side.

"No, I know that." My eyes widened in fear. Nausea washed over me yet again, and I sat down with my head between my knees.

He waited patiently and then crouched down beside me.

Once the nausea subsided, I pulled my head up.

"I really don't want to go to the doctor." Futile, but I gave it one last stab.

"Well, you're going," he said bluntly.

"I just don't feel comfortable with this."

He waited, and I started to feel cold sweat under my arms and at the back of my neck.

"I've never been to a male doctor before. My aunt is a doctor, I've only been examined by her."

"There's a first time for everything." He dismissed my protests.

I could tell he was used to taking control and getting his way.

"I don't want to have a man... examine me... it's silly..."

"Very silly. We're going. Shall I carry you downstairs?"

"I can walk." I stood up on shaky legs while he hovered, in case I collapsed again. I wiped at the cold sweat at my neck, and he frowned.

"You are really pale." He lifted his hand to check my forehead.

I cringed and ducked.

He took a step back.

"I was just going to check to see if you have a fever." His voice was very quiet, very calm. "You are safe with me, Shannon. I am never going to hurt you."

I moved back further and took a deep breath.

"I'm sorry. I'm just jumpy today, I guess." One tear had escaped my right eye, so I casually tried to brush it away in hopes that he hadn't seen it.

He saw it. The frustration that had been surfacing in his eyes softened to sympathy.

"This is a lot to... it's a lot to take in... I'm sorry I am reacting out of character... of course you aren't going to hurt me, what a thought..."

Stop prattling, Shannon!

Cole said nothing while I stood up straighter. He patiently waited until I gave him some indication that I was alright. I smiled to let him know the panic was over.

"Good." He smiled broadly.

I tried to find a reason to stall, but could think of nothing. *If I clung to a door frame would he just peel my fingers off and carry me out of this 'hotel'?* He looked determined enough, so I didn't risk it.

Once in the lobby, I moved closer to him as we passed the saloon connected to the hotel. I strained to see beyond the swinging doors. The men sounded drunk already. He frowned as a scuffle broke out and a man was thrown out of the saloon into the lobby. He landed about three feet from me. Cole took my arm and quickly moved me behind him. Before he could intervene, another man dragged the drunk off the floor and pulled him back into the saloon. The eyes of the drunk man flicked over me, so I quickly ducked back behind Cole. Cautiously, when I was sure they were back in the saloon, I peeked around Cole's arm in time to see the doors swing shut behind them.

"I think now is a good time to beg you not to recount anything that happens here to Lady Harper." Cole placed a hand at the small of my back to guide me to the waiting carriage.

"I won't say a thing," I promised.

"Good, before we go, you need to put this on."

He pulled out a very ugly knit hat and handed it to me.

"Not on your life."

"Listen, it is brutally cold outside, and your hair is wet." His lips were thin from the effort of keeping his patience. At some point his patience would be exhausted, so I took the hat and pulled it on.

Very gently, he tucked any stray wet hair up under the hat. Satisfied that all my wet hair was safely tucked away, he pulled the hat down securely over my ears. Next, he produced a scarf uglier than the hat. He wound it around me so only my eyes were showing. He carefully tucked the scarf into my coat.

"There we are." He smiled, clearly satisfied with his handiwork. "Now you are ready to face the Manitoba winter. Let's go."

The cold's icy fingers found any exposed skin and quickly froze it, making me grateful for the hat and scarf. The intensity of the icy air made me feel stiff as Cole lifted me out of the carriage.

Inside the hospital, we waited by a wood stove. He laid his hand on my cheek.

"You feel warmer. While we wait, you should try to get your hair dried out."

I took off the hideous hat and scarf. By the time the doctor was available, my hair was partially dry. I wiped the palms of my hands against the skirt of my dress as I looked at the doctor with fear.

"Don't make me do this," I whispered to Cole.

"Do you want me to go in with you?" His head tilted to the side, forehead creased with concern. I could tell he was worried I might completely fall apart.

"No." I didn't want him to know I was attacked exactly six weeks ago and made pregnant by that attack. What would he think? Would he leave me here? Would he react with disgust? Would he listen to the reason?

The nurse beckoned me in.

"Dr. Clark will see you now," she said.

I stood up, so weak with fear of being examined by a man that I swayed. Cole caught me and carried me into the room. The room was small. Two walls and then two sheets pulled together to form some semblance of privacy. These people seemed to use sheets constantly.

"Are you her husband?" the doctor asked Cole.

"No, I am escorting her to Oakland in the morning," Cole answered politely. "I'll be right outside the door if you need me."

The doctor was thorough. I tried hard not to cry as he felt my stomach.

"Are you married?" His lip curled with derision.

"No."

"Date of your last menstruation?"

"September fourteenth." Tears formed in my eyes and dripped into my ears. But the attack was September twenty-ninth. I'd been all over this for weeks. Trying to add and re-add the dates. Hoping to come to a different conclusion. I knew as well as he did why I was vomiting all day every day.

"September fourteenth, and today is November

tenth, that makes you approximately eight weeks pregnant."

I had never been with a man before the twenty-ninth. I knew with certainty I was exactly six weeks pregnant, but I didn't argue with him. Six, eight, who cared? The damage was done.

"I was..."

"I am not interested in any lies you have dreamed up." His voice was so cold and condescending it cut straight through me. "Listen, my dear, I've been doing this since the dawn of time. It's always the same thing. You are pregnant and not married. You are immoral."

"I... no... I..." I stammered.

He moved to feel my abdomen again, and I said, "No!"

"No?"

"Don't touch me. Take your hands off me."

"I'm examining you." His hands were hard on my stomach.

"I want a different doctor," I protested.

"I'm the only one here," he said so dismissively, I tried to move away from him and pull my clothes together. He didn't stop.

"I said, don't touch me!" Hysteria turned my voice into a screech. I heard Cole at the door.

"Miss Stone? Are you alright?"

"No," I called out, loud enough for him to hear me.

He entered the room so swiftly the doctor dropped his hands. Cole moved between us. I pulled my clothes into place.

"She's hysterical," the doctor sneered.

"She's been vomiting all day and she fainted." Cole moved closer to the doctor until he backed him into a corner. "She's crying and in pain." Cole's hands clenched with fury, yet his voice sounded restrained.

"She's hysterical, but what can you expect..."

"You need to write a prescription and apologize to her immediately." Cole's voice was low and dangerous. "We will be filing a complaint with your superior."

"Does he know?" The doctor directed this question to me.

"No." Humiliation made my voice weak.

"There is not a lot I can do for this..."

My eyes, even though they were full of tears, met his and held his gaze. Nothing hysterical about the look I was giving him now. There was a hardness in me I had never felt before. My jaw clenched, and I held his gaze until finally, he looked away.

"This can go one of two ways," Cole said calmly and clearly when he saw our staring contest was over. "You can write a prescription and apologize, or I will ask Miss Stone to leave the room and the two of us can come to an understanding."

The doctor's face flushed red with fury.

Cole tilted his head to the side and leaned casually against the examination table. I watched the doctor size him up. Cole was a head taller. The doctor sighed as if this whole situation were so beneath him he couldn't be bothered to deal with us any further.

Cole made room for the doctor to go to his small desk, but he was careful to keep his body between the doctor and me at all times. Dr. Clark pulled a brown bottle off a shelf and handed it to Cole.

"She should take this before she eats," he said to Cole, not to me. "It will help with the nausea."

I struggled to sit up, and Cole handed me the bottle. I read the label to be sure it was the correct tincture.

The doctor already had his hand on the doorknob.

"You're forgetting something," Cole growled.

The doctor turned on his heel. "Sorry," he said and slammed the door on the way out.

I jumped at the sound of the door slamming shut. Cole turned to me as I wiped my tears away.

"What happened?"

"A misunderstanding," I answered through clenched teeth.

"I don't understand. What did he do?"

"Can we talk about it later? I just want to go."

"If he touched you improperly I need to know and I'll deal with him."

"No, please, let's just go," I begged.

"Shannon." He said my name so gently, I knew he was exercising great patience. "Shannon, where did he touch you? Where did he hurt you? I need to know. I have to deal with this."

"You don't have to deal with this, Cole," I said so harshly his jaw clenched.

I felt guilt wash over me. Cole was trying to do his job; I was overreacting.

The salty, tight fist of a sob crawled up my throat. I put my hand over my mouth to try to stop it from escaping. My heart was beating so hard in the aftermath of the confrontation, I couldn't catch my breath. I pressed a hand to my chest to try to stop my heartbeat from racing; nothing worked. Cole gently placed a hand on my shoulder, and that kindness, that touch undid me. A sob burst out of me. I covered my mouth, hoping to stop another one from surfacing.

"Hey," he said so softly I wept even more.

He shifted so that I could cry into his shoulder.

Pull it together, Shannon.

This was the first time anyone had touched me with sympathy in six weeks. I clung to him like a life raft in a stormy sea. But the storm was me, and he was the only solid thing in sight.

"Please, I just want to go," I whimpered into his shoulder.

"We'll go, if that's what you want." His voice was soft in my ear. "Whatever makes you stop crying, that's what we'll do." He was so soothing that it helped calm me down.

I tried to get off the table, but my knees buckled.

Cole caught me and carried me out again, and I began to think this night was never going to end. He settled me into the carriage.

When we arrived back at the hotel I told him I could walk, but I took his arm because of the leering men in the lobby. This was like a nightmare that I just couldn't wake up from. I saw leering men everywhere. Or were they? Was I just crazy now, seeing danger everywhere?

When we got upstairs, I drank the tincture right out of the bottle.

"Classy, I know." I wiped a bit off my chin.

"We have sheets for walls. We're just trying to survive here. Forget classy." Cole laughed, and I laughed with him. It felt good.

"How does it feel? Is it working?"

"Yes."

"I'm going to get you some food and I'll be right back. Lock the door."

Because no one will think to come through the sheets.

Fear gripped me when he left. Cole was the only thing between me and chaos.

He was quick; he came back with a tray piled with plates of stew, a basket of bread and butter, and a big pot of tea for me, whiskey for him.

Tentatively, I ate a piece of meat. I waited to see how my stomach reacted. So far, so good. I added a piece of buttered bread soaked in gravy.

"How's the stomach?" He took a small sip of whiskey.

"Better," I said and smiled at him.

He poured me a cup of tea and added sugar to it. I was surprised to see a china tea cup in the midst of all this crudeness. "I'm sorry that the doctor upset you." Cole buttered more bread for both of us.

"He accused me of being immoral," I said dully.

His eyes flashed black and green. I'd never seen eyes do that.

"I should go back."

"I think we've been through enough for one day. You can't go back and leave me here alone. You handled him well. Let's just put it behind us."

"I am very sorry this happened."

"You could not know. Don't worry about it." I finished my tea, and he refilled the cup.

We ate in quiet companionship. I was famished, but I needed to pace myself.

"Did he touch you inappropriately?" Cole asked again. I could tell he could not turn the constable part of his brain off. "If he did, then we need to file a complaint with the hospital."

"He examined me," I said but could tell Cole was not going to drop this. "Which was fine, but then I thought he was done, and he questioned my morals. I didn't want him to touch me after that... but he continued to examine me, and I completely overreacted."

"If you tell a man not to touch you, he stops. That's how it is." His simple logic was refreshing and optimistic. I wasn't sure where this man came from, but clearly not from where I hailed from.

"He's a doctor."

"A man doesn't touch a woman who has said no," he repeated.

"That's how it should be." I tried to draw that part of the conversation to a close. I was getting tired.

I carefully sopped up any remaining gravy with a piece of bread, leaving my plate completely clean. Cole finished his whiskey and switched to tea. He poured it into a big, ugly tin mug.

"Were they out of tea cups?" I asked sweetly.

"You got the only tea cup in the whole establishment, Miss Stone." He grinned.

"I think you should just call me Shannon, please. We've been through way too much already for that formality," I said.

"Please, call me Cole. You should drink up. Tea is supposed to fix everything for the English, right? Everything from upset stomachs to distressing events."

"I've never heard that," I said.

"That's what I've heard. Quite frankly, until I met you this afternoon, I've never had so many distressing events in my life." He took a big sip of tea from that terrible mug. I wondered if it was even clean.

"Thank you, you're charming," I said dryly.

"Well, I've never been accused of that." He casually leaned back in his chair.

A gust of wind and ice beat against the panes of glass in the window. Cole stood up to put more coal on the stove.

"That tincture is working," I said as I lay down on the bed.

"You're alright then?"

"I am."

"You should get settled for the night. I'll go to my room. Do you need anything else?"

"Listen. Something you should know." I was embarrassed because my voice actually caught.

"Yes?" His voice was gentle.

"Just, those men saw where I was going. If you're not here... well, what if they got in here..." My voice trailed off, and he crouched down by the bed.

"I'm going to be here," he said reassuringly. "No one is coming in here tonight. Did something happen to you?"

This intimate of a question was surely inappropriate. Somehow, being in a hotel with sheets for walls causes people to lose a lot of pretense.

I held my breath. "I just can't—"

"You don't have to say anything, just listen. You are safe here. No one is ever going to lay a hand on you. Understand? I promise. If anyone lays a hand on you, I will lay two fists on them. You have my word on that. No one is coming through these sheets. They would have to come through my room first."

I nodded. "You're right. I have been through a bit of an ordeal, and sometimes I wake up screaming. So, I'm apologizing in advance if I wake you up." My face flushed hot with embarrassment.

"I see." His face softened. "I'm just on the other side of this sheet, so if you need anything, just call. I'll stay in the hallway until you are in bed. I'm going to come into the room to put coal in the fire though during the night. This is the only heat source for your space and mine. Unless you want to switch rooms. I know it must seem inappropriate, but I wanted you to have the warmest and most protected space."

"Thank you," I said, and I meant it.

He picked up the tray and left the room. I worried that he would freeze to death without a heater in his space. I pulled off my dress and corset and crawled into bed, pulling the blankets with me. For the first time in weeks my stomach was full, and I felt safe. No more vomiting from fear.

Chapter Three

I woke up in the night once and looked around. Cole was quietly putting coal into the heater again. He had lit a lantern on his side of the sheet. I watched as the muscles in his shoulders moved under his shirt as he worked. He had been so professional, so cautious with me; I shouldn't look at him like this. He turned, and his eyes met mine.

"Are you warm enough?" he whispered.

"Yes," I whispered back. I heard dripping; the ice was melting off the wall beside my head.

"Do you need anything at all?"

"No, thank you."

"Go back to sleep then," he said as he made sure the blankets were tucked in against my back. "Everything is taken care of."

"Are you freezing on the other side of the sheet? Maybe you should open it up so you get more heat in your room."

"That would be most inappropriate," he said as he straightened up.

"We just need to survive this night," I reminded him. "Whatever you think."

As I lay there and couldn't sleep, he tied the sheet back so we still couldn't see each other, but he would get more heat in his room. My thoughts kept snaking back to the whole reason I was in this mess... the night

Jedediah Watt came to the clinic. Even from this far away, I could hear the venom in his voice.

Til's convictions had gotten us in trouble... again.

***

The door flung open late in the night as we were finishing a difficult birth. Exhaustion dragged at Til's movements as she checked vitals after stitching up the mother.

Mr. Watt called for Til, and Til didn't care if the Pope, King, and Queen were waiting, she didn't rush her work. She was fastidious. Satisfied her patient was comfortable, she straightened.

"Should we see what all this commotion is about?" Til asked me. That was my cue to go with her. I wished the floor would open up, but it didn't. Nervously, I followed Til into the waiting room. I didn't love confrontation the way Til seemed to.

If Mr. Watt thought he could intimidate Til, he was in for a surprise.

Til said nothing. That was her great move. Imperiously, her eyes swept over Mr. Watt, and two distraught women. My eyes were on Til, and my heart was in my throat.

"I found this in the possession of my daughter." Mr. Watt tossed a pamphlet explaining how to use a diaphragm on the desk between them.

My eyes slid shut as I saw what he had thrown at her.

"I have a busy night." Til looked down her nose at Mr. Watt. "You can't prove that is from my clinic."

Jedediah Watt took a step toward Til.

Til took a step forward, lifted her chin created a challenge without saying a word. "You take a step back and leave this clinic. I am an advocate for women's health. You can't prove anything, so take your leave."

"My daughter says she got this filth from this clinic and she will testify to that in court."

"Her word against mine. Does she have any witnesses?" Til shot the young woman a hard look.

"She isn't married. You are promoting this *filth* to women who aren't married!"

"I am promoting nothing." Til didn't back down an inch.

"You are promoting *promiscuity*!"

Til laughed at him.

Mr. Watt vibrated with rage.

"Promiscuity? I promote the *best standard of women's health* I can. We don't ask if women are married or not before we assist in birth. We keep them alive. That is all we care about. Checking on marital status is far too tedious. I'm a doctor. Not a priest."

"This is about the *promotion of birth control*. Their *husbands* are not being asked for permission..."

Til drew herself up to her full height. "We have a difference of opinion. Keep it for the pulpit. No need for that talk here."

"You admit to giving birth control to married women?" Mr. Watt reached for her.

Carson, the security guard we employed, made his presence known by clearing his throat from the doorway.

Til shrugged, she didn't dignify his question with an answer.

Mr. Watt's face flashed purple with rage. "You will pay for this," he hissed.

"Mr. Watt, nobody comes into my clinic and tells

me what medicine I will practice. You should leave before Carson throws you out."

"You have no idea who you're talking to," Mr. Watt said dangerously.

I held my breath with fear as Til stood toe to toe and inches from Mr. Watt. Fearless— she spoke with such condescension I winced, worried he would hit her.

"I've come up against worse than you," Til countered, her voice like ice over iron. "You think you're the first person to threaten me? The first to try to make me compromise and throw everything I've worked for away? You are not the first, and you will not be the last."

"I will see you behind bars." Mr. Watt vowed.

"Better men than you have tried, and they have failed. Carson, take them out."

As the security guard, Carson held the door open. Fuming, they left.

Til sat down.

"Til!" I exclaimed. "You never should have handled him like that."

Til pulled her hands over her face. "Like what?"

I frowned at her. "You know what! You just made a huge enemy." I dared to scold her. "Why can't you just get along? Why does everything have to be a fight?"

"Are you not seeing what I am seeing? Jedediah Watt is a self righteous bully and I will not stand down to him. The oppression of women must come to an end and someday when you are a woman and not a little girl..."

Ouch.

"I hope you would stand by your convictions and not snivel and try to placate bullies like him."

Shame made my face hot as she spoke; I was terrified of Mr. Watt. I was terrified of the entire Society he represented. I wanted Til to tip toe around them. She refused.

Satisfied that I was chastised, Til continued, "I've lost my patience, Shann. I'm tired of rich men having opinions that oppress poor women. It's his wife that infuriates me more. The women of the Society are worse than the men."

"What do you mean?"

"I've tangled with Mrs. Watt and she's just as much a fanatic." Til waved her hand dismissively. "I've been dealing with them my whole life, Shannon. They are all spoiled brats. They are not women. They are little girls. They do nothing. They contribute nothing to society. Spoiled girls who grow into spoiled women, who don't get their hands dirty. They don't advocate change. They are the obstacle to women like us." She looked hard at me to see if she could lump me in with her and her kind.

Who was her kind? I'd never met anyone like Til... never.

"They dismiss everyone's rights and freedoms." Her voice escalated. "They believe that their ideals are more important than the health of the poorest classes. I hate it. I have watched it all my life and I can't stand it."

"You've made a terrible enemy, Til." I couldn't stop the fear from creeping into my voice.

"I have so many enemies, I've lost track," she said calmly. "We are going to do our part. Don't forget that. We stand down to the Society for the Suppression of Vice, what next! They want to infringe on the rights of all people. I refuse to allow it in my clinic. You remember that we have sisters in this fight, sitting in jail cells, doing hunger strikes, demanding to be treated as equals. If one of us compromises, it hurts the whole crusade. You cannot just be on the front line. You have to *hold* the line. Hold it and while you're doing that, figure out a way to advance it. There is no stepping back."

I poured Til some tea as she looked at me with exhaustion stamped under her eyes. It concerned me. She was looking tired more often now. The hours she forced herself to work were wearing on her.

"What you are doing is good, Til." I plopped two cubes of sugar in her tea.

She just looked at me. Til was a rare breed who required no validation from anyone. Certainly not me.

"Someday." She took a sip of her tea and then looked me square in the eye. "Soon, they will look back at this fight for contraception. They will laugh that women actually had to fight for it. The ability to give women a choice to be pregnant or not. They will shake their heads and say this was oppression. Women giving birth to fifteen children, not to mention countless miscarriages. Ridiculous, when we have the means to stop it. Contraception is available to rich men and by extension to rich women, but not to the poor? This work has to continue."

"You have some big enemies, Til." I heard the fear in my voice, and so did she.

"Listen to me, Shannon. Listen carefully. If you have learned nothing else from me, I want you to learn this. Know this," she demanded as she leaned forward to make sure I was listening. "If you do the right thing, you will have enemies. Don't ever forget that. If everyone loves you, you are not being true to yourself or your cause. When we stand up to tradition and oppression, especially the place men have assigned us, the enemies get bigger. A woman who wants to prevent a pregnancy that could kill her can't find a doctor to prescribe contraception? Barbaric. This cause will rock the very foundations of our society, and I say it's a little late in coming. Make no mistake. It will take women like us to stand up to this ridiculous 'Society'. I expect with what you have seen here, in this clinic, in this practice, that you are as concerned about women having choices as I am."

"Of course I am," I agreed. It was the truth. I had seen so much here in ten years. So much suffering, pain, and agony.

"Then we do our work and we do it well. We do not worry about the bullies." Til sipped her tea. She made a face at me. "No brandy to lace this with?"

Til's only weakness was tea laced with brandy after a difficult birth.

"Of course." I jumped up to get it. Til worked hard, she deserved it.

I poured the brandy into her mug and looked at her. She was a warrior. I wondered, not for the first time, if I would ever measure up to her. I handed her the mug, and she smiled.

"I am proud of you, Shannon. You are turning into a doctor that is worthy of the title. I wish I could say that of all the doctors I know. If you were my own daughter, I couldn't be happier with you." She said it so sincerely that immediately my throat closed with happy tears.

I couldn't speak. She noticed.

"Except for all this constant weeping. You have got to get your crying and emotions under control.

They'll hold you back. Stop feeling. Start thinking."

Typical Til. And with that, the moment was gone.

***

I brought my mind to the present. Cole was moving around on the other side of the sheet. My last thought that night had been that I liked him and I trusted him. For the first time in six weeks, I forgave Malcolm for sending me away and I thought I might survive.

Chapter Four

Before the sun was up the next day, Cole brought me warm water, soap, and a towel with breakfast. We ate fried eggs, toast, and tea for me, coffee for him. The sheets did nothing to mask the sounds of snoring from rooms occupied with drunk men from the night before.

"I'm sorry this is all so crude." His eyes crinkled as he smiled at my look of obvious horror from all the snoring behind the sheets. How these men slept through it was a mystery.

"It's an adventure!" I was determined not to test his patience today. "I feel better this morning. The tincture is working. All is well." I smiled at him encouragingly.

He smiled back.

"The stage coach leaves at ten a.m., so you have an hour to get ready. I'll be outside in the hall."

He left to give me privacy while I washed up and then dressed carefully. Today I would meet Lady Harper. Nerves made my heart beat hard as I checked myself in the cracked and pock-marked mirror over the basin. My toffee-coloured hair was piled high, now that it wasn't weighed down in grime from traveling. The few freckles on my nose stood out against very pale skin. My eyes were the same colour blue as before, but they had lost their sparkle in a gutter in England.

Would Lady Harper see a beaten woman or an accomplished midwife?

I straightened up to my full height.

Stop sniveling, Shannon. You are an accomplished midwife, with two years of training as a doctor.

My hand hesitated on the door knob as I took a deep breath before opening the door to Cole, who looked a little worse for wear. His jawline was covered in black stubble, and his black hair was standing on end. I felt bad; he was so busy making sure I had what I needed, he was clearly neglecting himself.

"You look really pretty." Cole's eyes lit up as he looked at me.

"Thank you."

"I mean it." He handed me that terrible hat again. "You can take it off once we get there."

The hat and scarf were becoming the plague of my existence. He grinned as he picked up my trunk.

"Alright," I groaned as I plunked that atrocious hat on. I followed him down the dark hallway. At the stage coach, Cole introduced me to Matthew Hartwell. Mr. Hartwell, who insisted on being called Matt, and Cole were good friends.

"Lady Harper is going to have your head for taking her nurse to this dump." Matt tightened the straps on my trunk while Cole handed me a lap robe.

"We've agreed that she doesn't have to know," Cole laughed.

"She'll find out," Matt said cheerfully. He slapped the reins down, and the horses took off.

The coach took us over a very flat prairie to get to Oakland. The snow the night before had blanketed everything, so it all looked clean and fresh. We turned toward a river bank where a foot bridge was suspended across the river with Hillcrest, the Harpers' home, right by it. *Who would dare to cross on that little bridge?* It didn't look very strong.

As we drew closer, it was obvious no expense had been spared in building Hillcrest. The brick was the colour of sand, and the stained glass gleamed with green, pink, and yellow.

Cole walked me to the heavy oak front door where he knocked, and the door was immediately answered by a butler. We were ushered into a parlour and tea was poured. We could not help but overhear the argument carrying on in Lord Harper's study.

"It's done." We heard Lord Harper say through the door. He sounded patient and reasonable. "This is my child, and I'm not having you kill yourself to get this committee up and running. There are capable women besides you!"

"It's my project!" she pleaded.

I looked at Cole and took his arm. "We shouldn't be eavesdropping," I hissed at him.

He smiled. "It's not our fault Jaffrey put us here, and I want to hear who wins!"

"No!" I tried to be firm but I laughed with him. "We should go!"

"How could you go to my committee and tell them I can no longer..." Lady Harper started weeping.

"I'm your husband!" He was losing patience.

"Oh, that's the wrong move," Cole said under his breath.

I stood up, so he grudgingly followed me back to the entrance.

"You never play the husband card. I think you

learn that the first day."

"You're married?" I couldn't keep the surprise from my tone.

I stopped talking because the flash of pain in his eyes was unmistakable.

He sat beside me on a bench near the front door, waiting for Lord and Lady Harper to end their fight. "She passed away a year ago in March, so a year and a half ago."

"I'm so sorry," I said quietly. I'd only spent a day with him, but I knew him to be kind and protective. Having a young wife die must have devastated him. I waited for him to elaborate.

He was quiet for a moment and then went on. "She got sick after she suffered from a miscarriage. It devastated her. I didn't know how to comfort her. I couldn't make her happy. Didn't matter what I did."

He rested his forearms on his thighs and rubbed his forehead. He tried to keep his elbows to himself, I noticed. "She just started to get sadder and sadder, and then she got sick with this terrible sore throat. I should have pushed her to go to the doctor sooner, but she said she was getting better. She didn't. She refused to go to the doctor, so finally I just picked her up and dragged her. I don't know if she died from the throat infection or from sadness."

We were silent for a moment. I didn't want to interrupt him if he wanted to share more of his pain about his wife. He didn't; he just sat there. After a moment, I placed my hand on his forearm; he looked at me and our eyes met.

"I'm really sorry," I said honestly. "I can tell you loved her very much."

"I did."

"To lose a wife and a baby is unimaginable."

"It still bothers me that I didn't insist on her seeing a doctor. She kept saying she was just tired and she needed some time to herself. I think she wanted to die, and I let her."

We sat together quietly while I tried to think of something to say.

"I don't know if this helps," I started tentatively, "but sometimes women who lose babies go into a sort of deep sadness. There's nothing anyone can do. Even women who have healthy pregnancies and healthy babies can sometimes react this way. We don't know why. I know it's hard to hear, but there is nothing you could have done. Some come out of it, and some don't."

He looked at me and nodded. As the light filtered through the window, it highlighted the green in his hazel eyes. "I have heard that. It's just difficult to believe that somehow it's not entirely my fault," he said sadly.

I wanted to touch his arm again, but thought it might be inappropriate, so we sat there a few minutes and listened to the argument that we could still hear, even though we had moved to the front entrance.

"I understand what Lord Harper is trying to do in there. But it won't work." He smiled as he looked toward the door they were yelling behind. "She'll get her way. No question."

I could tell he wanted the mood lightened. No more talk of dead babies and wives.

"Spoken like a beaten man. Sounded to me like he was winning." I laughed.

"Oh, we're all beaten men. Can't you tell? The

women run roughshod over us in this community. We can't get a moment's peace. They're always telling us what to do. Do you think I wanted to spend my only free day this week dragging an obstinate midwife-almost-doctor across the frontier? No. Did I? Yes, because what Lady Madeline Harper wants, Lady Madeline Harper gets."

"Obstinate? I thought I was a delight."

"Oh, yes. Let's see— vomiting on my shoes, fainting in a public bathhouse, refusing medical treatment, and then making me threaten a doctor. You're a real peach!"

"Actually, I am a real peach," I said with spirit. "I'm sorry that was your only day off."

"Well," he said, stretching his long legs out in front of him. I watched him settle in as Lord Harper's voice escalated in the other room. "This is a sleepy village where nothing happens. I am a constable and have the easiest job around. Occasionally there's some crime, but not much. Dealing with that doctor was the most fun I've had in a long time. I wish you would have let me go back and finish what I started."

"I don't like violence," I said primly.

He chuckled at that. "Me neither. I avoid it at all costs, but I don't hesitate to throw my weight around if it's necessary."

"Is it warranted very often?"

"No. It isn't. Sometimes just the size of me stops a fight before it starts. I take my coat off, and it diffuses the situation rather quickly."

"Take your coat off?"

"It's sort of a universal symbol that a fight will break out. I'm not sure how many fights you've participated in, but the first thing you do is size up your opponent and compare them to yourself. I am not a violent man, but I am a bit of a giant, so people usually just opt not to fight."

"I'll remember that." I grinned. He knew I wasn't worried in the least.

"See that you do." He tried to look menacing but failed.

I laughed outright, but was cut off abruptly when Lord Harper came to the door. Both of us stood up.

"Cole, would it be possible for you to settle Miss Stone into the carriage house? Lady Harper and I are not available to receive visitors just now."

"Of course," Cole said.

"I don't know if Jaffrey made sure the fires were started, would you check into that?"

"I'll look after it."

"Thank you. Welcome to Oakland, Miss Stone. We're delighted to have you. Will you join us for supper?"

"That would be lovely."

"Cole, would you come, too? We'll settle things up later."

"Of course."

"If you need anything, please ask Jaffrey and he'll help you out. I'll see you at six."

Out to the carriage house we went, Cole dragging my few possessions along. While I set things in order, he stoked fires. We worked peacefully, no need to talk.

"I'll leave you to have a rest and get settled," he said. "I'm going to chop some wood for you before I go, so if there's nothing else you need?"

"No, nothing."

He smiled then. "Except for the aforementioned vomiting, it was a pleasure to meet you."

I went to him and held out my hand. "Thank you for everything."

His very hard hand engulfed mine and gave it a firm shake.

"I know you'll be fine here at Harper's," he said. "If you look out your front door, I live at the second door to the south. I'm your closest neighbour, so if you need anything and you don't want to hassle Jaffrey, let me know."

"Thank you, and if you need anything, I'm here."

I could tell he didn't want to leave, and I didn't want him to either. Both of us heard a bell clanging at the same time.

Chapter Five

"What is that?" I asked.

"Fire," he said grimly. "I have to go."

And with that, he was gone. I shut the door behind him and looked over my little carriage house. I was thrilled to have this private space to myself. I had never had a place all my own.

At supper, the butler led me into the dining room. No expense had been spared. Lit candles covered the middle of the beautiful, huge oak table. I shook Lady Harper's hand before sitting. Lord Harper was helping with the fire, so it was just Lady Harper and me at the huge table.

Lady Madeline Harper was beautiful. Dark hair and violet-coloured eyes, but her colouring was a little high for my taste. I worried about that right off.

"I trust the carriage house is sufficient?" Lady Harper asked as we were served stewed vegetables.

"Oh, yes. I love it. Quiet and cozy."

"You must think we're overreacting?" she asked nervously.

"I don't know much about your situation," I said gently. I could see the pain in her eyes as she looked at me. "So, I'm not sure if you're overreacting."

"We were married three years ago, and I've had four miscarriages in three years. Each time I'm more devastated than the last. Lord Harper is just so hopeful this time."

"You're not?"

Her eyes filled with tears. "I've given up hope. I don't know what to think anymore. He wants me to quit all my committees, and that's all I have. It's all I contribute."

She stopped talking then. I understood that women of her class didn't speak openly about such things.

Biddy, Lady Harper's maid, whisked into the room. "Shall I bring you something?"

"Please," she said wiping at her tears.

Biddy took off like a shot and returned with a cup of something.

"What are you taking?" I asked Lady Harper as she took a long sip of whatever Biddy had given her.

"Just something to calm me down. My doctor prescribed it a while ago."

I reached over and smelled the contents of the cup. They both stared at me as if I had peeled off my blouse.

"Biddy, would you bring me the box?"

"It's from her doctor," Biddy protested.

"I'm sure it is. I'd like to see it. Some herbs are not to be taken during pregnancy. I would like a list of everything she takes."

Biddy didn't move and looked to Lady Harper for support.

"Biddy, I need to see the box or container this came from." My voice was hard.

"Miss, you're only a midwife," Biddy said haughtily. "A *doctor* prescribed these herbs for Lady Harper's well being."

"I have two years of medical training as a doctor,

and ten years as a midwife. I don't feel that I am making an unnecessary request." I'd heard Til use this tone numerous times before and I waited for her to leave and do what I asked.

"Please, Biddy?" Lady Harper asked, and Biddy went out of the room in a huff.

She addresses a servant with a please? What is going on here?

"After supper I would like to examine you, if possible?"

"Certainly," Lady Harper said and looked at the cup skeptically. "Do you think that this could harm my baby?"

"I have no idea until I know what you are taking, so I would request you take nothing until I can look at the prescriptions."

Lady Harper put down the cup and looked at me fearfully.

"No need to worry! I'll check the ingredients." I heard Biddy come in behind me and I added for her benefit, "Because of the delicate nature of your previous pregnancies, Lady Harper, I will be the only one to administer any medications, herbal or otherwise, from now on. I'm sure you understand?"

"Of course," Lady Harper agreed. "That makes perfect sense."

Biddy put the box down beside my plate, and I could feel the coldness emanate from her to me. I scanned the ingredients and saw there was nothing to cause alarm.

If this is, in fact, the package of herbs she put in the drink.

Biddy was vibrating beside me with rage. *How*

strange.

Why was she angry that I was double checking ingredients to make sure Lady Harper brought a baby to full term?

Something wasn't right here. Biddy was clearly a bully, and I knew how to deal with bullies. Stand up and make it quick.

"I don't mean to be offensive, Biddy. I've traveled many miles to assist Lady Harper, so I will be taking full responsibility for her health. I trust you understand?"

Outraged, Biddy turned on her heel and stalked out of the room.

"Forgive her. Poor old Bid doesn't like change. She tried to talk Lord Harper out of having you come. It was odd. I just reminded him that she was my nursemaid as a child. I am all she's got. I think she worried that I would come to depend on you instead of her. I don't know. She doesn't like to share me."

"How does she feel about Lord Harper?"

"She tolerates him. He's so good though. He wanted to send her away, but I wanted her to stay, and generally he puts my needs before his own."

"That's nice." She didn't realize I'd overheard their argument.

"Except for today!" she exclaimed and reached for a slice of meat. "I am part of the Women's Christian Temperance Union. We have been working tirelessly to start a cottage hospital here in Oakland. I was to speak at a fundraiser on Friday evening, and Lord Harper has requested that I hand that over to someone else."

"I see."

If that was a request, what was a demand?

"Would you take my place? You stood up to Biddy,

and no one does that! I think if you took my place on the committee, if the committee agrees of course, I could relax knowing it was in good hands."

"Oh, Lady Harper." I smiled. "I know all there is to know about getting money out of people to further my interests."

"That doesn't sound good at all!"

She laughed with me then I gave her an overview of what Til had accomplished in London. Carving a women's clinic out of nothing. Bringing contraception to those who desperately needed it. Lady Harper's eyes were beaming when I told her how successful we were.

"I miss Til. We knew each other briefly in England. Then I read about her clinic in a newspaper, which caused me to write for assistance. I had no idea she would send her niece. I'm so grateful. I bet she's popular?"

"You love her or you hate her. She doesn't have a personality that's easy to simply tolerate," I said dryly.

As we finished up our supper my stomach started to act up, so when we stood up to leave I asked her to give me a minute.

"Of course."

I stepped outside for some fresh air, and then I went to examine Lady Harper.

The smell of herbs was strong when I entered her room. She had a cloth over her eyes.

"What happened?" I exclaimed.

She groaned. "I'm not sure. I just got hit with a blinding headache. I don't know, I was fine and then I came upstairs and..."

"I smell herbs."

"Biddy offered to rub my back and temples."

Biddy stepped over a line by disobeying a direct order.

"I smell herbs," I repeated.

"She makes special oils for me."

Does she?

"Let's have a look, shall we?" I forced my voice to be gentle.

"Alright, but before we start, I have your word about the fundraiser?"

"Of course. I will be happy to do it. We'll get together, and you can tell me what to say and who has the deepest pockets."

"I'm married to the deepest pockets." She smiled at me and then rubbed her temples.

"Any cramping?"

"No, no cramping."

A thorough examination showed a healthy first term pregnancy. She was in her tenth week.

"Lady Harper, you are only ten weeks along. You sent that letter to Til in July, what happened?"

"I lost that baby," she said with such sadness that I sat down on the bed beside her. This was inappropriate because of her class, but I couldn't see this sort of sadness and not do what I could to sooth her pain.

"We're going to do everything we can to make sure this pregnancy is safe," I promised. "What was the date of the start of your last menstruation?"

"There is a calendar on my writing desk."

I went to her desk and picked up a calendar that had been marked all over.

She took it from me. "Yes, September fifth was the last time I had a menstrual cycle."

"That was the first day?"

"Yes."

"So, you are in your tenth week, your baby is due…" I calculated using the calendar, "June 12, 1905."

"June twelfth," she said softly. Tears dripped from her eyelashes. "If I don't lose this one… I feel like such a failure as a wife, as a woman. Look at this place! It should be full of children, and I keep losing these babies. What if I can't have a child? What will he do if I can't have a child?"

"You have a healthy pregnancy, so far. We are going to take very good care of you, Lady Harper."

I handed her a handkerchief that was heavily embroidered and rimmed with lace.

She gave me a watery smile. "I just wish I could get rid of this headache."

"I'll get a headache remedy." I met Biddy who hovered in the hallway.

"It's cruel that I can't give her something to ease the pain," she spat it at me.

"It's a headache, Biddy." I tried to sound patient. "Pregnant women get headaches. I have examined her, and she is fine. Can you bring her some water?"

"Water isn't going to do much."

"I have a headache remedy that works wonders. I can give you the recipe, but she needs to take it with a full glass of water."

When Biddy returned, I dismissed her and stayed in the hallway as she gave me one last furious glance. She turned on her heel and stalked to her room when I refused to back down. I smelled the water and realized it was laced with something. I took a tentative sip and couldn't figure out what was in it. *Biddy is poisoning Lady Harper's unborn children!* The thought of it caused the back of my neck to tighten with anxiety. *What did Biddy put in this water?* My hands trembled as I went downstairs to get a fresh glass of water. I returned to Lady Harper's room and mixed up the headache remedy.

"When did the headaches start?" I handed her the glass.

"Hmmm?"

"The headaches," I repeated. "When did they start?"

"Right around the time I got married."

Jaffrey brought up hot water and towels so I could make a hot compress for her forehead. She sighed with relief as the heat from the compress relieved her headache.

It took an hour, but the headache finally eased.

"Could we talk for a minute?" I asked gently as I replaced the cooling towel with a fresh one.

"Yes," she said as I massaged her hands. Sometimes a hand massage calmed patients down.

"Before marriage you seldom got headaches, and they started *with* marriage. Do you find that you suffer from nerves since marriage? Are you happy?"

She pulled the cloth down to look at me with one eye. "I've never been happier in my life."

"Headaches are a symptom of something," I said. "Sometimes stress."

"I love my husband, and he loves me. We're happy, except we can't have children."

"Yet," I said with confidence. Biddy had added something to her water, and I would bet my last penny it was something to cause a miscarriage.

"Yet." She pulled the cloth back over her eye.

"Before you got married, what was your menstrual cycle like?"

"What do you mean?" She blushed with embarrassment.

"How often was your monthly cycle? Twenty-eight days, thirty days? Do you remember?"

"It was about thirty days, I guess. I don't really know. It's so sporadic now. Sometimes it is very delayed and the pain is very great."

"Did that change happen after marriage?"

"Yes, shortly after I got married, I got more headaches and I started to get more cramping with my cycle. It seemed to come sooner or much later."

"Just so I'm clear." I placed her hand on the bed beside her and went to my bag to pull out a note book. "Before you were married, you had a normal cycle, every thirty days. Cramping?"

"A bit."

"Enough to confine you to bed?"

"No, I was fine to go to school."

"After marriage?"

"My cycle got shorter or much longer." She sounded puzzled. "I started to get severe cramping."

"Did you ever wonder why this happened after your marriage?"

"No, I never gave it much thought. I just thought maybe I was getting a little older and that things were getting more difficult..." Her voice trailed off.

"I don't want you to fret. You just rest. We're going to get this sorted out."

"Thank you."

I left her and knocked on Biddy's bedroom door. She opened her door and closed it behind her swiftly as she faced me in the hallway.

"Biddy, I expressly asked you not to give Lady Harper any herbs or medicines. There was something in the water you brought her."

"Remember yourself, miss," Biddy said venomously. "You might be able to watch her be in pain, but I am not that sort."

She wouldn't listen to me for a second. There was no use wasting my time speaking to her further.

"I'll retire for the evening now. If Lady Harper needs anything, please don't hesitate to come for me."

"I'm sure that won't be necessary. Don't concern yourself. It was Lord Harper's idea to bring you here. My Madeline didn't want or need you."

My Madeline. An odd way to phrase it. I felt a cold finger of fear on my neck.

This was Lady Harper's tenth week of pregnancy. According to her timeline, this is typically when she would miscarry. I didn't feel comfortable with Biddy and the contents of the glass in my hand.

"Has Lord Harper told you when he will return?"

"He went to assist with the firefighting. I don't know when he'll be back." Biddy looked at me with such unveiled hatred I wanted to take a step back.

"Goodnight, Biddy," I said dismissively.

She turned on her heel and slammed her bedroom door shut behind her.

I dressed to go outside so I could intercept Lord Harper where no servant would overhear. As I slipped out into the night, I saw a knot of men and horses. Lord Harper was probably in that group. I started toward them.

The fire was basically out by the time I arrived.

The men looked exhausted, streaked in sweat and soot. As the only woman there, I felt a bit conspicuous. The men looked at me wearily. Cole came to my side quickly.

"Hey! What are you doing here?"

"I'm looking for Lord Harper. I have a matter that is urgent."

"Already?" His eyebrow raised in alarm. "What is going on?"

"Yes, already. I need to speak to him. Is he here? It is really urgent."

"I'll find him. Why don't you step back over here?" He moved me to a safer place, and I waited for him to find Lord Harper.

Moments later, they both emerged from the smoke.

"Is she alright?" Lord Harper asked with concern written all over his face.

"When I left her, she was recovering from a headache," I said. "I treated her, and she is fine. We need to speak privately, tonight. Now, if possible."

"This is all in hand, Cole?" Lord Harper wiped soot off his forehead.

"Of course." Cole looked me over. "You're alright, though?"

"Yes, thank you. I'm fine."

Lord Harper and I walked back to the house briskly because the air was so cold I was shivering.

Upon arrival, he escorted me into his office, and I shut the door behind us.

"I am going to speak plainly," I started as he poured himself a brandy.

"Want one?" he interrupted me.

"No, thank you." I waved the drink away.

He tipped his head to the side.

"Your maid is interfering with my job."

"Lady Harper's maid," he corrected.

"Biddy has been giving Lady Harper herbal remedies and prescriptions. That stops tonight."

"I'm sure you just got off on the wrong foot... she is very difficult." Lord Harper settled some tobacco into a pipe.

If I were a man bringing the same concerns forward, would he take me seriously?

"Many herbs bring about miscarriage, and Biddy is not trained as an herbalist or a doctor. Lady Harper's care needs to be left in my hands."

His head snapped up at the word miscarriage.

"She's had four miscarriages. I don't want her to hurt or be sad anymore. If you're worried about what Biddy gives her, I am, too," Lord Harper said firmly.

We sat quietly for a minute while I thought about how to word this. He needed to take me seriously, and I couldn't be dramatic as I presented my concerns.

"Your wife is experiencing symptoms consistent with miscarriage that is brought on by herbs."

His face was mottled with anger. "You're sure?"

"You should have four babies, Lord Harper. I suspect that the water I intercepted had an herb in it that would cause a miscarriage."

His eyes met mine as I spoke.

"It's my job to make sure she brings this child to birth and I intend to do that. I am trained in this, but I need your support. I need you to intervene here. If you don't, this maid will cause another miscarriage."

"I will deal with it." He swirled the last of his

brandy in the bottom of his glass. "I'd like to have her arrested tonight. I don't suppose we have any evidence."

"No. I detected something in that glass of water she tried to give her, but it could have been anything."

"This is an abominable business." He huffed from behind his desk.

I shifted in my chair and leaned forward before I spoke. "Do you know what happened to force me to leave England? The events that forced me to take a year of absence from my studies, from my career?"

"I know about the arson, I can guess the rest."

No, you can't. You're a man, a very powerful man who has known only privilege.

Our eyes met, and I wasn't the one to look away first. Til had taught me well.

"Those circumstances are tough, Lord Harper. A maid who doesn't know her place is not so tough. If you can't handle it, I know I can."

I saw something flicker in his eye, and I daresay it looked a lot like respect.

"Has Lady Harper recruited you to speak for the women's union?" He changed the subject as he took a sip of brandy.

I smiled at that. "She has. My aunt singlehandedly keeps her clinic in London running with money she persuades out of rich people. I'm not new to this."

"Sounds like you have it all well in hand."

I shrugged. "I intend to be persuasive."

We were quiet for a moment before I stood up to signal the end of the meeting. It wasn't hard to just become Til when I was unsure of what to do. I'd seen her end meetings just like this, with far more difficult participants.

"Very well, I'll retire for the evening. Thank you for your consideration of this matter."

I turned and went to the door, and then turned to face him again.

"About those circumstances, that forced me to leave England. Any possibility that we can keep that between us?"

"Of course." Lord Harper pulled his attention back to me.

"What did Malcolm tell you?" I hated the fear and shame in my voice. My hand shook on the door handle.

Lord Harper finished his brandy and stood.

"He told me to take care of you."

"What does that mean?"

Lord Harper came around the desk, and I took a step back toward the door. I had no reason to, but that step back answered every question.

"He didn't tell me specifics. He told me you had been injured fleeing from arson. Your aunt was incarcerated. The injury incurred? Not hard to figure out, and nothing to be ashamed of."

Silence stretched between us while I processed his words.

"Are you up to this?" he asked bluntly as he saw me turn the door knob. "My wife cannot go through another miscarriage. Clearly, you have been through a lot. Should we be looking at another midwife, or can you handle this, and by this, I mean handle Biddy until we gather evidence against her?"

"I can handle it," I reassured him. "Good night, sir."

"Good night." He drained the last of the brandy in his glass.

It was not to be a good night. Only three hours later, Jaffrey came for me. Lady Harper was suffering from severe cramps; they were both terrified.

Chapter Six

We rushed to the house. Lord Harper's face was white with fear, Lady Harper was weeping, and Biddy hovered in a corner of the room. Her eyes narrowed as I approached the bed. Lord Harper moved to give me space.

I ignored Biddy and moved my hands over Lady Harper's abdomen, feeling too much heat. I turned her to her side and checked her lower back.

"So much heat. Is there a lot of cramping?" I asked her, cautious to keep the worry out of my voice. I didn't want her to tense with fear.

"Yes." Her voice trembled. She was already too close to panic.

"Lord Harper, you may wish to leave the room so I can examine Lady Harper." I kept my voice calm. "Biddy, you are dismissed for the evening." I went to my doctor's bag and found the calcium carbonate. I needed to mix it with water, but didn't trust any of the water or tea in the room.

"She needs me," Biddy protested. She looked to Lord Harper for support.

"Biddy, you are dismissed," he said with such authority Lady Harper flinched.

Biddy hesitated.

"Can we clear this room, please? I'm not asking again."

Lord Harper held the door open, and Biddy reluctantly exited before him. I carefully measured calcium carbonate and looked for some water to mix it with.

I picked up a glass of water and sniffed it. This was not just water. A finger of anxiety crawled up my neck. This water contained some sort of herb or medicine. I could smell it, but couldn't place it. It was possibly a combination.

What is in this glass? Why isn't Lord Harper taking me seriously? He should have intervened if Biddy brought this.

I went to Lord Harper who was pacing in the hallway. I asked him to have Jaffrey send up fresh drinking water, and a separate basin of water and vinegar to wash with. Lord Harper went at once; I returned to Lady Harper.

"You need to relax." I deliberately made myself sound more confident. She needed to be calm. My speedy examination revealed no blood. That was good. As soon as Jaffrey brought the water, I gave her the calcium carbonate.

"Just lie still. Try to take a deep breath and hold it a few seconds and let it go. We're going to stop this cramping. Breathe with me. In... hold it... now out... in again..."

I did another examination once the pains had calmed somewhat. I caught a scent that made the hair on the back of my neck stand up. Her nightgown smelled of pennyroyal oil. She was slathered with pennyroyal oil!

Pennyroyal oil... oh mercy... what is going on here? Pennyroyal, to induce a miscarriage? On its own, pennyroyal rubbed into the skin would do very little. Combined with other herbs, though, it was dangerous in pregnancy. *What combination has Biddy given her? What herbs are in that glass?*

"We have to get the herbal oils off your skin." I washed her abdomen and lower back with the warm water and vinegar. As soon as I was satisfied all traces of the oils were removed, I helped Lady Harper out of the bed and quickly remade the bed with clean sheets. Once she was redressed in a fresh nightgown, I saw relief in her face as the calcium carbonate did its job.

"The pains are stopping." She wiped tears from her eyes. "Oh, thank heavens, the pain is over. My baby is safe."

I asked Lord Harper back in the room so he would be reassured that his wife was fine. He stroked a stray hair off her forehead and kissed her hand.

"Lord Harper, with your permission, I would like to stay right here with her tonight. I will be on site to render assistance if the pains start again."

I have to keep Biddy away from her. Pennyroyal!

"Of course. I'll send Jaffrey up with some bedding for you."

Jaffrey brought up a cot that looked like it had survived a war, along with a pillow and blanket.

After the door shut behind him, I sat down on the bed and took Lady Harper's hand. "There is no blood, and the pains have stopped. Everything is going to be just fine. I am going to stay right here on the cot by your bed. I will check on you all night, Lady Harper. I am convinced that Biddy is actually causing you harm with her herbal concoctions."

"They were prescribed by a doctor." Her voice was weak.

"Lady Harper, she may be acting with good intentions, but you are in good hands now. Either you commit yourself to my care or to Biddy's. I will not share responsibility for this pregnancy with a housemaid. I'm trained. She is not. Can I have your word? No more treatments from Biddy?"

"She is hard to deal with," Lady Harper warned.

"You just leave old Bid to me. You just focus on having a healthy baby. I have your word. No more treatments?"

"You have my word."

"If the pains start again, I am right here, so wake me up."

"Thank you." She sighed and pressed her face into the pillow.

I met Lord Harper in the hallway.

"It's Biddy, isn't it?" he asked.

"I told you that."

"I just have such a hard time believing that she would do this to Lady Harper. She is the most devoted maid."

I took a deep breath and let it out slowly. My patience was ready to snap.

"The changes to Lady Harper's cycle indicate that she either suffered physical harm shortly after marriage or she is being given herbs or treatments that are inducing miscarriages."

Lord Harper reddened at the talk of Lady Harper's cycle.

"There was pennyroyal oil on Lady Harper's abdomen. While pennyroyal is not enough to induce a miscarriage on its own, we need to figure out what is really going on here. Until we do, I will be the only one administering anything. I'm the only attending physician or I get back in that stagecoach and I go home tomorrow. I'm not tiptoeing around a housemaid." I waited for him to respond.

Anger and pain flashed in his eyes. "I agree. I'm relieved you're here."

"Me, too." I took another deep breath.

"How do you wish to proceed from here?" Lord Harper asked.

"We need proof to have her arrested, and right now we have no proof. We will wait and gather evidence."

"Be careful," he said quietly. "Regardless of my own feelings regarding Biddy, Lady Harper thinks of her as a mother. I do not want my wife distressed. A false accusation would stop us from prosecuting her and would hurt Lady Harper. We will keep this to ourselves and be very careful, very cautious. After all, you could be wrong."

I'm not wrong! I wanted to shout at him. "This is my field. This is *all* I know. A woman giving a pregnant woman pennyroyal, and who knows what else, is acting recklessly. There is no other way to look at it. Who knows what else was intercepted tonight in the water or tea?"

"This is just outrageous, isn't it?" His face was almost purple with rage.

"We will get to the bottom of this whole thing," I assured him.

"Thank you," Lord Harper said through clenched teeth. "If you are right..."

"I am right."

Finally, our eyes met. We were partners against Biddy.

"Patience," I cautioned. "Once we find evidence,

she will be out of Lady Harper's life and put away so she cannot harm her ever again."

"I leave my wife in your capable hands," Lord Harper said in a tone that brought our conversation to a close.

"Good night, sir." I returned to Lady Harper's room to guard her from Biddy and make sure there were no after effects of whatever Biddy had given her in the night.

I tucked myself into the cot. Tonight, Biddy had been thwarted. The baby was safe. For now.

Chapter Seven

The cot was not comfortable, so I awoke early. Lady Harper had slept through the night. She was still peacefully sleeping, so I quietly left her room and asked Jaffrey to bring our breakfast up. I instructed him that under no circumstance was Biddy to touch anything on that tray. Jaffrey was as deadpan as I expected. He required no explanation.

I settled her breakfast tray on her lap in bed.

"It would be best if you just stayed in bed today." I poured her tea and gave her another dose of calcium carbonate.

"The temperance ladies are meeting in an hour. I guess you'll have to meet them on your own. Are you alright with that?" Lady Harper took a delicate bite of toast. "Priscilla was to fit me for a new hat. Please let her know I am indisposed. She's absolutely darling. She's opening a finery shop on Crescent Street, called 'Hope in Oakland', and I am to be her first client!"

"I'm perfectly able to meet the ladies on my own," I assured her.

"I am sad not to be giving my speech." She frowned.

"There is nothing to worry about, Lady Harper. All is in hand." I tried to calm her since she was beginning to get flustered.

I asked if she would like a book to read, and she

requested a book of poetry. Biddy tapped on the door to bring in wash water. One look at me, and Biddy's eyes narrowed. Her face reddened with fury. She hated that I was tending to Lady Harper and encroaching on her territory. Her movements were angry as she poured the wash water into a basin.

"Biddy, I am going to be resting today. No need for a dress. I'll stay in my nightgown," Lady Harper said as she took a hot wash cloth from Biddy and washed her face. I hovered until Biddy had no reason to stay in the room.

"Are you staying here all day? Don't you have better things to do?" Biddy sneered at me.

"Oh, Lady Harper is my only priority, Biddy. I'm happy to be caring for her today. After all, I'm the one confining her to bed." My eyes were hard as I watched her tidy up the wash water and soiled towels. "I'll follow you out with the dishes."

Biddy was shaking with rage as I waited for her to leave the room first.

As members trickled into Hillcrest, Jaffrey settled them in Lady Harper's parlour. I slipped out to my carriage house and quickly changed. I brushed out my hair and carefully tied it up, noticing my face looked pale when I checked my appearance in the mirror. As I tightened the corset, I wondered how long this dress would fit. At eight weeks pregnant, the swelling was still easy to conceal with corsets.

Don't think about it yet.

I ran back down the path to Hillcrest, and Jaffrey let me in. I took a deep breath to settle my nerves before I made my way to the parlour to meet the ladies.

Conversation floated out into the hall. This was

the world of women; I was comfortable here. I entered the parlour and saw six ladies visiting over tea and scones.

"Good morning, ladies." I smiled at the group of lovely women dressed in their best to attend Hillcrest.

The lady closest to me stood and held out her hand. She had to be around fifty years old; she was thin from hard work; her grip was strong. "You must be the long-awaited Miss Stone. I am so happy to meet you. I am Ada Bennett, the old midwife you are so graciously replacing." She smiled at me, and I found her so engaging I smiled right back. "Once we get you introduced, I'd like a word with you?"

"Of course." I turned to meet the five other members.

"Priscilla Charbonneau is one of our newest members. She's opening the millenary shop on Crescent. You can have all your clothes and delicates sewn by Priscilla."

I stepped forward to shake her hand. She was lovely with black curly hair and black eyes. We shared a smile, and I knew we would be fast friends.

"Lady Harper is thrilled to be the first client in your shop. Today, unfortunately, she is indisposed. Before you go, may I order a hat and scarf, something appropriate for the weather here?"

Something that is not hideous.

"Of course you can, and let it be my 'welcome to Oakland' gift to you," Priscilla offered. The smile that passed between us was one of tentative new friendship.

"Now, let me introduce you in order of operation," Mrs. Bennett redirected my attention to the other ladies in the room. "I am vice president to Lady Harper, who is of course our president. Mrs. Rood is our secretary. Mrs. Holt is the mayor's wife and our treasurer. Mrs. Daindridge and Mrs. Carr are in supportive roles."

I shook strong, calloused hands belonging to hard working women. Their presence spoke to their deep sense of community.

"A word, Miss Stone?" Mrs. Bennett asked and I left the room with her.

Jaffrey was busy bringing in more tea and scones. We waited for him to enter the parlour before she spoke.

"There was not another miscarriage, was there?" Mrs. Bennett surprised me with her bluntness.

"No, some cramping, but I stopped it with calcium carb and bathed the abdomen. She is fine, but I thought it best if she rests today."

"Very wise," Mrs. Bennett agreed. "Keep a close eye on her. I am worried about her emotional state now. She is feeling like she is failing as a wife and woman, so we must do what we can to build her confidence."

Mrs. Bennett was a no-nonsense woman. I loved her immediately.

"These ladies are going to ask you to do the speech, so I thought I would run that past you, so you aren't blindsided."

"Thank you. Lady Harper already asked me, and I am happy to do whatever needs to be done."

"Let's return to the ladies, shall we?" Mrs. Bennett asked, and we returned to the parlour.

"I think we should brief Miss Stone about the speech tomorrow," Mrs. Daindridge said to the group as she smiled at me.

"Of course," Mrs. Bennett said as Jaffrey refilled her

tea cup.

"I'll find out where that speech is later," I assured them. "Why don't you tell me a bit about your project?"

"We had a mass meeting with the town. As a result, the town council asked us to put together a hospital, so we decided a cottage hospital would suit the needs of the community. We have rented a home with four beds." Mrs. Bennett sipped her tea.

"So, we are fundraising. Hopefully, we will make enough on the night that you are giving the speech to purchase the beds." Mrs. Daindridge slathered jam on a scone.

"Who will run the hospital once we get the funds to operate?" I asked the group.

"We will, of course." Mrs. Holt raised her eyebrow at me. "We've done everything up to this point. This has been a huge project."

"Wonderful!" I said. "Are you sure an outsider should be appealing to the people of the town?"

"Ah" —Mrs. Daindridge met Mrs. Carr's eyes conspiratorially— "you're going to be quite a draw."

I cocked my head to the side in question.

"Everyone wants to meet you." Mrs. Carr grinned at Mrs. Daindridge. They had clearly discussed this at length.

"Mr. McDougall hasn't had a smile on his face for a year and a half. Everyone wants to know who put it there." Mrs. Daindridge and Mrs. Carr's eyes gleamed at me.

Mercy, they have us together already!

"Oh! I'm sure that's not true…" I sputtered.

"Mrs. Daindridge," Mrs. Holt said coolly, "let us not interfere and be busy bodies."

Mrs. Daindridge stuck out her tongue at Mrs. Holt. "Just a bit of fun. Cole McDougall needs a woman in his life. If not this one, another one."

"Mrs. Daindridge, you are relentless!" Mrs. Holt's lips thinned. Mrs. Daindridge clearly tried her patience.

Mrs. Daindridge rolled her eyes and shrugged, but I noticed her eyes lock with Mrs. Carr's. They looked like cats that got the cream.

"Please, tell us about yourself." Mrs. Holt directed the attention back to me.

"Lady Harper tells us you have two years of schooling as a doctor." Mrs. Carr leaned forward, eager for information. "We understand you've spent the last ten years working with your aunt, who is a gynecologist. It seems impossible. You can't be more than twenty-five."

"Twenty-four. She adopted me at the age of fourteen. My aunt put me in private school, but every minute I wasn't at school, I was her right hand in the clinic. She wanted me to work as a midwife first, before becoming a doctor."

"What brought you here?" Mrs. Carr fired the questions almost before I could answer.

"Lady Harper wrote my aunt requesting a midwife to assist with this pregnancy. My aunt is unavailable, so I was sent in her stead. Aunt Til trained me herself, so I'm the next best thing."

"She's unavailable? Why?" Mrs. Daindridge leaned forward with Mrs. Carr to wheedle for more information.

I can't tell them she is in jail!

"She was not available. As it is, I was barely able to come either." I thought about Til's upcoming trial.

Yet, the way Mrs. Daindridge looked at me caused me to fear a newspaper article may have reached out here. No, it was impossible... I felt panic crawl around my stomach nonetheless. I shifted uneasily under their scrutiny. I opened my mouth to speak and then snapped it shut again. Mrs. Daindridge frowned.

"Go ahead, dear, tell us about your aunt. It all sounds so fascinating." Mrs. Daindridge was not about to drop it.

I forced myself to smile warmly and looked around to see if anyone would save me and change the subject.

Mrs. Bennett took my cue. "I am so glad you are here to help Lady Harper at her time of need. We are pleased to have you as well."

I smiled at her gratefully and allowed myself to relax.

"Other business?" Mrs. Bennett asked the ladies.

"The matter of Thomas and Emily Wheaton?" Mrs. Rood was so soft spoken we had to strain to hear her.

The manner of the ladies immediately changed; apparently, this was serious.

"Yes," Mrs. Bennett said and put down her cup. "I am increasingly concerned for Emily and Ivy's well being."

I was confused, but didn't say anything. When Mrs. Bennett talked, everybody listened. She was the steel backbone of this group of women, nothing frivolous about her.

"Has anyone spoken to the constable about this?" Mrs. Holt asked the ladies, as forthright as Mrs. Bennett.

"I don't mean to be a busy body?" I fiddled with the handle of my tea cup.

"He beats her." Mrs. Bennett stood up and moved to look out the window as if the river held the answers. "He's a drunk, so he drinks every penny he can get his hands on."

If they thought they had shocked me, they'd never experienced the brutality of the mean streets in London. I didn't blink, I didn't exclaim, I simply waited for them to collect their thoughts and continue.

"We can't do anything about that until she wishes to leave him." Mrs. Rood stood up and moved to Mrs. Bennett. She placed a hand on Mrs. Bennett's arm to calm her down. I watched as a look of long-time friends passed between them. No words were necessary to show mutual support for each other. Mrs. Rood continued softly, "We do try to make sure that they have enough to eat."

I knew about the generosity of people; I'd seen it, but this was a whole new level. Mrs. Daindridge's mouth pursed in obvious contempt for poor Emily Wheaton. She caught Mrs. Carr's eye. I recognized two old gossips when I saw them. I would not trust them with personal information. Every gossip needs a side kick, and these two were clearly in cahoots.

"Mrs. Bennett, what does she need?" Mrs. Holt took out a note pad to write out the list of essentials. She sat there poised with a pencil, ready to write.

I warmed to both of them as I saw they did not allow the conversation to turn to bashing Emily Wheaton, regardless of her situation.

"Meat and flour. She and I spent a lot of time canning and preserving, but she has no meat and no flour." Mrs. Bennett sat back down next to Mrs. Holt.

"I will pass that on to Mr. Holt. He can quietly in-form the council, and they will address her needs privately," Mrs. Holt said as she wrote down the request.

Their manoeuvring fascinated me. I had never seen anything like this in my practice in London.

"How do you know Emily?" I asked Mrs. Bennett.

"She lives across the river from me," Mrs. Bennett said as she sat back down. "She is my nearest neighbor. I assisted her in childbirth with her daughter, Ivy, and am the only person allowed in her home. Her husband is very controlling and terribly abusive. I have begged her to leave, but until she decides to do so, I do my best by her. Unfortunately, the laws of this land are not in favor of our women. If she left, she would have no rights over Ivy. The thought of leaving Ivy there with that... monster... she's in a desperate state."

"Well" —Mrs. Carr sniffed— "once you've made your bed..."

"You have to lay in it," Mrs. Daindridge finished in agreement.

Spiteful cats!

"No one should be living in fear of their health, certainly not with a little girl suffering, too." Mrs. Bennett's mouth thinned with suppressed anger. Mrs. Rood placed her hand back on Mrs. Bennett's forearm. "We cannot turn a blind eye to a little girl in our community who is on the brink of starvation."

Mrs. Daindridge and Mrs. Carr looked sufficiently chastised, and Priscilla looked grey. Mrs. Bennett reached for Priscilla's hand and gave it a squeeze. *Such solidarity in these women!* I wondered why Priscilla was so upset, but looked away. No need for me to intrude on this moment between Mrs. Bennett and Priscilla.

"If you could get her measurements, I would like

to make Ivy a little coat for winter and new long underwear. I cannot stand the thought of her being cold." Priscilla had tears in her eyes, and her voice shook.

Was she upset about Ivy or was there something else bothering Priscilla?

"Of course, and we'll say they are hand-me-downs from my girls. You are so generous, Priscilla," Mrs. Bennett said with such approval and love, I wondered what the story was there. There were enough busy bodies in this room, I would never pry.

"Any other business?" Mrs. Bennett asked the rest of the ladies.

"Thankfully the fire was detected early enough that the Howards were evacuated and no one was hurt." Mrs. Daindridge sipped her tea.

"Do they need anything at all?" Mrs. Holt asked Mrs. Daindridge.

"Not to our knowledge." Mrs. Daindridge looked at Mrs. Carr who nodded in agreement.

If they didn't know, no one would!

"Matt moved to the barracks and gave the Howards his home until they can find something to rent." Mrs. Daindridge put down her tea cup.

At the mention of Matt Hartwell, Priscilla looked up. A hint of a love interest there. Our eyes met and we smiled at each other. Mrs. Daindridge and Mrs. Carr looked at each other and raised their eyebrows.

"Any chance we'll be watching you march down the aisle any time soon?" Mrs. Carr asked Priscilla sweetly.

Priscilla stiffened and went pale as she became the object of scrutiny.

"What an extraordinary question!" I exclaimed,

trying to deflect the conversation.

Priscilla looked grateful.

"Certainly we'll be among the first to know." Mrs. Holt stared down Mrs. Carr and Mrs. Daindridge.

"Well, long engagements are not typically appropriate," Mrs. Daindridge said rather self-righteously. "We would not want to see your reputation in any way compromised."

"What she means is…" Mrs. Carr tried to interject.

"We know what she means." Mrs. Bennett stepped in to deal with the situation.

"Just that Priscilla has been married before…" Mrs. Daindridge let that statement hang in the air without finishing it.

What did that mean? What were they implying? Were they saying that since Priscilla had been married previously she couldn't control herself around Matt? This was like watching a lamb being slaughtered. Priscilla was a gentle soul; she didn't deserve this.

Priscilla stood up to leave; the tears in her eyes dripped down her cheeks. Mrs. Bennett stood up beside Priscilla to stop her, taking her hand.

"Matt and Priscilla have impeccable reputations. Their reasons for waiting to be married are entirely their business." Mrs. Bennett directed her comment to Mrs. Daindridge and Mrs. Carr. Her voice was so icy, even I looked to the ground.

"We just don't want anyone to talk." Mrs. Daindridge implied people were in fact talking.

"No," Mrs. Bennett said bluntly, "we certainly would not want anyone to talk, especially anyone close to Priscilla."

"We meant no offense, dear," Mrs. Carr said soothingly.

Priscilla wiped her cheeks and tried to smile.

"Please, sit back down," Mrs. Daindridge begged, "we're just concerned at the lengthy engagement."

"Typically it's a short engagement that is talked about." Mrs. Bennett indicated this conversation was over. She spoke with such finality that both Mrs. Daindridge and Mrs. Carr snapped their mouths shut.

"About Howard's house," Mrs. Holt said, steering the conversation away from poor Priscilla and back to the matter at hand.

"They will be starting to rebuild shortly," Mrs. Rood confirmed as she jotted down notes.

"It has been confirmed that there are two barmaids at the saloon," Mrs. Holt informed the ladies.

Their mouths were a grim line. Here, they were clearly all in agreement.

"What does that mean?" I asked, as there was no more information forthcoming.

"We would love to shut the saloon down. Up to this point, the saloon has never employed... well, it's been a place to drink, which is bad enough. Now with women there, well one wonders how to address this," Mrs. Holt stammered with moral outrage.

"How could you shut down the saloon though?" I asked and looked to Mrs. Bennett.

"We can't. We have protested in the past, but we haven't for a while," Mrs. Bennett said.

"It's pretty cold for a protest, right?" I asked.

They chuckled at that.

"Wait until January and February when it actually gets cold." Mrs. Holt laughed and the rest of the women joined her.

I shivered at that.

"We'll table the discussion about protesting, but we will decide what to do at the next meeting when we have more members present." Mrs. Bennett took her seat again.

With business out of the way, it was time to socialize. Socializing in these parts included work you could do sitting down.

Out came the sewing things. I was hopeless at sewing, but these women refused to sit idly. I was sure that every waking moment was filled with some form of work. They brought out a quilt that was simple yet beautiful.

"We collect scraps and make quilts for just this sort of occasion. Someone has a home burn down, new baby, a hard stretch of luck..." Mrs. Bennett explained to me then stopped to thread her needle. "We take care of our own out here. Our success has always relied on hard work, willing hands, and a strong love of our neighbors. There's nothing between us and complete destruction but each other."

I felt inadequate, but they weren't derailed by my lack of experience. I was handed a thimble, a threaded needle, and we got down to work.

"I'm glad you're here." Mrs. Bennett threaded a needle.

Her words were so simple, so straightforward.

"Oh?"

Her fingers moved deftly across the fabric; she worked swiftly and neatly.

"I am impressed with you already. I look forward to seeing what you can accomplish here." Mrs. Bennett smiled across the quilt at me. "Just having someone to step into my shoes is a relief for me. This has been a hard year. My health just does not allow me to be out at these births late at night. Not so bad in the summer, but I have been very tired this winter."

"How long have you been a midwife?" I asked as I readjusted my thimble.

"My mother was a midwife and taught me everything she knew. I haven't been able to help Lady Harper, though. I feel terrible for her having to endure so many miscarriages. But you're here now and you will help her, I am sure." Mrs. Bennett tied a knot at the end of her thread.

"Thank you. I appreciate your kindness." I felt my heart warm at her confidence in me.

"Make sure your stitches are small," she said quietly.

"Oh, sorry. I'll pay more attention." I immediately looked closer at the quilt.

We worked in quiet companionship for a few minutes.

"There was trouble last night." I lowered my voice even though we were sitting together at the end of the quilt. Instinctively, I knew Mrs. Bennett could be trusted, and I did not want Mrs. Daindridge and Mrs. Carr to overhear. The gossip mill needed no fuel. "I smelled pennyroyal oil on Lady Harper's nightgown."

Mrs. Bennett's forehead creased in concern, while her eyebrow rose.

"That's unusual," she murmured with polite correctness.

"That's what I thought."

"Who would have given her that?"

"I believe Biddy concerns herself greatly with

Lady Harper's well being." You could take that statement and read it off to a court of law, and it couldn't be used against me.

"Hmm," Mrs. Bennett said, her voice no more than a whisper. "You'd do well to keep your eye on that."

"Yes," I said quietly.

"I have wondered in the past if Biddy was interfering," Mrs. Bennett's voice was low. I leaned in a little closer.

"What would cause you to think that?" I whispered back, but kept my eyes on the sewing so no one would know we were deep in conversation.

"Biddy's father was an apothecary," Mrs. Bennett said, again so softly, I strained to hear her.

My head snapped up at the mention of an apothecary in Biddy's background. Our eyes met and held. Sewing was forgotten. I broke out in a cold sweat. I took the thimble off my finger before the sweat made it slip off and fall to the floor.

"Apparently, there was a falling out, and she was sent from his home. She worked for Lady Harper's mother when Lady Harper was born. Unfortunately, Biddy's illegitimate child was removed from her care so that she could work. I believe she couldn't emotionally handle those unfortunate events. When Lady Harper was placed in her care, I think she looked at her as if she was her own daughter. She despises anyone who gets close to Lady Harper. You would do well to watch yourself." Mrs. Bennett was not a dramatic person, making her words all the more ominous.

"Why would I need to watch myself?" I asked a little breathlessly.

"Biddy sees you as a threat." Mrs. Bennett picked

up her needle again.

I slipped the thimble back on and looked down the quilt.

Is Mrs. Daindridge trying to read our lips?

"I'm not sure what she will do with a threat to the relationship between herself and Lady Harper. She barely tolerates Lord Harper, but a *woman* who might threaten the closeness Biddy seems to crave from Lady Harper? Well, be careful."

"Should I make these concerns known to Cole... uh Constable McDougall?" I asked.

"I already have, dear." She patted my arm to re-assure me. "Lord Harper retained him to protect you from Brandon to here, but I believe Lord Harper has spoken to Cole about your protection in the area if you are to be out at night. I filled in a few more blanks. Be prepared. He'll be your shadow. He probably knows we're talking right now."

I actually blushed at that, and Mrs. Bennett chuckled softly.

"You like him." Her voice was soft.

"Hard not to," I admitted.

We got back to work. I stole a look at her bent head from across the quilt. She didn't know I was watching her. My heart warmed to her. In Mrs. Bennett, I found a mother to replace mine. Til by no stretch could be accused of being maternal. I hadn't realized how much my heart had yearned for this kind of empathy and warmth of spirit until it was sitting in front of me.

"Those stitches are perfect. You are a natural," Mrs. Bennett complimented me.

I clung onto that praise like a life raft and hung on every word; I felt inadequate compared to these women. My skills involved administering chloroform, delivering babies, and stitching skin not fabric.

The ladies left at eleven, after finishing three baby blankets and almost completing a quilt.

I checked on Lady Harper who was resting in her bed.

"How are we doing?" I asked.

"I am fine. No pain, no headache. I feel a little silly lying here while my committee was hard at work downstairs!"

"We have everything all in hand. I will let you rest," I said and left her. I was hardly down the stairs when there was a banging on the door. Biddy was still out on errands. Jaffrey opened the door to a distraught man who looked a lot like Cole, but was clearly not Cole.

"Is Miss Stone available?"

"Yes," I said as I motioned him inside.

"No time, Miss. I'm Cole's brother Nathan. My wife is in labour, and they said that you could help. Mrs. Bennett has requested that you take over Hannah's delivery, if you would?"

"I'll grab my bag. Jaffrey, please let Lady Harper know where I went. I will be back to check on her as soon as I can. Remember, Biddy serves her nothing. Nothing. I have your word?"

"You can rest assured that I will be sure that Biddy doesn't even bring her a glass of water, Miss."

"Thanks, I hate to leave her. Be careful, Jaffrey, be very careful. If she enters Lady Harper's room, you need to alert Lord Harper immediately. She cannot be with Lady Harper without supervision. Can you do that?"

"I'll take care of it," Jaffrey nodded.

Chapter Eight

Cole's brother and parents lived three miles north of town. The horse flew across the field with such speed I fought nausea.

Nathan pulled the horse to a stop in front of a beautiful home.

"Your home is lovely," I commented as he flew out of the cutter.

"This is my parents' house. Hannah and her mother had tea with Mom when she went into labour here. No need to move her." He took the doctor's bag from me, and we hurried into the house.

We brushed past Mr. and Mrs. McDougall. Once in the spare room, I found his wife deep into the second stage of labour.

Hannah's mother's face was white with worry. I leaped into action, requesting more hot water and more towels. Keeping the birthing room as calm as possible was always important. I dug into my bag and brought out some chloroform and a mask, automatically doing the math to give the exact dose to take the pain down and yet leave her conscious. I measured the dose and brought it to her.

After I slid the mask over her face, I performed a quick examination.

"You're doing great," I said enthusiastically. "This is going to take the edge off the pain."

Nathan and I both watched as she visibly relaxed from the chloroform.

"Oh, thank heavens," she wept. "I couldn't take anymore."

"It's all going to be just fine. This baby isn't going to be joining us right away, but this takes the edge off in the meantime."

Nathan let out a breath he had been holding in.

"You can leave now, Mr. McDougall. She's in good hands."

"I'm not going anywhere." Nathan went to Hannah's side and took her hand. "I'm not having my wife screaming in pain in another room. I'm staying right here."

"Really?" I asked both of them. This was unheard of.

"Nathan..." Hannah moaned and squeezed his hand hard.

"I want to help. I can't stand the thought of her going through this alone," he insisted when he saw me hesitate.

"Hannah, do you want him to stay?" I administered another very light dose.

She clutched at his arm and moaned into his shoulder. I took that as a yes.

"You stay at her head. I'll stay down here." I increased her dose of chloroform just slightly.

"Right." He held her as she relaxed with the dose of chloroform.

I carefully swaddled her abdomen in a very hot towel, and she sighed with relief. I listened to the heart beat strong and steady against my ear. Now that the chloroform was taking the edge off the pain, she was able to talk a bit. I knew she had hours to go yet, but sometimes the chloroform caused the birth to progress faster.

"Everything is perfect, Hannah. You are doing great. We're going to get you up so that the head can put pressure on the cervix and help move things along here." I helped Nathan put her in a position to help her body open up fully. I arranged him to support her and then administered another very light dose of the chloroform.

There is an art to chloroform. John Snow had perfected it; Til had run with it. Why more doctors didn't use it in delivery always made Til wild. I still hear her ranting whenever I see a bottle of chloroform.

"You know, they say that God cursed women with increased pain in childbirth, so they withhold pain medication for women. So many men in medicine are misogynistic!" she would say as she rebelliously slipped the mask over a woman's face. "Thank goodness for John Snow breaking through all that nonsense. I wonder sometimes, is that why so many women name their sons John?"

I watched as Nathan very gently wiped the sweat from Hannah's brow. He was so kind; it put a lump in my throat. He pressed slivers of ice between her lips. Watching them, I found myself re-evaluating if men should be allowed in birthing rooms. Late in the afternoon, she was fully dilated, and we got down to the business of a baby being born.

The birth proceeded without incident, and soon I held a perfect baby boy in my hands.

I laid their son on Hannah's abdomen.

"He's gorgeous, Hannah." Nathan had tears in his

eyes.

I blinked back tears. I should be able to get through a birth without all this emotion, but it's such a miracle that I couldn't help myself. It's especially breathtaking when the couple is so completely in love with each other and the baby, even before they've seen it.

A pang of pain sliced straight through my heart. I would go through this alone and didn't love the baby growing in me. There was no time to think about it, as I checked to be sure the placenta had completely delivered. After the baby was all washed and wrapped securely in a blanket, I handed him to Hannah. The love they felt shone from them, and this baby basked in it.

"Everyone is desperate to meet him," Nathan said to Hannah.

I piled all the soiled laundry and tidied up the room. I smiled at them both. This baby was in good hands.

"Shall I show off little James to his new family?" Nathan asked her.

Hannah smiled, and off he went to show off his son.

"You did amazing, Hannah. Good work." I returned my tools and implements to my bag.

"Thank you so much," she said. "If you hadn't been here with that mask…"

"Oh, I am happy to be able to help," I said. "It was my pleasure. It all went well. I'm going to make you a tea to help with the pain, and I'll be right back. I usually stay to make sure the baby has nursed and then I follow up the next day. I'll get you that tea."

I slipped into the kitchen. Cole had come out at the news and was holding his brand-new nephew, clearly besotted. Nathan hovered protectively behind him. The look of pure love in Cole's eyes as he reached forward to kiss his tiny nephew stopped me for a moment. I was certain there were tears in his eyes, and it made me pause.

Was he thinking of his own child who hadn't made it? Did this delivery remind him of his wife's? What was he thinking as he held that precious little baby in his hands?

Making sure to be quiet, I put the kettle on for the tea I was making for Hannah. I did not want to interrupt this moment.

The grandparents "ohhed" and "ahhhed" as grandparents do when Cole finally released little James to Mrs. McDougall. I felt another pang but shook it off. This happy and loving family didn't need me snivelling and ruining their day. I pulled my professional mask back down.

I bustled around making tea, forcing myself to smile. Finally, Nathan took little James because he was starting to fuss, and I followed him with the teapot. Time to see how James would do with his first meal. I heard the grandmothers making supper as we worked with mom and baby.

"The pain is normal," I said as I massaged her womb. "It's your womb going back to the proper size."

She sipped at the tea with added laudanum. "When will this start to work?"

"Soon." I wrapped a flannel around her abdomen to keep pressure on the womb and help it revert to its normal size.

James finally got the hang of latching on.

"The tea will help the womb constrict. It works

with the baby's suckling. This should take the pain down a notch."

Once the baby was done nursing, I asked Nathan to help her out of bed. He simply picked her up, as I quickly stripped the bed and remade it with fresh sheets and blankets.

I had him bring in more hot water so I could help her get cleaned up.

"Would you give us a minute?" Hannah asked her husband shyly.

"Of course." His eyes were soft with sympathy as he looked at her. "I'll take James with me."

He picked up his son and left us together.

I helped her get cleaned up and into a fresh night-gown. Once she was tucked into bed, he returned with James.

He brushed the hair back off her face and kissed her softly.

When I was sure mom and baby were settled, I smiled at her again.

"I need to check to see if the womb is reverting to its proper size. Let's have a look, shall we?"

Everything felt in order. I rewrapped her with the flannel to make sure the pressure stayed firm.

"I'll be back to check on you tomorrow." I tucked her back in.

"Thanks so much." She snuggled down into bed with her baby.

"My pleasure. Get some rest. You did a great job. You're a natural."

"That's too bad." She smiled at me as she snuggled down with the baby. "I am never doing that again!"

"Ah, I've heard that before!" I joked with her, and it

was a delight to laugh together. Back in London, I never had time to laugh.

When I tried to pass on supper, there was an uproar. They wouldn't hear of it.

"Alright," I relented, "I'll stay!"

The grandmothers had whipped up a ham and scalloped potato masterpiece, which I devoured. You'd think I had done more than assist. They poured wine after I assured them I worked with the temperance union, but was not a card-holding member. My glass was never allowed to be empty.

Cole's mother was a sweet woman who had born and raised seven sons. She fluttered over the meal until finally Mr. McDougall told her to stop fussing.

"We have everything we need, dear. Come on, sit down." Mr. McDougall clearly loved a good laugh, the skin around his eyes creased from the permanent smile on his face. He looked like Cole. They were the same height, same hazel eyes, but where Cole's hair was black, Mr. McDougall's was salt and pepper. Cole's parents were the most hospitable people I had ever met.

"Eat up, girl, that was an honest day's work there," he commanded from the head of the table.

I was anxious to get back to Hillcrest in case Biddy was planning another attack, but I pushed it out of my mind. Jaffrey and Lord Harper were apprised and would be vigilant.

Mr. McDougall nodded to Cole to fill my wine glass again. I tried to protest, but Mr. McDougall wouldn't hear of it.

"Half a glass," I whispered to Cole.

"I'll help you drink it," he promised and once he'd filled it as per his dad's instructions, he took a gulp for me. I looked at him gratefully.

"If I drink any more I'm going to pass out under the table, and that's just a terrible impression for all involved," I whispered into his ear.

"I'll get you some water." He brought back a huge tumbler of water, and his father smiled at us.

"A woman doctor. Doesn't that just beat all?" Mr. McDougall passed the potatoes back to Cole to clean up the last of them.

"Not a doctor yet, sir." I took a big gulp of water and wished the room would stop spinning.

"But you are in school to be?" he prodded.

I felt like an exhibit. Everyone was watching me. Women doctors did not exist here on the frontier.

"I have completed two years. I have another two to go. When I return to England, I will resume my studies at that time."

Please do not let me slur my speech!

Cole casually took my wineglass and sipped some more. I squeezed his arm gratefully. His eyes smiled at me as I polished off the ham on my plate.

"Can I get you anything else?" Mrs. McDougall jumped up to bring me more ham.

"Oh, no ma'am, I could not eat another bite. I am very full! I've had enough of everything."

"I'll pack you a lunch for tomorrow." She went to the kitchen. "You hardly ate anything, and I'm packing a lunch for Cole anyway."

Hardly ate anything?

Hannah's mother, Mrs. Rook, was lovely, gentle, and quiet. She got up to assist Mrs. McDougall in packing lunches for Cole and me.

"Your mother does not have to," I protested

quietly to Cole.

"Let her. It's easier to just let her smother you. If you protest, she fights back, Dad gets involved— just take the lunch," he advised.

This family clearly loved each other and respected one another. I loved them on sight. The conversation swirled around me, and my exhaustion made it hard to concentrate. My eyes felt full of gravel. I turned to Cole. "I'm falling asleep. I'm sorry, but I have to go home."

"Sure, I can take you home." Cole stood up. "Dad, we have to get home. Thanks so much for supper."

"Heaven's, no! The night is just getting started! We have a new grandson to celebrate!" Mr. McDougall protested.

"We haven't even started on dessert. It's chocolate cake, Cole. It's your favorite." Mrs. McDougall stood there with a piece already on a plate.

Cole wavered beside me, and I tugged at his sleeve. "Please, you have to get me home," I whispered to him.

He grinned. "You're going to have to toughen up."

"Very likely!" I agreed. "After I check on Hannah, I really have to get going. I am so sorry, Cole, but I am not feeling well. Please."

"Of course. I'm sorry. I didn't realize you weren't feeling well. We'll go right now. Pack extra cake for me, Mom. We have to get going," Cole said to his mother.

I peeked in on Hannah. She was cradled in Nathan's arms with little James contentedly breastfeeding. The sight was so breathtakingly intimate, I couldn't interrupt. If she needed me, she'd call. I crept away so they would not be disturbed.

My heart broke looking at them. *I am ruined. No man will cradle me like that.*

I shook those thoughts away and blinked back the tears that threatened to spill. With a smile plastered on my face, I re-entered the dining area.

"Thank you so much, Mrs. McDougall, Mr. McDougall. Supper was lovely."

Mrs. McDougall wrapped her arms around me and hugged me hard.

"You keep up the good work, girl." Mr. McDougall hugged me so hard he lifted me right off the ground. "Thank you for your assistance. That is a beautiful little baby you just helped into the world."

"Ah, that's Hannah's work. I just was there to catch him."

Mr. McDougall and I smiled at each other as Cole picked up my doctor's bag and I carried the lunches. We went out of the warmth of their beautiful home into the icy cold cutter.

Does this family realize what they have? They are so giving, so generous with each other. I didn't see this in London, and yet I think the vast majority of this small community out here on the frontier had it.

The cold air bit into my eyes. Finally, I had to close them, and not long after, I was sleeping. I woke up as Cole carried me into my home. This was unusual. I had never been carried anywhere. Ever. By anyone. Until him.

He laid me down on the settee and immediately lit a fire in both the fireplace and cook stove.

"Are you alright?" he asked, once all the fires were blazing.

"It doesn't seem to matter how many babies I assist with. It's always brand new." I unwound my heavy scarf and took off my coat. "It takes my breath away.

I don't know how to explain it. It's so beautiful." I refused to tell him the real reason for all this emotion and valiantly tried to blink the tears back out of my eyes. He came to me with a handkerchief, which I gratefully took.

My head went to war with my heart. To tell him, to let this burden out, let someone else carry it for a while. To just be honest about what I had been through. Would he understand if I told him I envied what he had —parents who loved him, a home. The women in his family, from what I had seen, were pure, clean, beautiful, and adored. Cherished. I could never fit there now. *Why am I thinking of that?*

Cole came to me and put his hand on mine, still and silent. I wondered if he would talk about the pain in his eyes.

My hand felt small in his. The tears would not stop. "Do you want to tell me what is really going on with you? Whatever it is, it's all fixable."

I put a hand over my eyes. This was not fixable.

He held my hand until I pulled myself under control.

I wasn't used to men in my world. My world was women. As I tried to gain control of my emotions, Cole went to the cook stove to boil water for tea.

While we waited for the kettle, I stood by the fire. He came up behind me and placed his hands on my shoulders. They felt hard and heavy. When I stiffened under the pressure, he let his hands drop and I turned to meet his gaze.

"I can't," I stammered "I can't seem to..."

"I shouldn't have touched you, I'm sorry."

I looked at him in agony. My desire for comfort and

fear of his disapproval fought in my heart. My shame, my story was so revolting I couldn't speak of it.

"What you have..." I started. The moment was so intense between us that when the kettle screamed, I leaped two feet in the air.

"Merciful heavens!" I exclaimed, and he chuckled.

"You *are* wound a little tight, aren't you?" He went to the cook stove and moved the kettle off the stove top.

"Yes," I agreed. "I am definitely wound pretty tight. That's an accurate description."

He made us both tea, and we settled down on the settee.

"It just hit me, how far I am from home, but even at home..."

He nodded his head in encouragement.

"I didn't have that, even there." My voice was a whisper. That wasn't the whole problem, but it was a big part of it.

"Family?"

"My mother died when I was fourteen, and my father was an alcoholic. My aunt swooped in and took me out of there. She raised me. I don't know what it feels like to have what you have, but it looks good."

"That's everything that's bothering you?" He handed me a lap robe and helped me tuck it in.

"It's a start." My eyes filled with tears again.

"Alright," he said. "That's a pretty big start."

We sat there in silence as my mind flew back to the day Til came for me.

"I was fourteen when I watched my mother die in childbirth." I took a sip of my tea.

That statement hung between us. He looked at me

to continue, but said nothing.

"Til landed at our tenement the next day," I said hoarsely. It was hard to talk about this kind of pain and anguish with anyone. I could remember everything about the tenement no matter how long I had been away. It haunted me. I formulated what to say to him next.

I remember looking up at her standing in the doorway. Everything in the tenements was grey like dishwater, so she stood out like a vision. Dressed immaculately in a dark purple day dress. Her amber eyes narrowed as they took in my drunk father. He had urinated in his trousers and had passed out in the middle of the floor.

Malcolm stood next to her; he was a big man, very broad through the shoulders, ready to step in if there was a threat, knuckles raw from a previous fight. But there was no threat here.

There was only me— a terrified, despairing child sitting at a table, and a passed-out drunk on the floor.

"Pack your things." Til's eyes swept mercilessly around the room. She saw everything. Every shameful thing. Towels and rags soaking to remove the blood from my mother's hemorrhage, empty bottles of whiskey, broken glasses and plates from my father's breakdown when my mother was pronounced dead. I should have cleaned up, but I could do nothing but sit at the table and cry.

My father stirred, and I watched as Malcolm put himself between my drunk father and Til.

"Hurry up. Pack your things," she said impatiently.

"She told me to pack my things," I recounted. "I

remember I had nothing to put anything in. I remember looking for a bag or even a pillow slip or something. We had nothing... We had nothing..." I felt that same poverty-induced pain crawl up from the pit of my stomach. I stopped to sip more tea and try to pull myself together.

My eyes slid shut as I remembered looking at my defeated father and then back to Til. Her lips thin with derision. This woman was used to giving orders that were immediately, obediently followed.

After I fled to get my few rags together. I brought them out in my arms because I had nothing to pack them in.

"That's it?" she asked.

"Yes."

"Leave it. There is nothing in that batch of rags that you need where you are going. You'll live with me now."

"Why? Why are you taking me?" The nerves in my stomach fluttered and then flared into full fear. I was terrified she was taking me out of here, away from the only life I knew, and at the same time terrified she would change her mind.

"I need an assistant," she said bluntly, and Malcolm must have seen my face fall. "You'll do."

"You just want me to work... to work for you? That's all?" My voice weakened from the threat of tears trying desperately to escape. More tears. I was weary of crying. Tears, tears, and more tears that turned the grey of this tenement to black wherever they fell.

"Til," Malcolm said sternly.

She looked at him and grimaced as she turned back to me. "You're Martha's daughter." I heard in her voice that she loved my mother. "I need an assistant, and you need a home."

I looked at my father, who was trying to get up and couldn't.

"She's not going...she's not going anywhere..." he sputtered, his speech still slurred.

I wanted to close my eyes so I didn't see his hand slide through the urine as he tried to drag himself up off the floor. My face flushed red from the shame of it.

"My Father was so drunk he couldn't get up off the floor," I said to Cole, not adding the bit about the urine, but so help me, I could still see him sliding through his own filth. I felt hot with embarrassment, even now, all these years later. "He didn't want them to take me, but he couldn't stop them."

"Did you ever see your father again?"

"No."

I couldn't stop the memories.

Til rolled her eyes at Malcolm, on account of my drunk father. She stepped forward to take my hand in hers. There was absolutely nothing soft about Til, not even her hand. She gripped me hard as she dragged me inexorably forward.

Malcolm stood back as she led me through the door.

Even as my father sobbed on the floor, she didn't look back, she didn't hesitate. She frowned at me when I did. Til had no use for weakness. She ignored it, stepped over it, or plowed through it. Like all men, my father let her have her way. Who could stop her? If there was a man that could stand up to Til, I hadn't met him. Until Mr. Watt...

"Do you miss your father?" Cole asked politely,

pulling me back into the present with him.

"I don't think about it," I said honestly. "He drank himself to death three years later. Malcolm took me to the funeral, but Til didn't go."

"Not even for you?" Cole's face was hard.

"Til doesn't do anything Til doesn't want to. Feelings don't matter to Til— hers or anyone's. Malcolm was there for me, but Til never really was. She considered my father a complete loser. Til didn't take time to attend a funeral for someone who wasn't worth it. She said she couldn't bear his last name attached to me and my upcoming career, so she changed my name from Mathis to Stone, same as hers."

"I see." Cole shifted so his arm was against the back of the settee.

I moved a bit so I was looking at him, careful not to get too close to that arm. Just holding hands felt outrageously intimate. If he put his arm around me I'd have been lost. I couldn't afford to be lost. I had to account to Til.

Would I ever get to make a decision that didn't involve her approval or disapproval?

"What about you? How do you feel about this new baby? Are you alright with all that?" I wanted the subject changed— enough about me.

Your brother, whose wife is healthy and happy with a new baby boy. Your brother, having all the things you thought you would have.

"Of course." He sipped the tea that was starting to cool.

Just as my wall was starting to crumble slightly, his walls were being reinforced. I needed to hide my shame, and he needed to be sure I knew he was strong, in control.

"Nathan is a good man. He'll be a great father."

"I think so, too," I agreed. "I just thought it's hard to see a new baby when you've lost one."

He pulled his arm against his body and shifted forward.

"I'm happy for him," Cole said with finality.

"It's alright to be sad. I told you my sad tale..."

"You told me some of it, but I can tell that's not all." He put his tea cup down. "I don't want to talk about Maggie or the baby."

"Why?"

"Because men don't talk about feelings, Shannon. I already told you everything." He got up and took his tea cup into the kitchen, shutting the conversation down. I let him. "There is nothing to talk about. My wife was pregnant, lost the baby, lost her mind. No need to discuss it."

So, I bared my soul, and he clammed up.

Wonderful.

"Oh." I had no experience with men outside of Malcolm and my drunk father. There was so much hurt in his voice; I wanted to help. It became clear to me as we sat there, that in Cole's world, women did not rescue men. Women did not swoop in and make the pain go away. That was the job of men. All fine and dandy if I was an emotional train wreck. That was alright. Cole, on the other hand, was not prepared to show me any weakness. I sat quietly beside him and watched the flames lick the logs in the fire place.

"I should go anyway," he said firmly. "I don't want to compromise your reputation."

I got up to walk him to the door.

"Good night, Shannon, I hope you sleep well." He opened the door, and icy air rushed in, billowing around me.

"Good night," I said.

Once the door shut, I rested my forehead on it. The tears welled up again. This time I could cry alone, without an audience. I let the pain wash over me as I sunk to my knees on the floor. I cried for what I lost, but in addition, this time, I cried for a man who couldn't.

Chapter Nine

The next day, I met with Lady Harper in the parlour. The sun streamed in through the windows, highlighting books, and the china tea set in front of her. *Deceptive sun.* The weather was bone chilling. The brisk walk across the grounds made my fingers numb. Grateful for the fire crackling in the grate, I settled into a chair closest to it.

"How are you? Tonight is the big night." Lady Harper's eyes twinkled at me.

"I'm trying not to think about it." I wished the butterflies in my stomach would calm down.

"Cole McDougall was here. You just missed him."

"Oh?" My heart skipped.

"He wanted to speak to Lord Harper about you." She grinned a little wickedly.

"That's strange, isn't it?" I was bewildered. "Have I done something wrong?"

"He had a long talk with Lord Harper. *Very* concerned about your safety." She poured the tea, waiting for a reaction from me.

I didn't give one. We weren't little girls on a school playground. If Cole was concerned, he must have a reason. Why was he talking to Lord Harper and not me though? Mrs. Bennett had warned me; he was going to be my shadow. We were together last night; he had ample opportunity.

"Safety?" I asked and couldn't hide the confusion.

"He feels it would be prudent to accompany you on any births outside the town limits. Up to this point, he thought Ada, uh I mean Mrs. Bennett would be doing all the country births. He ran into her at the post office this morning. He told her about Nathan and Hannah's new son and was wondering why she hadn't been called. Apparently, Ada has informed the new mothers-to-be that they are to call on you. She was thrilled you were here to give her a break. She has not been well, and all of us worry about her. Anyway, Cole is concerned that you might run into some trouble."

"Why is he talking to Lord Harper about this?"

"Well, you're technically under Lord Harper's roof, I guess."

"I don't understand this." I reached for a cookie from her tray.

"You're from a different world, I think." Lady Harper picked up her tea cup and frowned because it was cold. She poured a new cup and settled back in her chair.

"Apparently!" I bristled. *I'm not a child. Shouldn't an adult speak directly to another adult?* "If he's worried about my safety, why isn't he talking to me?"

"Lord Harper takes full responsibility for your safety because you are living here, technically under his roof. If you need anything, he would provide it. So if Cole has a concern, he would go to Lord Harper with that concern. I don't know how else to put it." She frowned as she struggled to find a better way to explain.

"This is fascinating." *This is stifling.*

"What about your Til? Doesn't she have a man

worrying about her?"

"Oh, yes. Malcolm is always there, making sure." I stopped. *The one night he hadn't been there—* The cookie I just ate turned to acid in my stomach. Thinking about that night made my hands shake.

"Are you alright?" Lady Harper tilted her head to the side in concern.

"It's just, Til fought her own battles and expected me to as well. I am not used to men taking over. Malcolm would physically protect Til, of course, but he would never make decisions for her or put limits on her. Men telling women what to do or making decisions for them, this is all new to me."

I'm not comfortable. I don't want to be stifled. He's too bossy! "I'll talk to Cole and ask him what has him so concerned," I said.

"Shannon, weather kills people out here faster than anything else. It's not even cold yet. We are facing months of brutal cold that would kill you in less than fifteen minutes. He cares about you, and I hope if you are not reciprocating that, you aren't encouraging it." She leaned forward to be sure I was listening. "I would hope you would not hurt him."

"I have no intentions of hurting anyone." I felt stung by her tone.

"Good." She smiled brightly.

"I didn't come all this way for a man." I put my tea cup down, determined to defend myself. *A man is the last thing I need!*

"Understood," she said and changed the subject. "Getting back to the speech."

"Is the speech here?" I asked.

"Biddy must have taken it to her room. Would you

get it and have a look? If there are any questions, I can answer them before the W.C.T.U. meets."

"It's alright to go into Biddy's room?" I hesitated. "She won't mind?"

"I'll tell her I sent you, but she's out for the morning, so have a look and tell me what you think."

Once outside Biddy's room, apprehension seized me, making my hand tremble on the door knob. No matter how much Lady Harper assured me, Biddy, if she caught me here, would be furious at my intrusion. The bedside table was empty, and her desk was cleaned off. She had a long, shallow drawer in her desk. Perfect for storing documents. Cautiously, so as not to disturb the contents of the desk, I pulled the drawer out.

No speech.

Instead there were bottles.

Many bottles.

I frowned as I pulled them out and lined them up on the desk. My hands shook when they landed on a blue bottle, Ergotole... ergot of rye... the fear in my stomach turned into revulsion. I felt sick looking at that bottle.

How did she have this?

I sat down. A thin finger of fear moved from my stomach to my heart. My pulse pounded, even in my ears.

First, don't panic.

Second, don't panic.

Telling myself not to panic wasn't working.

Here was the proof Lord Harper requested, right here, sitting on this desk. Biddy was the cause of Lady Harper miscarrying. The headaches, the increased cramping, the shortened menstrual cycle, or even more telling, the brutal end to a long absence of a menstrual cycle.

Ergot of rye fit every symptom. Every heartbreaking, painful, terrible symptom. Ergot of rye was a powerful medicine, which has saved countless lives. The ability to increase uterine contractions and to stop hemorrhage. In the hand of a skilled physician, invaluable. In the hand of a maid who is completely deranged, though? I shivered at the thought of how brutal the cramping would have been. I marvelled that Biddy hadn't killed her.

There was no speech anywhere, more medicines, though. Mercy, if she were running an abortion clinic, she would have had fewer of these potions and powders. I looked at all the medicine and oils and the female corrective powders. Cold sweat broke out all over me. My hands shook as I put everything back, exactly as I found it, and quickly went to join the ladies.

A few of the W.C.T.U. ladies had arrived in my absence, and Jaffrey was busy filling tea cups. The same happy sunshine streaming through the windows mocked me; there was nothing happy about what I had just uncovered. I took a minute in the doorway to breathe deeply before entering the drawing room to address the ladies. I put my hand on my stomach in an attempt to calm it down. It didn't work. I forced myself forward anyhow.

"Sorry, Lady Harper, I cannot find that speech anywhere." I sounded like I was out of breath.

"Try my desk. Maybe Biddy returned it," Lady Harper suggested.

"I'll be right back." I fled upstairs to retrieve it. When I returned, we got to work.

Twice I left to throw up in the backyard. My precious tincture was in the carriage house, and in this whirlwind of activity, I didn't have a chance to go and get it.

"Is this too much for you?" Mrs. Bennett asked the second time I excused myself to calm down.

"No." I smiled nervously. "I'm just fine! I'm a little worried about all the people, but I'm fine."

"Are you sick, dear?" Mrs. Carr asked sympathetically.

"I have a slight headache." My neck was so tight with nerves, the headache would not be far behind.

The back door slammed, and I knew it was Biddy. She was the only occupant in this home that slammed doors. I immediately stiffened in alarm and felt waves of hot and cold wash over me.

Would she know I'd been in her room?

My hands trembled as I held the speech. The ladies thought it was anxiety about tonight. No need to correct them. My nerves were shattered; who cared what the reason was? I had to pull it together; the Harpers' baby was at stake.

Finally, we had the speech organized. It hit all the points the W.C.T.U. wanted clarified.

The ladies were ushered out to prepare the supper for the fundraiser, and Priscilla Charbonneau came in to do a fitting with Lady Harper. I left Lady Harper in her capable hands.

I flew to my cottage and gulped down a dose of tincture for my stomach then raced to the barracks.

I pounded on the door, and Cole answered immediately.

"Have a minute?"

"Of course." He looked behind me as if expecting to find someone else in close pursuit. He pulled me in out of the cold. I took off my boots and went to the cook stove to warm up.

The constable's quarters were neat, clean, and sparse.

"I'm in a pickle." I put my hands over the heat and pretended it was the cold making them shake.

"Already?" Cole's forehead creased in concern. He tidied up his papers and fiddled with his notepad, clearly uncomfortable with me in his space.

"No need to be smug. This is serious. How can we get you and Lord Harper into Biddy's room without her knowing?"

"What happened?" His face changed. His eyes stopped smiling at me and became dark; his jaw clenched.

"She's in possession of something questionable. Can you make it happen or not?"

"Did she hurt you?" He moved closer to me. "I worry about you in that house with her."

"I'm worried, too. Can you make this happen?"

"Of course."

Within half an hour, Biddy had been dispatched to a neighbor, and I stood at Biddy's desk between Lord Harper and Cole.

"Lady Harper asked me to check Biddy's desk for the speech that I'm giving at the fundraiser tonight. That is why I was in her room."

Lord Harper impatiently waved my explanations away. He didn't care.

"Instead, I found this." My hands shook as I pulled out all the bottles and boxes of medicines.

Both men blinked and looked at each other, back to the boxes, and then at me.

"These herbs and powders are for women," I stammered a bit due to the terror that Biddy would return any minute and all manner of chaos would ensue.

"Well, Biddy is a woman," Lord Harper said gently. He checked his watch, cleared his throat, and his eyes met Cole's.

They think I'm an idiot.

I looked at Lord Harper and shook my head.

"These herbs bring about menstruation."

This caught their attention. Now both men were as uncomfortable as me. *Good. Equal footing.*

"I see." Lord Harper's face went completely red with embarrassment.

They still didn't understand. I scratched my head and began again. In spite of these two men having been married, this was uphill all the way.

"These herbs are sold to women who have had their menstruation suppressed in some way. Biddy is past the age of childbearing. She no longer has menstruation to contend with. The only reason she would be in possession of these herbs is to cause a miscarriage."

Their heads snapped up at the mention of miscarriage.

"She could say anything." My voice trembled with nerves. "I have no proof. She could say they were left over from when she did menstruate."

Lord Harper grimaced, and Cole cleared his throat.

"I'll stop saying menstruate," I said rather feebly.

"We're all adults here." Cole straightened and took control of the situation. "Let's take this conversation into the library, shall we? If Biddy comes in, this could get ugly."

Lord Harper picked up every bottle. He was so angry; I thought he'd hurl them at the first person he saw. Both Cole and I stood back as he shredded Biddy's room, leaving not a speck of powder *anywhere*. His mouth settled in a grim line as he marched out of her room, leading the way to his study. Cole shut the door firmly behind us.

Cole took out his notepad and wrote down the name of every oil, every powder, carefully listing the symptoms and side effects of each medication.

Finally, Cole handed me the bottle that said Ergotole.

How on earth would Biddy Baxter in Oakland, Manitoba get her hands on ergot of rye? How had she not killed Lady Harper outright?

"My question is, how would Biddy get this?" I asked.

Lord Harper rubbed his eyebrows.

"Could it be mailed?" I demanded. "Does she often get packages from Baltimore? This is Ergotole, from Sharp and Dohme in Baltimore."

I stood up with the bottle in my hand. What did we know? We knew that Lady Harper was miscarrying in the first trimester, we knew her cramps had increased, we also knew that Biddy was in possession of Ergotole.

"What does it do?" Cole asked me, his hand poised ready to take notes.

"Ergot of rye is also called birthing powder when it is in powder form," I said and opened the bottle. It was nearly empty. Not enough left to do any damage... is that how Lady Harper had escaped a miscarriage this time around? Biddy didn't have enough to do the job?

"It's a fungus that grows on rye. Ergot of rye was discovered many years ago by European midwives. They noticed cows would miscarry after eating rye that had been infested with ergot. They were the first to use it to bring about contractions. I took notes about Lady Harper's symptoms."

"I'm not sure we should discuss these delicate and intimate details of Lady Harper's person," Lord Harper interrupted me. His face was beet red with embarrassment.

"I'm sorry, sir." Cole gripped his pencil, ready to take extensive notes. "We can't ignore any evidence. Biddy will have to be prosecuted. Promoting abortion is a criminal charge. It's life in prison, if she is convicted."

Lord Harper moved to the sideboard to fill his brandy glass. Drink in hand, he sat back down in his chair, so far out of his comfort zone he was making me even more nervous. He waved his hand at me, indicating that I should continue.

"It fits." I skimmed my notes. "Lady Harper has had increased cramping, pain, and shortened menstrual cycles since marriage. Prior to marriage, no adverse effects from her uh... cycle according to my notes."

Cole looked confused. "When would Biddy administer this then?"

"She would have to know Lady Harper's cycle." Cole still looked confused, so I clarified. "To know when she... uh... bled... each month..." Lord Harper looked at me sharply. "She would likely wait a few days, even a few weeks. I am not sure. According to my notes, Lady Harper's cycle was on time or became much longer. Biddy must have been just administering this every four weeks and blaming the acute pain to a difficult menstrual cycle. Sometimes she stopped administering it and Lady Harper would get pregnant. Maybe her conscience bothered her? Maybe she ran out of ergot and the shipment took too long to come in? It is unknown why, at times, Biddy let her get pregnant. Biddy is mentally unstable, and we cannot guess why she would do this at all in the first place. When she did leave off administering the ergot and Lady Harper was pregnant, well, ergot causes extreme cramping. The miscarriage would have been traumatic. Very, very painful."

Poor Lord Harper looked like he was on the verge of a stroke. This topic was not normally discussed, not even hinted at.

"That is why Lady Harper kept requesting doctors to attend her," Lord Harper said vehemently. He paced over to the window, his fists balled at his sides. The full weight of what Lady Harper had endured from Biddy, under his nose, sunk in. His face went from red to purple as he vibrated with rage.

"The pain would have been atrocious." I winced, confirming his worst fears. "It's a miracle she didn't kill Lady Harper. Biddy would have to know exactly *when* to administer this, though. She couldn't possibly be that close?"

"She's that close. She's obsessed with her." Lord Harper kept his back to us.

"She's dangerous," I said to Cole. "Please conduct this carefully."

"I don't know how to thank you for finding this." Lord Harper finally calmed down enough to face us. He picked up the bottle of pennyroyal oil.

"Never mind the pennyroyal oil." I stood up and took it from his hand. "That's child's play compared to this. This is the real killer, right here. Every effort must be made to keep Lady Harper comfortable and calm. Calm, Lord Harper, calm is of utmost importance."

Lord Harper stood up and poured himself another brandy. He offered one to Cole and one to me. But we shook our heads. We had a battle ahead of us.

"How do we proceed?" Lord Harper sat back down at his desk.

"I'll arrest her on charges of promoting abortion and take her in today," Cole said, closing his notepad with a snap.

"I want to see her hang." Lord Harper said ominously. "Pressing charges will have to be enough. This can't be known to the community, Cole. Use discretion."

"The most we'll get is life in prison for promoting abortion, but only if we can prove it," Cole warned him.

"How do we protect Lady Harper in all of this?" I asked. "She and the baby are all that matter."

"I'll deal with that." Lord Harper drained his brandy.

"So, now we confiscate the herbs." Cole gathered the herbs together. "Then we bring her in for questioning. I'll question her with a witness present, and we'll get to the bottom of this."

"Of course," I said handing him the ergot that was in my hand.

"I'll get Dr. Davies to come in and assist in the interrogation."

I opened my mouth and then shut it. This was a

wise course of action. The less I had to do with it, the less emotion would be involved. They were right to be concerned with my professional reputation.

"I don't want you associated with this in the slightest." Cole braced himself, expecting me to have a problem with his decision. "If we don't have grounds to prosecute, she's so unhinged she might come after you next. You will not be involved, nor will you breathe a word of any of this to anyone."

I looked at Lord Harper and then at Cole. They were both resolute, faces as hard as stone. Lord Harper was still visibly upset; he rang for Jaffrey to bring him a bag for all the medicines.

"I'll handle it from here," Cole repeated as he took the bag Jaffrey brought and carefully placed everything we had found in the bag.

"Of course." I turned to Lord Harper, who looked completely devastated.

"She's going to be alright, Lord Harper. This is good news. Now we know what's causing the miscarriages. This baby is safe."

I opened the library door to find myself facing Biddy standing there, enraged.

Chapter Ten

"How dare you?" she screamed, as she lunged at me.

Biddy landed one hard blow before Cole could grab her and drag her off me. He clamped his hand over her mouth, and she bit into it. If Cole was in pain, he didn't show it. He dragged her kicking and screaming out of the house, across the road, and into his office.

"Merciful heavens," Lord Harper exclaimed as he lifted me up off the floor. "You're in it now. Let's go."

I gathered up all the evidence and bolted across the road to Cole's home, which was also the police station and office.

Even restrained, Biddy tried to lunge at me again. Cole dragged her into the interrogation room, and I took a deep breath before following them in. She spat at me as Cole sat her down in a chair. I took a seat across from her as Cole hovered behind.

"You've been trying to come between us since you got here!" Her face flushed purple as it twisted with hatred.

It took my breath away. She spat at me again and tried to grab me across the table. Cole caught her and pulled her back into her chair. She struggled against his iron grip until she finally relented.

My eyes met his, and I shook my head slightly to let him know to let her go. He shook his head no. I realized I wasn't going to win, so I turned my gaze to meet hers. She had flecks of spit at the side of her mouth.

"Ever since you got here, you have been trying to steal her from me! Everything I do for Madeline, you destroy. I cure her headaches and her woman problems and pain. Me! Not you. She doesn't need you. Madeline is mine. She's mine!" she screeched hysterically.

"What woman problems, Biddy?"

She blinked in confusion. I made my voice soft, professional—the tone I use with people out of control with pain. Clearly, Biddy was driven by her emotional anguish. Again, I signaled Cole to let her go. His eyes narrowed, obviously reluctant. He needed a confession, and I was going to get it for him. I held his gaze until he stepped back, though he stayed close enough to drag her off me if necessary.

"What woman problems was she suffering from?" I kept my voice soft.

Cole's hands relaxed until they finally dropped to his sides.

"Her monthly courses were too painful if they were suppressed," Biddy sneered at me, triumphant that I needed to ask.

"Has she always suffered with painful menstruation?" An easy topic, no blaming Biddy. She might think she could lie and not be caught.

"Yes... ah... no, not always." Biddy shook her head and stared vacantly at the wall for a minute. She looked at me; she blinked as if she wasn't sure why she was in an interrogation room. "Yes. Always terrible menstrual pain."

"I see." I pulled out my notepad.

Liar.

"According to Lady Harper, she had regular menstrual cycles prior to marriage, but after marriage those menstrual cycles got a little shorter or much longer and much more painful. Maybe you can help me, since you know Lady Harper so much better than I do."

Cole looked ready to pounce again. I kept my eyes down and fiddled with my notes, playing at being unsure. I wanted Biddy to feel in control. She'd feed off my insecurity. Unfortunately, Til and I had dealt with too many of her kind before.

Cole looked puzzled, and I did not look forward to the conversation we would be having later. Apparently, women's hygiene was a mystery to him. I pressed on.

"We both want Lady Harper to be happy and healthy. I know you love her. Biddy. Please tell me how you were helping her, so I don't make any mistakes."

Her chest swelled as the power in the room shifted to her.

"I don't have to explain anything to you." She spoke to me like I was incompetent.

"How long did you wait until you gave her these medications? Say her menstruation was due on the fourteenth of the month?" My hands trembled as I lined up the powders and tinctures on the table between us.

"Then I started the powder on the fifteenth of the month."

The powder, but not the tincture. She has to confess to the ergot...

"The instructions on the pills ask married women to be certain they are not pregnant before taking the medication. How would you be sure Lady Harper was not pregnant before administering any powders?"

Confession to the powder is safe. Let's talk about the tincture.

She shifted.

"I would never give Lady Harper anything that would hurt her. She wanted assistance with difficult menstrual pain. I did what any maid would do."

"Can you explain what this is? I am unsure of this tincture... this ergot of rye..." I deliberately let the sentence trail off.

"I don't know what ergot of rye is."

Liar!

"Can you tell me how this ergot of rye came to be in your room?"

"You're the midwife." She blinked at me. "Likely you put it there to blame me when my lady miscarried."

She knows what it does. Oh mercy. She's been killing these babies, and that was almost a confession.

"Biddy," I said very cautiously. "You told me you didn't know what ergot of rye was."

Cole tensed, ready to spring into action.

"She didn't want a baby!" Biddy's entire countenance changed, rage erupting from her inner most being. "She didn't want a baby! I know what she needs."

She's evading this. She knows we need her to confess to ergot of rye... she knows it.

"But you must have held her when she cried. Every time the bleeding started, Lady Harper was devastated, another month, no pregnancy." I pushed her hard.

Biddy looked angry enough to rip me apart. She slammed her fists on the table over and over again. "She couldn't bear those children. It was too much for her! She would get weakened. She could die."

"You wanted to protect her," I whispered. I leaned in to look her in the eye. Cole tensed. "You love her more than Lord Harper. You know what happens to women who bear too many children. You were only protecting her. You're all she has."

Come on, how did you protect her, what did you use? Say it... say it...

"Yes!" she shouted triumphantly.

"How did you protect her, Biddy?"

Tears rolled down her face. "He doesn't love her, and you don't love her. You don't. No one loves her like I do."

"How?" I felt on the verge of tears myself.

She ignored my questions. "You think I'm a fool. I know what you're doing, but I will destroy you."

I stood up and backed away. Cole looked wound like a spring. We couldn't let her stop her rant.

Let it all out. Let us put you away.

"Really?" I tilted my head and leaned back against the wall. "And just how do you plan to do that?"

She smiled then— terrifying to see.

When had this woman last been sane?

"You won't see it coming." Biddy shifted in her chair, ready to strike out at me like a snake.

Cole gathered her arms behind her back and said, "Biddy, you're charged on suspicion of procuring miscarriage by unlawfully administering noxious drugs."

Chapter Eleven

Cole escorted her to the jail cell in the basement where he left her ranting and screaming. He returned to me in the interrogation room, after taking the stairs two at a time. I was still shaking in my chair.

Lord Harper dragged a chair in and sat down heavily beside me. "I could hear everything." His eyes were wide at what we just witnessed. "I knew she was odd, but she's absolutely insane. Are you alright?"

Cole's eyes darkened with worry.

"Of course." I scrubbed my hands over my face. "That was all rather shocking."

"I need to return to Lady Harper. Are you sure you'll be alright?" Lord Harper looked at me. An unspoken signal passed between him and Cole, who stood beside me, strong and solid. I started feeling safe again.

"Yes, please go to Lady Harper. She'll be worried about Biddy. You'll have to come up with a story."

Lord Harper left, and I turned to Cole.

"I would like to go home, please. I don't want to hear anymore of her ranting and screaming from the basement."

"Of course." Cole escorted me thirty steps across the road to my carriage house. I sat down wearily as he made a fire in the hearth. He started the cook stove then slipped outside. Upon returning, he knelt down in front of me and handed me a tea towel full of snow.

Now that the interrogation was over, I was shaking uncontrollably from the depth of Biddy's hatred.

"Can I put this against your cheekbone?"

"Sure." The more I tried to stop shaking, the worse it got.

"You were outstanding in that interrogation. I take my hat off to you." He brushed the hair away from my face tenderly.

I closed my eyes in relief as the icy tea towel spread coolness on my aching cheekbone.

"I failed," I groaned. "I wanted her to confess to the ergot. She only confessed to powder. She'll have a story, and she'll get off. That interrogation was a disaster." I held the tea towel of ice and snow against my cheek.

"You're shaking. Come here. I can't stand to see you terrified."

He wrapped his arms around me, careful of my cheek. I was stiff and awkward. He was the only man in my life who had done this, promised to use his superior strength to protect, not harm. It was soothing. Malcolm was always proper with me. We were not the sort that hugged.

Cole mistook my stiffness for fear. "It's alright now. No need to be afraid. She can't hurt you. She's safely locked up."

"You have no hard evidence. You'll never convict her without it. It's all circumstantial. She didn't admit to the ergot." My words were muffled against his chest.

"Are you a lawyer, too?" he joked to lighten the mood.

I tried to relax into his hug, but it felt so foreign, I didn't know how to respond. He rubbed his hand up and down my back.

"No, Til's man, Malcolm, is a lawyer. A good one. He'd have this thrown out of court in a minute."

I closed my eyes and rested my cheek against his hard and broad shoulder then relaxed against him. It was like a sort of miracle. My body instinctively knew it was safe in his arms. In that safety, I molded against him.

"I know." He held me even tighter. "I know you were scared. It's alright now. I promise that. Absolutely nothing to worry about. We have enough evidence to convict her of assault. She's all locked up and can't hurt you now."

As hard as I tried to pull myself together, I couldn't. Not only did this pregnancy make me vomit constantly, I was crying at the drop of a hat.

"I feel so stupid. I can't stop crying." I reached for the proffered handkerchief in his hand.

"You're not stupid and you don't have to stop crying." He continued to rub his hand up and down my back.

My heart wanted to stay right there in that embrace. My mind made me pull back a little. His eyes searched mine. Looking for fear or passion? I looked away. As much as I wanted to meld into him, I didn't have that luxury. This baby was going to ruin me, and by extension him, if I let things go too far. What I'd felt, looking into his eyes, terrified me. Maybe I wasn't completely damaged, maybe I could love a man. Unfortunately, that scared me on a different level. A different kind of vulnerability, letting a man have any control over my life. It was terrifying.

Oh, Til, get out of my head.

"Am I bruised?" I asked, desperate to ease the tension in the room.

He very gently took my jaw in his hand, so he could see it in the light. "Hmmm."

"Curses! I am speaking tonight at the fundraiser!" I frowned at him.

I went to the mirror and craned my neck so I could get a good glimpse of my cheekbone; a huge bruise bloomed there. I wiped the tears from my eyes. This was serious. I could not ask for money looking like a street fighter.

"What am I going to do?" I put the ice back on my face as I collapsed on the settee.

Cole held his hands out helplessly.

"How many people are going to see this bruising?"

"Maybe it'll be dark enough." He sounded hopeful.

"It won't be pitch black! Now I look like I was in a fight." I was nervous to begin with.

"Let's go to Lord Harper." Cole pulled me up off the settee.

Together we went to Hillcrest, and Jaffrey escorted us to Lord Harper's study. His lips thinned at my bruised face before he closed the door behind us.

"What happens next?" I asked Cole.

Lord Harper leaned forward to hear what Cole had to say.

"I'll take Biddy to Brandon for processing first thing in the morning." Cole paced over to the window.

"Are you still able to do the speech for Lady Harper? It's late to enlist anyone else," Lord Harper asked.

"I'm fine. It throbs, but I've been through worse."

Oops, that slipped.

Cole turned around, wanting to know when and

who and where — it was written all over his face. Lord Harper caught the look in my eye and swiftly changed the subject.

"Do you have something appropriate to wear tonight? Lady Harper wondered if you needed to borrow something. Maybe you should go to her."

"What have you told her?"

"The truth," Lord Harper said with a glint in his eye. "I told her Biddy is sick and needs to be examined. Dr. Davies felt that she needed some rest, and I would handle all the arrangements."

I leaned forward and put the mostly melted ice down. It left streaks of water all down my arms.

"Brilliant." I wiped the water off my arms. "I'm going to poke around for a dress in Lady Harper's closet. Please excuse me, gentlemen."

They stood as I moved toward the door.

"One more thing," Lord Harper said as I stood there, ready to leave.

"Yes?"

"Cole and I have talked about this at great length. You are not to leave the town limits without either him or me as an escort. I am not as available, so Cole will accompany you to any births taking place outside the town limits, or you simply won't go."

I raised an eyebrow at them. "At what point were you thinking of asking me my opinion on this?"

"Shannon, it's a dangerous time of year. It is so cold. Minus-Forty-five can kill you quickly. I don't think you have ever faced cold like it. The storms can come up really fast, too. Not to mention there could be criminals as well waiting to prey on a woman on her own. No. Absolutely not." Cole tried to come to Lord

Harper's aid.

"So, if a woman is dying in childbirth, I'm supposed to say no, I need an escort."

"I told you she would never agree," Lord Harper said to Cole.

"Your safety is my concern, my job, actually." Cole crossed his arms. "I live exactly thirty steps from your front door. You can come to me at any time of day or night. I do not want you out in the elements."

"You both need to try to find a way to trust me. I was raised in the worst circumstances you could imagine. I'll let you know if I need you."

"And nothing ever happened?" Lord Harper asked quietly.

That statement stopped me as if he'd physically hit me.

"I answer to *Malcolm* as to your whereabouts and safety. I say you will be accompanied by Cole. That is the end of the discussion. I will not have an altercation or a problem on my hands. I have enough to deal with," Lord Harper said, while pouring himself a brandy.

My eyes met Cole's, and he was resolute.

"So, my opinion or my thoughts don't matter to either of you?" I asked and felt a little betrayed. "I will not have a woman suffer because I don't have a baby sitter."

"Body guard," Cole corrected me. "Your safety is my primary concern."

"Fine." I narrowed my eyes. "The next time you are making decisions regarding me, do me the courtesy of inviting me to the conversation. Can I go upstairs to get ready? Or would you like to check for monsters under the bed?"

"Of course, you may go and get ready. You should hurry. The fundraiser starts in two hours." Cole opened the door for me.

I seethed. Clearly sarcasm was wasted on him.

***

I pushed that altercation to the back of my mind and found Lady Harper in her dressing room. She was sick about her maid, but she rallied for the good of the community and found me a gorgeous gown that I looked forward to wearing. Bruise and all.

Priscilla arrived in time to help me dress.

"How are preparations?" Lady Harper asked Priscilla.

"Everything looks amazing!" Priscilla's excitement was contagious. "You will be so proud. The meal is lovely."

"What are they serving?" I asked.

"The men shot thirty geese for us," Priscilla said as she examined my face.

"Which men?"

"Well, the husbands of the W.C.T.U. and a few of the suitors."

Lady Harper smiled at her.

"I think the word you are looking for is fiancé," she said to Priscilla.

She blushed three shades of red. "What happened to your face?"

"Oh, clumsy, slipped on ice." I rolled my eyes.

"We'll have to cover it." Priscilla rummaged in her bag. "Here's some paste. This should do it."

I ran my hand over the velvet of the gown Lady Harper had chosen for me — beautiful, heavy black velvet with ivory lace detailing at the bodice.

"Let's lace you into this thing, shall we?" Priscilla held up a corset specially designed for the dress.

I undressed and slipped the corset on. Thankfully, still so thin I could see the pregnancy, but no one else did.

"Some would wonder why you are making poor Matt wait so long," Lady Harper said mischievously as she poured us all some tea. "A long winter pining for you, no marriage until spring. You are a cruel fiancé."

"I am starting a business." Priscilla adjusted the laces on my corset. "I cannot start a family right away, and I want my business to succeed first. You maybe don't realize but it will take six months for the divorce to be final."

Divorce was so unheard of; I stifled my look of surprise. I made a mental note to discuss contraception with her in case she wanted to wait before starting a family, even after marriage. Priscilla carefully adjusted my corset.

"It's good to make a man wait. If it's too easy, they lose interest," she said lightly. "I am going to start pulling this tight."

Start!

"You might want to hang onto the bedpost. Breathe out please."

I breathed out, and she pulled those corset strings so tight I thought I would never breathe in again. Finally, she was satisfied with my shape.

"Perfect! Let's put this gown over your head, and I'll start with your hair."

She worked magic. My hair was naturally curly, but she used hot tongs to exaggerate the curl. Then she carefully covered my bruising. "Does it hurt when I touch it?"

"It's not too bad."

I didn't recognize myself when she was done. My toffee-coloured hair was piled high, making my neck look longer and more fragile. The corset formed me to look whip thin and delicate. She had left half of my hair down and curled tightly.

"That curl will relax, so I thought we should start off tighter." Priscilla adjusted some of the curls on my shoulders.

I examined myself in the mirror. Other than the shadow of the bruise, I blinked in surprise. Priscilla knew what she was doing.

This dress was like wearing a sculpture. It accentuated the swell of breast and hip by making my waist look tinier than it was. The clever dress designer deliberately exaggerated the fragility of a woman's body. I had never felt so beautiful in my life.

"It's perfect." I hugged Priscilla hard.

"I have something more to add." Lady Harper rifled through her jewellery box and brought out a heavy black and garnet necklace, earrings, and a bracelet.

When they were done with me, I stood up, and Lady Harper clapped her hands with happiness.

"You look perfect!"

"Thank you, both."

I left them so Priscilla could help Lady Harper dress. From the top of the stairway I could see Cole at the entrance. I decided to forget our altercation; we could hash that out later. He cared about my safety; I could work with that. Previously, I had wondered why the manor house had this extravagant sweeping staircase; it seemed excessive. As I descended, his eyes lit up. A slow smile of appreciation played across his lips as his eyes took their time, sliding down the length of me and back up again. I couldn't stop a smile from slipping across my face. Now I understood the purpose of the staircase.

I should stop this, shut this down right now.

I couldn't do it. My eyes lit up looking at him. While my gown was cut to accentuate my fragility, his suit was cut to make his naturally powerful body appear bigger, broader. My heart hammered in my ears at the sight of him.

"You are stunning, Shannon," he said when I finally descended the whole length of the staircase.

"Thank you." I caught my breath, partly from looking at him and partly because the corset cut into my lungs. "We can finish that discussion we just had in the study later."

"I am sorry." He held his hands out in surrender. "We handled that poorly. Both of us are used to different sorts of women. I apologize. We'll figure out a solution that works for you."

Our eyes met. I looked for any evidence he was playing with me. There was nothing.

"As I said, that conversation can wait. I have enough on my plate. You agree to discuss it later?"

"Promise." He opened my coat to help me into it.

This was an elaborate operation and I wanted nothing squashed or flattened. I carefully held my curls up so the coat would not ruin Priscilla's careful work. I let my hair go and did up the buttons on my coat.

I had never in my life tried to catch and keep a man's attention. Flirting was new to me. "You look great, Cole. Very different."

"Well, I shaved, so that's usually an improvement. Shall we?" He offered me that terrible hat again.

"Absolutely not!" I pushed it away. "Nothing can go on my head! Look at the beautiful job Priscilla did on my hair! It will ruin it! Get that hat away from me!"

"I was kidding. You won't freeze in two blocks." He grinned.

I picked up my speech and took his arm. He then navigated us around snow drifts and ice patches to the community hall.

He opened the door, allowing me to enter ahead of him. His hand at the small of my back guided me through throngs of women working hard to put this event together. He led me toward the back of the stage area. They all smiled at me as I worked my way to the stage. The W.C.T.U. had forty-six women members, and they were all there. The tables were set with their best linen and china. Nothing matched, and it didn't matter. They had pine boughs and candles everywhere. It was beautiful.

"I'll leave you back here. I have to help with making sure people know where to put horses and carriages. Will you be alright?"

"I will be fine." I fought the waves of nerves in my stomach.

He left me there to pace around behind the curtain, and my mind flew back to the last fundraiser I attended with Til.

***

I'd watched Til Stone charm money out of men since I was fourteen years old. When she entered the room, every eye stopped to look. The men looked, and their eyes widened. She was five feet nine inches of stunning. The women looked; their eyes hardened— they couldn't hold a candle to her. They knew it; worse, they knew *she* knew it.

The richest and most powerful men in London were there, but the veneer of civility in the room was thin. The men of the Malthusian league wanted Til to succeed. The elite were here in this room at their invite. Til made sure their wives knew that she offered birth control with chloroform. At a premium price of course; the women in this room would pay more and she would channel the proceeds back into the slums. If Robin Hood had been a woman and a midwife, this would have been his deal. Provided, of course, he was drop-dead gorgeous and as ruthless as a serial killer.

The mean streets of London would benefit from these men. Til intended to get as much of it as she possibly could.

Her eyes moved coolly over the men at the fundraiser.

If a member of the Society for the Suppression of Vice infiltrated, I worried about Til not being discreet. I remember feeling terrified Til would take this too far. She *always* did. Malcolm and I watched as she moved from table to table, advocating as if she didn't have a care in the world. As if we could promote birth control without fear.

My breath caught as I saw Mr. Watt hover near the entrance. Malcolm stopped him from entering the ballroom. I remembered the fear as it curled through me. Desperate to stop her, I signalled to Til. She smirked at me and kept working. With Malcolm by her side, she never felt fear. I was different, I never stopped feeling terrified. I knew what The Society could do and it made me shake with worry.

***

A continent away wasn't far enough. My stomach felt sick with fear at the thought of the society. I needed to calm down. *No more thoughts of England tonight. I'm safe in Oakland.*

I peeped out from behind the curtain, and my eyes swept over the room. This was a friendly fundraiser. I'm not in need of a body guard, and we are not pushing the limits of what is legal. I don't need to be Til to do this.

Chapter Twelve

I smiled as the crowd, dressed in their finest, took their seats, and I picked out faces I knew. Though I tried to breathe deeply to calm my nerves, I could only get a little air into my lungs. The corset was a medieval torture device I couldn't wait to get off and fire at a wall. Instead, I paced around until Priscilla joined me.

"How are you doing?" Her face was creased in concern.

"A little nervous. I wasn't expecting two hundred people out there! I usually work a smaller crowd."

Actually, come to think of it, I usually stood and smiled while Til worked the crowd like a shark.

"You look great, if that is any consolation."

"It would help if I could breathe." I moved my hands over the corset that didn't budge. "I feel like I'm encased in iron."

"You'll be fine." Priscilla, as a dress designer, was big on form over function. No sympathy from her! "The band is almost set up. Supper starts in fifteen minutes. You will address everyone in about forty-five minutes."

"I hope so." I closed my eyes and tried to take a deep breath.

Lord Harper, as master of ceremonies, came behind the curtain.

"Small change in plan. Why don't you eat now with Cole and the first table. I'll call you up before dessert? That way, as soon as everyone is done eating, you'll be ready to address them."

"Alright." Immediately, my stomach fluttered with nerves.

I went to join Cole, Priscilla, Matthew, and the Bennetts. The men settled us into our chairs first and then took their own seats. We were the first table called to dish our plates. As Cole and I went to the buffet table, he maneuvered me in front of him. This was fascinating. He made sure I was seated first, filled my plate first; Cole was a gentleman. He frowned when he saw I was hardly taking any food.

"You are going to starve to death," he said when we were halfway down the buffet table.

"I can barely breathe, let alone eat anything," I whispered, even though we were a little behind the rest of our party. He stopped and bent down to speak right into my ear.

Ohhhh... Mrs. Daindridge and Mrs. Carr are going to have a field day with this.

"I'll have an extra plate sent to your cabin for tonight when this is all over." His breath was warm against my ear, and my stomach flipped against the hard wall of corset.

"Can you do that?" I whispered back.

"Of course." His voice in my ear made my knees feel weak. "When you get done here, what would you like to eat?"

"I would like some bread and more goose, extra stuffing, and those stewed vegetables."

"Is that all?" he asked dryly while piling stuffing on his plate.

"Could you bring a little wine?" I moved my

mouth closer to his ear.

Is this having the same effect on him? Is he weak in the knees, too? He looks completely unaffected.

"If I promise to snag you some wine, which will be tricky at a temperance union fundraiser, but it can be done, can I ask you to do a favour for me?" His voice was a combination of liquid chocolate and gravel at the same time.

Anything. As long as you keep speaking in my ear like this...

"Sure." I tried to be casual.

"Can you pile your plate up, and I'll eat what you can't?" He grinned like a school boy. "Mrs. Holt makes the best stuffing in the province. I'll need at least two helpings."

Stuffing!

My heart plummeted. I was a swooning mess, and he wanted more stuffing!

"I'm starving." He placed an extra dinner roll on my plate. "This is going to be a long night."

Clearly, your knees aren't weak and you aren't melting from this very intimate whispery conversation at a buffet table like I am.

"It *is* going to be a long night." I grinned wickedly. "We have a fight scheduled for later..."

"Not a fight," he corrected me, and scooped another helping of stuffing on my plate, for *him*. "A discussion, a clarification of how things are going to work between us." He moved a little closer and his lip actually touched my ear. This was the undoing of me. My breath caught, thankfully, the corset kept me ramrod straight, or I would have pooled at his feet. "There is never going to be a day that I have a fight with you, Shannon."

Oh mercy... I'm done.

That's it. Right here, at this buffet table in front of two hundred people, I've handed my heart to Cole McDougall of Oakland, Manitoba, Canada.

My mind scrambled to get the situation under control. I took a step away to create a little distance. My breath was so shallow, I worried I might faint.

"Don't forget that wine." I could hardly breathe enough to speak.

Cursed corset, cursed emotions! I was swooning like a school girl.

"Miss Stone, it would be best if you would stop trying to get me into trouble with the temperance ladies," Cole said with such disapproval I burst out laughing, working wonders on my nerves.

We laughed as the tension between us ebbed so I could think again, but the feelings remained.

Once he stopped whispering in my ear, I could concentrate on piling food on my plate. He helped me to my seat where we all started eating right away.

"Have they talked to you about pledging yet?" Mr. Bennett asked.

"No." I smiled at him. "I won't be here long enough to fully participate. I am happy to support them, though, however I can."

Our conversation was cut short by Lord Harper's arrival at our table.

"You have thirty minutes," he said before moving on to another table.

The band started playing softly in the background. When I was finished, one of the ladies came by with a choice of pie or cake. I declined both. When everyone had started their dessert, I made my way behind the stage. I wiped my palms on my skirt and tried to breathe as deeply as I could.

I cursed that corset for the hundredth time.

"I would like to introduce to you our guest speaker tonight, Miss Shannon Stone," Lord Harper boomed to the audience.

Somehow, my feet propelled me forward until I stood at the podium.

"Ladies and gentlemen, welcome to the W.C.T.U. cottage hospital fundraising initiative!" The speech I clutched was damp from the icy cold sweat that slicked my palms and trickled down my back.

The entire audience gave me a round of applause. Miraculously, I felt the worst of my nerves dissipate.

"Lady Harper has sent her regrets she couldn't de-liver this speech tonight. I am honoured to speak on behalf of the W.C.T.U." Lady Harper caught my eye and gave me a beaming smile. She appreciated that I men-tioned her.

"As you know, our town council asked the W.C.T.U. to organize and institute a cottage hospital." My eyes locked with Mrs. Bennett's, and she nodded her encour-agement to me. I stood up straighter. "Your donations up to this point, along with their careful allocation of funds, have allowed them to secure a cottage and begin to make it ready.

"By being here to support the ladies of the W.C.T.U. tonight, we have raised six hundred dollars!"

Mrs. Daindridge and Mrs. Carr stood up and started cheering. This brought everyone to their feet, and I felt an overwhelming love for this community. When they stopped clapping and cheering, they sat down. My palms were dry, and my voice was strong as I finished.

"Thank you, generous citizens!"

The W.C.T.U. started the clapping again. Their way of saying thank you to the community they worked for.

"I am thrilled to tell you that the cottage hospital, as some of you know, the old Byron home, is to be under construction this week, and the ladies promise to have things up and running three weeks after the construction is finished."

The room burst out in applause again. I clapped with them. I caught Cole's eye; he gave me a huge smile.

"Citizens, without your kind support, we would not be on the verge of our first hospital. I am in awe of what a small community, who cares about each other, can accomplish. Thank you to the men who so generously donated these geese. Thank you to the supporters who pledged a dollar early on to get this project started. On behalf of the W.C.T.U., I would like to extend a sincere thank you to all of you here tonight and those who couldn't make it but supported this initiative nonetheless. Thank you, from the bottom of our hearts!"

The crowd stood up as they erupted into more applause. People loved praise. Obviously, I spoke for a well-respected group of women.

As I moved away from the podium, Mayor Holt came up beside me. He shook my hand then took over the podium.

Cole and Priscilla met me behind the curtain.

"You were wonderful!" Priscilla beamed at me. "Thank you."

"You did amazing out there!" Cole hugged me so hard he picked me up off the ground.

Priscilla slipped away, leaving us behind the curtain alone.

He set me down and then righted me as I tried to catch my breath. I was still in his arms when I looked up at him. He looked like he wanted to kiss me, so I gave us a little distance. I wasn't ready for this yet. I needed this to slow down.

Too late.

"The ladies want to congratulate you. Let's get back to the crowd." He held out his arm. I linked my hand in his elbow, and we rejoined the group.

Lady Harper grasped both my hands in hers. "I couldn't have done it better." Her eyes shone with happiness.

"That felt so good. Was it good?" I asked nervously. This was her speech after all.

Lord Harper hovered in the background, worry about his wife written all over his face.

I smiled at him encouragingly.

Before I knew it, I was mobbed by the W.C.T.U. members.

The men moved chairs, and the band switched from dinner music to a waltz. Cole brought me a glass of punch, and I took it gratefully.

"Is my bruise showing?" I tilted my face so he could see it clearly.

"No." He scrutinized my face carefully, taking longer than necessary.

"Priscilla covered it with a paste." I touched it to make sure it was still on.

"This has been quite a day." Cole took my empty punch glass and set it down. "Care to join me on the dance floor?"

Lord and Lady Harper left at ten, but we stayed

and danced every dance. Around eleven I started to feel nauseated; I needed some air.

Outside, I tried to fill my lungs with the ice-cold air frosted with large snowflakes. I leaned up against the side of the building and pushed a stray hair away from my face then lifted my hair off my neck so I would cool down quicker. Two men followed me out to smoke; Cole surfaced soon after. I began to feel sick again, so I forced myself to breathe in slow and controlled breaths. I longed for my cozy bed.

"Ready?" Cole handed me my coat.

"How did you know?"

"You look tired. This has been a difficult day. I'm exhausted, too, and *I* didn't address the village like a pro."

You're not pregnant either.

"I'll walk you home." He set down a huge plate of food and helped me with my coat.

"I thought I was alright to be unescorted in town limits." I narrowed my eyes at him. "This is new to me."

He stopped and looked at me in confusion. "It's new for people to care about your safety?"

That threw me a little, so I looked at him quizzically. "No, I mean, Malcolm cared. I'm just not used to this level of... I don't really know how to put it. I don't think you should tell me what to do. I would prefer if you spoke to me. It irks me that you went to Lord Harper instead of coming to me. It's like you don't trust me to be reasonable."

"I apologize." His eyes met mine, and I could see he was sincere, not making fun of me.

Cole took a step toward me. "You on your own out here terrifies me. I'm as nervous as an old grandmother.

Well known for it. You'll have to just put up with me. I'm your closest neighbor, and as such, I get a voice in all that happens in your life."

"Hmm," I said. "That's all?"

"Of course." He picked up the plate and opened his coat to show me that he had tracked down a bottle of wine. He grinned as he held his arm out for me.

His stride was too long; I almost had to jog to keep up. I pulled on his arm to slow him down. "I can't breathe, remember?"

When we arrived, he opened the door to my carriage house then moved to the fireplace to rake the coals together while I took off my coat and scarf. He started a fire in the cook stove automatically.

"Well, I'm glad our discussion is over. After watching your interrogation skills, I'm terrified of you." He finished with the fires and found two glasses for the wine.

"Terrified?" I raised my eyebrow. I put my supper in a cast iron pan to warm it up.

"Scared stiff!" He poured a glass for him, a glass for me.

Corset or not, stomach crushed to the size of a walnut, I was starved. I sat down at the table and now that my nerves were calm, I ate right out of the pan.

"Classy," he commented.

"I'm starving! You are right, about this stuffing. How does she make stuffing like this?"

"I think it's a carefully guarded secret. I have to tell you, Shann, that dress is a real stunner." He handed me the wine. His eyes skimmed down me and then back up to my eyes.

"It's Lady Harper's. She let me borrow it. I didn't

pack anything this extravagant." I sipped the wine.

I wanted desperately to be out of this dress and into an extremely comfortable nightgown. Unfortunately, I owned the ugliest flannel nightgowns known to mankind, and my vanity would not let me slide into one.

I finished supper while Cole poked at the fire and got the flames going higher to take the chill off the room faster. I wasn't sure how to address the fact that the corset was cutting me in half, and if I didn't get out of it soon, I would faint. I put the pan in the sink and picked up the wine then went to the fire.

I felt tiny standing next to him.

"You were wonderful tonight. You delivered that speech like you were born on a podium."

"Thank you." I sipped my wine. "That was my first speech in front of that many people. I've spoken before, of course, but the size of the crowd was overwhelming. Once I got into it, I actually enjoyed it."

"You weren't nervous?"

"I was for the first sentence, but as soon as the crowd applauded, my nerves fled, and it felt good to kind of work the crowd... I'm not sure how to put it."

"I think it will be the first of many."

I shrugged. "I'm not sure."

"I have a question, and I didn't want to ask it in front of Lord Harper." His tone of voice changed, so I knew we were changing this conversation drastically.

"Oh?" I braced myself for the inevitable.

"The herbs in Biddy's room. It would help if I knew how exactly she would have known when to administer those herbs."

I looked at him to see if he was kidding, but

clearly, he was not. Here it was: the conversation I had been dreading.

"I'd love to answer, but I have to breathe to do it. Let me get out of this gown, if you could just excuse me a moment?"

Vanity or not, I needed to breathe.

"Oh, right, of course." He settled on to the settee to wait for me.

I went to my room and took off the gown, but then couldn't reach the corset ties.

Curses! I can't get out of this torture device!

Priscilla hadn't thought forward to me taking *off* the gown. She'd tucked the ties in neatly so they wouldn't show up under the dress. This corset was designed for a lady with maids. I had a constable in the living room and not a maid in sight.

I put on a long robe and hesitated at the door that separated us.

How do I ask him to undo these corset lacings?

Taking a shallow breath, wishing desperately it was a deep one, I finally opened the door and crept into the living room.

"This is grossly inappropriate, but I cannot get out of this corset."

"Oh?" His eyebrow arched, and a smile played across his lips.

"Could I impose? Would you please untie this infernal thing?"

"Certainly." He got up and followed me into my room.

"Don't get any ideas," I warned him.

He held up his hands in surrender.

"I am a gentleman," he assured me.

After I carefully arranged my robe, he untied the laces then pulled at them until I could finally breathe.

"Thank you. That was actually cutting me in half." I slumped onto the bed, letting my lungs fill with air.

"You don't need this." He went to the door. He was creating distance between us so I didn't have to. "You're fine without it."

"To get into that dress, I did need it!" I protested weakly.

"Whatever you say." He left me so I could pull on one of the hideous flannel nightgowns Malcolm had packed. *Am I really going to face a man wearing this terrible thing? I have to go see what Priscilla has in stock.*

I squared my shoulders to face the conversation waiting for me in the next room. If he was blinded by the horror of this flannel get up, I hoped he was gentleman enough not to let on.

"You were a married man." I re-entered the room and picked up my wine. I joined him in front of the roaring fire and settled onto the settee with a big blanket.

"I was raised in a house of seven boys, and I was married for less than a year," he said to explain his ignorance. "I understand the only thing that suppresses menstruation is pregnancy?"

Maggie must have gotten pregnant days after getting married. I sighed. He was so sincere and innocent. We had a lot of ground to cover.

"Did you ever notice Maggie was sad or easily upset or had pain on a monthly schedule?"

"Yes," he confirmed. "Before we were married she told me about that, but she didn't go into any great detail. She would have times she wasn't well, and that worried me. I would ask if she was sick, but she called it a feminine complaint, and we never discussed what that meant. Honestly, she didn't talk about it. I respected her privacy. Maggie was just naturally a private, quiet person so I didn't ask. She was pregnant right away, so I don't know a lot. I never lived with a woman who had to... uh... deal with a menstrual... what did you call it? Oh yes, a cycle."

I shifted on the settee so we were facing each other before I launched into an explanation. We needed more wine.

Unfortunately, there was not enough wine on the frontier for this conversation.

"Biddy was carefully watching to be sure Lady Harper's menstruation," I paused, and Cole went pale, "was never delayed for much more than a day. She would be watching for symptoms every twenty-eight to thirty-one days. It seemed like if Biddy missed that window, she waited until around the eighth week. I am not sure why she did that. It's possible she understood that the ergot can cause serious complications, so she wanted to be sure of pregnancy before... I'm not sure of the word... I guess administering the ergot. That level of obsession is quite obviously an indication of insanity. She is an incurable, Cole."

"It would be hard to figure that out though, right? I mean, how would Biddy know if she was... well, having a cycle?" He cleared his throat in embarrassment, and I wanted to die.

"A lady's maid would know exactly when her lady would be dealing with her time of menstruation." I soldiered on for the sake of justice. "Four to seven days of bleeding... no lady's maid would miss that..."

Cole's face flushed red. He took a sip of wine and

then looked at me in disbelief. "Four to seven? You're right, Biddy wouldn't miss that."

"Worse, if it was *absent*, she would notice. Most women are like clockwork. If she missed even by a day, Biddy would know and she would be there with ergot of rye to make sure that the pregnancy didn't progress."

"How did *this* baby escape the ergot of rye?" Cole put his wine glass down.

I pulled a blanket around me to try to cover the atrocity of my nightgown. "The bottle of ergot was nearly empty, and she had to ship it in from Baltimore. Possibly the package was delayed, lost in the mail, or the package broke in shipping?"

"I'll have to find that out." He reached for a notepad in his breast pocket but there wasn't one. "Have you ever heard of such a thing in your life?"

"Oh, I've heard of procuring miscarriage through chemical interference, of course. But never a lady's maid administering them!"

"Well, hopefully this baby is going to be alright." His voice hardened. "What reason will Biddy use to explain these herbal remedies? What do you think is coming at us at trial?"

"Biddy has some knowledge of how it works. You need to find out how she learned about it. Mrs. Bennett said her father was an apothecary. You need to investigate that angle. She said she wanted to keep Lady Harper's menstrual pain to a minimum— that's what all those powders and concoctions promise. It makes it legal to advertise it. For the majority of those remedies, it's simply false hope."

"What sort of pain?"

Oh, please let us be done with this conversation soon!

"Well, when the uterus contracts, it's very painful. It's called cramping. Cramping typically accompanies the... bleeding."

"Let me see if I have this right. Biddy is claiming that she had to administer the ergot to make sure the menstruation was started on time to ensure Lady Harper was not in terrible cramping pain, but the ergot *causes* cramping pain."

"Excruciating."

"So, Lady Harper would have agreed to take it in the hope that her pain would be decreased because the menstruation was induced on time." Cole got up and found paper and a pencil and took notes. He returned to the settee and moved so that he could face me straight on.

Because this conversation couldn't get any more awkward.

"Yes, you have it. I'm certain that is how it worked between them. Lady Harper would be devastated to know her maid was causing her to miscarry on purpose." I scrubbed my hands over my face. I felt weary. "She *might* claim that delayed menstruation increases pain." I pressed my fingertips into my eyebrows to relieve the stress building there.

"Does it?" he was in constable mode and not a stone, cycle, or symptom would be disregarded.

"Not enough to go to these measures. A married woman who is desperate for a child certainly wouldn't. Either you have pain or you don't. It's pretty consistent, but the pain is different for everyone."

His face creased in concern. "What about you? Is it bad for you?"

"Uh... I have pain, yes, it's not terrible ..." My face

reddened. This was never discussed between men and women. I was hot with mortification.

"Sorry, that made you uncomfortable." He put his arm across the back of the settee. His fingertips were exactly nine inches from my shoulder.

I put down my empty wine glass and tucked my hands under the blanket. "To kill a fetus, you almost have to kill the mother. Ergot works, but it's dangerous. The only thing that changed Lady Harper's cycle was marriage and Biddy's overwhelming need to control Lady Harper. She was terrified someone would interfere in their relationship. A baby certainly would."

We were quiet for a moment; we listened to the fire snap in the grate as the weight of that statement settled around us.

"Would you write all that out, so I have it for the file? I might have missed something in my notes. We'll need a doctor to approve it, but you were there and on site. It might help convict her. Whatever details you can think of, please put it in the report." He put more wood on the fire then settled back on the settee and turned to look at me.

"If you hadn't been there today, I'm not sure what I would have done, Shannon. I could not have interrogated Biddy without you. You were amazing."

"There is one more angle to this, Cole," I said quietly. "This is not my field, but part of me wonders if Biddy let the pregnancies progress so that the devastation Lady Harper felt was more intense."

"Why?" Cole looked genuinely perplexed.

"I've run into women like her. They are so miserable, so mentally unstable, they feed on the misery of others. They crave it. The times that Lady Harper would have needed Biddy the most would be when she was devastated from a miscarriage, therefore feeding Biddy's need to be needed. It's a theory."

"Good grief." Cole shook his head. "Women are far more complicated than I originally thought!"

Mentally or physically?

"Whatever her intentions, she is safely in jail and she can't hurt this baby. Thank you for interrogating her. You were amazing. Without your knowledge of, well... I couldn't have done what you did."

"No. Not amazing. I just wanted justice for the Harpers and I am educated in these matters. It's easier for a woman to talk to a woman. It was nothing."

"I knew Biddy was guilty, but when you started on her, it was obvious. No doubt. I saw what you did. You shifted all the power in the room to her. That's why you wanted me to let go of her. That terrified me by the way. I was so scared she would hurt you. How did you learn that?"

"Cole, I have so much experience with crazy women."

He looked at me to continue, but I didn't want to.

"I have worked with women and for women for the last ten years. I've seen it all. It's unfortunate she didn't confess. It makes your job harder. She *thinks* she loves Lady Harper. She is obsessed with her. I just exploited it a bit."

"Well, thank you, again."

I yawned and stretched.

"I hate to go, but I better get out of here." His face softened again; he was worried about me. "You look exhausted."

"I'm alright." I wondered what it would take for

those fingertips to navigate the nine inches between us. "I'm glad that conversation is over," I confessed. "Did you get enough stuffing?"

"No, there is never enough stuffing, especially if Mrs. Holt made it!" Gallantly, he accepted the change in subject.

He got up and pulled on his coat and boots.

I got up as well and walked him to the door.

"Get a good rest. This was a big day." He tucked a stray hair behind my ear.

I looked up at him, and he smiled.

"Thanks for clarifying all that," he said softly.

"I'll write it out tomorrow so we never have to have that conversation again," I promised.

"That would be great. Good night, Shannon." He opened the door and slipped out, shutting it firmly behind him.

I locked the door and crawled into my ice-cold bed, too tired to pull the bed warmer through it.

Sometime late in the night, someone began pounding on my door, loud enough to wake the dead.

Chapter Thirteen

"Gentlemen, to what do I owe this honour, at this time of night?" I leaned against the door frame to keep upright while rubbing my eyes. So exhausted, I couldn't focus on the men in front of me. Cole, Matt, and Councilman Carr shuffled into my carriage house.

"Sorry to wake you in the middle of the night. Would you be willing to assist us? Katie Ross's father is asking for assistance from a midwife. He's accused the hired man of being inappropriate with Katie... against her will. Mr. Ross has run the man off the property. We thought it would be best for Katie to be examined by a woman," Cole said then looked at the other men, Councilman Carr and Matthew Hartwell. "She is young. She would likely feel more comfortable with you than Dr. Davies."

"Of course. Give me a minute to change and get my bag together."

Cole followed me into my room, which made me turn on him with a raised eyebrow.

"Matt and I are going after the hired man. Would you go with Councilman Carr? Do you feel safe if I send you with him?"

I rubbed my eyes again and yawned.

"Sure."

"Alright, I'll wait outside. I know you are tired and it's really late, but we have to get moving." Cole left the room to join the men.

Once dressed in my warmest and heaviest clothes, I grabbed my doctor bag, making sure I had all the necessary equipment for assault. Cole was pacing; Matthew stood with Councilman Carr by the door.

"Don't kill him." Finished with my bag, I pulled on my boots. "I mean it. You look like you are ready to rip him apart limb by limb. Sometimes these things aren't what they seem at all. Please listen to me, Cole, be careful. I don't want you in a cell beside Biddy. I won't be there to protect you." I grinned.

He reached out and adjusted my hood. "If he did, if he actually did force her... well, heaven help him."

He's not just over protective with me; he's over protective with all women.

Thin snow drove across the prairie like needles; the snow was coupled with a deep cold that numbed everything it found exposed.

"Will you be warm enough?" Cole asked as he lifted me straight up onto the back of a horse. I couldn't get my feet in the stirrups, so he adjusted them to a length that was comfortable.

"What is going on with this saddle?" I held the horn on the front of the saddle as the horse danced under me. Cole caught the reins.

"It's a western saddle." He smiled broadly, even though he was impatient to get going. "This isn't England. We do actual work with horses here."

"Alright, never mind," I said dryly. "Let's ride."

"It's a hard ride." Cole doubled checked the reins. "She's obedient, so you need to give her lots of slack in those reins. She's nearly dead, so no need to worry about her taking off. I didn't want to put you on anything that would be challenging. Are you warm enough?"

He couldn't see the shrug because I was wearing too many layers. "You worry too much. Besides, I can't put on any more layers."

"I know that I worry. You are right to call me an old grandmother. It's my wife— she was so frail, and that's all the experience I have." Cole's face was creased with concern that he was asking too much from me.

"I'll be fine," I assured him. "I'm not frail. If I thought I couldn't do this, I would tell you. How far?"

"Twenty minutes, give or take."

My eyes widened.

"I can bring Katie to you if you aren't up for it," he offered when he saw my face.

"Cole, I'm fine." I shifted in the saddle. "Let's ride."

"Shannon?" Cole said after he had mounted his horse.

I looked at him as my horse moved unsteadily beneath me.

"Take detailed notes."

"Of course."

With that, he was gone into the vast, black prairie night. I followed Councilman Carr straight to Mr. Ross's house.

Carr's horse plowed through the drifting snow ahead of me. My stomach became queasy. If I ever got off this horse, I would never get back on. Finally, at two in the morning, Councilman Carr dragged my frozen body off the horse and ushered me into the house. Mr. Ross took me straight to the cook stove and helped me out of all my outer clothes. As I thawed out by the wood stove, I listened to Mr. Ross's account of things.

"This is a terrible business," Councilman Carr agreed with Mr. Ross.

"When I get my hands on him..." Mr. Ross trailed off because men didn't speak of violence in front of women. "I'm sorry to drag you out of your bed at this time of night."

"I'm a midwife, sir. I'm used to being dragged out of my bed at all hours of the night." I flexed my frozen hands over the fire. "Would you mind telling me how you came to find them?"

"I wasn't sure what was taking him so long at the woodshed. I thought he might be hurt and thought I better check. As soon as I poked my head into the woodshed, she started screaming blue murder."

"Screaming before you opened the door or after?"

I watched realization hit him and then get replaced with sheer fury. "After."

"What reason would Katie be in that woodshed, unless he dragged her out there or she went willingly?" I peeled off another layer.

His face went red with rage.

"I don't know who I want to kill first." He hung my coat up by the fire to dry out. "If this gets out, it will ruin her."

"Mr. Ross, things happen. This is not the first or last girl and hired man to find themselves in this situation. Let's get her checked out. We don't know anything for sure, yet. May I see her?" I asked as soon as my fingers were thawed enough to examine her.

When I entered Katie's room, her back was to me. Only one candle glowed on the stand by her narrow bed; the room felt cold. I put my hand on her shoulder and she turned to me; eyes red and swollen from weeping.

"Are you in pain, Katie?" I pulled the blanket up around her.

She blinked in confusion.

"Your father told me that you were hurt."

Her face crumpled.

"I'd like to help you."

She launched herself into my arms, and I held her while she wept.

"It's going to be alright," I said as she clung to me.

When that storm was over, she lay back down.

"In England," I said gently to help her relax, "I went to school to be a midwife first and then a doctor. I'd like to examine you to make sure that there is no damage."

"You're a doctor?" She wiped her eyes and looked down.

"Almost, I still have two years of training to complete."

"Women can't be doctors."

"My aunt is a doctor, and she wants me to be one, too."

"Do you want to be?" She looked at me timidly.

"Yes, I do. I like helping people. I'd like to help you." I sat down at the foot of her bed keeping my tone soft, no accusations, and no judgments. Just here to make sure everyone was healthy and no one was falsely accused.

Her eyes welled with fresh tears.

"Did John Marsden force you to have sex with him?"

She cried harder now, and I understood from her weeping there had been no forcing. She was scared all right, but not scared of what a man could do to a woman, more of what her father was going to do to them in this state, at this age.

"Constable McDougall has asked me to check for bruising. That's all."

She shook her head no. I heard the front door open and the heavy boots of men entered the house.

Her eyes widened in fear. She turned to the wall and refused to let me near her or speak of what had happened.

I left her room, and Cole left John Marsden with Matthew and Councilman Carr to meet me privately in the hallway.

"Was a rape committed?" Cole's jaw clenched so tight I worried his teeth would break.

"I think not. She won't allow me to examine her."

"We'll go into her room together." He reached for the door knob, but I stepped in front of him.

"Don't scare her." I pressed my hands against his, stopping him from opening the door.

"I don't know if this man is guilty or innocent," Cole said in a low voice. "She will talk, because if he's guilty, so help him."

"I'm pretty certain, from the facts I've gathered here, Mr. Marsden is innocent."

Cole's face changed. It went from granite hard with anger to confusion.

"Calm down, please. Your face is scaring me. You'll terrify her. Let me try once more."

Cole took a step back. My hands dropped to my sides. "Once more, and then I go in."

When I entered the room, I realized she had heard through the door.

"He didn't rape me." She trembled as she allowed

me to examine her. No bruising, no tearing. She looked like a woman who had had consensual sex and was six to eight weeks pregnant.

"You're pregnant, Katie." I pulled her clothes back into place. "When was your last menstruation?"

"I don't know," she wailed.

"You must know," I insisted. My patience had snapped. She had let her father drag us all out here in the middle of the night instead of telling the truth.

She's young.

"You need to talk to your father. He needs to know you're having a baby. You have to tell the truth now, or things are going to go very bad here for Mr. Marsden. Constable McDougall is not going to walk away from this and ignore it. You heard him out there."

"Will you talk to my dad? Tell him I love him?" she whimpered.

"I will sit with you while you talk to him, and I'll stay until it's all worked out."

So, at three in the morning, I sat with Mr. Ross, his pregnant daughter, Katie, the guilty and sheepish John Marsden, and a stern-faced Cole McDougall. Councilman Carr and Matthew had left after John had been apprehended.

When we arrived, Mr. Ross had been furious. By four in the morning, the truth came out.

"John and I are in love, Dad. We want to be together, but we know I'm too young..."

"You are too young. John, you'll have to leave in the morning." Mr. Ross banged his fist on the table.

Katie and I jumped.

"Katie." I looked at her sharply. "Shall I tell him, or will you?" My stomach rolled with nausea. The baby

I carried did not like being up and around at four in the morning. Exhaustion wore at me; I wanted this resolved and I wanted to go to bed. Cole and Mr. Ross looked at me with confusion.

"John and your father have a right to know," I said impatiently.

Cole looked at me with concern as he moved closer to me.

"I'm pregnant." She covered her face with her hands.

Mr. Ross's face fell in disappointment.

John wanted to go to Katie, but didn't dare.

"You'll have to be married immediately." Mr. Ross was grimly determined to resolve this matter for the baby.

Katie pulled her hands away from her face and looked at John with so much hope and love I wondered how Mr. Ross hadn't seen the feelings growing between them.

Cole's jail cell would remain empty. The matter was resolved.

Exhausted, I looked gratefully at Cole as he picked up my heavy doctor's bag. I forced my arms to drag on all my outerwear. A cutter had been provided for our return trip, and I felt weak with relief. Twenty minutes' hard ride sounds fine if it's not a million below with wind. Mr. Ross came out with me and put hot rocks at my feet and handed me a hot rock for my hands.

"We'll come back for the horses when this cold snap breaks." Cole pulled a heavy lap robe over me.

"Thank you for coming and helping us through this." Mr. Ross patted my shoulder. "I apologize for my angry behaviour."

"Of course," I murmured. The cold had already numbed my lips.

Cole slapped the reins down on the horses, and we took off into the night. I hunched over the hot rock, grateful for it. Cole stopped the horses and turned to me, opening his coat. I looked at him completely confused.

What is he doing?

He pulled me onto his lap and I curled up against him, my face pressed against his chest. I tucked my head under his chin, and he arranged his coat and the lap robe to block the wind. In this cocoon the rock warmed me, and I fell asleep.

I didn't wake up until we were at my home, and even then, everything felt like a dream. Cole carried me into the house. I must have participated as he took my heavy outer clothes off for the second time that night, but I had little recollection of it. He pulled the bed warmer through the bed and then put me in the bed with a hot water bottle at my feet and another for me to hold onto. I heard him making sure the fire in my room was stoked to the highest heat.

"Do you need anything else?" he whispered into my ear, pulling me back to consciousness. He carefully stroked my hair back from my ear. The man was examining my bruised cheekbone, again. I heard him tsk under his breath. Any mark on me bothered him.

If a bruised cheekbone bothered him, what would he do with the rest of my tragic tale?

"Does it hurt?" he whispered. "Should we put some more ice on it?"

"Hmmm," I mumbled into my pillow.

"Is that a yes hmmm or a no hmmm?" he stroked

my face.

I shifted in bed. He carefully moved the covers so my back wasn't exposed.

"Thank you, Cole, I'm fine. I'm just so tired."

"You were great tonight. Thank goodness you were there. I'll let Jaffrey know you are not to be disturbed tomorrow. Sleep as long as you can."

"Thanks, Cole." I closed my eyes and burrowed deeper into my pillow.

Instinctively, I knew he wanted to stay. To crawl into bed right beside me, pull the covers up over both of us, shut the world out. He behaved like a gentleman, no crawling into beds of almost-doctors.

"Sleep well. I'll check on you in the morning."

I didn't even hear him leave.

Chapter Fourteen

Priscilla stopped by mid-morning and found me still in my robe, drinking tea by my fire.

"You aren't dressed." She went to refill the kettle in my kitchen.

"I got called out last night." I put down my tea cup and raked my hands through my hair, trying to look more awake than I was. "After all the drama of the day before, I am exhausted."

"Poor thing, what happened?" She made a fresh pot of tea and placed warm scones and butter in front of me. She topped up my tea cup.

I couldn't tell her about Biddy or about Katie.

"An altercation that needed a midwife." I slathered butter on a scone and sunk my teeth into it.

"Oh! A new baby?"

"No. I am not a doctor yet, but I respect that code of confidentiality. All is well. The matter is sorted out."

"Good! Of course, it's nice to know you don't say anything. I just wanted to check on you and let you know that we are planning a pie box social. We want to raise some funds for baby blankets and clothes for newborns at the hospital. Can we count on you to provide a pie?" Priscilla asked.

A shiver of apprehension made my heart beat hard at the suggestion. Left to my own devices, any pie I put together would be a disaster, and I would be sitting alone. Worse, it would be purchased, and my failings as a woman would be on display for the entire community. "I have never made a pie in my life."

Priscilla looked at me blankly.

"Can you make one, and I'll just buy it from you?"

She frowned at me. Apparently, this was not done. Women baked pies; men bought them. That was the rule.

"I can learn." I straightened up on the settee, ready to face a new challenge. "How hard can it be? You read a recipe, and you make it, right? What is a pie box social anyway?"

"All the ladies submit a pie, and the men pay for it, and the lady eats the pie with them. Only single ladies, of course."

"Of course," I agreed.

If these women knew how hopeless I was at homemaking, what would they think of me? Why didn't Til get someone to teach me how to bake? What am I thinking? Til? Baking? Oh my heavens... not on your life.

"Would you like to come over and make one with me? I can sort of guide you along," Priscilla offered.

"I think that would be the best solution."

A week later, I made my way to Priscilla's to bake after I picked up the requisite cream and coconut, an extravagance. She assured me it was a money maker.

Baking turned out to be quite fun. Once I learned impossible terms like 'rub lard into flour' and what a 'sprinkle' or 'pinch' was, it wasn't as daunting as I thought. She sprinkled, I rolled dough and obediently stirred filling in a pot. At the end of the afternoon we had two perfect pies anyone would be proud of.

"Now you know how to make a pie!" she declared and poured tea for both of us.

"I'm so grateful to you, Priscilla. I think I could have figured it out, except the 'rubbing in the lard.' That really threw me." I sipped my tea.

"It's a skill most girls have, though. Were you rich in England?" Priscilla added a sugar cube to her tea and then blew on it delicately.

"Well, I was being groomed to be a doctor by my aunt. If she knows how to bake, she didn't pass that skill to me. She put all the emphasis on medicine. I wasn't trained to do much else."

"I see," Priscilla said politely. "That coconut cream pie is perfect. You'll make a lot."

"Oh, well, as long as whoever shares it with me knows I'm here only until Lady Harper's baby is born." There was a warning in my voice.

"Oh?"

"Yes, once Lady Harper's baby is born, I'm back in England for school." I fiddled with the tea towel and found myself wondering about Til, how was her trial...

"Hmm," Priscilla said.

"I have to." I stood up to tidy the dishes. This conversation was making me uncomfortable.

"I just thought... I thought you and Cole maybe... were... getting serious?" She got up to help me wash dishes.

My conscience plagued me.

When this pregnancy shows, what will I do? What will happen to Cole? I should have stopped this!

"I don't know how else to put it. I have to go home. Things between Cole and I just sort of escalated, and I don't really know where we stand." I filled the sink with hot water from the kettle.

"Does he know this? I love Cole like a brother, and I don't think he knows."

"I have been honest about returning." I felt sick at those words. I hadn't been honest about everything. Bile raised in my throat. If I didn't come clean soon, I was going to have an ulcer.

"You know what Cole's like, Shannon, fiercely protective. He thinks women are fragile and helpless. I know you wouldn't take advantage. Just be careful. He's got a big heart. I don't want him to get hurt." She took the bowl I had carefully washed and dried it.

Am I here to make pies or be warned?

Be serious about Cole or let him go. The situation with Katie had nearly sent Cole over the edge. Cole would have destroyed John Marsden if he had forced Katie. He'd never guess the women of this community were ready to go to battle for him in their own way.

Did men know women were as protective of them as they were of us? Did Cole have any idea Lady Harper, and now Priscilla, women he looked at as fragile and helpless, were ready to battle me to the death if I hurt him?

"I don't speak of it, but Cole protected me and helped me at a very bad time in my life. I want you to be sure about how you feel and make it clear to him. I see how he looks at you." Priscilla took another bowl.

"I promise I'll be careful with him." I turned to her. "I appreciate you telling me how you feel about this. I really do. Cole and I need a conversation. Soon."

"Good." She smiled her approval at me. "I hope he convinces you to stay here with him."

Oh Priscilla, that isn't even on the horizon as an

option!

"We'll see." I wrung out the dishcloth, and we poured another cup of tea.

"I have an offer for you, Priscilla."

"Oh?"

"You mentioned you did not want to get pregnant right away, once you are married. I can help you with that."

She looked at me, and her eyes filled with hope. "It's not that I don't want to have a baby. I just can't yet. I know Matt would understand, but I... I just keep putting off the wedding because my business is so new."

"I can't bake a pie to save my life, but I can make sure you don't have a pregnancy unless you want one." I took a cookie and handed her the plate.

"I'd say that's a much better skill." She took a cookie and grinned at me.

***

The pie box social was a huge success. I wasn't in the same dramatic outfit as before, so I could breathe. When Cole out bid everyone for my pie, we shared it companionably at the same table as Priscilla and Matthew.

I tried to soothe my conscience.

No one thought we were courting. He bought a pie I made. Big deal. Priscilla noticed things between us, but only because she is so close to Cole.

Mrs. Daindridge floated by and stopped to whisper in my ear. "You two make a beautiful couple. I loved Maggie, but I dare say if I had to pick a wife for Cole, you are the exact girl he needs."

I smiled at her while my throat closed with anxiety. People were looking at us and smiling and nodding. At first I was a little flattered, and then it hit me.

No, Mrs. Daindridge! Don't think that! This pregnancy he doesn't even know about is going to be blamed on him... this is a disaster.

My conscience beat me with waves of hot and cold. I was sweaty and clammy at the same time. I felt sick. A lump started in my throat, and I could not get any more pie down, even though it was absolutely delicious.

I had to tell him, but hadn't I suffered enough?

I watched him laughing with Matt and Priscilla, and tears stung at my eyes.

I pushed away from the table, and Cole and Priscilla looked up in alarm.

"Are you alright?" Priscilla asked as she laid a hand on my arm.

"I have to go." I tried not to let the tears drop from my eyelashes to my cheeks. The least I could do was minimize the damage. If I kept him at arm's length, maybe people would forget we had been close.

Cole stood up when I did, frowning with confusion.

I dashed to the cloak room and pulled my coat and boots on. I wiped tears from my eyes and was out on the street when he caught up with me. Now that I was away from the crowd, the tears could flow unchecked down my cheeks. Cole came up behind me.

"Shannon, what's wrong? Are you sick?" He took me by the arm just as I started to slip on ice.

This cursed country! Can't run from anything. Ice and snow everywhere.

I wanted to grab onto that explanation like a life boat, but it would be more lies. I couldn't do it. I couldn't lie to him.

"I have to go home." I carefully stepped away from him as I pulled my arm out of his hand. He took my arm again as I tried to march away from him.

Tears kept falling down my face, and Cole looked at me helplessly. I felt sick keeping this pregnancy from him. I hadn't realized that the town had us basically married already. All these people that respected him, and I was going to ruin him. No solution presented itself except the truth. How could I do it? How could I tell him and watch his face change, watch him pull away? I needed to talk to Lord Harper; he was the only person who knew the truth. But every time I thought of it, my mouth went dry. How could I talk to him about this, not wanting this baby that was a result of violence, when he yearned for one? The more I thought about it, the more my stomach churned.

"I need a minute." I took a few steps away from Cole.

He stood there and made no move to leave me. "Shannon, please just tell me what is wrong. Did someone say something to upset you?" He made a move toward me again, but I held my hand up.

"Please, just go back inside. I'm sorry. I just need a minute." To my utmost mortification, I dropped to my knees and threw up. I threw up every speck of that beautiful pie, so I cried about that, too.

"Shannon!" Cole dropped to his knees beside me.

"Please, I don't want you to see me like this," I said through my sobs.

He knelt there motionless. I was certain he was asking himself 'how do I deal with this woman?' Weeping, I tried to cover my vomit with snow.

Gently, he rubbed his hand up and down my back and he took my hands in his. My vomit-covered, snowy hands didn't stop him. He didn't seem to care.

Please, God, let me die right here.

"You are going to freeze to death, Shann." He pulled out a handkerchief and wiped my tears and the vomit I had missed on my chin. I felt fresh mortification wash over me.

"Whatever this is, I want you to tell me right now, and we're going to face this together," Cole commanded.

I couldn't do it. To unburden all of this would be a relief, but the consequences would be dire. Once Cole knew, there would be no more parties, no more speeches, no more midnight romps across the prairie to assist teenagers with unwanted pregnancies, no more assisting me out of gowns with ridiculous amounts of hooks, eyes, and buttons.

What would he do?

He would be stoic. He'd do the right thing; get me in touch with the right doctor. Someone discreet who would make arrangements for adoption, make sure that I had what I needed. The look in his eye when he saw me would be gone. The fierce need to protect would be gone, too. What would be the point of protecting what was soiled and destroyed? I closed my eyes for a minute, allowing all my muddled thoughts and feelings to wash over me.

"I'll take you home." I could hear disappointment in his voice as he stood up.

I stayed there kneeling on the ground.

"Have you ever felt..." I whispered.

He turned to crouch down beside me again. "Have

I ever felt what?" He placed a hand on my shaking shoulder. He almost added darling. I was sure of it, and that would have sent me right over the edge. You can't come back from a 'darling' or a 'honey' or a 'love.'

"Worthless and ashamed?" I looked down at the snow between us.

"Someone *did* say something to you." He took me by the upper arms so I would face him. I kept my eyes down, focusing on a button on his coat. "I knew it. Was it Mrs. Daindridge? I saw her whisper something to you. What did she say?"

If I looked at him, if our eyes met, I would be undone.

"Shannon, what did she say to make you feel so ashamed? I can't think of a thing that you could have possibly done."

"She said—" I sobbed.

"Oh, honey," he whispered as he put his arms around me.

There it was... *honey*... we were doomed. He'd be blamed for this pregnancy. I'd leave him here with a damaged reputation and a broken heart.

I covered my face with my hands and tried to remain as stiff as possible in his arms, but my traitorous body softened, leaned into him, and started to melt.

"What did she say?" He held me right there in the snow bank.

Finally, I pulled it together enough that I could pull away from him. If anyone saw him holding me in a snow bank, it was only going to make things worse. I noticed his knee was dangerously close to the edge of all that coconut cream vomit.

"She said I would make the perfect wife for you."

My breath was coming in short little gasps.

"And that made you feel worthless and ashamed?" His forehead was creased in confusion. "I don't get it."

Cole looked up and saw Priscilla coming toward us. He stood up and helped me to my feet as Priscilla approached.

"What's wrong?" she asked Cole.

"Shannon is not feeling well." Cole held onto me, even though we were both standing. "I'll take her home."

"Shall I come, too?" she asked me, obviously concerned.

I looked at her dully through my puffy eyes. "I just need some time alone. Maybe stop by tomorrow."

"Of course." She slid her arms around me. "I love you."

My heart warmed. "I love you, too." I hugged her back. "But I need to go home, and I want you to stay and enjoy your night, please. I would feel worse if you left."

"I'll come by in the morning," she promised.

I turned to walk away, and Cole reached for me.

"I should walk home alone," I protested.

"Not on your life. We have a conversation to finish," he said grimly.

"I already said too much."

"You hardly even started. We're not done with this."

We walked to my carriage house, and it was so cold when I opened the door, Cole started the ritual building fires in my room, living room, and in the cook stove. He put on water to boil so I could wash up before bed. It didn't take long for the chill to leave the air, and I could finally take my coat and boots off.

My clothes were cold; I stood by the fire and tried to warm up.

"I got hurt in England." I couldn't look at him. I focused on the fire in front of me. "And I feel bad about it."

Cole scratched his temple and put another bucket of water on the cook stove. He finally came to me at the fire and ran his hands up and down my arms to warm them up.

"I don't understand. Did *you* hurt someone in England? I think that would cause shame, not getting hurt."

Fresh tears gathered in my eyes, and I tried to will them to stop.

Will I ever stop crying about this?

"Who hurt you, Shannon?" he asked finally.

I stepped away from him. He had the decency to give me the space I suddenly needed. I felt vulnerable, completely exposed.

"My aunt has powerful enemies, and the night they came for Til, the clinic we worked out of was burned down, and I ran away and I got... I got hurt," I whispered the last few words.

I saw his eyes change from concern to a slow realization of what had happened. He was too decent and too kind to push me to tell him. To make me formulate the words that had devastated me right to my core.

"Oh, Shannon." He moved closer and took my hand in his. "I'm so sorry, Shannon. But I'm not sure why that means you need to push me away. Are you afraid of me? Do I scare you?"

"No, you don't scare me. I... please... I don't think..." I felt more bile crawling up my throat. "I'm so sorry, but that's all I can say..." I ran to the only bucket left that didn't have water in it and tried to throw up again. The stress of sharing something so traumatizing took everything out of me.

"It's alright," Cole said patiently from the living room as I wiped my mouth. "You don't have to tell me anything, Shannon."

I picked my head up out of the bucket and I felt sick again at the defeat I heard in his voice. Tentatively, I crept back into the living room. He didn't move until I was close enough to touch him. I took his huge hand in mine.

"Thank you, I appreciate that." My stomach calmed down, and I took a deep breath.

He squeezed my hand in his. Not so hard that it hurt, of course, just enough to be reassuring.

"I'm going to stay long enough to pour you a hot bath, and then I'm going to ask Mrs. Bennett or Priscilla to come and talk to you tomorrow. If she can't come in, I'll take you to her." He tugged at me to sit beside him on the settee. "I think you need a woman to talk to, not a man."

His kindness and empathy unraveled me. I covered my face with my hands as I fought the sobs crawling out of my blackest depths. He asked nothing. He reached for me, dragged me onto his lap, and held me while I broke into pieces. He ran his hands over my back and arms. We both heard the water boiling on the cook stove at the same time. He didn't move, waiting for me to indicate I was calm.

Eventually I sat up, still on his lap. He handed me another handkerchief.

"You have a lot of these." I wiped my eyes and blew my nose.

"Good thing," he said softly.

"The water is boiling." I moved off his lap so he could pour the bath water into the tub.

Once the bath was poured he turned to me. "What-ever this is…"

I turned to look away, so he gently stroked my face to get my attention. This time I didn't flinch.

"Shannon, honestly, whatever this is, it's going to be alright. Unless you killed someone, everything else in this world is fixable."

"I didn't kill anyone," I whispered.

"Oh, good. I didn't really think you had. So, when you are ready to talk about this, I'm ready to listen."

I nodded, and he pulled his coat and boots on. He'd stayed too long as it was.

"I'm really sorry. I'm so sorry. I can't speak of it yet," I said so piteously his forehead creased in concern.

"Try to have a good sleep tonight, everything seems better in the morning," he said reassuringly.

"I'll try."

Once he was dressed for the weather, he came to me and tucked some hair behind my ear. "I hate to leave you when you are so upset. Don't feel sad, please. What-ever this is, we're going to face it together."

I said nothing as he kissed my forehead. My traitor-ous body leaned into him again.

"Good night, Shann, take something to help you sleep. I'll be back tomorrow with Priscilla," he promised.

I nodded in agreement.

With that, he was gone into the night. I closed the door and leaned my forehead against the hard wood. "I'm so sorry," I whispered into the wood. "I can't speak of this. I don't think I ever will be able to. When you know the truth, what you feel for me will die."

Chapter Fifteen

I woke up to Jaffrey making me a big breakfast and leaving lunch and supper in my kitchen. *Did he hear about my ridiculous outburst last night? Did Cole send him here to make sure I ate breakfast?* On my breakfast tray with warm toast and poached eggs was a note from the Harpers.

"Thanks, Jaffrey." I opened the note and scanned over it.

An invitation for an informal evening of skating and a bonfire on the river behind Hillcrest.

"May I ask your shoe size, Miss Stone? I'll have a pair of skates ready for you."

"Size seven, thank you."

"Of course." Jaffrey bustled around making sure I had everything I needed then left me to eat my breakfast.

After breakfast, I had just settled on my settee with tea, a blanket, and a book when there was a tap at the door. Both Priscilla and Cole had arrived. I asked them in and pulled my robe tighter.

Cole looked at Priscilla and then he moved forward to me.

"Please talk to Priscilla," he suggested gently in my ear.

"Alright," I whispered back.

"I'll leave, and you ladies can have a chat." Cole

firmly pulled the door shut behind him.

"Are you alright?" Priscilla went to pour herself tea while I put more wood on my fire. We settled down on the settee together.

I opened my mouth to speak and promptly closed it.

Why does speaking of this make it more real?

"Oh, Shannon, just tell me what on earth is going on." She hugged me hard.

"I haven't spoken of it... I don't know if I can... I..." I stood up and paced over to the fire.

"I can tell you what happened to me then you can decide if you should open up to me or not."

I turned to look at her. She patted the settee, and I sat back down. We sat together a minute while I watched Priscilla gather her thoughts.

"Almost two years ago, I married a man so rich, so powerful I was swept off my feet by him until he hit me. The first beating was three months after our wedding. I thought he would stop. He didn't. The last beating terminated my pregnancy. I ran from him, but my escape came too late to save my baby."

We sat there silently, as I imagined the loss she must have felt. Tears gathered in her eyes. She pulled out another handkerchief. I reached out to hold her hand.

"It's a long story for another day, but I spent the first three months here in this carriage house and at times in the basement of Hillcrest. I worked for Lady Harper. Because of this community, I have a business and a life of my own. Richard can't hurt me anymore. This community came together, and they gave me what I needed to survive and finally be done with him.

It was a long battle, and without Matthew, and my dear friend Cora, I don't know what would have happened."

"I am so sorry!" I squeezed her hand.

"It all worked out. That's why my business is called 'Hope in Oakland'. My hope was restored here. So, why don't you tell me what brought you here?" Priscilla reached for her teacup. She was so serene, there was no hurry.

"My aunt runs a women's family planning clinic, and there is a Society in London called The Society for the Suppression of Vice. This Society accused her of promoting obscene literature. The leader, Mr. Watt and his wife came by to threaten her to stop promoting birth control and the pamphlets with the diagrams of how to use the birth control. She refused.

"Oh! So, what happened next?"

I sipped at my tea.

"I believe Mr. Watt and his followers in a fit of zealous rage burned down the clinic and had Til arrested. While they were busy doing that, she told me to run so I wouldn't be arrested, too, as an accomplice. So, I ran, and I don't know who attacked me. I eventually was unconscious from the attack. My uncle found me and sent me here so my reputation wouldn't be muddied with Til's."

She took my tea cup when I covered my eyes with my hand.

"I am so sorry." Priscilla's eyes filled with tears of sympathy.

"I am pregnant and no one knows but you. I haven't been able to speak of this."

"Oh, my dear." She put both cups on the tray and opened her arms to me. Until that moment, I had no idea what it felt like to have a sister, and now that I have experienced it, I don't know how people live without them. She stroked my back as I wept against her.

"Oh, Shann." She held me tighter.

After a while, I pulled myself together and mopped my face.

"So, now you are worried that Cole will be blamed for this pregnancy, since he has shown an interest in you?" Priscilla's eyes were soft with sympathy.

"Exactly. Mrs. Daindridge said we made a beautiful couple. It's all just so awful. He is such a good man. He is so honourable. This will ruin him here." I pressed a handkerchief to my eyes.

"Well." Priscilla patted my shoulder. "Cole's a big boy. He needs to know. You obviously care about him, and he cares about you. He truly needs to know everything."

"I know," I groaned. "I feel really confused because I have to go back to England. I should be shutting this relationship down anyway."

"Life is messy, Shannon." Priscilla picked up her tea again. "That's what I have learned. We can plan things out so carefully, and then religious zealot or a mean husband throws a wrench in things. Sometimes you can't plan everything, and you have to trust your gut a bit. Cole is a good man, and they don't come along every day. Tell him and let the chips fall where they may. You could run this by Lord Harper, too. He might be able to come up with a solution."

"What solution?"

"Well, he has more money than anyone in the land, so maybe he sends you both away to have your babies, and then they adopt yours. Who knows what he would come up with?"

"I never thought of that." I clung to hope for the first time since I woke up on that ship leaving England. "Can you tell Cole I'll meet him tonight? We'll go to the bonfire together, but I want a meeting with him and Lord Harper in the morning. Can you do that? I just want one more night before having to deal with this whole mess."

"Of course, I'll set that up. Don't worry about a thing."

"I don't know how to thank you for coming here and listening to all of this."

"We're friends." She gave me another hug. "I am always here for you."

***

Cole came by around seven. He had two pairs of skates slung over his shoulder.

"Sorry about that emotional outburst last night." I pulled on my boots, allowing me to look at the floor instead of at him.

"That's alright." He pulled my coat off the hook and held it open. "Are you feeling better today?"

"I had a big talk with Priscilla, and I think she told you that I want to meet with you and Lord Harper tomorrow."

"She did tell me that." He helped me into my coat.

"You were right. It really helped to talk to a woman. I actually feel a lightening of the spirit." I wound a scarf around my neck. "Let's just have fun tonight, alright? I can see you are concerned, but let's just enjoy the night."

Before I break your heart tomorrow.

"Done! One fun night coming up." He held out his

arm.

He helped me down the bank of the river with his left arm and held the lantern with his right. The path through the snow was very narrow. We slipped and laughed until we reached the river. There was a path of candles to the cleared patch of ice. Off to the side there was a bonfire so huge I couldn't see the other side of it.

Lady Harper was there, wrapped up against the chill in a heavy fur blanket.

"This is nice!" I sat down beside her and worked my boots off my feet. Cole handed me the skates, and I slid them on. Thanks to Jaffrey, they were a perfect fit.

Lady Harper said, "I'm not going to be here long. I can assure you! This is tradition. He always throws a huge skating party for the town. This is the pre-party!"

She looked beautiful tonight— her eyes clear and snapping, cheeks red, and a broad smile on her face.

We laced up our skates, and off we went.

There are different degrees of cold. Tonight was a mild cold, so I didn't need to bundle up to the point I couldn't move. We skated and skated until finally I pulled on Cole's arm.

He turned to me.

"I'm frozen," I stated through lips numb with cold.

He smiled and led me back to the fire. Couples clumped together. The older ones had already gone home. The cold became fiercer now the sun had gone down.

"Sit here." He helped me onto a log and crouched down in front of me. He unlaced my skate and held my frozen brick of a foot in his hands. He rubbed until there was feeling in my foot again. There was nothing like the feeling of a frozen foot being put in a boot after being released from the tight confines of a skate. It's a bit surreal.

When I was warm by the fire, he went to the table of treats for the skaters; he got hot chocolate for both of us. When he returned, he pulled a heavy fur lap robe over us, and we sipped the chocolate in silent companionship.

The stars were diamond bright in the expanse of black. I thought about Til, wondering where she was, how she was, if she looked at these same stars, wondering about me. I worried that the pamphlets would be traced back to our clinic and she would be facing two years in prison. I worried about the rest of the staff, where would they be working out of? I tried to console myself, Malcolm would handle things, but he wasn't Til. The midwives would all miss her as their leader. Would the Malthusian league help her? I tried to put my fears about Til aside.

"What are you thinking about?" Cole asked.

"I'm thinking about my aunt. I wonder if she's looking at the same stars that I'm looking at. I hope she's alright."

"I hope so too," Cole murmured politely.

It was cold enough I needed to warm up my back against the fire.

"I'm a little surprised your aunt sent you here, on your own."

"Aunt Til raised me to be independent. As long as I don't get tangled up in a relationship, she isn't worried about me."

"Oh? Why is that?"

"She doesn't trust men."

"What about you? Do you trust men?"

"Some of them," I said slyly. "She's taught me to keep men in their proper place."

He laughed out right.

"I have to admit," I said ruefully, "that was a much easier exercise when we were talking about hypothetical men! Not so easy when they are right in front of you. It's especially difficult when they are nice to you and keep you alive."

"It's easy to be nice to you, Shannon. You're lovely. I like keeping you alive, too, it's the highlight of my day." He reached out to brush some hair back from my eyes. "I will never let anything happen to you, Shannon."

"I am not used to this. I never had anything like this." I tucked the hair firmly behind my ear.

"You should get used to this because you deserve to be happy. You're one of the best people I know. Don't start crying, I can't handle any more weeping. Last night was terrifying." He grinned.

Lord and Lady Harper stood up to go home. She was unsteady on her feet, and Lord Harper instantly stabilized her. He nodded to Cole and me as he passed by us. "I'll see you both at eleven a.m."

Lady Harper smiled mischievously, and I smiled back. Slowly, couples faded into the night until only two other couples were out by the fire with us. I was trying not to shiver, even though I felt frozen.

"I'll take you home," he said finally.

"Thank you," I said. "I feel like my lips must be blue."

A young man ran onto the ice toward us. Cole stood up to see what was going on.

"Constable McDougall?" he asked.

"Yes," Cole said as he went to meet Shane, the Bennett's hired man, on the ice.

"Is Miss Stone with you?"

"I'm right here." I got up to go to him.

"Mrs. Bennett apologizes for the lateness of the night, but she has requested that you come to her tonight. She is very sick, Miss."

"Of course." I looked at Cole.

"I'll get the cutter," Cole said. "How much time do you need?"

"I can be ready right away. I just need my bag."

"What are her symptoms?" I asked the young man fidgeting with urgency.

"A bad cough. She's pretty sure it's pneumonia, Miss."

As soon as Cole had helped me up the river bank to my carriage house, he and Shane went to get the cutter. I filled my bag with medicines for pneumonia and packed clothes for an extended stay. When Cole returned, he put a hot rock at my feet and gave me one for my lap to keep my hands warm. We'd become like a well-oiled machine. We swiftly cut across the prairie to the Bennetts'.

When we arrived, I found Ada's pulse was weak and rapid. "When did the symptoms start?" I pulled out a stethoscope.

"Late this afternoon I felt a chill and a headache. I thought it just a cold, but then the chill turned into a pain in my chest. I've had pneumonia before. I know the symptoms. It hurts to breathe, so I sent for you."

I warmed up the stethoscope and then placed it gently on her chest. I could hear the tell-tale crackling sound.

"I'll be right back." I went to the kitchen to get her some water to drink, so I could prepare a full dose of quinine. Cole waited for me to ask if I needed to stay or go home.

"You may as well leave me here." I poured a glass of water. "She's sicker than I thought. She will need round-the-clock care. Can you cancel our meeting with Lord Harper tomorrow, and we'll resume that as soon as I can leave Mrs. Bennett? I would expect I'll be here a week. If Lady Harper would prefer me to come back, she needs to send a doctor or a nurse to care for Mrs. Bennett. She cannot be here without help. Please send Dr. Davies here in the morning. I will require a second opinion."

"Certainly." Cole pulled on his coat. "I'll be back every day to check on you."

"Alright, have a safe trip home."

I went back to work. After administering a full dose of quinine to reduce her temperature and produce perspiration, I went to the kitchen to prepare a mustard plaster. I flew up the stairs with it and then carefully arranged it on her chest.

"What would we do without a good old mustard plaster?" I bathed her forehead with a cool cloth. "Let's see if we can get that chest to loosen up a bit."

I hit the pneumonia as hard as I could, mixing up one-one hundredth of a grain of tartarised antimony because she was in the first stages of pneumonia. I waited for the body to fight.

I dozed in a chair by her bed, changed her mustard plaster, and kept her dosed with quinine, tartarised antimony, and actinilid all night. By the morning, she wasn't better, but at least she wasn't worse. Even though a course of carbonate of ammonia was to be started in the second stage, I debated its use and decided on five grains in syrup every two hours.

Within hours of administering the carbonate of ammonia, her lungs seemed to fight back. Encouraged by its success, I increased the dose to ten grains every two hours. I continued treatment with the mustard plaster and was increasingly concerned her fever was not coming down. My field was midwifery, not pneumonia, so I watched the clock. Around ten a.m., Shane let Dr. Davies into the house.

I met Dr. Davies at the top of the stairs, briefing him on my course of treatment before we went into Mrs. Bennett's room together.

"This fever is still high, even with actanilid." I cleared the mustard plaster away so he could listen to her chest.

"Good work, Miss Stone." His eyes met mine, and I couldn't stop a smile of gratitude from flashing across my face. My heart warmed at his praise. "This was the perfect course of treatment. Keep going with the actanilid. I'm glad you started that when you did."

"Thank you, sir." I nodded. "I appreciate your second opinion."

"You can go ahead and increase the dose to one fourth of a grain three times daily." He started to pack up his equipment.

"Yes, of course." I helped him tidy up.

"I'll leave her in your capable hands. Where are Mr. Bennett and the girls?" He stood at the door with his hand on the door knob.

"At a piano recital in Winnipeg." I straightened up. "I'll see you out. I need to make another mustard plaster."

We went to the kitchen, and as I made the plaster, he pulled his winter clothes on.

"They say there is a bad storm coming. If you are short on any supplies, make sure you send Shane for supplies today."

"Thank you, I'll check the pantry."

"Don't hesitate to call for me if you need me. Good day, Miss Stone," he said cheerfully and left me to keep battling pneumonia with Mrs. Bennett.

To my relief, the fever finally broke the next day at eight p.m. I helped her into a bath to get her cleaned up. Three days of fever had left her exhausted. She bathed while I stripped the sheets off the bed and remade it. I got her redressed in a fresh nightgown then sat her by the fire with a bowl of chicken soup. After her meal, I settled her into her fresh bed with a hot water bottle at her feet and one at her hands.

She fell asleep as soon as her head hit the pillow. I felt it safe to leave her a few hours, so I went downstairs and made myself a very late supper.

I was tidying up the kitchen when the door burst open. Shane held a woman in his arms so bruised and bloody I dropped the dishcloth and ran to assist him.

Chapter Sixteen

Shane laid the woman on the bed in the spare room.

"Emily Wheaton?" I asked as he left her there and went to the front door.

"I can't stay, her daughter is home alone, and I have to go back for her." Shane's face was hard.

"What happened?" I asked.

He hesitated, with his hand on the door knob. I went to my doctor's bag for some anesthetic to take the edge off her pain. "You know about her man?"

"I know that the situation is less than ideal."

He snorted. "He's beaten her bloody more times than I can count. I check on her from time to time."

"Thank goodness you found her." I put a pot of water to boil on the stove.

"She won't leave him." His jaw clenched. "You'll patch her up, just like Mrs. Bennett, and she'll be back with him as soon as she can stand up. Better for her if she died. I'll go find Ivy and bring her here."

"Thank you. Please find Cole, too. He needs to know this assault has taken place, and we need protection in case Mr. Wheaton returns. Hurry."

I put Shane out of my mind and set to work. Exhaustion dragged at my hands and shoulders as I worked.

Terrible cramping pain caused her to moan in her sleep then curl in a ball to protect her unborn child. I adjusted the morphine. She bled from a gash above her eyebrow, her lip was split, and she had finger marks around her neck, indicating she had been strangled.

"I need to examine you, Mrs. Wheaton. You look around five months pregnant? I need to see if we can save this pregnancy."

She said nothing, but when I helped her up to remove her clothes, the bruising on her abdomen and lower back had to be deliberate. I shuddered at the thought. The amniotic fluid and blood on her skirts told me she was well along into miscarrying this child. As the cramping labour pains ripped through her, I made her as comfortable as possible. She must have been trying to get to Ada for assistance.

I'd seen horrendous assaults and degradation in my time, but this was so vicious, I blinked back a look of horror.

As the pains came closer together and with more intensity, she whimpered in pain.

"Not long now." I brushed hair back from her face and administered more pain relief. "Shane went to find Ivy... We'll have you all cleaned up and comfortable right away."

She looked away from me.

At 11:18 p.m. Emily delivered a stillborn daughter. I worked on cleaning Emily up, taking detailed notes of all her bruises. After administering more morphine, I carefully stitched the gash above her eyebrow then set and taped her dislocated finger. She barely made a sound.

"Shane is bringing Ivy right away." I irrigated the wound above the eyebrow with carbolic acid before carefully bandaging it.

She didn't speak.

"Do you know where your husband went?" I applied salve to her skin where the snow and wind had burned it.

Nothing.

I stopped talking. I had seen women in all levels of depression and abuse and could tell she didn't have the strength to speak. The trauma was too great.

After helping her bathe, I dressed her in one of Ada's flannel nightgowns. Silence filled the room around us as I tucked her into a clean, warm bed. I tucked a hot water bottle against her abdomen.

"Was it a girl or boy?" Her voice was raw with pain.

"A girl," I said.

Tears sprung to her eyes. "He doesn't mean it." She was prepared to defend him even after all this horror.

Oh, Emily, why are you defending this terrible man?

I kept my thoughts to myself. This was not my fight; I'd seen this before. There'd be no reasoning with a woman this far gone; I'm sure she'd heard it all before. There had to be a way to prosecute this. He'd nearly killed her.

Shane returned with Ivy. He handed her to me, and I could hardly stand the smell of her.

"Shane, can you please put on water to boil? She needs a bath before bed."

After battling pneumonia with Ada then assisting in a miscarriage with Emily, I was bone weary.

Ivy was cold, hungry, malnourished, and exhausted. She ate the food, and when she thought I wasn't looking, she hid some in her skirt pockets. My heart broke to see this little child stealing food.

Pretending I hadn't seen her squirreling food away, I helped her into a warm bath. After washing her lank hair and thoroughly cleaning her nose and behind her ears, I scrubbed that little three-year-old within an inch of her life. She was so filthy, surely someone would intervene. Cole, Lord Harper, and Mayor Holt could not allow this to go on. As soon as I was back in Oakland, I would address Ivy's condition. Emily may choose to stay, but Ivy could not. Ivy's filth and neglect went into my notes.

"You must not wake her," I whispered as I helped Ivy into bed beside her mother. She clutched the toy bear I tucked into her arms and pressed her toes against the hot water bottle at her feet. I went back to the kitchen and made a plate of snacks for her. Her eyes followed me as I set the food and a glass of milk on the nightstand by her bed.

I crouched down to whisper to her. "If you wake up and get hungry in the night, my little darling, you eat all of this." I pulled the blankets up and around her and tucked her in tightly, the way my mom used to do for me, neatly all the way down her back so there would be no draft. I stayed and stroked her hair until she slept.

How could a mother justify keeping a daughter in this state? How would Ivy ever survive this abuse? Who would teach her to demand better when it's her turn to find a man?

Tears stung at my eyes. Could I take Ivy? Could I adopt her? Til adopted me; maybe it was my turn to return that favor to someone else.

The house was peaceful, everyone sleeping. My eyes flicked over the sleeping form of Emily.

Stop judging her.

Really, what options did Emily have? Uneducated, far from home, and very far from her own family support. I knew nothing about how she had been raised. If she left, she had no rights over Ivy.

I couldn't leave a child with an abusive man; why would I expect that from anyone else?

Hot tears of frustration gathered in my eyes and spilled down my cheeks. The outright unfairness clawed at me. Emily abused, Ivy abused. A baby girl dead tonight at the hands of a man who had sworn to love and cherish her mother. The baby in my womb moved, the result violence. The suffering men could inflict on women crushed me, made it hard to breathe.

I crept out of the room, knowing my tears would not help anyone.

I breathed in deeply and out slowly. Once in the privacy of my room, I pulled off my gown and corset then rubbed my hands over my pregnant belly. My lower back ached in exhaustion. I could not hide this pregnancy any longer. I wore bulky sweaters and laced as tight as I could, but I was almost four months along.

I forced my thoughts to change to something more positive. This was a part of my life, this pregnancy, but not my whole life. If the Harpers wanted this baby, they could have it. I felt no guilt when I thought of giving him or her away; it made me feel relief.

But what will Cole say? What will Cole do?

Dead tired, I pulled on a nightgown and smoothed it over my abdomen. If Cole couldn't get past this, well that would be his failing, not mine. Crying over this trauma was exhausting and accomplished nothing. Five more months and I'd hand this baby away to a couple who desperately wanted one. I knew the

Harper's did. I would speak to Lord and Lady Harper as soon as I was home in Oakland. I pulled the covers over me and put my hands over my face.

After blowing out the candle by the bed, I took another deep breath and slowly let it out. I burrowed into my pillow. I'm not sure how long I'd been sleeping when a window downstairs smashed.

Chapter Seventeen

"Emily!" a drunken voice screamed downstairs.

I rushed out of my room and down the stairs.

"Emily!" Thomas Wheaton screamed as he crashed around the living room. Emily emerged from the spare room, Ivy right behind her.

"Oh, no," I whispered as she willingly went to him.

Hot and cold waves of anxiety pulsed through me as she stepped close enough for him to slap her right across the face. She was so weak, she dropped to the ground.

She had just miscarried a five-month-old baby... a beating could kill her, cause her to hemorrhage.

Fury took the place of anxiety as I dashed across the living room and tried to wedge myself between them. In the background, Ivy wailed. He swatted me away like a fly.

"What are you doing here?" he roared at her.

Emily cowered as he shook her.

"She was hurt. She needed a doctor," I leaped back between them again.

Turn your attention to me, not her. She can't take another beating.

"I'm not talking to you." He threw me aside again. He stood by her. "Get up, Em," he said in a sick, sing-song voice that made the hair on my neck stand up.

"Don't touch her. You'll kill her!" I threw myself

between them again.

Finally, his attention shifted from Emily to me. He loomed over me as I shook with fear. My worst nightmare came to life in front of my eyes. My heart pounded as terror washed through me. Shaking with fear; I didn't back down. I coulnd't. A woman's life was at stake.

"I'll look after her." My eyes locked with his.

He hit me so hard and fast I had no chance to brace myself. His hand split the skin on my cheekbone. He yanked me up off the floor and threw me across the room. I tried to break my fall with my arms, but I landed right on my stomach. The wind knocked out of me, and the world faded to black.

***

Slowly, I regained consciousness. I blinked as Cole's worried face came into focus along with Ada's.

"She's coming around." Ada spoke reassuringly.

Cole turned from me, satisfied that I was going to live, he pounced on Thomas, and dragged him out of the room.

From the fury on Cole's face, the only thing saving Thomas Wheaton's life was the fact that he was already unconscious. After handcuffing Thomas Wheaton, Cole turned back to me.

"Shane," Cole barked. "Escort Emily and Ivy to their room and then drag this animal to the basement."

Ada slumped into a chair. She let the frying pan clatter to the floor, no longer strong enough to hold onto it. She must have hit Thomas over the head.

Cole hugged me tightly against him until I stopped trembling.

"Shannon, look at me. It's Cole. You're safe, you're safe."

Cole tried to help me up, but I pushed him away and curled on my side, whimpering. Cole stayed crouched down beside me.

Shane closed the door on Emily and Ivy but hesitated to move Thomas.

"Take him to the basement and lock the door. Get him out of my sight, Shane," Cole growled.

"He's unconscious," Shane protested.

"Throw him down the stairs then! I don't care. Just get him out of here, I don't want Shannon to have to look at him."

Shane mercifully dragged Thomas' body into the kitchen, out of Cole's sight.

"Boil some water, Shane," Ada called out wearily.

"You're alright." Cole rubbed my back as I fought my way back to sanity. He reached for a blanket from the settee, he settled it around me as he rubbed my back and arms until I calmed down and my breathing was steady once again.

Cole wanted to move me, but Ada said she needed to look over my injuries. Cole turned his back to maintain my privacy.

Her examination was speedy, but thorough. Her skilled hands moved over my abdomen and her eyes locked with mine.

"Have the pains started?" she asked quietly.

I moaned my answer.

"Darling, you're miscarrying your baby."

Chapter Eighteen

Cole's head snapped up at this pronouncement. He turned around to look at me, modesty tossed aside.

My eyes met his, and I saw so much hurt, so much outrage; it was more than I could bear. I closed my eyes as the cramping intensified, and I moaned louder.

"A baby! Ada, what happened? Tell me right now! What do you mean, a baby? How is she losing a baby? How is she pregnant?" Cole's face was purple with fury.

Ada stood up and held her hands out. "Stop it," she shouted at him.

Cole walked away from her, his hands clenched into fists that he slammed against the wall. I jumped in fear.

"You're terrifying her." Ada's voice was hard.

"I want to rip him limb from bloody limb, Ada," Cole roared. He pulled his hands over his face. "I could put my fist through this wall!"

"Pull it together, Cole." Ada's voice was like ice on steel. "Shannon is miscarrying a baby. Thomas Wheaton will go to jail for this, if we do it right. You killing him tonight will accomplish nothing. Pull yourself together or get out of my house. I don't have the energy for the night ahead of us with you screaming and shouting."

Cole closed his eyes in disbelief, and a part of me died as I watched it. Shame and guilt engulfed me.

You don't deserve this. I should have told you. I'm so sorry. You will never know how sorry I am.

"I need you to take Shannon upstairs." Ada's voice softened. "Cole, I'm so sick, I can hardly stand up. You're going to have to do this."

"Ada. I can't do this," Cole's voice was ragged.

"If *she* can bear this, *you* can bear it. She needs to be taken upstairs." Ada stared at him, willing him to pull it together.

Another pain ripped through my abdomen, and I moaned. Ada moved toward me as Cole visibly unclenched his fists, rolled the tension out of his shoulders. He dragged his hands through his hair and finally joined Ada at my side.

Her fingers were gentle as she found fractured ribs. I groaned and tried to pant through the pain despite her care. Cole cursed under his breath. Distressed, I thought he was cursing at me. My eyes flicked over his face. He was under control again. Fury was simmering behind his eyes, but he was back from the edge.

"Cole's going to lift you up and put you in bed so I can get you in position to deliver this baby," Ada gently brushed hair back from my face. "Darling, I'm too weak. Cole's going to have to help. Careful of her left side, Cole, I think her ribs are fractured."

More pain ripped through me, leaving me shaking and sick.

"Shannon," he said so quietly, right into my ear. "It's me. It's Cole. Ada says that your baby is coming."

His voice, his hands, everything was so gentle, it broke something in me.

"I'm so sorry," I wept.

"Shannon, you've nothing to be sorry about. We're

going to get all this sorted out. May I pick you up and take you upstairs? I'm not going to do a thing unless you say yes." His voice was soothing in my ear.

I nodded; the pain was taking the fight out of me.

He gently picked me up and took me upstairs.

As soon as Cole laid me on the bed, Ada went to work, sending Cole to get hot water, cloths, and my doctor bag. I'd only brought things for pneumonia, not for a miscarriage, so had nothing to contribute but anesthetic. Unfortunately, I was the only one who knew how to administer it.

"Wrap hot towels around her back and abdomen. The heat helps with the cramping," Ada said to Cole. He was quick to comply. I had been redressed in a long nightgown, which would have been dispensed of if it were just women in the room. I couldn't bear to be naked and miscarrying in front of Cole. Ada made sure when she examined me she kept my privacy and dignity as carefully guarded as she could.

It was going to take hours of pain for the tiny baby to deliver.

"Go to bed, Ada," I said after panting through the pain of the last contraction. "I'll ask Cole to come for you when I need you. You don't need to help with the pain. I'm fine. Please get some rest."

"Shannon," Ada protested.

"I do not want you to have a relapse. This is just cramping. I know when to call for you, and I will. Please, Ada, please go to bed."

She didn't want to, but she left, leaving Cole and me.

"Are you up for this?" I asked through clenched teeth as I breathed through the worst of it.

"Don't worry about me. Tell me what to do. There has to be something in this bag for the pain." I heard the frustration and rage in his voice.

"The pain brings the baby," I said, as I panted through a contraction.

Eventually though, I couldn't stand any more pain.

"Cole," I groaned. "Can you get that mask and place it over my face? Please hurry."

"Should I get Ada?"

"No, just the mask."

He slipped it on over my face.

"Put one drop of that chloroform on the mask, just one," I explained.

His hands shook.

I breathed in and slowly felt the pain in my body loosen. "If I pass out, take off the mask."

His eyes locked with mine.

I'd never seen him scared. "It's alright. You'll be fine."

I nodded and he administered one drop to the mask. "Another one."

He added another.

"That's all." I curled onto my side. He replaced the hot towel on my lower back.

"Now, we just wait. Nothing we can do. It won't be long now," I murmured.

He replaced the towels as they cooled and helped me sit up to drink water. When the pain started to come back, he gave me one more dose of chloroform.

I felt my womb constrict and bring with it a feeling that I needed to push. Too soon and I could tear. I needed Ada to examine me.

"It's time for Ada to come back." I took the chloroform mask off my face. I wanted to be mentally present for the pain, to work with it.

Cole rushed to get her and they came back into the room together.

"Cole, we'll need more hot water." I was relieved Ada knew what she was doing.

Once he was out of ear shot, I clutched Ada's nightgown. "He's going to insist that he stay in the room to support me, and I don't want him to see this. You and I know this is going to be ugly."

"I understand." Ada nodded.

We heard him carrying the hot water up the stairs.

"You aren't ready yet." She pulled my nightgown back down. "Not dilated enough, but you're almost there."

Cole came back in the room.

"Help me up off this bed." I tried to pull myself up.

"That can't be right," Cole protested and looked to Ada for support.

"Help me. I want this over with." I grabbed the footboard to hold myself up. Cole leapt to my side. "If I walk, the weight of the baby will help open the womb."

"Shannon, this can take as long as it needs to," Ada said softly.

"I want it over!" I wept as the pain made me drop to my knees. "I just want this over, Ada. I can't stand it."

Cole thought I meant the pain, but I meant all of it. I wanted it done.

"Can I give you more of the chloroform?" Cole asked me and then looked to Ada. He was right there on his knees beside me.

"No." A contraction roared through me, so I had to

clutch him to stay upright.

"What can I give you for this pain, Shannon? I can't watch this." I heard fear in his voice. He sounded like he was on the verge of tears.

"Spread your legs apart, Shannon, and lean against Cole," Ada instructed. "That also applies pressure."

I can't let you see me like this.

"You have to go," I said to Cole. He looked wounded as I pulled away from him. I had seconds before the next contraction to arrange myself. I pulled away from him and moved to the mattress.

"I'm not leaving you," he protested.

Kneeling with my legs spread apart, I held onto the mattress and moaned in pain.

"No." I breathed through the contraction. "It's time for you to go." I would have this birth on my terms. "I'll be fine. Ada will call you when it's over. It won't be long."

He looked to Ada, and she nodded.

As soon as he grudgingly left, I asked Ada to examine me again.

"You're ready."

It didn't take long from that moment. With each contraction, I pushed with the pain. The agony in my ribs made it unbearable, but all I could think was once this baby was delivered, I could put everything behind me. Cole paced on the other side of the door. As soon as the baby was delivered I shook with shock.

"You're almost there. Once the placenta is here, we'll get you cleaned up and comfortable."

I couldn't stop shaking.

"You're alright. It's almost over." Ada's voice was gentle in my ear. "There you are. Placenta is out. It looks whole. Breathe, Shannon, it's all over."

I pressed my forehead into the mattress while Ada took the placenta away. She laid a heavy towel on the bed.

"I would like to ask Cole to come in and help you back into bed... I can't do it. I'm not strong enough."

"Of course." I tried and failed to make myself stop shaking.

She opened the door, and Cole immediately came to my side.

"Can you put her back on the bed? It's done," Ada said as Cole lifted me up and very gently set me down on the mattress. "At three fifteen this morning, January 28, 1905, Shannon Stone gave birth to a stillborn son," Ada said to Cole. "You can add that to the report."

A son.

I closed my eyes as that sunk in. I had lost a son.

She walked away from us so she could examine him and the placenta to be sure there was nothing left inside me. Then she came back to the bed and massaged my womb to help lessen the bleeding.

"Let me see," I insisted as she massaged.

"Are you sure?"

"If anything remains in me, Ada..." My voice was weak in my ears.

"There's nothing left in you, love. This is all over now." We examined the child together.

As soon as I saw the baby, I started to shake again. Cole gathered me up and pressed my face into his shoulder.

"It's all over now," Ada repeated.

I clutched at Cole as the pain and the horror of this hit. I wept for this baby, for me, for my ruined life.

Chapter Nineteen

"It's time to clean you up and get you settled for the night," Ada said briskly. "Cole, she needs a hot bath and something to eat. Shannon, can I leave you with him? I can't stand up, I am so weary."

"Of course, Ada."

Cole stroked his hand down my back. I didn't move.

"I'll run a bath and come back for you," he said softly.

"Not yet," I whispered.

He moved us so he could lean against the headboard. His body cradled me so that I could weep against him. He didn't ask anything, just stroked my matted, sweaty hair, rubbed my back gently...

"I'm so sorry, Shannon, so sorry I wasn't here sooner."

I pulled away so that I could blow my nose. I lay in a pool of blood. There was blood all over him, me, the bed. I felt humiliated.

"Don't worry about it. I'll clean it up," he whispered as I settled back against him. "Everything is alright."

"What are you thinking?"

"I am thinking that I never want to see you in that kind of pain again. As soon as you're sleeping, and as soon as Thomas Wheaton regains consciousness, I am going to go down, and we're going to come to an understanding. I am a law man, so I can't beat him to death. But I can and I will beat him *nearly* to death."

"You can't beat him at all, Cole."

"I absolutely can. Never mind that, you should have told me, Shannon, you really should have. This was too much for you to bear on your own."

"Can I have that bath now?" I didn't want to talk about it anymore.

"Of course," he said. I could tell he didn't want to leave.

"I'll be alright." I pulled away from his shoulder to look at him. My eyes begged him to believe the lie.

"Right." He hurried to get the bath poured. He was back in record time.

"Wait. I don't want to be anywhere near Thomas. Is he still in the kitchen?"

"He's in the basement. I dragged him down there and then started the bath. He's still unconscious, you have nothing to worry about."

Very gently, he picked me up, ignoring the blood.

"How come all this blood doesn't bother you?" I asked timidly.

"I was raised on a cattle farm. I've seen lots of birthing in my time. Never broke my heart like this though."

"Are you calling me a cow?"

"Never." Cole carried me downstairs to the kitchen in front of the cook stove where there was a screen for privacy. The bath was steaming and scented with lavender.

"Take your time." He put me down by the tub.

I peeled off my bloody nightgown and sunk into

the bath.

"There is a nightgown here, and Ada left you some other things…" he trailed off.

Thank goodness for Ada.

When I was through bathing, I redressed in a fresh nightgown and got ready for bed. I peeked around the screen. Cole picked me up like I was made of glass and carried me back upstairs.

I thought I respected him before, but now he was in a whole new category. I could trust this man with my life; I knew it right down to the depth of my soul.

He settled me in a fresh, clean bed then stepped out. Ada hovered, double checking that my womb was reverting to its proper size.

"There are plenty of absorbent rags sewn into pads in the top drawer. Call for me if the bleeding increases. You're going to be fine now."

I looked into her eyes and wanted to believe her. She went to the door and asked Cole to enter.

"Cole, I expect you'll stay here with her tonight. That chair is pretty comfortable." She smiled at him. All of us knew he would not be sleeping in that chair.

"Of course, if she wants that."

"She will. You make sure she gets this in two hours. It'll help with the pain."

Ada came back over to me. She held my hand and stroked my hair back from my face. She pointedly looked at Cole as he stood by helplessly, and then at me.

"This does not define you," she said firmly with what seemed to be the last of her strength. "You are an honourable woman, and you will come out of this. You will be happy again."

My eyes welled with tears.

"I mean it. Women make this mistake all the time. Somehow, they think how men treat them or what men praise in them, that's where we base our worth. Don't make that mistake, Shannon. You decide your own worth. You will heal and you will succeed. You will find love."

I couldn't get any more words past the lump in my throat.

"I would stay with you all night, but I am exhausted. Cole is going to stay right here in this room. He's going to give you your medicine. You are not to worry about a thing," she spoke with such authority I believed her.

With that, Ada was off to bed, and I faced Cole.

"You deserve an explanation." I wiped at my tears and tried to sit up. This was not a conversation to be had lying down.

He arranged the pillows behind my back and said, "I don't deserve anything. You have done nothing wrong." He stoked the fire in the room and then he turned to face me. "Let me give you this for the pain."

He gave me the tincture that Ada had left for me. It was morphine. I felt it dance in my blood stream, unlocking the dull cramps in my abdomen.

"Are you warm enough?"

"Yes."

"I'm so sorry, Shannon, I don't know what else to say." His eyes were anguished in the dim light.

My hands shook again; he noticed and he put his huge hand over mine.

My eyes filled with tears again.

Would I ever stop crying over this?

Cole closed his eyes and pulled me forward until I

was on his lap.

"I might get blood on your pants."

"Too late," he said ruefully. "There's blood every-where. I don't care."

"You already know about... well... the night they came for Til, they took me, too."

He turned to face me, and the pain in his eyes broke my heart.

"I tried to run away. I don't remember everything because I passed out. I was on a ship and halfway here when I figured out that I was pregnant." I shuddered.

He didn't say anything. I knew he was enraged, disappointed — or worse — disgusted. I couldn't read his face; it was like looking at granite.

I covered my mouth with my hand to quiet the sobs. I was weary of the shame, the lingering horror I still felt as I thought of that night.

"I'm so sorry, Shannon." His eyes, full of misery, flicked over my face.

"Me, too." I wiped at my eyes, and he handed me a handkerchief. "Will you stay with me?"

"Do you want that?"

"Yes, but not if you're disgusted..." I was curled up on his lap, and my head was resting on his shoulder. The steady beat of his heart slowed me down. Made me calm.

"Disgusted?"

"I saw the women in your family. The woman your brother married... your mother. They're so pure, so beautiful. They've never done a bad thing in their life. Now that you know...it must change the way you look at me. I feel... I feel... filthy. Worse, I've lied to you for months. All those times you thought I was sick, and I could have told you and I didn't. You must be disgusted and disappointed."

Cole took the glass out of my hand.

"Please say something, Cole. I…"

"There's nothing to say," Cole said.

I started crying even harder.

"Listen to me, Shannon. Listen now." He cradled my bruised and battered face in his very big, hard hands. "You are as beautiful and pure as any woman I've ever met. What has been done to you was a crime. How could I look at you with anything other than respect? You are one of the most honourable people I've ever met, Shannon. I mean it."

He carefully and tenderly dabbed at my tears with a clean handkerchief.

"This has been a horrible day, and we're in the middle of a three-day storm. We're going to go to sleep now, and we'll talk about it in the morning. Do you want me to stay in the room with you?"

"Do you want to?"

"I would like to. I'll stay in the chair," he offered.

"Or maybe you could just stay right here?" I suggested timidly.

"Of course, if that is what you want." He smiled before he kissed my forehead.

He put a pillow behind his back, and I shifted until I was comfortable in his arms. The morphine made me calm; I tried to fight the exhaustion so I could remember this night. Surely, tomorrow he would come to his senses, but I would always be able to remember *this* night.

Much later in the night, he woke me to take the pain medicine as Ada instructed. The morphine made me sleep so soundly the nightmares slipped into my dreams. I bolted awake, at one point panicking, but he held me tighter, talked to me until I focused on him.

"You're alright, you're safe now."

"Where is he?" I shook with fear.

"Nobody is here but me. I'm the only man in the room." He held me as tight as he could without hurting my ribs.

"No, where did you put him?" I broke out in cold sweat. "Where is he in the house?"

"He's in the basement. He's tied up. He's not going to hurt you. As soon as the storm stops, I'll take him out of here, and you will stay with Ada until you feel better. There's no rush. No reason to leave until you're ready. Is that alright? Nothing is going to happen now."

I felt my body calm down, and I settled closer into him.

"Let me refill your hot water bottles. The heat helps the pain, right?"

"Don't you dare move," I said against the hard wall of his chest. Again, I focused on the beating of his heart. I pulled his arms around me tighter.

He leaned down and kissed my forehead very gently.

"Shannon Stone, you are the toughest girl I know."

"I don't feel very tough," I said sadly, "but thanks." The morphine made the world fall away.

When I woke up, he was gone.

Slowly, I crawled out of bed to clean myself up. He couldn't see me lying in a pool of blood. The pain in my ribs caused me to sink to my knees by the bed. That's where he found me.

"What are you doing out of bed?" Cole put my

breakfast down on the dresser.

"I wanted to get cleaned up before you saw anything."

"Shannon, I've seen it all, and I'm still here, and I'm not going anywhere." He helped me to my feet, and he saw the blood on my nightgown at the same time I did.

His mouth was a grim line.

"What should I do?" He did a good job of hiding his panic.

"I know I had a bath last night, but could I trouble you to draw another?"

"If you wanted me to lift the house up and move it twenty feet east, I would. Anything you need, I will do it."

"I'm still cramping..." I felt my eyes fill with tears. "Is he still downstairs?"

"He's still in the basement, Shannon." Cole's eyes softened with sympathy.

"I can't stand that he's in this house with us." My voice trembled with fear. "I hate this. What if he gets out of his handcuffs and comes up here?"

"He'd have to get through *me* to get to you, and I won't let that happen. You have nothing to worry about." Cole's hands curled over my upper arms as he held me up. "As soon as this storm stops, I'll get him out of here. It's not ideal, but he can't hurt you." He rubbed his hands up and down my arms.

I told myself sternly to calm down. Hysterics wasn't going to accomplish anything.

"Why all this blood, Shannon? Something must be wrong. Should I get Ada? That is so much blood..."

"It's normal, Cole, it's normal..." I tried to sound confident and failed. Weak from blood loss, I swayed against him. His hands tightened on my upper arms. His face creased with concern, he waited patiently for me to tell him what was going on.

"It's normal," I finished lamely.

"You're not just trying to be brave?" He tilted his head to the side.

"No. I ran out of brave quite some time ago."

"Are you in a lot of pain?"

"Yes," I said tightly. "Is Ada alright?"

"She's still weak, so you're stuck with me, unfortunately."

"Well, we'll have to make the best of it."

"I'll get that bath drawn."

I took a long time in the bath. I didn't want to rush. There was nothing to do anyway. This was day two of snow. The world stopped; the snow falling seemed like a veil of silence around us. We couldn't go anywhere, and no one could come to us. The hot water eased the cramping. Finally, I struggled into my nightgown, and he tucked me into bed. He reached for the salve Ada had left out for me and gently rubbed it into the bruising on my neck. I couldn't help it, his fingertips on my neck and shoulders made me catch my breath. His eyes met mine as I opened the top of my nightgown.

"Ada didn't tell me about this." Despite his anger, with teeth clenched in outrage, his fingertips stayed gentle, moving the salve along the mark, Thomas had left there.

"We're pressing charges. A court of law needs to know exactly what he did and attempted to do to you. We don't want him going home to Emily and little Ivy."

He could have just said Ivy. He didn't. He said *little Ivy.* My heart warmed to him.

He took notes on everything, from when Shane brought Emily to the house, to the miscarriage.

"Cole, maybe that doesn't have to go in the report?" I suggested.

He looked at me and back down to his notes.

"Everyone will know," I whispered.

"It's up to you." He was in constable mode. Zero emotion. "Two babies died at his hand last night. He knew his wife was pregnant, and he beat her until she miscarried anyway. He's a murderer. But it's the same sentencing with one or two."

"What if you are blamed? What if they hear my testimony and blame you for this pregnancy?"

"Shannon," Cole said patiently and rubbed his forehead. "We are people of integrity. We don't hide facts because small minds might make assumptions. If people choose to think that then they don't know me and they don't know you. They are not the sort of people we want in our life. They should know that we are honourable people."

"Right, of course. Would you bring me a hot water bottle?" I asked.

"I'll be right back."

When he returned, I opened the blankets and took it from him and laid it against my aching womb.

His eyes were sympathetic. "Does it hurt a lot?"

"It's getting better."

"Really?"

"No."

Cole sat down on the bed and took my hand in his.

"This is all very hard, but I look forward to charging him and locking him away. With your testimony and miscarriage, we can finally put him away for life.

Emily never would press charges. I hated letting him go, knowing he would do it all over again, especially with a little girl in the house. Every time I wondered if this was it, would he kill her next time? I cannot, for the life of me, understand a woman that would stay and take that kind of abuse."

"Whatever happens with Thomas and Emily, Ivy need to be protected from both of them."

"She will," he promised.

"Well, I am glad you will lock him away this time."

"We'll talk again before I submit the report. I need to take that nightgown for evidence, if that is alright with you?"

"Of course, it's destroyed anyway, and it's hideous on a good day."

"Take your pain medicine before you go back to sleep," he said softly in my ear. He helped me sit up and pressed the spoon into my mouth. Twice. "Is it enough?"

"Yeah."

"Sleep well. If you need anything, I'm right here. I'm not going anywhere."

That night I woke up and studied him. He was in the chair. The storm lashed ice and snow against the windowpane. The room was getting chilled; I stirred in bed because it was so cold in the room I was shivering, which hurt my ribs.

He woke up suddenly when he heard me moving around. "Sorry, it's freezing in here." He raked coals together into the fire, and soon a blaze took the chill from the room.

"I can't sleep." I made room for him on the bed. He hesitated. I patted the mattress beside me, and he sat on the covers. I moved into his arms and laid my head on his chest.

"Do you think I should name the baby?" I asked.

"Of course," he replied.

"It's pretty terrible, isn't it? His life began and ended in violence." A tear slid from my eye. "I kept thinking of him as something that was ruining my life. He was going to ruin things with you. The village would despise me, judge me, the worst thing is *you* would get blamed. I never really thought about him. Until..."

I stopped to pull myself together, and Cole held me closer.

"Until I saw him. His tiny little body, so vulnerable, so still and blue...." We were quiet for a minute. "I was going to give him away."

Cole kissed my temple. "You don't have to explain anything to me."

"No, you need to know everything. I feel like I've been lying to you by omission, and I despise lying."

"Shannon, I'm so sorry." He moved me so that I fitted even tighter against him; like he was trying to give me his strength.

I curled against him. He got comfortable. It was time to talk.

I sighed. "My grandfather's name was Harold," I said softly, reverently.

"You cannot call a child Harold. That's the worst name I've ever heard in my life."

I laughed. I couldn't believe it, but he was so sincere that I laughed right out loud. Then Cole laughed, and we kept laughing.

"What was your grandfather's name?" I asked him.

"Ebenezer."

"It is not," I protested.

"I swear it. So, I'm wrong. Harold is the second worst name in the world. Ebenezer takes first place."

I couldn't help myself. We looked at each other and laughed harder.

"Alright, not Ebenezer either! Uncle Malcolm's middle name is Dathan. Maybe I should call him Dathan."

"Very nice. I like Dathan. Sounds just like him." Cole stroked my hair back from my face.

"Alright." My breath caught. "Dathan Stone."

Silence. As his name settled around us, I thought about him, his tiny blue body. He'd been as vulnerable as I'd been...

Goodbye, Dathan.

Giving him a name made me stop thinking about the attack and just think about him. If Lord and Lady Harper had wanted him, I would have happily handed him over to them. Pain curled around my heart and made me swallow an ache I didn't know was there.

"I think taking Dathan's life should be prosecuted. I want it in the report. I want it all in the report. Dathan should have had a chance."

"I'll put it in the report, and I think you're making a wise decision. Thomas Wheaton should have to pay for the death of both children."

We didn't say anything after that. We just lay there. I breathed in the scent of him, let it calm me. I didn't let my mind slide to the monster in the basement. I didn't think about anything but my breath going in and out.

I sorted through feelings of relief, guilt, and sadness, a new confidence surfaced in me. It didn't matter that he had overpowered me and I lost; it mattered that I came out swinging and I would do it again.

I traced the fingers of Cole's hand. This hand that dragged Thomas from me.

"There is one more thing to talk about." Cole shifted me in his arms so he could look at me. As soon as there was some distance between us, I missed the heat from his chest.

"What is that?" My eyes met his.

"I know you're still upset. I just have to address this now, while we have time and privacy. Ada said you stepped in between Thomas and Emily. He didn't come after you. You went after him." I heard the disapproval in his voice.

"That is correct." No justification or excuses from me.

"Shannon, what were you thinking?" He cradled my face in his hands. "You took a terrible beating. What if Ada hadn't been there to knock him out? What if I hadn't gotten there?"

"I was thinking that Emily had just miscarried, and if he hit her in the abdomen, she would start to hemorrhage and she'd die. I could not stand by and see a man beat a woman to death and not do all that I could to stop it. You would have intervened, too."

"Of course, I would have intervened. I would have beaten him senseless. We're not talking about me. I'm a man. That's my job, to protect anyone that cannot protect themselves. We're talking about you."

"It's my job to protect those who can't protect themselves, too. She didn't get hurt. It worked."

"But you did!" Cole's patience was wearing thin. "I

want a promise from you, right now, tonight, that you will never, ever put yourself in harm's way again. Next time you see something like that, you wait for me."

"Oh, Cole." It was my turn to put my palm against the hardness of his cheek. "I cannot promise that. My job puts me in danger all the time."

"Then we should figure out a different job..."

I stiffened.

"We need some ground rules." Cole rubbed his forehead as he thought. "You cannot go out at night by yourself. Scratch that. No going out alone. Ever. Night or day. Trouble seems to find you. You can't attend anyone whose husband might be dangerous unless I am with you. There will be no protests. I get that you have strong convictions... but it's too dangerous... so no protests... from now on, if I can't go, *you don't go*. You never, ever put yourself in harm's way again. Ever. You never step between a man and his wife."

I stroked his cheek. "No."

"What do you mean, no?" He was stunned, used to unquestioned obedience from a docile woman.

"I mean, no. I have to live and work and enjoy life. I can't do that if I'm living with all these restrictions."

"I cannot watch a woman I..."

Love.

That unspoken word hung between us; our eyes locked.

"I can't watch a woman in my life get hurt. I watched Maggie die, and I cannot go through it again."

Shocking both of us, I leaned forward and kissed him very softly on the lips. His entire body jolted. The feeling of his lips against mine rocked me to my foundation. He pulled back first, holding me at arm's length.

His breathing was ragged, and I was thankful I was sitting because my knees were weak.

"That's a mean and very dangerous way to win a fight."

"I won, then?" A smile played on my lips.

"You win." He frowned and took a deep breath. "I'm furious about you stepping in between Emily and Thomas, but I understand why you did. I'm going to *try* to calm down. You can't *ever* do it again. I mean it."

My smile broadened. "Cole, no. Don't be like that. You can't say no to me. We're supposed to be a team. We're supposed to work together. It won't happen if you are forbidding me morning, noon, and night."

Cole took a deep breath and let it out slowly.

"I will try to support you and not stifle you. You use the word stifle quite a bit."

"Bossy, too. You could work on that while you're at it."

He scowled at me. "It's going to be a battle. I'm going to make mistakes, lots of them."

"I'm going to make mistakes, too, so you're in good company. While we still have some privacy, I want to thank you."

He waved my thanks away.

"I mean it. Thank you for everything. You helped me through hours of cramping and pain. If you hadn't showed up when you did…"

"No." He smoothed hair away from my face. "Don't think about it. It's done."

He pulled me back against him, arranging me so I was tightly curled up in his lap, head on his chest.

"You're not going to sleep in that chair?" I asked mischievously.

"This is it. Tomorrow we go back to real life. I want one more night with you in my arms," he said. "This is the only way I know for sure you are safe. You scare me to death."

I sighed. I didn't want to think about real life.

"It's going to be alright. You'll get used to it."

Chapter Twenty

The day the storm let up, Cole packed up the Wheaton family. He took two other men with him to put Thomas in jail. Emily insisted she and Ivy would stay with Thomas' brothers. Cole and Mayor Holt spent two hours trying to talk her out of it. He didn't trust them; it was the hardest thing he had ever done, leaving Ivy there with the Wheaton brothers. Finally, he came back for me and dropped me off at my carriage house. Cole stoked my fire and reluctantly prepared to leave.

"Are you going to be alright, here on your own?" His face creased with concern.

"I'll be fine," I assured him.

He passed the bed warmer through my bed more than once. He filled three hot water bottles, and once he'd tucked me in, I snuggled down into the extra feather tick he had pulled onto my bed.

"Are you sure? You're almost a doctor, right? You could claim this is a medical emergency and order me to stay." His eyes crinkled up as he smiled.

Things had shifted between us. There were no secrets now. He knew everything. Every sordid, shameful thing, and he'd taken the news stoically. I'd never imagined he would take all that evil in stride. Even when I was a vomiting and bleeding mess. He just boiled more water, brought more clean towels, spooned more pain medicine, stroked, and reassured. There was no complaining. No shirking the duty he'd assigned himself. I considered not returning to London for the first time since I'd come here. Fresh guilt washed over me, as I thought about abandoning Til and her crusade.

"You need to regain your strength. I don't want you to get sick." He was worried about that.

"I won't get sick. I'm going to be fine."

"Do you still have any... um cramping, though?"

"It comes and goes," I admitted. "The cramping has stopped for now. I know I need to rest, or it'll come back."

"I'm glad they've quit. Those cramps seemed rather vicious."

"Yes. They are terrible."

"Hmm." He tucked the blankets in so I couldn't move. "Maybe we should have held onto some of those powders that Biddy was administering. I don't want to ever see you in that kind of pain again. It's late. I better get moving. I have a lot to do tomorrow. You'll take it easy?"

"Yes," I promised.

He kissed me on the cheek and went to put his winter clothes on.

"Tomorrow I will check on you and make sure Jaffrey can come to stoke fires throughout day. Please give me your word that you will stay in bed and rest."

"Jaffrey has enough to do at the big house. I can do it."

"Shannon, you need to rest. You have been through a lot," he said sternly.

"Of course. I'll rest. Relax, Grandma. I'll be fine," I teased.

He came back and kissed me. "I'm not your grandmother."

"I don't know. That kiss seemed a bit grand-mother-ish."

He kissed me again.

"What about that one?"

"Hmmm."

This time he attacked me, yet mindful of the cheekbone.

I smiled as he dragged himself away.

"Be safe tomorrow," I said as he left the room.

"I'll be back to check on you."

Chapter Twenty-One

The light shining through my curtains woke me up. I lay there assessing my various pains. My ribs were by far the worst; it hurt to breathe. My face ached, and the cut on my cheekbone throbbed. The cramping, aching pain in my womb made me feel weak. Slowly, carefully, I pulled myself up to reach for the morphine and cried out in pain. It didn't matter; no one was here to hear it.

A timid tap at the door startled me.

"Shannon, are you up? Can I come in? I have a breakfast tray ready for you."

Mrs. McDougall? What is she doing here?

"Please, come in." My voice was hoarse.

"You're up!" Mrs. McDougall's cheerful face fell when she looked at me. "Oh, my dear! Cole said you had an altercation with Thomas Wheaton. Altercation! Oh, my darling! You're black and blue!"

I finally got my hands on the morphine and took a quarter of a grain. "I am in a lot of pain." My voice sounded raw. I laid back and hoped the morphine would work quickly.

"What do you need, darling?" Mrs. McDougall sat down on the bed.

Her compassion swept me away. Once the horror of my face had worn off, she was cheerful and happy to help. This was the world I was used to— women looking after women.

"Oh, what did he do to you? What did Cole do to him? Has my son seen *all* this? He'll kill him." Her voice, gentle with an edge of steel, calmed me.

"He didn't kill him, but I think he wants to," I reassured her.

She was outraged on my behalf, and I loved her for it. The softness of her touch undid me. The cramping pain in my womb made me curl into a ball. She held me while we waited for the morphine to work. "You're going to be alright, honey. This is all going to heal, and you are going to be just fine. I promise it," she murmured as she brushed hair back off my face.

"The pain is so intense. I'm not sure I can handle much more."

"Come on, take a little more of this." Her hands were gentle as she helped me take another dose of morphine. She helped me lie back down with my head on her lap. It should have been awkward, but it wasn't.

This place is full of moms and sisters. Thank heavens for them. Thank heavens Cole sent his mother today.

When the morphine finally took the edge off, she settled me back against the pillows.

"That is terrible cramping if it requires morphine." Her eyes were guileless. She took her seat near the fireplace and picked up her tea cup.

I looked at her to assess what she knew.

What has he told you? Do you know about the miscarriage or just that maybe this is a typical cramping that would accompany a menstrual cycle?

"It's better now." I fought to keep my eyes open.

"You've become close with him?" She sipped her tea and waited for me to speak.

"We are close," I agreed.

He held me while I miscarried my son then stayed that night to make sure I wasn't alone after I told him the truth of what happened the night they came for Til. He made sure I felt safe all night.

"We haven't talked about any sort of understanding," I added softly.

Except last night we kissed, and I thought my heart would burst with happiness.

"Do you want one?" she asked quietly.

I didn't know how to answer that. I looked at her as I thought carefully.

"I have to return to my life in England." I tried to sit up a little straighter for the conversation we were about to have. I fought waves of drowsiness from the morphine. "I am to finish my education. My aunt expects me to assist her in rebuilding her clinic." No need to tell this lovely lady that she was currently in jail on ridiculous obscenity charges.

"You sound committed." She stood up and arranged the pillow behind my back.

"I am very committed," I said truthfully. "However, I didn't expect to meet Cole and feel like this. When I am with him, it's like he's filling in all the pieces that were missing. We make a good team."

"You love him, Shannon." Mrs. McDougall leaned forward, her face creased with sadness. "I know my son. When he was begging me to come look after you today, well, he loves you, too."

"It's too soon to make decisions like that, Mrs. McDougall. This is the wrong time for me."

Her eyes filled with tears. "You'll find a way. Cole will, if you don't."

She brought the tray to me. Now the pain had edged off enough I could stand the thought of eating.

"He's different since you've been here."

"Is he?" I took a tentative bite of toast.

"Yes." Mrs. McDougall refilled my cup of tea.

"I don't know what he thinks. I just know that he has now officially seen me at my worst, and he hasn't run away."

Mrs. McDougall very carefully put the pot of tea back down on my tray. "Cole has never run from anything in his life."

"Did he tell you what happened? About England?"

"No." Her eyes met mine, and she sat down on the bed. "You don't need to tell me either. He says you got hurt. If you want to talk to me about it, I'd love to listen. If it would help."

"A man hurt me in England."

Her eyes met mine and neither of us looked away. "I see."

She did. I could see it in her eyes. She could see everything.

"I almost got… uh… hurt again at Mrs. Bennett's. Cole was there just before…"

"I see that."

"Thomas Wheaton."

"I know about Thomas Wheaton." She could see I was struggling, so she came back to sit on the bed and took my hand. That simple act of kindness unraveled me. My face started to crumple with feelings of shame that started in the pit of my stomach and washed over me until that was all I could feel. Shame, fear…pain.

"Try not to think about Thomas Wheaton." Mrs. McDougall squeezed my hand in silent reassurance.

"He's been arrested, and he will face charges. Cole was wild that you stepped in to protect Emily. I listened to that rant for, oh, half an hour. He's bossy. You already know that. This is going to stop hurting so much. You just need some time to recover. You should try to go to sleep."

"Right."

I spent that whole day in bed after Mrs. McDougall stripped the sheets and helped me bathe. I woke up late in the night to find Cole there, in my room. He was stoking the fire, his back to me. I watched him rub his neck as he watched the flames grow.

"Thank you." My voice was scratchy from lack of use.

He turned and stood up.

"How are you feeling?" He placed his hand on my forehead, worried about fever.

"I'm better."

"Is the cramping, um, stopping, or how is that?" He was clearly embarrassed, but asked anyway— noble of him.

"It's better if I just stay still." I struggled to sit up. "We need to talk, though."

"We don't need to talk until you are ready." He helped me sit up, wincing with me when my ribs ached from the movement. I settled back against the pillows that he propped for me.

He poured us each a glass of brandy.

"I want to touch you, but there is nothing on you that isn't bruised or hurt." He sat on the bed facing me.

I took a deep breath and then a sip of brandy. "We need to talk, though," I whispered.

"There's really nothing to talk about."

"Listen to me. I don't have the strength to fight with you. I just need to say this," I pleaded. "You know the worst thing about me."

"I don't know the worst thing about you," he countered. "I know the worst thing that someone did to you. It's a big difference."

"I know that you have feelings for me," I faltered. Here it was.

He was silent, waiting for me to continue. Tonight, there had to be an understanding. We both knew it.

"When I look at you, Cole, you're one of the best people I know. I think that everything you do is honourable, true, and good. I don't feel like I can live up to that now."

"You don't feel like you are honourable, true, and good, too?" he asked quietly.

"No." My face started to crumple. "I feel dirty all the time."

I looked away to get control of my emotions. He rubbed his forehead.

"So," he said cautiously, "you think what happened to you makes you who you are?"

"I just think things happened between us really quick." I struggled to sit up straighter. "I didn't tell you what happened and *I let you feel for me*. It's like a sort of lie, and now that you know I was violated, maybe that means you stop and think."

"Think about what?" His forehead creased in confusion.

"Think about whether or not you want... uh... that sort of woman." I took a shaky sip and picked at a loose thread on the quilt.

"The sort of woman that wasn't able to defend herself against a man?" His eyebrow arched. "You think you should have somehow protected your own virtue?"

Now a tear did escape as I focused all my concentration on the loose thread as if it held an answer.

"Darling, a woman up against a man... any man, I'd say the odds were against you. You think I should feel different about *you*? What happened to you was a crime and not your fault." Cole's simple logic was refreshing.

"When you put it that way, it sounds ridiculous." I took a long sip of brandy to dull the pain. Not just the physical, the emotional, too.

"I had feelings for you the minute you first threw up on my shoes. It was impossible to stop wanting to protect you from everything. In the bathhouse, when you were so terrified. You know now, if a man came anywhere near you I would have stopped him. You wouldn't let me deal with that doctor, remember? I listened because I already respected you. When you exposed and helped prosecute Biddy, I was in awe. Even *Lord Harper* couldn't stand up to her, and I've seen him in action with men twice his size. Then you stepped up to the assignment to address the town on behalf of the W.C.T.U. You went and looked after Ada when she called you, made sure Katie Ross was safe, and warned me not to do anything rash... I'm only describing what I have seen in the last few months. Honour, true, and good. I think that is you in a nutshell."

"But, I heard about Maggie." I looked back down at the quilt. I felt the fear of inadequacy wash through me. Compared to Maggie, I would be a complete disappointment to him. She was everything a man wanted—

quiet, demure, and probably obedient. "She was beautiful, pure, and perfect. If you said jump, she probably said 'how high?' I'm not perfect."

"Maggie was not perfect." Cole's eyes softened in sympathy.

"She was pure though."

"This is not a competition. She wasn't perfect. It will shock you to know this, but I am not perfect. You don't have perfect to live up to."

"It's just we're so different." My eyes flicked over his face, and I watched as I asked the next question. "If you laid down that list of rules to Maggie she would comply."

"That's true," he agreed.

"She could handle your bossiness." I took another sip.

His eyebrows were both arched. "Bossy?" he protested.

"Very bossy. You expect immediate compliance. I *know* she deferred to you, and I can't promise that. I know myself now. All the horror I've been through has changed me. I'm a fighter." I tried to move and gasped at the pain in my ribs.

"Maybe you should leave the fighting to me." He rearranged the pillows so my ribs would not ache.

I tried to stifle my cry of pain. After he helped me settle into a somewhat comfortable position, he took a long sip.

"Bossy or not, I'm trying to keep you safe and I haven't been doing a very good job." He gestured to my beaten body.

"When Thomas went after Emily, I just reacted. All I could think is 'a beating after a miscarriage would kill her.' It's not your fault. It's just wrong place, wrong time. You can't protect me from everything."

My determination to act on my convictions tried his patience. His teeth clenched together; he was not happy about this. "I want to protect you from everything."

"You can't." I shrugged. "I want to just say that I didn't tell you about the baby because I knew it would change everything."

"It did change everything. I don't think I realized what you meant to me until Ada said 'you are going to lose this baby' and I thought, 'oh no, she has a man.' I didn't put all that together. Honestly, that was my first thought. I feel like a naïve idiot."

He got up to add more wood to the already roaring fire. He needed some space, and so did I. He poked around and built the blaze higher. When he was done, he sat back down on my bed. His profile was highlighted by the light from the flame. Tired and scruffy, his face was covered in stubble. His knuckles were raw.

"You are not an idiot. You're a good person who expects goodness from others."

I focused on his knuckles as I traced over them with my fingertips. "What if that baby had lived, if Thomas hadn't hurt me? What would you have done?"

"I don't know."

"Well, that's honest." I pulled my hand away and took a big sip to try to drown the pain that radiated from my heart.

"Shannon." Cole stroked my face softly so I would drag my eyes away from the fire to look at him. "It would have depended on what you wanted. If you wanted to give him up, I would have helped you do that. If you wanted to keep him then I think we would have had to move. People here are pretty judgmental."

"*We* would have to move? What *we*?"

"Shannon." He reached out to hold my hand. "Since I met you, everything changed. You changed everything."

"I don't understand."

"We need to know each other better before we rush into anything. I'm not rushing you, but if you needed to leave here to have a baby, you wouldn't be leaving alone." His hand covered mine.

My eyes filled with new tears.

"I kept thinking 'tomorrow'," I said, despite the knot in my throat. "I'll tell him tomorrow and then it will all be over and I will deal with this alone. I didn't know what to do. It was lying, lying by omission."

"You must have been terrified." He ignored the confession. He didn't care about lying by omission; he cared about me.

"I knew I was going back to England, but I was afraid for you. For your reputation. I should have pulled away. I put you in a really bad place."

"Me?" He frowned.

"I knew you would be blamed. That's why I was vomiting all over the place after that pie box social. Mrs. Daindridge said we made a beautiful couple, and it hit me that you would be blamed for this pregnancy and run out of town. I was sick about it. I was such a chicken. I couldn't bring myself to be honest with you. My conscience was killing me. The vomiting was eighty percent baby, twenty percent conscience. Everyday my conscience was making me sicker. I was going to tell you. Now, I wish I had."

"Shannon, that's noble of you, but it's not your job to protect me. It's my job to protect you. You don't seem to understand how things work between men and women."

Does anyone know how things are supposed to work between men and women?

Cole gently brushed the hair back off my forehead. "You're tired," he said quietly.

"Yes," I agreed. "I wish you could stay."

"I can. Jaffrey is in your spare room to ensure you and I are chaperoned." He kept stroking my hair back. "Finish your drink. It'll help you sleep. Are you in pain?"

"A little."

I measured out some more morphine.

"So, what is this?" I asked cautiously as I handed him back the spoon and bottle. "What are we deciding here tonight?"

"What do you want?" he asked simply. "You're the girl. You call the shots. I want to see where this goes, but this is your decision."

"I have to finish school, and I have to go back to England," I said. "How is that going to work?"

Priscilla's voice came back to me. *Life is messy, and people throw wrenches in your plans. Sometimes you just have to go with things.*

"I'm not sure," Cole admitted.

"Do you want a professional woman in your life? I work super long hours. I work in contraception, making powerful enemies. Til is in jail right now because of our work."

"I can't handle you going to jail."

"But you should see what I have seen, Cole." I felt

the morphine unlock the cramps, and relief slid over me. "You saw a tiny taste of it with Emily Wheaton. I have seen women die in childbirth who should never have been pregnant. The body can only withstand so much, so I'm left standing with ten little children around me and no mother. These families get ripped apart. The father cannot possibly take care of the children. They're sent to orphanages and work houses. There is so much suffering that contraception can fix. The obscenity laws are ridiculous! The pamphlets have diagrams because the women can't read! Saying we are promoting vice is just... it's insanity!"

Cole said nothing. It was obvious he wanted to say 'change your work.'

He was learning.

"I started working with Til when I was fourteen. The poverty, Cole! The poverty is so desperate that I used to cry when Til took me to work with her. She'd frown at me and tell me to stop snivelling. I learned *not* to cry. I'm not sure if you can make the leap from Maggie to me." I felt inferior to a dead woman. "I know though, Til gave me a gift. To heal people and to alleviate suffering. I can't have this gift and not use it. I'm told I'm good at what I do. I think it's because I started so early. Midwifery is like breathing to me. It's part of me. Can you handle that?"

"Yes." His eyes locked with mine. "I can."

"Are you sure? It's not going to be an easy life. You'd have to relocate. I can't have children right away."

"Well, if you can't have children right away, good thing you're in this line of work. All that birth control and diagrams are going to come in handy!" Cole smiled wickedly. "Can we please just be together and see only each other and decide closer to the day? We do not need to make any big decisions tonight."

"I don't want to get hurt. You might decide that a nice, chaste girl who has never seen the horror I have seen, who has no ambition in life besides making you happy—"

"Shannon, she doesn't exist." Cole finished his drink and put the glass down.

"You had it before," I whispered.

"I did not. I had a lovely wife who let herself die from sadness." He scrubbed his hands over his face and scratched at the stubble on his chin. He didn't want to talk about Maggie anymore. I knew this gesture now.

"Shannon, it's fun to watch you in action and to be there to make sure you have the protection to walk into the scenes you get yourself into. I know when you show up, you know what to do, and I get to make sure you can do it. We're already a great team, so let's just see where this goes and stop over thinking this whole thing. Can we just say we're a couple and see what happens?"

"What does that mean, 'we're a couple?' How does that work?" I couldn't keep the suspicion from slipping into my tone.

"That means, no more pie box socials for you." He leaned in closer.

The nerves I had been feeling dissipated as we laughed together.

"Just so you know up front," I said after the laughing had died down. "I have to go back, and I have an alarming tendency to over think everything."

"Shannon!" he groaned, "You're killing me! I know.

You're going back. It's all in the open."

I could hear the resignation in his voice.

He leaned forward to kiss me. "Get some sleep. I'll check on you before I go to work tomorrow."

Chapter Twenty-Two

A week after the attack, I was finally well enough to check on Lady Harper. I found her playing solitaire in the front parlour. The curtains were drawn back to give us a view of the snow-covered river. The branches of the trees were black against the grey of the sky. I was grateful for the light and warmth of the fire on such a grey day.

"Shannon!" she exclaimed as Jaffrey left us together.

She stood up to greet me and looked at me with horror. "Oh, Shannon, how are you?"

"I'm healing. How are you, Lady Harper?"

She gestured to me to sit by the fire with her. "I'm fine, I think. A little bored with all this cold weather."

"I think I should do an examination, make sure you and baby are alright. I've been gone for two weeks."

"Of course," Lady Harper agreed as we ascended the staircase to the master bedroom. "How is Mrs. Bennett?"

"Mrs. Bennett is on the mend. Mr. Bennett got home with the girls from that piano recital, so she's in good hands." I listened closely to the baby's heart. "I wish there was a way for you to hear this strong, steady heartbeat. This baby is happy and healthy."

"Really?"

"There is nothing to worry about, from what I can

tell," I assured her as I straightened up.

"I am so excited." She moved her hands over her pregnant belly, smiling with delight to feel the movement of the baby under her hands. "Pregnancy is such a gift." Her eyes glittered with tears of joy.

My heart ached at her joy. *Will I ever experience this?*

I forced myself to smile at her as I put my tools away in my bag. She was unaware of what I had endured, leaving me raw and sad, guilty and relieved. In short, a disaster.

"Lord Harper left you a note. He wants to meet with you and Cole this afternoon at three." She got up off the bed and readjusted her gown.

"Certainly," I agreed. "If that is all, Lady Harper, I need to lie down."

"Yes. That is all. Make sure you pick up some lunch and supper supplies from Jaffrey. He's been cooking up a storm all morning."

"I will, thank you."

***

"I heard what happened," Priscilla said when she came to check on me later that day. She made tea so I didn't have to get up. Cole had so many women floating through my house, it was hard to get a nap in. Recovery took as long as it took. No speeding up the process, but I was impatient to feel well. I lay on my settee and tried to regain my strength.

"Cole won't tell me," I said from the settee. "What is going on with Emily and Ivy? Has she left the Wheatons? He just keeps saying to focus on getting better."

"Emily is still with the Wheatons." Priscilla set the tea tray down in front of us. Her brow furrowed with concern.

"What?" I sat up too quickly, and everything hurt.

Priscilla winced in sympathy.

"Cole took three extra men to drop her off. He wasn't sure he would get out of there alive if he went alone. It's terrible." Priscilla poured the tea then settled into the rocking chair.

"What is Emily thinking?" I asked incredulously.

"Cole begged her to stay with the Bennetts. He asked Mrs. Bennett to intervene. He even went to the mayor to see if he could set up assistance for her. She refused and said she wanted to be as close to Thomas as possible. She said the Wheatons look after their own."

"Oh, no," I groaned. *No wonder Cole wasn't talking.* "Poor little Ivy. I hate to think of it."

"Cole warned her that he will be checking on Ivy's welfare. If he sees anything then he will step in. What else can he do? Emily is the mother, and she's too proud to take assistance. It's dreadful. He's out there right now actually. He took Matt with him even though I didn't want Matt to go."

"She is likely in shock, right? She'll come around?"

"I don't know. She's a very abused and sick woman. It's hard to say. I know the men will keep their eye on the situation, and Cole won't hesitate to intervene." Priscilla took a sip of her tea. "How are you feeling, though? This has been quite the event."

"Relief that the pregnancy is over. Guilty that the pregnancy is over. Sad that the entire event happened. Worried for Ivy. I can't stop thinking about Cole. When he's coming back… I'm a disaster."

"This too shall pass…" Priscilla looked at me in sympathy.

"I hope so." I settled deeper into the pillows.

Cole came for me at exactly ten minutes to three. Priscilla bade me farewell, and Cole set about helping me into my coat and boots.

"How is the level of pain?" he asked as he knelt and tied my shoe laces. It hurt too much to bend over.

"Tolerable." I wound a scarf around my neck. "I didn't take anything because I wasn't sure what this meeting was about, but I will take something after."

"Whatever he is expecting of you, you can say no." Cole held my coat open.

"You told him I didn't need to meet with him anymore?"

"I did."

We slowly made our way to Hillcrest where Jaffrey greeted us and served us tea in the parlour while we waited.

Right at three, we were summoned into Lord Harper's study.

"Please, sit." Lord Harper gestured to the seats across from his desk.

"I wanted to brief you both on what is going on." Lord Harper picked up a letter. "We have a meeting with the lawyer who is prosecuting Biddy on Tuesday next week. Cole, would you be available to take Shannon into Brandon to meet with the lawyer?"

"Of course." Cole turned to me. "Will you be well enough to travel to Brandon in a week?"

"Yes," I said.

"Are you sure?" Cole's face frowned with concern.

I waved his concern away. It was time to get Biddy safely behind bars.

"Now, about Thomas Wheaton. It grieves me that

Emily has chosen to take Ivy back to Thomas' brothers. That is a desperate business. I want that child out of there as soon as possible. I want you to go out every day and *find a reason* to remove Ivy from Emily's care."

"Can you do that?" I asked Cole.

"Yes, we can," Lord Harper answered for him. "If Emily cannot protect her child, the council will do it for her."

This stunned me. How could the council step in between a mother and her child?

"There are laws for this?" I asked.

Lord Harper frowned. "The law of humanity, Miss Stone, will not let us sleep at night if a child is being harmed or neglected. We will resolve this and face whatever backlash comes at us."

He looked firm and determined. Ivy's situation was wrong, and he intended to right the wrong.

"What if she protests? I mean, she could fight this..."

"Then she fights it, and we fight back. We will not allow Ivy to suffer further," Cole said in support of Lord Harper's decision.

My heart warmed as I looked at the grim resolution on the faces of Lord Harper and Cole.

They would fight to the death for this little girl, both of them.

"I can be there every day, but they will get agitated." Cole stood up and paced over to the window. He rolled his shoulders as if he were preparing for battle.

"How many men do you think you should take tomorrow?" Lord Harper asked.

"At least three." Cole turned around to face Lord Harper. "I talked to Matt already. I'll take Holt."

"You really think Mayor Holt needs to be involved?" I asked.

"He'll want to be there. This situation involves municipal assistance, and we may need to intervene further, so best if the mayor is there to see it firsthand." Cole sat down beside me and turned his attention back to Lord Harper. "If you want to come, too, that would be enough. We'll take Mrs. Bennett if she is well enough, and we will try to persuade Emily to allow Mrs. Bennett to care for Ivy until this matter of Thomas' trial is over."

"I think that would be best," Lord Harper agreed. "If you take Mrs. Bennett, Mr. Bennett will be there, too. He was delayed due to the storm, but he's home now. I saw him at the post office. He won't let her walk into that mess without his protection. Good. That is settled."

"Just so we're clear." Cole leaned forward, resting his forearms on his knees. "She hands over the child, or we will be there to inspect every day."

"Yes, that is the message," Lord Harper agreed. "Back to the trip to Brandon. I have made arrangements for you both to stay the night with the mayor, better accommodations than you had last time you were in Brandon."

"I said nothing!" I held my hands up in defence.

"Don't worry, Lady Harper doesn't know. We will stay at the mayor's as well, but we will take our own carriage. I don't want Lady Harper to be up and about that early in the day."

Lord Harper stood up, indicating the meeting was over. He shook Cole's hand and then mine.

The next day, I was on edge, terrified Cole was

going to get killed. There were four men and Ada, but I knew how much damage one Wheaton brother could do. Two of them facing Cole made me so terrified I couldn't sleep. Finally, he came by after supper. The relief I felt was so intense. Tears gathered in my eyes as he entered the carriage house.

"Hey! What is all this?" He closed the door behind him and took me in his arms.

"I thought they would kill you. I was scared to death all day."

"Shannon, I'm huge." Cole was genuinely perplexed. "I can take on two Wheaton brothers and not even break a sweat. What is this?"

"I don't like you putting yourself in these positions."

"I said the same thing to you, and you brushed it off. 'Don't stifle me,' you said! You, who clearly couldn't fight your way out of a paper bag! You dare to be scared for me! Who is stifling who?"

"It does seem a little irrational," I agreed as I wiped my eyes.

"A little!"

I sat by the fire as he brought us both a drink. Brandy for me, whiskey for him. If he was drinking whiskey, it was worse than he was letting on. I peeked at his knuckles. No rawer than the day before. Good sign.

"You had nothing to worry about. I knew the brothers would be out when we went to see Emily. I planned that carefully. You should have seen it, Shann. I had back up, and every man was armed to the teeth, ready to battle for Ivy, but in waltzed Mrs. Bennett and a very small orange kitten. She politely reasoned with

Emily and encouraged her to think of how much happier Ivy would be if she could have a 'vacation' at the Bennetts'. Ivy fell in love with that kitten, of all things, and would have followed Ada to the ends of the earth. I would never have thought of it. Honestly, all of us just watched her in awe. Ada Bennett is fearless, ingenious. She is amazing. She packed Ivy's few possessions up and walked out of there with Ivy, and there was no fuss."

"I am so relieved." I let my breath out in a long sigh.

"Me, too. I wasn't sure what we would be walking in on. I told Emily I would be by to make sure she was alright, but she didn't seem to care."

We both took a sip of our drinks. A log on the fire exploded on the grate and I moved so I could curl up against Cole.

"Can you tell me, why would a woman stay in a situation like that?"

"There are few options for women like her, Cole." I pulled a blanket over both of us. "If she leaves, she has no legal recourse. No money and no rights to Ivy. You know how this works. The husband retains rights to the child. Always."

Cole's face was granite hard thinking about that. He took a sip and went back to watching the fire. He had to go. I knew it, and he knew it.

"How are you feeling today?" he asked.

"I am healing well." I sipped the brandy.

"Good." His eyes flicked over me. "I worry about you."

"I'm fine." I patted his hand to reassure him. "Now that I know Ivy is safe, I can relax."

"I wish I could relax." He trailed his fingers down my arm and back up again.

"I think you should change your work," I mocked him. "It seems to place you in danger."

"Listen, woman." Cole pretended to be outraged. "I have put up with a lot from you, and I'm at the end of my patience."

It hurt to laugh, but I had to.

"It sounds ridiculous when I say it, but you think you can get away with it?" I protested.

"Shannon, if we end up together, I have a feeling I'll never get away with anything ever again."

Chapter Twenty-Three

Cole and I boarded the stage coach on Monday morning. I was grateful Matthew had supplied hot rocks for my feet and hands; the cold of February was as intense as January. My ribs ached from the shivering.

"I wonder if Lord Harper warned them about your face," Cole said as he arranged a lap robe around me.

"Oh, the mayor's wife has never had a black eye?" I curled against him for additional warmth.

"Not to my knowledge. I don't know of many women who could take the beating you took and get up and hit back at life the way you have." He linked his hand with mine. We had so many gloves and layers on; I wanted to take my glove off and feel the hardness of his fingers against mine. But it was too cold. That kind of gesture had to be saved for spring.

"Aren't you freezing?" I burrowed down further into my scarf. A nice one, custom made by Priscilla.

"I am pretty used to this. I have about three layers on." His eyes were sympathetic as I shivered beside him.

"I don't think I'm going to make it all the way there. I'm going to die from this cold. It's vicious."

"I know." He shifted so I could curl closer against him.

"That's better." I settled against his chest.

"Miss Stone, I believe you are trying to tempt me."

He pulled the lap robe up and tucked me in against him.

"Mr. McDougall, I believe you are slow at picking up the hints!"

"Try to get a little rest." He adjusted my hat over my ear. "This is going to be a trying day."

I did fall asleep. Cole gently woke me when we reached the mayor's mansion. The coach dropped us off at the door with our bags. The butler greeted us and took us to the parlour. Almost immediately, the door flung open.

"Miss Stone!" a maid asked me wildly.

"Yes." I stood up and clutched my doctor's bag from sheer habit. "Is everything alright?"

"One of our guests requires your immediate attention. Please, follow me." We ran down the hall to the spare room. "Mary Varsdon, the mayor's niece, has just delivered a baby, and we are terrified she will bleed to death."

A midwife looked up at me as she massaged the womb. Her voice was high with fear. "I've done all I can. I can't stop the bleeding."

"Did you give her ergot?" I dropped my bag to the ground and pulled out the ergot.

"I don't have any." Her voice shook with fear.

I mixed the ergot in water and helped Mary drink it.

Cold sweat broke out on my forehead as I calculated how much blood she had already lost.

Once the ergot of rye was ingested, the cramping pain intensified, but the uterus would begin to constrict. I massaged the womb and worked with the tincture to slow down the bleeding.

"That pain is stopping the bleeding. This is all very

normal. I know it hurts. As soon as this bleeding is under control I'm going to give you something for the pain."

The bleeding wasn't stopping as quickly as I hoped, so I gave her another dose of ergot of rye and continued to massage. The mayor's wife came in to the room. She stood by the bed and wrung her hands.

"I know it's terrible. Hang on. The bleeding is starting to stop. As soon as we get this bleeding under control, we're going to hand you that new baby. You just hang on."

Cole appeared at the doorway.

The last dose of ergot did the job; the bleeding slowed. I didn't take my hands off her womb, applying hard pressure.

"Put the baby on his mother," I instructed the midwife. "Help him start to nurse."

"Cole, we need more hot water, please," I said as the midwife helped the baby latch on. When he touched his mother's skin, his crying stopped.

The blood slowed more. Breastfeeding would help the womb constrict, and she needed all the help in this regard as she could get.

Now that the crisis was averted, I wiped the cold sweat off my forehead with my arm and kept one hand pressing hard on her womb. I breathed a sigh of relief. Mary Varsdon was deathly pale; she had been so close to dying, I didn't take my eyes off of her. I checked to see how much blood was still flowing. Normal amount now. She was in immense pain. Ergot of rye created tremendous cramping.

"Would you please apply pressure?" I instructed the midwife who replaced my hands with her own.

I went to get the chloroform mask.

"You're all right. I know it hurts. Let's take the edge off." I slipped the chloroform mask over her face and gave her the lightest dose.

"Thank God, you were here," she said as the pain eased off.

"Shhhhh. No talking. Just take it easy. The bleeding is normal right now, but we need to get you to a hospital. Let this baby eat all he can. The suckling causes the womb to constrict, and we need that. It helps stop the bleeding."

"You just saved my life."

"Shhhh, never mind that. You are going to be just fine. Weak but fine."

Cole appeared at the doorframe again. "The carriage is here to take her to the hospital."

"Oh, good." I smiled at him. He was as pale as Mary.

"The hospital has been advised that she is on her way," Cole said as I scratched my brow, leaving a streak of blood across my forehead.

"Please, come with me," Mary pleaded.

"Cole, I should go and make sure she is settled."

"I'll let the lawyer know we'll be late." He wiped my face with a warm cloth to remove the streak of blood.

"We need a driver to take me to the hospital. I'll make sure she is alright and then go to the lawyer from there," I suggested to the mayor's wife.

"Of course."

"I'll come with you," Cole said.

I went back to my patient on the bed and held her hand, administering another light dose of chloroform to keep her somewhat comfortable.

I turned to the midwife, who looked crestfallen.

"You did a great job. You were doing everything right. Ergot of rye constricts blood vessels and stops the bleeding. Did you make a note of the dose?"

"Yes." She poured fresh water into a basin so I could get cleaned up.

"I have a spare bottle. I'll give it to you. Remember though, only to be used when the cervix is *fully* dilated. If not, the contractions will push the baby against the cervix so hard that it will cause tearing."

Together we washed our hands in carbolic acid.

"Let's get a tight banding around her abdomen before the ambulance gets here. What is your name?" I asked the midwife.

"Kathleen." She handed me a long, narrow cloth to wrap the pelvis to assist in constricting the uterus. Cole came into the room with fresh, hot water. Kathleen and I worked together to clean up Mary to the best of our ability.

When the orderlies came for her, I wrapped the little baby within an inch of his life and took him in my own arms.

"Wrap that blanket around me. I want my face on his face. He cannot breathe in this icy air."

Cole wrapped our heads in one blanket and led me to the carriage.

Doctor White met us right at the door. The mayor's niece got the red carpet treatment. I told him exactly what I had done. He frowned at the ergot of rye. I didn't defend myself. Incorrectly used, it caused many casualties, but I knew how to use it and had been administering it successfully since I was fifteen years old. The baby started to cry in my arms.

"He needs to nurse again," I said. "Shall we take him to his mother?"

"Certainly," the doctor agreed. I followed him down a shiny clean corridor. The familiar smell of antiseptic smelled like home to me.

"We will keep a close eye," he assured me. "You saved her life."

"Yes, it was close."

"Where did you learn that?"

"My aunt is a gynecologist in London, and I have been her assistant for the past ten years. I have completed two years of training as a doctor. In June, I am going back to England to attend university in the fall to finish my training."

"A woman doctor?" he asked. I listened for the usual condescension but didn't hear any. "I've heard of it, but never met one."

"Well, I'm only two years into my schooling."

Cole came up behind us, and the doctor shook his head. "Do not underestimate those years of experience. What you did here was amazing. Well done."

"Thank you." I could not stop the smile from crossing my face. First, Doctor Davies complimenting my work and now Dr. White. I felt my confidence grow.

"If you are looking for a place to do a residency, I would be honoured to have you on my staff."

"Thank you, I really appreciate that." My smile was ear to ear. Til was so sparing with praise; I always wondered if I was any good or not.

Doctor White shook my hand then I peeked in to see Mary once more.

"I can't stay," I said to Mary as her baby nursed. "You are in excellent hands here. Your baby is happy and healthy."

She nodded.

"Sleep well." I took her hand. "When the lawyers are done with me, I will be back to check on you."

"They say you saved my life." Mary started to cry.

"You're a fighter." I patted her hand. "You're going to be just fine."

She nodded, and I left the room.

I gave Kathleen the ergot. She looked crestfallen, so I put my hand on her arm.

"You can't use a tool you don't have. The only difference is I had the ergot and knew how to use it. You did your best in that birth. I would recommend you to anyone. Be careful with this."

"Thank you." She smiled as we shook hands.

"Ready?" Cole asked me, and I took a deep breath.

"I am, but what will I do? I don't have a change of clothes."

"We're out of time. We'll have to go as we are." Cole shrugged. "After you."

Cole held the door open, and we left together.

Chapter Twenty-Four

We were escorted to a dark, dusty hallway outside the lawyer's office. Nerves made my stomach flip around, so I got out of my chair to pace. Finally, we were called into the office. His desk was covered in paper. The lawyer, Mr. Cairn, looked over my bloody clothes and bruised face. Immediately he looked hard at Cole.

"He didn't do this," I said quickly.

"Oh, I was going to ask what on earth is going on here?" He frowned at us both.

"Sorry, I was caught up in an emergency before I got here," I said self-consciously.

"Please, sit." He was so formal and dry I felt a little nervous.

Once we were seated, he turned his attention to the notes in front of him. He read through them swiftly.

"Biddy threatened to kill you?" Mr. Cairn asked me.

"She did," I confirmed.

"She struck Miss Stone and would have done further damage had I not intervened." Cole moved forward in his chair. He sounded like a police report.

"Yes," Mr. Cairn droned. "I see that in the report."

My eyes met Cole's; this man was like talking to a machine.

We waited in silence as he read further.

"I have here, I'm to meet with the doctor. That

can't be right. What are you exactly?" He looked me over, clearly confused. "You're the nurse or the midwife. You can't be the doctor."

I could hear Til in my head. *'Being a nurse or midwife is not enough. You have to be a doctor.'*

I stiffened. Mr. Cairn scrambled through paperwork trying to figure out why a woman was sitting in front of him.

"Here it is. Yes, meet with the doctor."

"I am a midwife and I have completed two years of training as a doctor." My tone was cold.

"So, technically not a doctor," he clarified. He scratched the clarification of my credentials on a form.

I know what I'm talking about. Don't dismiss me.

"I have ten years of experience as a midwife and a nurse. I have seen ergot administered countless times." I tried to defend myself.

"So, this ergot of rye, how can you be sure she administered this?" Mr. Cairn asked.

"Her symptoms of increased menstrual cramping are consistent with being dosed with ergot of rye. Ergot of rye causes miscarriage. Lady Harper suffered from multiple miscarriages."

"Women do experience increased cramping and miscarriage for reasons other than ergot of rye ingestion, I presume? I know very little about this, but I will be double checking this information with a doctor."

A real doctor, a male doctor.

"...that the defence will likely call as witness."

"Of course," I agreed. "I assure you, sir, I have extensive experience with ergot, and I know exactly how it works. If Biddy is freed, she will absolutely be back to Oakland and Lady Harper and her baby would be in danger."

He's not taking me seriously.

"Miss Stone would be in danger as well," Cole said, trying to add weight to my testimony.

"Did you actually see her administer any herbs?" He was poised to write down any information I could add.

I bristled at his tone. He was treating me like an overreacting, hysterical woman. If he didn't care, no one would, and Biddy would be released. Someone as obsessed with Lady Harper as she was would not stay away. She would be back. The baby Lady Harper carried would not be safe, and neither would I.

"I did not. She put something in the water she gave Lady Harper."

"Something," he droned. "Can you be more specific?"

Frustrated, I picked my words carefully. "No. Unless I had a lab. I couldn't be positive what it was."

"Why did she carry this baby so far?" He cut straight to the point.

"Biddy actually ran out of ergot. The bottle was empty. The night I intervened, there was increased cramping, but not enough to bring about a miscarriage."

He made yet another note.

Cole stepped in because he felt the undercurrent of dismissal from the lawyer. "It sounds like you are not interested in prosecuting this."

"Unfortunately, Miss Stone did not see her *administer* this ergot of rye. She has it in her possession, but her lawyer will say it was planted by Miss Stone. He will say she had it left over from her own menstrual discomfort. He will come up with half a million reasons why that ergot of rye was in her room. What else is ergot used for?"

"Migraine," I replied weakly.

"So, she'll claim she suffers from migraine. This entire case will depend on whether or not Lady Harper will testify against her. You have given me all the information I need. I'm going to speak to another doctor today, and we'll all meet tomorrow morning with the Harpers and we will decide how to proceed. Would you like to press charges for the attack? At this point, that is about all we can successfully prosecute."

I felt a shiver of fear. Biddy on the loose terrified me.

"Yes, absolutely press charges for the attack," I instructed him. "If she gets out, my life will be in danger, so whatever you need to do to get her off the streets." I looked at Cole, who was frowning at the lawyer.

"We'll see what the Harpers say. Thank you for coming in so I can run all this by a doctor this afternoon. I'll see you at the mayor's residence tomorrow."

I stood up. "It is my medical opinion that Biddy Baxter caused multiple miscarriages to her Lady over the past four years. The emotional suffering and loss of life is something that should warrant a thorough investigation." My voice sounded icy.

"I'll make a note of it." He didn't even look up. "I'm here to see if I can build a case. Emotional injury is not in my field. Good day, Miss Stone."

He's not taking this seriously. He's not taking me seriously!

Cole escorted me out. His hand firm on my arm, prepared to stop me from going back in there and giving the lawyer a piece of my mind.

We said nothing as we made our way down the narrow corridor to the carriage that was waiting to take us back to the mayor's residence.

As we approached the carriage, we looked at each other.

"He thinks I'm a hysterical woman! Overreacting. I'm furious!" I rounded on Cole. "I have ten years' experience in the slums of London! Ten years, Cole." My rant was just gathering steam as Cole sat me down in the carriage. "I've seen *everything*. Every miserable thing a woman can experience. I've been administering ergot, with supervision, since I was fifteen years old! Did you see how he treated me?"

"I saw." Cole's mouth thinned as he crawled into the carriage beside me.

"Do you have any idea how infuriating it is to be treated like that?" I demanded.

"No," he admitted. "I've had people question my word, but not like that."

We sat quietly while I fumed. The coach lurched forward. I looked out the window at the huge brick buildings. Lawyers, merchants, pedestrians, everyone going about their day without a thought that there was this sort of evil in the world that we could not successfully prosecute.

"You are so beautiful when you are furious."

"Do *not* try to placate me," I warned him.

"I wouldn't dare." Cole held his hands up in a show of surrender. A big grin crept across his face.

I couldn't help it. Despite myself, the anger dissipated, and I smiled back at him. "Do *not* make me laugh," I begged him. "My ribs can't take it."

Cole couldn't stop himself. "I'll make a note of it," he said as he burst out laughing, and I held my ribs because I couldn't stop myself either.

"Were we just there to make sure he had an audience to read the papers?" I wiped my eyes.

"I think so." Cole rolled his eyes. "Back to the mansion for you. I have some errands to run, and I'll join you for supper."

"After I check on Mary."

I looked in on Mary and the baby. When I was satisfied that all was well, I was dropped off at the mayor's mansion, and Cole carried on.

In my room, a servant drew a hot bath; within minutes of arrival, a hot meal and chilled, white wine were sent up. I ate everything on my plate, refilled my wine glass, and then sunk into the huge, hot tub of water.

After I put my wine glass down on the rim, I scrubbed the cuticles of my nails to get the blood out. So many times, I watched Til scrub her hands just like that. My mind wandered to the first time I had ever seen Til in action with ergot of rye. The night had been so traumatic; it was permanently etched into my mind.

It was the first time I had ever seen Til's hands shake.

Chapter Twenty-Five

Til's hands never shook.

Crisis averted, both of us breathed a sigh of relief.

Til sat down, and still shaking, poured each of us brandy. It sloshed over the rim of the glasses, but neither of us cared. I took it. No pretense of tea this time. We sat together silently. She instructed me, and we had saved a life.

I looked at her with a whole new respect. She massaged a womb to stop a hemorrhage, administered ergot of rye carefully and consistently. It was easy to back off when the pain was intense, but Til was not emotional. She was fearless.

Finally, Til spoke.

"Twenty years ago, I watched my mother bleed to death. I didn't know how to stop it." She took a shaky sip, her grief so intense she could barely form the words. "Just the two of us. I didn't know what to do. I held my hands against that flood of blood. All that blood. There was nothing I could do as the blood washed over my hands and she died."

We both took a gulp.

"It was exactly the same problem we just fixed." Her voice was husky with unshed tears.

I closed my eyes to block the memories of watching my own mother die in childbirth. It didn't work. Tears pricked behind my eyes as I opened them to focus on Til.

She took another sip, so I did, too. The brandy made me numb.

"You know what people think about me?" Grief switched to anger as she challenged me to answer. I remained silent. "Everybody thinks I'm a humanitarian. That I love women, want them to succeed." She paused to gain control of her thoughts. "They don't know me. I did this, all this education, so that I am *never* helpless again."

Oh Til, you don't feel angry, not really. This is all just pain. Let yourself hurt and put away all this anger. Let yourself be happy. You didn't lose your mother. It's not your fault. Til.

I held my breath. This was it. This was the day the mask and the walls would fall, and I would see the real Til. Complete with fear, pain, and tragedy. She took a breath and soldiered on. That was the thing about Til. She left no room for weakness. It was her greatest gift and her saddest tragedy all in one. She could build a practice out of nothing, defy convention, but at the end of the day, she was hardened. She had built a wall around herself that protected her from pain and from freedom.

My heart ached, Til's soul was raw with pain.

"I wonder what my mother would say about the choices I have made." Til pressed her fingertips against her temples to release some of the tension she felt.

"I think she would be like the rest of us, in awe of you... scared of you a little bit." I poured more brandy into her glass.

"I wonder." Til took another sip.

"I think you are amazing," I said honestly.

"I'm not amazing." She sighed, looked right at me. "I'm educated."

She let that statement hang between us.

"Imagine what women could accomplish if education was not the exception but the rule? When you have days where you want to quit, and you will, I want you to remember we saved a life tonight because we knew how. Not because we are humanitarians. Everyone should be a humanitarian." Her voice was rough. "Not because we love women and we're all sisters or any of that nonsense. We're educated and we need more educated women. *Not* more mothers and wives."

The ice in her voice made me wonder if she was actually a bit jealous of women who were content as mothers and wives. Women who didn't push so hard. Who could allow a man to take the reins and not be terrified of losing control.

Silence settled over us once more. I clutched my glass and held my tongue. This was hard for her, baring her heart.

"Tonight is why your education is not negotiable. I did not save you from the slums so you could end up back there married to a half-wit who won't let you work in your field. Or the opposite, married to some rich idiot so insecure he would be threatened by a woman who might be more than just useless decoration on his arm."

And that, unfortunately, was how Til viewed women. *Oh Til.*

"To be able to do what you just did, what else could I do?"

Til shrugged at that. "I care about my work. I care about my reputation. I think these women deserve better than this. This is my passion, but I don't know if it is yours."

How could she question that?

Til never trailed off. Never. She was concise. Right then, at that moment, she looked tired. I had never seen her tired before. A battle raged inside her, but I wasn't sure what the problem was.

"Malcolm wants children."

Ah. There it is. Press on with her crusade or have children with Malcolm.

"What do you want, Til?"

She looked up and held my gaze. "I want everything."

That was Til in a nutshell.

"What is in your control?"

"Ah." She laughed. "You are wise."

"Til, what you've created here is amazing, but you deserve happiness, too."

Even exhausted, she stood up and paced over to the window. "I'm turning thirty-eight. I've put him off as long as possible. It is time to start this. I know."

"Til, it's not a business contract!" I dared to reprimand her.

She turned to face me. Til Stone was stunning on a good day, but covered in blood, triumphant from staring down the face of death and defeating it, she was breathtaking. She held her brandy in a hand she hadn't taken time to wash, so the blood had soaked into her skin, dripped down her arms. She looked like a warrior straight from the front lines of battle.

"No, it's a sacrifice!" Her voice bit into me with such ice I rubbed my arms for warmth. "You remember this if a man wants to marry you. It's called an *altar* for a reason. Altar means *sacrifice*. I married him but told him children were not possible. There are too many that are starving in the streets. We're good the way we are. We're happy."

"I might get married." I challenged her. "There must be some benefit to marriage."

"Oh, it's a great benefit to *men*," she said furiously and sat back down. "A husband has all the rights in this world, and a wife has none. A husband can forbid you to work, he can beat you, and not a court in the land will intervene. None whatsoever. In England, right now, there is a stiffer fine for beating a dog than beating a wife. You should look at the laws. It's devastating." Her eyes flashed at me. "Any woman who gets married without contracts and trusts is willingly abdicating all her rights. It's *foolishness*."

"Create those unnecessary contracts regarding children." I leaned back in my chair and put my feet up.

Til looked at me sharply.

"You're much wiser than I give you credit for. While I'm indisposed with children draped all over me, who will run this, though?" Til's eyes narrowed at me as if it were partly my fault she was facing this decision.

I struggled to imagine Til draped with children!

"I will. You'll get nannies. You'll get a team of servants. You can have a lot, maybe not everything, but you make him happy, and you need him."

"Shannon, I do not *need* anyone." She corrected me with such arrogance I winced.

Poor Malcolm.

"Til, you know that's wrong. He's kept you alive on more than one occasion. How many times has he stepped in and saved your life?"

"Who's counting?" Til gave me a shadow of a smile. She knew when she went too far and acknowledged it with that small little smile. "Men are useful for that," she conceded.

She looked at her brandy.

"Malcolm loves your strength. He loves your passion, and he is not going to change because you have children together. He knows you, and he loves you anyway."

She burst out laughing at that.

"Only one child," she said mulishly.

"I'm sure Malcolm will concede to your wishes. He always has."

"Not always, Shannon. He does get his way on occasion." Til sighed.

"I've never seen it." I rolled my eyes at her.

She sniffed at that and turned from me to wash the blood off her hands.

"Is that all that worries you? How your life will change? There must be some other hold up. What's the problem?"

"It's just so... ordinary. Me, with babies! Mercy. I can't even imagine it. I'll lose my edge."

"Til, you won't lose your edge." I dared to contradict her.

"I fear the memories of... Memories of who I left behind might surface when I hold a child of my own." Sadness flashed across her face. Not sadness. Devastation.

"What do you mean? The ones you left behind?" I watched her to see if she would finally let me in on what haunted her.

"I don't speak of it." Til dried her hands and tossed

back the last of her brandy. She held her teacup out for more.

I filled her cup. I watched her eyes for a tell tale sign of what she left behind. Her face was a mask of professionalism. She refused to speak of it and I didn't pry.

**

My memory of that night sank away as I dragged myself from the bath and settled into my bed. I hoped Til was winning her legal battle and would be out of jail soon. There was so much I still needed to learn from her. To be able to step in and stop a hemorrhage was only one gift Til had to give me. The learning was not done. My longing to see Til brought tears to my eyes. I missed her ruthless determination. When the chips were down, that's when Til really began to shine. Where I used to feel wearied by her relentless drive, now I felt it surface in myself. I had it, too.

I could not stay here and disappoint Til. Not negotiable.

A thought of Cole stabbed through me; I didn't want to leave him. This was an impossible choice. Maybe he would come with me? Could he walk away from his family and everything he had here? Life was messy and getting messier by the day. My heart couldn't leave him, but my head couldn't stay.

'Marriage and children are the ultimate sacrifice, Shannon,' I could hear Til in my head. 'You will lose yourself — to give a man that much power over you is terrifying. Think with your head, not your heart. All these women we patch up and sneak birth control to... they trusted men. Married them.' She shuddered. 'Look at them. They are exhausted and beaten.'

Get out of my head, Til. Those decisions are yours. I

have to decide for myself. Your fear has crippled you, crippled Malcolm. I don't want to be a casualty, too. Your anger has pushed you forward, but it's held you back. There are good men. I have a choice to make — mine. I'm not afraid of Cole, of letting him into my life. He doesn't hold me back; he propels me forward.

It was one thing to fight with Til in my head, quite another to stand up to her in person. If whatever decision I made took me off her carefully crafted plan, there would be hell to pay. I put Til out of my mind, settled into rich sheets with such soft bedding my rib didn't hurt so much, and sighed with relief that this day was over.

***

After breakfast, Cole, Lord Harper, and I met Mr. Cairn in the drawing room. The opulence of this room dazzled my eyes. Sunlight filled the room, pouring in through stained glass windows.

"It's purely circumstantial," Mr. Cairn said to Lord Harper. "The ergot of rye is clearly what caused the miscarriages, but how do we prove Biddy administered it? Any lawyer can get this acquitted."

Lord Harper's face reddened with rage. "There must be something you can do."

"What would it take to ensure she is no longer a danger to Lady Harper or indeed Miss Stone?" Cole interrupted. "If we investigate further..."

"To prosecute for the alleged promotion of abortion, we need Lady Harper's testimony," the lawyer said. "We need to hear it from her."

"Miss Stone has her testimony," Lord Harper protested.

"Apparently, a maid with ergot of rye in her

possession and a woman losing multiple pregnancies under her care isn't clear enough evidence." I kept my voice unemotional. Disappointment settled over the room, followed closely by worry.

What would Biddy do if she wasn't jailed? When would she return? What would a woman full of rage do if she made her way back to Lady Harper, and indeed me?

Cole moved closer to me and rested his arm across the back of my chair.

"She's right." Mr. Cairn nodded in my direction. "We can try, but I have to suggest you let your wife on the stand or we plea bargain."

"No." Lord Harper stood up and put his hands on the table, towering over Mr. Cairn. "I cannot put Lady Harper through that."

"Put Lady Harper through what?" Lady Harper asked from the doorway.

Lady Harper looked beautiful in the morning sun. It shone through her dark hair, lit up her creamy skin. Her pregnancy was showing; five months had whizzed by. Lord Harper turned to her as Mr. Cairn and Cole leaped to their feet as she made her way into the room. Lord Harper pulled out a chair for her. She settled in and looked at us curiously.

"Honestly, I have no idea what all the cloak and dagger is about. This is silly. If something is going on that I can testify about, I think I should know about it," she chuckled.

We all sat silently.

"Lady Harper, you have been through a lot. There is no reason for you to be distressed." Lord Harper reached for her hand.

I poured her some tea.

"Is this about Biddy?" Lady Harper asked me directly. "Was she the cause of all the miscarriages?"

My eyes met Lord Harper's as I put down the tea pot.

"I am an adult. If I want information that pertains to me or my household I think you, of all people, would have the decency to let me be informed and not treat me like a child," Lady Harper said directly to me.

"Biddy was administering abortifacients to you. That's why you had such increased pain at times." I met her eyes, watched the pain flash through them and her face pale as she realized what I meant. "She is responsible for every miscarriage. No one saw her actually give ergot of rye to you. Also, those potions and drugs usually are ineffective unless the person using them knows your... well, knows you intimately. There is no reason to have ergot of rye except to bring on a miscarriage, to speed up labour, or to stop a hemorrhage. It is helpful with migraine, but no doctor would prescribe ergot to a pregnant woman or a married woman, for that matter. It is deadly to the unborn fetus."

She went completely pale at that, and I stopped talking.

"What are you saying?" Lady Harper's eyes filled with tears.

"Darling, this is too much for you." Lord Harper put his heavy hand on her narrow shoulder. "We need to focus on this baby. This baby is all that matters."

Your wife matters, too.

"I knew something was wrong, and I thought it was me. She let me think it was me! All these years!" Lady Harper collapsed into tears.

Lord Harper gave me a hard look.

"Darling. You don't want all this to be paraded in front of a judge and jury. We will plea bargain."

I can't handle the shame of this, so you must bear it.

"She should be prosecuted." Lady Harper wiped at tears. "I don't care if we lose. She needs to know this was monstrous. So much suffering she brought to me. What if she does it to someone else?"

"She won't," I said firmly.

"How do you know that?"

"I interviewed her." I waited for the backlash of emotion.

"And you kept this from me." Betrayal flashed across her face.

"Yes." There was steel in my tone. "You were at a very delicate state, Lady Harper. I could not be sure if it was the herbs Biddy was putting in your drinks or if it actually was you."

She stood up in outrage, which brought all the men to their feet. "How dare you?" Her face was red with fury. "I brought you from England to ensure the birth of this baby!"

"I didn't know you. I didn't know Biddy. I realized my mistake."

You don't know what I've seen desperate women do. You have no idea the messes I've cleaned up.

Lady Harper moved to the window, away from all of us to try to calm down. Cole's eyes were on me as I went to her. It was my turn to appeal to her.

"Lady Harper, until I knew the reason you were miscarrying those babies, I really couldn't do anything. It was a time to just observe, but now I *know* Biddy was poisoning you. Once she stopped caring for you, the headaches were gone, the cramping was gone. You are successfully carrying this child to term. I can't prove it, but I know without a doubt she caused you many miscarriages. More than you know."

"I will testify." Lady Harper turned to the men, and her eyes locked with Lord Harper.

"You will *not* testify in open court about such intimate details of your person," Lord Harper said so harshly she winced.

Suddenly, I realized another side to this class of women. They had everything materially, but almost no say in their lives. Til should not have been so hard on them. Til plowed through life without a thought for anyone. She looked down on the Lady Harpers of the world. The strength to carry on when you have little say in your life, to accept decisions you wouldn't personally make, that took a certain kind of strength, too. They may be spoiled and pampered, but they were raised to submit to very powerful men. These men overrode their thoughts and feelings and didn't give it a thought. Raised to be masters of their domain and as such did not look at their wives as their equals. This was a tragedy, and Til would have shriveled in that environment. Women like Til, me, and Priscilla, we might be working our guts out while these powerful men considered us inferior, but when we spoke, some of them listened. Eventually, more of them would.

Would Cole trample my rights the way Lord Harper had just trampled Lady Harper's?

I watched Lady Harper carefully put a mask over her feelings. I marveled at her strength of will, to push such strong feelings away and not react to this injustice. She was a lady. No one would know her true feelings on this matter.

"Of course," she acquiesced to Lord Harper. "Whatever you think is best."

He didn't ask her opinion. Her opinion did not matter.

"What will happen to her?" Lady Harper asked the lawyer. Her voice was carefully modulated, no emotion in her tone.

"If I might," Cole interjected. "Lord Harper, it's your job to keep Lady Harper happy and healthy, but I heard Biddy threaten Shannon. We have it on record that she threatened to end Shannon's life."

"Maybe we could discuss this when Lady Harper has been..." Lord Harper interjected.

"Biddy threatened to kill you?" Lady Harper raised her eyebrow at me.

"She did." I took a step closer to her.

"Listen." Cole directed his attention to Mr. Cairn. "I do not want Shannon's life in danger from this incurable."

"I will meet with her lawyer." Mr. Cairn took a note of it.

"Take me with you," I said to the lawyer.

"Shannon," Cole said sternly.

I dare you, try to trample my rights... try it... see what I'm capable of.

"Cole, if I'm in the room, she will go crazy. I don't think Biddy should be in jail. I do think she needs to be in a sanatorium so as not to bring harm to herself or others. Those sanatoriums are pretty brutal, but what she is capable of is brutal, too."

"Well, you're not going in there alone." Cole moved closer to me and crossed his arms over his chest.

"I will come with you."

"I have enough to get her off the streets." Mr. Cairn interrupted us. "I'll let her lawyer know we are pressing charges for the assault, and the death threat is in the notes. Her lawyer doesn't need to know that Lady Harper will not be participating in trial. I can keep that information to myself and use it as leverage."

Mr. Cairn tidied his papers up, and Lord Harper turned to Cole.

"Could I have a word with you?" Lady Harper asked me.

The men took the cue and left us in the drawing room.

"You were acting in my best interest, and I am so sorry." Her eyes shimmered with the tears that she had just suppressed. "I shouldn't have let my feelings get the better of me."

"We hardly knew each other. I walked in and had some suspicions, and I acted the best way I knew how. I am sorry, too. I could have told you everything when Biddy was arrested, but I worried that your concern about Biddy would cause you unnecessary stress."

Lady Harper waved my apology away. "We'll call it even."

She put her hand on her baby, and we smiled at each other. This baby was safe.

At the end of the day, Lord Harper, Cole, and I had one final meeting with the lawyers. Both prosecution and defence. Cole stood behind me while I reiterated my concerns about Biddy.

"This is all circumstantial," the defence lawyer, Mr. Harrigan, said to Mr. Cairn. "A midwife brought these concerns forward. What training am I supposed to believe she has?"

I am being dismissed, again!

"A charge of procuring a miscarriage with noxious drugs, that is seven years in prison, sir," Mr. Cairn countered. "Imagine what will happen when Lady Harper takes the stand in court." He let that sink in. "Say we draw, oh I don't know, Judge Antoinne. Do you want to gamble on what the judge would do with a charge such as this? Ergot of rye in her possession, her father an apothecary, which gives her access and knowledge on how to use it..." Mr. Cairn let that statement hang there.

I'd underestimated Mr. Cairn. He was clever and emotionless. He might have spoken down to me, but he spoke down to everyone and bluffed so convincingly, I almost believed him. The defence attorney clearly did.

"Motive?" The defence attorney made one last stab at getting her off completely. "Hard to prove motive. Miss Baxter loves Lady Harper."

Mr. Cairn leaned forward on the desk. "But, she despises Lady Harper's unborn children." The pause for effect was perfect. I wanted to applaud him. The defence lawyer went pale. "Do you think the court will worry about motive if Lady Harper takes the stand?"

The defence crumbled at the suggestion.

"What are you offering?" the defence asked weakly.

"Six months, a gift. For the assault and repeated threat on Miss Stone's life." Mr. Cairn didn't even look up. He was writing on an affidavit.

"Done." Mr. Harrigan frowned.

Just like that.

"Are you alright with that?" Cole asked as we left the room and walked down a dark, dusty hallway.

"Sure." I shrugged. "The baby will be born by then, and I'll be back in school in England. She won't be hopping on boats to come find me, I'm sure."

England was a word I tip-toed around, but I couldn't any longer.

"I underestimated Mr. Cairn. He's very good." I tried to build a bridge between us, find some common ground.

"I was impressed, too. I wouldn't want to come across him in court," Cole agreed, accepting the peace offering.

"I'm going to be completely honest with you." Cole took my hand in his.

I looked at him and waited for him to speak.

"When we first met, I thought I could persuade you to give up England, give up being a doctor. I really did. I wanted you here, in my life. I couldn't imagine why a woman, a beautiful woman like you, would put yourself through all this study and work. You know you could have any man you wanted."

"That's rather disturbing," I said frankly.

"I agree. I was completely out of line in my thinking. Good thing I never said it out loud. I had no idea what you were capable of until I saw you in action with Mary Varsdon. I stood watching in awe. You knew exactly how to stop a hemorrhage. Everyone else was terrified. You handled the near death of a woman as if it were afternoon tea. If you hadn't been there, the mayor would be planning a funeral. The baby would have been motherless. I've never seen anything like it." His hand squeezed mine. "You can't stop the path you are on. You must go back, and you have to continue. I have no idea how to make this work on my end or if you want me with you, but *you* can't stop."

I felt my heart soar with his words and smiled as I leaned forward to kiss him.

"Miss Stone, you are playing with fire." He pulled me closer and kissed me again.

"Playing with fire is fun." I pulled my gloves off so I could stroke his face before I leaned in to kiss him again.

Chapter Twenty-Six

Cole and I took our new understanding home and got back to work.

The cottage hospital had been transformed. Every inch of wall had a fresh coat of paint. The beds were arranged, two downstairs and two up, made with crisp white linen. Everything was stacked and organized neatly.

"This is amazing!" I was stunned by the amount of work that had been accomplished in such a short time. "Your W.C.T.U has done more than expected! I am so proud of everyone!"

Lady Harper teared up as Mrs. Daindridge came in with extra baby blankets. The births would happen at home, but if a baby was sick and needed extra care, there were special blankets here of soft yellow flannel to keep them warm and comfortable.

"We did it!" Lady Harper gave Mrs. Daindridge a hug.

"We need to celebrate. All the ladies at my house tomorrow afternoon. This calls for a tea party!" Lady Harper announced.

We all assembled at Hillcrest promptly at two p.m. the next day.

"Ladies, I have some difficult news to share with you." Lady Harper twisted her wedding ring and bit her lip as the ladies turned their attention to her.

They set their tea cups down to brace themselves for the bad news.

"The paper is full of the news. The people are requesting a different group to run the hospital."

"You and your women put this together from the ground up. This isn't right," I protested.

"Just read it."

She handed the paper over, and I read it quickly then focused on some specific points.

"Irrational W.C.T.U!" I looked up from the paper at her. "How is putting together a hospital irrational?"

"Chester Manning." Mrs. Carr stood up and held her hand out for the paper. Her eyes flicked over it. "Anonymous. Of course, it's signed anonymous. *Typical* Chester Manning."

"I don't understand." I looked from Mrs. Carr to Lady Harper.

"Chester Manning owned the saloon when we protested. He went to our husbands and asked them to, how did he put it?" Mrs. Carr asked Mrs. Daindridge. It was as if they shared a brain for gossip, anything one forgot the other remembered.

"Get your women under control." Mrs. Daindridge handed the paper to Mrs. Holt.

"He's been wild at the W.C.T.U. ever since." Mrs. Holt stood up to refill her tea cup. "He protested my husband running for mayor because he is married to me and I might have some control over how he handles business matters with people who sell alcohol. Little does he know, I couldn't control Harris Holt if I held a gun to his head. He's the most stubborn person on earth. Anyway, Chester Manning is a crazy loon. He'll calm down."

"He doesn't run the saloon now. I understand Roger Hanover does." I looked from Mrs. Carr to Mrs. Daindridge to be sure I was correct.

"Yes." Mrs. Holt's mouth was a thin line.

"Chester Manning gambled the saloon one night and lost it to Roger Hanover." Mrs. Daindridge's eyes gleamed imparting that piece of gossip.

"It hasn't improved his mood." Mrs. Carr's lips pursed.

"Never mind Chester Manning." Mrs. Holt pointed to a line in the newspaper. "The operation of the hospital cannot and will not be handed over to a 'bunch of women'."

"Anonymous again?" Lady Harper asked.

"It's in more than one column." Mrs. Holt narrowed her eyes. She bristled at the terminology 'bunch of women' like all the ladies in the room. "It seems as if it were a consensus."

"What should we do?" Mrs. Daindridge straightened her shoulders.

"There is more here. They want the broadest base represented." Mrs. Bennett finally spoke up and everyone listened. "I think that means some of us can be on the board, but not all W.C.T.U."

"Women on a board of directors with men?" Mrs. Carr said waspishly. "They'll never agree to it. They will say running this hospital would be too stressful for women."

"They are saying that if we are not elected to run it, we can't be removed. They want to be sure that we are accountable." Mrs. Bennett was taking the attack out of it and focusing on the only thing in the newspaper that warranted attention.

"They were happy enough to ask us to do all the work." Priscilla stood up and held her hand out to read the paper for herself.

"Would you meet with the council for us?" Lady Harper's eyes were full of concern as she came to me and laid her hand on my arm. "Lord Harper is absolutely going to have a fit if I address this, and nobody else will want to address council."

You're the only one that doesn't have a husband to stop you.

"We need you to go. But after this ordeal, I'm not so sure," Mrs. Rood said softly.

"I still look like a street fighter, Lady Harper," I warned her.

"We need a street fighter, I think. Can you meet with them tomorrow?"

"Of course," I said firmly. "Priscilla, can you help me get ready? I would feel better if you could do all that paste again. I hate to go in with all these bruises."

"I'll be over. When does Shannon need to be ready for the meeting?"

"She needs to be ready by two p.m. at the council chambers."

A tap at the door interrupted us. Jaffrey went to answer.

"There is a woman here to see you." He frowned at me as I went toward the door.

"Lady Harper, I'll go and attend to this. I'll be back tomorrow to get ready."

With that, I left to meet the woman in the entry way.

"Can I help you?" I asked the woman who was clearly ill at ease standing at the door.

"It's my sister, miss," she kept her eyes lowered. "They said you would know what to do."

"What is happening?"

"She has a very high fever. I'm scared. I've tried everything." Tears fell down her face, soaking into her scarf. "But, she is at the... in the... saloon." Her voice dropped incase anyone might overhear.

I took Jaffrey aside.

"Let Cole know where to find me please," I said as I pulled on my coat and scrambled into my boots.

Jaffrey bristled with indignation. "Of course, but Mr. McDougall would *insist* you wait for him." Jaffrey crossed his arms. He was uncomfortable with the woman in front of me and the thought of me following her.

"There is no time. Would you find him and send him for me? This sounds like an emergency."

He opened his mouth to argue, but I was already following the woman out the door. I made one quick stop to pick up my doctor's bag, and we raced to the saloon.

Chapter Twenty-Seven

On the top floor of Roger Hanover's saloon, a feverish woman writhed in agony on the bed. I rolled up my sleeves to do an examination.

"I'll need hot water." I felt her forehead. This fever was very high.

"You have to work quickly. He's gone to Brandon, but he could be back at any minute. He can't know I contacted you." She wrung her hands in fear.

"I'll do my best," I promised. "I need hot water so I can help. What is her name?"

"Ruby."

"Real name?"

"Martha," she said sheepishly. "You must be horrified, a lady like you."

"Not at all." I took her pulse; it was rapid. "Please, get that water as quickly as possible."

She fled as I moved to the foot of the bed.

"Martha," I said quietly. "Martha, I'm here to help you. You need to tell me what happened."

"I can't," she whimpered.

"Martha, I am a doctor and I am here to help you, but I cannot help you unless I know what happened."

"She had a miscarraige," said the woman who had let me in.

Oh Martha... this is a bad fever...

"Your name?" I asked the girl as she brought in the

water.

"Enid." She didn't bother with her fake name.

"I'm Shannon." I held out my hand for her to shake.

She looked at me skeptically.

"We've got a lot of work to do here, Enid. We may as well be friends."

"Will she die?" Enid was on the verge of tears.

"Well, let's see what we can do."

After scrubbing with carbolic acid, I did a full examination.

I could tell just by the fever that she had retained product of conception that had gone septic.

Enid's eyes widened as I straightened up and washed my hands. "I need to do a procedure. A piece of the placenta has remained inside her. It has become septic and I need to get it out immediately. I need as much hot water as you can carry up here."

Enid brought water as I readied my tools. Before I began, I asked her to leave.

"No." Enid grasped Martha's hand tightly. "I want to stay."

"If you stay you can't faint or cry, you have to be tough." I heard Til in my head.

Be tough...

Enid nodded.

"This is a chloroform mask, I want you to drip one drop on this mask every minute. The chloroform makes the pain bearable, can you do that?"

"Yes." Enid took the bottle of chloroform in her shaking hands.

"He might get back before she is done. Is there any-thing we can do to speed this up?" Enid was so scared, her voice shook with fear.

"The constable will be here soon and we don't need to worry about Mr. Hanover." I got to work as fast as I could, as carefully as I could. I wished for a surgical room with all my tools placed where I liked them and worried that I was turning into Til with all my requirements.

Enid put another drop on Martha's mask.

She was afraid of the man she worked. I'd seen this before. The sound of heavy boots sounded outside the door.

"Oh, no! He's back." Enid's body trembled in fear.

"Shannon?"

"It's alright. It's Constable McDougall." I hoped she would calm down, but the mention of Cole seemed to make her even more nervous. "Cole I need fifteen more minutes, keep everyone out of here."

I could hear him pacing with what was very likely fury. I ignored Cole, finished my work and then filled a fountain syringe to make sure I flushed the womb to kill as much infection as I possibly could.

"Your face looks... terrifying." Enid's voice trembled.

"Does it?" I didn't look up, I concentrated on my work. I prayed this would work.

"Yes. I am scared, is she going to live?" Enid bit her lip.

"We are going to do our best." I promised as I placed a hot towel on Martha's abdomen and then washed my hands with carbolic acid. "I'll be right back."

I slipped out into the hallway, pulling the door shut firmly behind me.

"What is going on in there?" His jaw clenched so

hard I thought his teeth would break.

"Retained product of conception. Martha miscarried and a piece of the placenta was caught, she is septic. I have done my best, but I fear she won't live until morning." I held my hands up to ward him off. He looked ready to grab me and drag me down the stairs.

A muscle in his jaw jumped, his lips thinned in anger. "This is not safe. We need to move her to your carriage house."

"I agree, but she is in a terrible state. We can't move her yet."

His stance widened as he glanced down the hall. "I'll guard the door. You go back to work. As soon as she is ready to move, we move her, and you are *never* stepping foot in this saloon again."

I bristled at his tone and then shook it off. I had work to do, and now I didn't have to worry about Roger Hanover.

With Cole guarding the door, I returned to Martha. Her fever raged. I put my soiled instruments in a bag and then tucked them away. After half an hour hoping the fever would settle, it didn't.

"We're going to relocate her to my home," I informed Enid. "You should pack some clothes for her.

Enid's eyes filled with tears. "You can't take her. He'll go crazy."

"She's not staying here. She will need around-the-clock care," I insisted. "I'm taking her to my home, and Roger Hanover can deal with me."

"You don't want Roger Hanover to deal with you." Enid shook with fear.

"I'm not afraid of Roger Hanover. Did you see the constable out there? We have nothing to worry about."

"I wish that was true." Her face was white with fear.

I opened the door.

"She is ready to be relocated," I said to Cole.

He found a man downstairs that was sober enough to go for Matt. In minutes, Matt was bounding up the stairs two at a time.

"Would you please take Martha to my carriage house and put her in my spare room? I just have to finish up here."

"Certainly." He carefully picked up Martha and began heading down the hallway. Cole stood by and waited for me to get my implements and medicines back in the bag.

I turned to Enid before I left.

"How did you come to be here?"

"We owed Roger money and we work as bar maids to pay it off." She shrunk back from me.

Acid turned my stomach at those words.

Bar maids... working to pay off a debt...

"Come with me, Enid. You don't have to stay here." I held my hand out to her.

Her eyes widened at the suggestion.

"He will never let that happen, we owe so much money." She bit her lip so hard I thought it might bleed.

"You are safe with me." I placed my hand on her shoulder.

"You don't know..."

"I think I do." I spoke gently. "Come with me. This is over, whatever it is."

"I'm scared to death of him." Enid's narrow shoulder shook under my hand.

"Did you see the man guarding the door?"

"I can't do it," she whispered.

I sighed. I had to go. I reached out to her and gave her a hug. She clung to me. "Whatever this situation is, we can fix it. You do not have to be afraid of anything." I squeezed her hand and then left the saloon in front of Cole.

Cole helped Matt settle Martha in my spare room.

I administered the highest dose of aconite for the fever.

I did everything I could think of; I tucked her in and smoothed her hair off her forehead. When I turned to leave the room, I caught a glimpse of Cole's stern face in the doorway. Fury made his face harden in a way that made me nervous.

"We need to talk." His words were clipped with anger.

"I know." I straightened my shoulders to face him in the other room. I gently pulled Martha's door shut.

You don't want to hear this...

Cole thanked Matt for his assistance, and Matt shot me a look of sympathy as Cole opened the door for him to leave. He kept his back to me for a minute; he must have been trying to calm himself down. I moved closer, no sense trying to get out of the lecture that was coming. Finally, he turned around to face me.

"The next time you are called to a drinking establishment, you will wait for me. You had no idea what you were walking into."

"Cole, it was an emergency."

"Emergency! It will *always* be an emergency, Shannon. You are a doctor! From this minute forward you wait for me or you don't go." A vein in his neck throbbed.

"There wasn't time." I lifted my chin and held my ground. "I can't always wait. I am sorry I worried you."

"Worried me?" He couldn't yell because he didn't want to scare Martha to death. He hissed instead. "You terrified me."

"I'm not used to this." There was nothing I could say to stop this rant except an apology, and he wanted more. He wanted a vow to put my safety ahead of a patient, and I couldn't promise that.

"Get used to it." His teeth clenched harder; I stood up straighter. He was wild with fury, but I knew him. He could never hurt me; I wasn't afraid of him.

A knock at the door interrupted us.

Lord Harper didn't wait for the door to open to him. He strode into the room. He looked from me to Cole and then turned his focus back to me. "I was coming down here to give you the lecture I realize I just walked in on."

Merciful heavens! I've been in a million drinking establishments!

"Jaffrey told me about your summons to the saloon." Lord Harper stood beside Cole, so now I faced two angry men instead of one. "Would you like to explain why you were racing to Roger Hanover's with no protection?"

I straightened my shoulders and lifted my chin. "I was doing my job."

"Your job is to assist my wife. You work for me."

My face went pale. I crossed my arms in front of me. "I am a trained midwife, and I know how to help women who are suffering from miscarriage."

"Miscarraige!" Shock splashed across Lord Harper's face.

"Sadly, yes. I know you would not turn your back on someone suffering. Why do you think I would?" I appealed to their reason.

"I'm not saying you have to turn your back on anyone." Lord Harper recovered and pointed his finger at me. "From now on, you wait for Cole or me before you set foot outside this door where it involves danger to your person. Are we clear on that? Or should we pack you up and send you back to England? I don't have employees that disobey direct orders. Your choice."

My eyes narrowed.

"I'm waiting to hear what you choose to do. Right now. Stay and do it my way or go. Which do you prefer?" Lord Harper's voice was cold.

I swallowed down my pride. "I apologize. I acted on impulse."

"From now on, you will wait for protection or you will not go. I'd like to hear you say it." Lord Harper wasn't backing down.

I gritted my teeth. "From now on, I'll wait for protection or I won't go."

"There, that wasn't so hard, was it?" Lord Harper turned from me to Cole.

Tears of humiliation pricked behind my eyes. I turned to my doctor's bag, pretending to look for something so he wouldn't see my face.

"Roger Hanover is a volatile person. Cole, you'll have to stay here tonight until Martha is returned. Since the two of you are courting, you will need a chaperone, so please ask Matt, and if he's not available, we'll send Jaffrey down."

"Martha will not be returning." Cole shook his head. "These women are being kept in the saloon against their will. Enid mentioned they owed him money and I believe an investigation is in order."

My tears and emotions were tamped down; I turned to face them both.

"I leave that in your hands." Lord Harper pulled his gloves back on. "I had been informed that they were barmaids, Miss Stone. In light of recent events, it is clear at least Martha is no such thing, and we will not have this *debauchery* in our community we will route it out forthwith. Let Cole and I handle this. I'll talk to the mayor in the morning, and we will come up with a plan of action."

"I am to meet with the mayor at two p.m." I went to the cook stove to put water on to boil.

"Of course, we'll reconvene in the morning." Lord Harper left as abruptly as he entered.

I turned to Cole.

"You alright? He was pretty tough."

"You were pretty rough, too." I frowned at him.

"I care about you and your safety."

"So you have said." I wanted the subject changed. "How does he know we're courting?"

"I spoke to Lord Harper about it. I'm waiting to hear back from Malcolm. I asked his permission, and there has been no response yet."

"Wrote to Malcolm? Without asking me first?"

"He's the only man in your life other than Lord Harper, of course, that I can see."

"Til will be wild when she sees that letter! You should have talked to me first. Why not just ask me? This is the oddest thing I've ever heard of!"

"Because I'm serious, Shannon," Cole nearly shouted. He couldn't stop his impatience from surfacing between us. Not just about rushing into Roger's. I wasn't getting it, and he was getting tired. "I'm not a boy."

I can see that. You're a man, no question.

"I've been married, and I want to be married again. I am serious about you. There is no way I could proceed without permission from the one man in your life who has your best interests at heart. If there is any reason he thinks that you are vulnerable or this is not good for you, or maybe this is too soon after... after what happened, then I should know and back off."

"Shouldn't I be the judge of that?" I rounded on him. We both heard the ice that crept into my voice. "Don't you see that all this manoeuvring indicates that I have no say in what happens in my own life? You think that I need men to make decisions for me?"

"Please don't take this the wrong way, but you're a woman. It's customary to..."

"Hang on." Anger made my heart pound. "Let me get this straight. You think that I am too what, *emotional,* to think for myself? You think that I don't know my own mind? Please, spell it out."

"You are vulnerable," he fired back. "You have been through a lot. You are far from everyone who loves you and knows you. I want to be in your life, but you have so precious few family members, I don't want to alienate any of them. We're courting, and I want more than that. It is only fair that Malcolm should be consulted."

"Well, that is honest." I folded my arms.

"I'm sorry you are upset. This is how things are done. I thought you knew. What's bothering you? That I didn't talk to you first?"

"Oh! I get to speak for myself!" Sarcasm clipped my words. "Cole, you are the most honourable person I know. We're adults. We can choose to court if we want to. You asking Lord Harper and Malcolm for permission makes me wild. It takes me, my thoughts, my feelings out of the equation. I am not a child. You have no idea the can of worms you just opened with Til. If she's out of jail, no one is safe. She'll be on the next ocean liner over here."

"It's just customary!" He held his hands out in surrender. "This is how men of honour interact. I thought you knew this! No one asks the aunt, that's preposterous."

"The whole thing is preposterous! Maybe I should speak to your mother," I said wildly. "Find out if this is the right time for you. Make sure I'm not taking advantage of you. You are so fragile, Cole. I would hate to overstep."

He burst out laughing at that.

"So, do you see how completely ridiculous that is?" I demanded.

"When it is about me. Yes. When it is about you. No."

I rolled my eyes, and he smiled and grabbed me by both arms.

"You want to be with me?" he asked in a tone that made my knees weak.

Every time you touch me I'm weak. No wonder Til warned me!

"I agreed to *court* you." My voice was cold. I had a patient to get back to. "Try things out. You're making this too serious."

"I want more," he said simply.

I scowled at him. He let his hands soften their grip. They moved up my arms and cradled my face.

Tenaciously, Cole tried to explain it another way. "Malcolm is the man in your life responsible for your wellbeing, and I want to be that man, to take that role. So, I'm asking his permission to take on that role. From him. That's all. You can still turn me down flat. You have complete control, Shannon."

"This is fascinating." I tilted my head. "I have some concerns."

He took his hands away and immediately I felt the loss.

"What are they?"

"How much of a say will you expect to have in what happens in my life?" I asked tentatively.

"I would expect to have a reasonable degree of input on what happens in your life. Just as you would have input into what happens in mine," Cole replied cautiously.

I felt a shiver of apprehension. What did *reasonable degree* mean? I heard Til in my head... 'Never let a man have any control over you... never... you can't trust them... you will get hurt.'

"That sounds very open to interpretation." I narrowed my eyes.

"You're going to have to trust me, Shann. Do you think you could trust me a slight little bit?"

I already trust you. That's the problem. One touch from you and I lose my senses.

"Maybe." I tried to sound in control. He was making a convincing argument. All this manoeuvring was to let the men in my life know he cared about me. He had left out Til, which was a disaster, but maybe Malcolm would calm her down. I felt my anger dissipate. He was a man of honour, and I was raised by a tyrant. What did I know?

"Does this mean I get to kiss you whenever I want? Demand things of you?" A smile tugged at my lips.

He smiled back. "Of course."

I moved in, and he held up his hands.

"I haven't gotten that letter from Malcolm yet. So, until then..."

"You are joking." My jaw dropped open in shock.

He laughed. "I wouldn't joke about that."

I sighed. "We kissed before," I protested.

"That was before the inquisition and hands asked in courtship. This would be different kissing." He made his voice sound like the lawyer Mr. Cairn. "This would be kissing with intent."

"Intent to what."

"Marry."

How does he do that with his eyes? Make one word into a promise? Hold it together, Shannon.

"I have school to finish. I have obligations to Til." Worry made my heart hammer.

"Marriage doesn't have to stop that," he said firmly, and meant it.

"I guess we will wait for that letter." I couldn't keep the disappointment out of my voice.

"I guess so," he agreed and picked up his coat to go.

He got as far as the door before he came back for me and swept me right off my feet. He kissed me in a way I had never experienced. I thought we had kissed before, but that had been as intimate as a handshake. This was kissing, possession, a whole new level of intent. When he finally set me down, he had to hold me up. Mortified, I swooned like a complete idiot. Exactly the kind of woman Til rolled her eyes at. My knees were weak.

Please don't let him notice.

"Can you stand up?" he whispered.

Oh mercy, he noticed!

"Not yet," I whispered back. "One more time..."

He complied, his lips claiming mine again.

Kissing with intent, indeed!

I pressed against his chest just slightly, and he stopped, created a little distance, and looked at me carefully. I marveled at this. All this strength, all this power, so tightly leashed.

I could stop him. One gentle push and he would stop. *I don't want you to stop.*

Boldly, I ran my hands across the tops of his shoulders, down the thickness of his arms. I watched as his eyes changed, went darker.

I thought men had all the power; I was wrong. Women are powerful, too.

"If we start this," he said quietly as his eyes locked on mine.

"If we start this, there will be no finishing it," I whispered.

This was no play-yard fling. He would not be content to be in my life without a marriage certificate. It was all or nothing. Marriage, children, working together, laughing, crying, the whole thing. He would be one-hundred-percent committed to me, but he would expect nothing less.

This is what Til warned me about.

I understood Til's fear. He would own me. My body would be his body, and his body would be mine. He would expect to call some of the shots. He was used to taking control, being relied on; he was used to a wife that was meek. *Heaven help both of us.*

"What if I am not right for you?" I barely whispered.

"That is what courting is for, Shannon. To figure out if we can stand each other."

"Stand each other!" I sputtered. "How romantic."

"I am not looking for a replacement for Maggie." He tugged me closer. "I am looking for a wife to share my life with. Every time I walk you home, it is getting harder to leave you. So, we do this or we don't. If it's not happening, Lord Harper needs to find someone else to guard you."

"What about London and school and all that?"

"It's all in the letter to Malcolm."

"When Til hears about this, she's going to swim here from England. She will stop this at all costs." My heart pounded in fear at the thought.

"Probably."

"But while we wait for that letter, having another kiss — a kiss like the last one — that's off the table?"

"It is."

"I see."

He grinned then, and I knew nothing was off the table.

"So, I better speak to your mother, and you better wait for that letter," I said primly.

"Alright."

He lunged for me, and I knew right then — I was in over my head and I didn't know how to swim. As his mouth claimed mine, as his arms held me hard against him, I was thrilled to be drowning.

The woman moaning in the spare room put an end to our embrace. He reluctantly let me go.

"Can I help?" he asked, setting me on my feet carefully.

"I need hot water and I need a carbolic acid solution." I went from courting mode to doctor mode.

"Done. I'll go up to the big house and see if I can get some supper from Jaffrey for the three of us."

"Great, make sure you get enough for Matt, too. We have a chaperone to think about now." I readied the fountain syringe.

"What on earth is that for?" He pumped more water into a bucket and put it on the cook stove.

"It is nothing you ever want to know about," I answered dryly. "Funny, I thought courting would be much more glamourous."

"Wait for it. Once we get the bad guys squared away you'll be blinded by all the glamour Oakland has to offer."

"I'm going to hold you to that." I grinned.

No time for anything untoward. It took everything I had to keep Martha alive through the night. The fever was worse the next morning when Lady Harper had Jaffrey come for me. I didn't want to leave Martha, but I couldn't refuse a summons to Hillcrest.

"Cole, the minute Doctor Davies gets back to Oakland bring him here to check on Martha. Her fever hasn't come down." I sponged sweat off her forehead for the millionth time. This fever was raging, and there was nothing I could do for her.

"I'll go for him right now. He got back late last night."

Dr. Davies returned with Cole.

After a thorough examination, he turned to me.

"This is the correct course of treatment. I appreciate you handling this. It is great to have another pair of hands."

"I just wanted to be sure I hadn't missed anything. I've been over every procedure and I am worried..." I couldn't keep the sound of defeat out of my voice.

"You thought of everything." Dr. Davies patted my shoulder. One doctor to another, we knew what it felt like to face death and lose ground. "Now we just wait, keep her comfortable, and hope she pulls through. Send Cole for me though if she takes a turn for the worse."

Which she will.

We left Martha to continue the conversation in the living room.

"Don't sign any paperwork." Dr. Davies picked up his doctor's bag.

Cole looked at him with confusion.

"Women doctors are often accused of procuring a miscarriage." Dr Davies directed his comment to Cole. "Miss Stone's reputation needs to be taken into consideration. Let me be the one to process this. If she doesn't make it, no one will look at me with suspicion."

"Thanks, I appreciate it." I moved forward to shake his hand. His hand was hard; he squeezed mine in solidarity. Dr. Davies addressed my fear with a practical solution. Relief washed over me.

"Good work here." Dr. Davies tipped his cap to me and left for his next patient. As Dr. Davies left, Priscilla was coming up the walk way.

"You knew your reputation could be affected. Your professional reputation, in addition to your safety being compromised, and you attended her anyway?" Cole sputtered.

Here we go...

"I do the right thing no matter what." I rounded on him. "They are all women to me, there is no class distinction."

"I'd like to remind you your aunt is in prison because of that exact attitude," Cole countered. "You should have called Dr. Davies."

"No." My voice was clipped. "Enid came to me. Martha felt more comfortable with a woman. I went. It's my job. I don't cater to bullies. I'm not discussing this any further. I have work to do!"

"I would love to stay and fight this out, but I have to get going." Cole furiously crossed his arms over his chest.

"I'm sure we'll revisit this another day," I snapped at him.

We both watched Priscilla pick her way around icy patches to get to my front door.

Cole opened the door to her gentle tap.

"I thought you might need another set of hands." Priscilla unwrapped her scarf, and if she noticed the tension between us she didn't mention it.

"Thanks." I went to her and hugged her hard. I was tired of men yelling at me. "I appreciate it."

"Good day ladies. Stay out of trouble, Shannon." Cole shot me a look of frustration before he left.

"Try to keep her comfortable." I dragged my outer wear on. "I have to run up to Hillcrest. I need a list of women who would like to be on the hospital board. I'll be back right away."

"Good luck," Priscilla said as I left her there with Martha and raced up to Hillcrest.

Chapter Twenty-Eight

Back at the carriage house, Priscilla met me at the door with worry stamped on her face.

"What happened?" I pulled my coat and boots off. Thankfully, Priscilla had hot water on the cook stove. I rolled up my sleeves and washed my hands before going to check on Martha. Her fever was still high; I checked her pulse.

"What can we do?" Priscilla wrung her hands. Anxiety made the back of my neck wet with sweat; I felt it trickle down my back. My mind raced through everything I had already tried. There was nothing left. Everything I used had failed.

"I will dose her with aconite again."

"Will it fix it?" Tears of sympathy filled Priscilla's eyes.

No.

"Maybe, we have to try." Priscilla's tears touched my heart.

Priscilla pumped fresh water, and I refused to admit defeat and gave her morphine and aconite to ease Martha's suffering.

Priscilla wiped tears away.

I swallowed hard. "If she is in pain, give her more morphine."

Priscilla nodded.

I raced into a new dress that wasn't soaked in

sweat from anxiety. I brushed my hair and re-pinned it quickly. As I placed a hat on my hair, my face stopped me. Face covered in bruises, my eyes were dull from the helplessness I felt as Martha slowly died in my spare room. I straightened up, pulled my shoulders back; no time for self-pity and worry.

"Aconite, a drop every half hour. I'll be back as soon as I can."

Priscilla dashed tears from her eyes as she took the aconite from me.

"I won't be long," I promised.

I picked up the papers from the dresser as I read through the legislation. I was so surprised I had to read it again.

"What?" Priscilla asked.

"Who put this together?" I straightened the papers.

"My dear friend, Cora Rood. Canada's first female lawyer, she's from here." Priscilla sponged Martha's forehead with cool water.

"It's perfect. It's exactly what I need."

Priscilla nodded. "I'm glad."

I drew the curtains closed to keep the room dark. Cole tapped gently on the door.

"I'm ready." I rushed out of Martha's room.

"You must be exhausted." Cole's eyes were sympathetic as he held my coat open. Clearly, our previous disagreement was tabled. "You were up all night."

"As soon as this is over and I check my patient, I'm going to bed." I wrapped a scarf around my neck.

"Let's go. Lord Harper said he would meet you there."

Flanked by Cole on my right and Lord Harper on

my left, I waited outside the mayor's office until he was done with his previous engagement. When we were called in to see him, he stood up and gasped at the site of me.

"Gracious!" he cursed as he came around the desk to take a closer look at my face.

"I apologize for my face."

"This didn't happen over this hospital thing, did it?" Mayor Holt asked incredulously.

"No," I assured him. "Thomas Wheaton. He's been apprehended and charged, so it's all been dealt with."

"Please, sit." The mayor directed me into the chair directly in front of him.

"How can I help?" he asked.

I pulled out the paper and watched his reaction as I showed him the article. "You've seen this?" I allowed the anger I felt creep into my voice.

"I have."

"So, what are your thoughts?"

"The subscriber makes a valid point. That the hospital should be represented by the broadest base possible."

"This sounds like a gentle way of saying 'we do not want women in charge of a hospital, but we cannot come right out and say it'." I made no attempt to mask my fury.

He looked away and fiddled with a pen.

I waited until he finally turned his attention back to me. "I will remind you that the hospital was not put together and *built* on the broadest base possible. When the work was being done, the community was happy to leave it in the responsible hands of the W.C.T.U. However, when the oversight is to take place, suddenly this group of women is what? What did he call us?" I rifled through the paper and stabbed the point in the paragraph. "Oh, yes. Irrational."

I put the paper down and met his gaze.

"The W.C.T.U. has worked tirelessly. To call them irrational is absolutely unfounded and downright reprehensible," I said without breaking eye contact.

"What do you want us to do?" The mayor held his hands out as if the situation were completely out of his control, and leaned back in his seat. He looked away. "The public is saying they want their own board to be elected to run it. It's unfortunate that women are not permitted to be part of that process."

"You might not be aware of this fact, sir, but since 1890, women who are land owners can vote in municipal elections. A board of directors for a hospital would fall well within that category."

Cole shifted uncomfortably at the ice in my tone.

Holt blinked in amazement. "Can I see that document?"

I handed it to him and watched as he swiftly read over the law.

"I had no idea."

"So, I can't vote in this election of a board, but I am confident many of our members can."

"They would have to provide proof of ownership."

"You can double check your tax rolls. Of course, as they can vote in municipal elections, we have a list of women here that own land who would like to be considered for the board of directors. We would expect half the board to be W.C.T.U."

"Come now." He held his hands out to me. "You know that's impossible. There are a lot of valid points here. They are not just saying they don't want a bunch of women to run it."

"They *are* saying that!" I picked up the newspaper and read it word for word, enunciating each carefully. "I quote, 'Operation of the hospital is being turned over to a bunch of women' and it gets worse, sir, 'the narrow-minded selfishness of these forty-six persons, in rejecting the committee's recommendations has, I believe cut them off from sympathy and support of three quarters of the community.' This is appalling and absolutely needs to be addressed. It is a travesty, that the outcry is so great they canceled their official opening!"

"May I direct you to the wording here, 'the citizens do not want the hospital to be run by a religious sect or society.'"

"They are not a religious sect for heaven's sake. Where were these citizens and their objections when the hospital was being put together? Why not raise their voices then? Why not say forty-six narrow-minded women might not allocate the funds properly! We should get involved."

"You're right. This is not fair, but it is what we are dealing with. The citizens are asking for a broad base to make up the board of directors. Miss Stone, this is a hospital that is publicly funded, and the public needs to feel represented."

"The W.C.T.U. agrees with that point," I said. "Specifically, they agree if the W.C.T.U. do not fulfill their obligations, they could not be removed if they had not been elected. I also understand that as a board that is elected, we can apply to the provincial government under chapter sixty-nine of the Statutes of Manitoba. This would allow the hospital to receive a government grant of thirty-seven-and-a-half cents per day per patient."

He blinked in surprise as I handed him another document.

"You have certainly done your research. This will be invaluable in the operation of this hospital. Why don't you leave this with me? I will make sure that this is brought to council. We'll run it by our legal counsel and we'll get back to you." Mayor Holt carefully printed 'add to agenda' on the top of the paper.

I don't want to be responsible for allowing women on a board of directors so I'll hide behind my entire council so you will never know which one shut this whole thing down.

"So, based on *these* legalities, we would expect that half the board would be W.C.T.U. members. I have a list of women here who own property."

"As I said, half is impossible." His tone might have intimidated me if I hadn't been raised by Til.

"What do you suggest?" I asked.

"I think the ladies who own land should apply, and the town will vote."

And I will get re-elected because no one can blame me for women running a hospital.

"I'll put a word in at the council meeting that you would expect no less than two members."

"Two?" I stood up and put my hands on his desk. "Of the sixteen members, you only want two members to be W.C.T.U?"

Now Mayor Holt stood up, and Cole got to his feet too.

"Two is better than the zero that you came in here with," Mayor Holt said calmly. "As I said, I'll lobby for it, but it's not up to me to decide which members will be voted in. I would really suggest that you take the personal attack out of this."

Cole moved closer to me to drag me off the mayor if needed. Lord Harper shifted a bit in his seat as I dropped back down into my own.

"You have no idea what it feels like to do the work and put your heart and soul into a project and then have to hand it over. It's appalling they had no help in starting it up, but now, when someone might get a hint of credit or have a speck of power, the insecure men among us need to make sure we know our place. The men who wrote this should be ashamed of themselves."

"Whatever our personal feelings," Mayor Holt said in his most soothing political voice, "the public is demanding an elected group to run it, and they will not vote for women."

I took a deep breath.

"But you realize you *cannot* disqualify them to run for the board."

"Once I've double checked the legalities, I will recommend any woman who is a land owner to run for this board." He breathed on his glasses and carefully rubbed them clean. "I cannot control how many will be elected, of course. I will have to run all this by council. Can the women handle losing?"

"They've already lost." I felt my shoulders slump. "This gives them some dignity at least."

"They did fine work." Mayor Holt's condescension grated on my nerves. "They'll always have that."

"Well, sir, you go and do your research and make sure no one blames you if any woman is voted in, and I'll be busy making sure land-owning women in this community are reminded to run for the board and to cast their vote." I straightened up and leaned forward. "Remember this. If these land-owning women can vote in this election, they will be watching how you run this. When you're up for re-election, you may want to keep in mind you have a large segment of your community wild about the mistreatment we have received thus far. Forty-six women in a community this size may not be a huge voice, but they will be *a* voice."

He went a little pale.

"Check your agenda. I am booked as a delegate at your next council meeting. You have a week to get your council up to speed."

"These land-owning ladies likely have husbands who don't want their wives overburdened. Don't be disappointed if they aren't permitted to run." The mayor took one last stab.

Permitted!

My teeth clenched. Cole closed his eyes. Lord Harper cleared his throat.

"I'll run that by the W.C.T.U. I'll be sure to pass on your concerns." My teeth clenched in rage.

Stay calm. Do not reach across this desk and try to strangle him. He's twice your size.

"Fortunately for you, this is a perfect opportunity for you to lead the way. Your wife wants to run for the board."

His face went completely white.

"You're surprised." I tilted my head to the side. "Hopefully you will *permit* that, and other husbands will follow suit."

The mayor cleared his throat, opened his mouth to speak, and then shut it.

"Don't take this as a threat. I'm not here to threaten you. Just a friendly warning. If we don't see some justice here and some dignity and consideration, there will be protests like you have never seen. I'll be the one in front."

The mayor's face flushed red.

"You have a week before the council meeting. I suggest you figure out how to make these ladies happy."

I felt Cole tense beside me.

"You just threatened to lead a protest! You are threatening me!" Mayor Holt stood up.

"Of course not." I stood up, too. "I'm letting you know our position. The hard-working women of this community are entitled to some dignity and respect. Don't be afraid of men not voting you in. Once I rally these women and advise them of their municipal rights, you will want to be known as the mayor who supported equality, whether you agree with it or not."

"I'm not saying I disagree with women running for the board," he protested.

"You're not saying you agree, either. You're a politician. You aren't *saying anything*. So, I'm talking, and I won't stop talking. Get your council up to speed because we're organized, we're educated, and we have no intention of taking this lying down. This 'bunch of women' will not be treated as door mats."

My words hung in the air as the mayor visibly struggled to come up with something to say that wouldn't make me angrier.

"You've raised some interesting points. I will go to the council with them."

Nothing is going to change, but I want you to go away, so I'll tell you what you want to hear.

When the door shut behind us I looked at Lord Harper and Cole.

"Are the women really going to protest?" Lord Harper gasped. "Lady Harper will do no such thing. I won't allow it."

I shrugged. "I will."

"So, you were bluffing?" Lord Harper's eyes widened.

"Is that what it's called? I am pretty certain I could rally the women to protest this injustice."

"I really don't like the idea of you protesting." Cole frowned.

"Oh, you won't *allow* it?" I challenged him.

Cole looked at me and then to Lord Harper and wisely said nothing.

"Gentleman, I have letters to draft and a woman dying in my spare room. If we're done here, I'll go home please, Cole."

***

It took until four for the ladies to assemble. Once I had checked to make sure Martha was comfortable, I joined them to tell them of my discussion with the mayor.

Forty-six W.C.T.U. women filed in angry, very angry.

Again, it was Ada that saved the day.

"We wanted a hospital for the citizens of this town, and it is ready to open its doors. We worked hard, and the end result is we succeeded. There is no irresponsible or irrational W.C.T.U. member. You are all hardworking and strong women. I am proud of the hard work that went into this project. Shannon, we want you to finesse this. When you meet with the council, make sure the council knows we are too dignified to fight. We will support the direction from the town's folk." The way she spoke was so gracious I was relieved she took over.

Due to Ada's gentle advice, the ladies agreed they would swallow their pride and hand over operations because the uproar in the community was too great.

I didn't want to contradict Ada, but I felt I should make sure they knew what was available to them.

"Ladies," I addressed all forty-six women in attendance. "I agree with Ada. However, legally whomever among you owns property in this community is welcome to run for the board of directors. If you do not wish to run, you can still vote in this election."

A ripple of excitement went through the women.

"So, please let me know whom you wish to represent you, and I will take that list to the council. I'm a delegate. Mrs. Holt, things went south in that meeting, and I mentioned you planned to run."

Mrs. Holt went completely white.

"I'm sorry. I panicked. Mayor Holt said the women could legally run for the board, but they may not be *permitted* to participate if their husbands felt that it would be too much of a burden. I said you were running."

Her face went from white to red. I thought she was upset with me.

"I told him that he could lead the way and support his wife. I was completely out of line."

"He said the husbands may not *permit* it?" Her jaw clenched and her eyes flashed in anger.

"That's what he said."

"Put my name at the top of the list," she commanded Mrs. Rood.

Mrs. Rood scrambled to find a pencil and carefully put Mrs. Holt's name at the top of the list for suggested delegates. I breathed a sigh of relief.

Relieved that there was progress, they broke out in applause.

"So, we won't fight, but we agree that every land-owning woman who can make time for this will run as a delegate?" Ada asked.

My heart swelled as I watched every woman who had her name on a tax roll stand up at Ada's invitation. They personally wrote their names down on the form. I wanted to stay and celebrate, but I had to go. Ada caught my eye as I slipped out, and we held each other's gaze. She nodded at me without words; she was saying thank you, and I smiled back because her thanks were not necessary.

Worry about Martha made me walk quickly to my carriage house. I gave her as much pain medication as I could. Exhaustion overwhelmed me, so I crawled into my bed to catch up on some sleep while the men met to decide what they would do with Roger Hanover and the remaining bar maid in his saloon. I slept too long. Martha's cries from the other room woke me, and I stumbled to her bedside to find her fever had spiked.

Wearily, I gave her morphine for the pain, aconite for the fever, but she was slipping quickly. The knock on the door came as I bathed her flushed face.

Merciful heavens, what now?

Cole, Lord Harper, and Mayor Holt stood outside the door with Enid beside them. Their faces were grim. Cole and Mayor Holt left immediately and I went to assist a beaten and sobbing Enid.

"Come in." I opened the door wider.

Lord Harper helped Enid sit on a chair in my kitchen. She winced in pain as she sat. I needed Lord Harper out of the way so I could examine her.

"Unfortunately, Dr. Davies is out of town, so I will leave Enid here in your capable hands. Can you get her stitched up? Cole will be back with Mayor Holt to question her tonight."

"They will *not* question her tonight." I gritted my teeth and gathered supplies to clean her wounds. "She will be examined, and they can wait to speak to her in the morning. I will document everything for trial."

"Miss Stone, Roger Hanover has been arrested, and we need to charge him."

"This woman looks like she is on the verge of collapse. The men can come for her in the morning."

She started to shake, and I took her hand, effectively dismissing Lord Harper.

"Enid, I'm going to treat your wounds."

Enid trembled as I lifted her hair to examine her cheekbone and temple.

Miraculously Lord Harper backed down. "We'll be back in the morning."

"Thank you. Could Jaffrey send some supper over for us?"

"Of course," Lord Harper said and left me to my patient.

I helped Enid take her clothes off and crawl into a warm bath. Her face had taken the worst of the beating, but there were bruises on her ribs and arms as well. After her bath, she dressed in a warm nightgown and wool socks. Her shoulders slumped as she sat on a kitchen chair.

She needed stitches on her face. The skin on her

cheekbone was split, so after giving her morphine as strong as I could allow, I carefully cleaned and stitched the wound. I bandaged the palms of her hands that were bruised from trying to defend herself.

"Let's go into the spare room, you'll feel better after you sleep." I helped her up off the chair and settled her in Martha's room on the other bed.

Jaffrey brought the food in and left again.

At nine p.m., I finally sat down to eat my own supper.

A gentle tap at the door interrupted me before I could take my first bite.

Now what?

I opened the door to Cole. "Come on in. I was just sitting down to eat."

He poured whiskey for himself and brandy for me while I dished him up a plate.

"You are absolutely not speaking to her tonight." I traded his plate for my brandy. "They are both sleeping and you..."

"Wouldn't dream of it." He held his hands up in surrender. "I came to check on things and couldn't resist Jaffrey's pot roast."

Taking a bite, I nodded. Delicious, Jaffrey was a miracle worker with roast beef.

"What happened with Roger?" I rolled my head around to try to ease the tension in my neck and shoulders, not sure I was ready for the next statement.

"We have Roger arrested. As soon as I can question the women, we will charge him. But, where will these women go?" He poured more gravy on his roast beef.

"There should be some sort of funding to help these women, Cole. They should be assisted to get some education so they can support themselves."

"I agree." He sipped his whiskey. "This is a tough world."

"Tougher for women than men, wouldn't you say? Mayor Holt will lobby the husbands of land-owning women to help them see that they can't handle the stress of running the board of a hospital they started themselves. Now I am treating two bar maids who were being held in a saloon on some sort of debt they could never pay. They *never* should have been in this position to begin with."

Cole sighed as my rant gathered steam. He leaned back in his chair with his whiskey in hand and took a slow sip. "Shannon, this is true. It takes time to change minds and attitudes."

"How long?" I cut into the pot roast. "How long before we see some the oppression start to ease?"

"Shannon, I agree with you. I am sorry that men are oppressing and persecuting women. I wish there was more I could do."

"It's just been a terrible day, Cole. It's discouraging to come up against this over and over again."

Cole's eyes softened with sympathy. "The men of this town, oppressive or not, just went and took Enid out of Roger Hanover's saloon. They know now, the girls are there against their will. We are not all bad people. This matter will be resolved."

I sipped my brandy and watched him over the rim.

"Will Martha and Enid be alright?" He poured more brandy in an attempt to calm me down.

"I've done everything I can think of, but I don't think Martha will make it through the night." Grief made me feel defeated.

I let out a long breath I hadn't realized I'd been holding.

"Who will help these girls?" My hands shook. I hadn't succeeded in getting W.C.T.U members on the board of directors. Their husbands could shut that down, and I was losing Martha. I felt sick to my stomach. All these women looking at me to speak for them, heal them, and I couldn't. We kept running into a massive wall of men saying 'no.' Over and over again.

He gazed at me sympathetically. "The W.C.T.U will sort it out. They always do."

"I heard about what they did for Priscilla."

"Exactly." Cole reached across the table and squeezed my hand. "They fixed that mess and they'll fix this, too."

Cole got up and rifled around my pantry for some lazy daisy cake. He cut us each a piece. "Are you nervous about addressing the council tomorrow?"

"No, I think we're ready to put this whole thing behind us. The hospital can open once the election of the board happens. That was the original plan. It will be good to see it through for the ladies."

"I am proud of how you handled the mayor. I wish the W.C.T.U. had been there to see it."

I shrugged. Cole arguing, I could manage; compliments were uncomfortable. "I care about them. I care about their project, and we used the law to our advantage. The husbands *will* have the final say though, and that is infuriating."

Cole tilted his head to the side.

"I know a lot of those husbands, Shann, and they want happy wives. If you ask them, they'll tell you they would have nothing without the hard work and support of their wives. Give these men a little credit."

"I will admit, I don't know them."

"My mother is not W.C.T.U., but if she wanted to run the country, my father would help her. My dad never makes a decision without her input. They're a team. As long as supper is on the table by five thirty." His lips curved into a mocking smile, and I shook my head at him. "Hang on, I'm not done. She runs the house, and he runs the yard. He doesn't make supper, but she doesn't clean the barn. They play to their strengths and they respect each other."

I looked at him warily. "Really?"

"Really. My dad would never make a decision before consulting her and vice versa. She's changed his mind more than once." Cole finished his cake.

"In my life, I've seen men shut women down, take their rights away. I don't trust these husbands to do the right thing." I pushed my plate away.

"Malcolm doesn't do that to Til, from what I understand." Cole finished the rest of the cake on my plate.

"True," I conceded grudgingly.

"The husbands might surprise you," Cole said. "You might want to cultivate some trust. It's a lonely life looking at half the population with suspicion. Including this half sitting right in front of you."

I thought about that and shrugged.

"You didn't seem the least bit intimidated by Mayor Holt." Cole pushed his plate away and picked up his whiskey.

"Cole, I was raised by a dictator. Mayor Holt is a walk in the park on a spring day compared to Til. I'm not afraid of confrontation. I don't love it, but won't shy away from it either."

We heard the moaning from the bedroom at the same time.

Chapter Twenty-Nine

"You should go. The fever is worse. I am just going to keep her comfortable."

While she dies.

Cole didn't leave, but rolled up his sleeves and brought water so I could bathe her face and neck to try to cool her down. The fever would not break. Martha's face flushed red; she moaned from the pain of the infection that ravaged her body. Enid wept beside her sister.

"Don't leave me, Martha, please don't leave me." Enid collapsed beside her on the bed. "Please, Martha, stay with me."

I checked for a pulse.

"She's gone." My heart sunk as I said the words. "Time of death is eleven twenty eight p.m., March 18th, 1905."

Cole stood back. His eyes met mine as Enid collapsed on the still form of her sister.

Her sobs filled the room. I closed my eyes. Enid's ragged sobs broke me.

Weariness from watching women needlessly die flooded through me. There was a time I would have wept right beside her. Now, the injustice of Martha's situation lit a rage in me, if left unchecked it would consume me. Martha was kept in a situation against her will and died because Enid was terrified to ask for help. Cole moved toward Enid and placed a hand on her shoulder. She flinched. He dropped his hand as he looked at me. This was up to me. Enid needed a woman, not a man. I pulled myself together.

What you feel doesn't matter, put your emotions away, do the right thing and you can process this fury later... I gave him a slight nod, trying to communicate that it was alright. He could go home and leave me with this grief. This was nothing new; I'd never get used to it, but I knew what to do.

"It's alright." I kept my voice soft as I put my hand where his had been. Gently, I pulled Enid off her sister and wrapped my arms around her. Cole stepped back further. I smoothed Enid's hair as I held her against my shoulder.

"I'll be back with Dr. Davies in the morning to have him sign the—"

"Of course. Thanks for your help."

Everything about him told me he wanted to stay; he worried I'd be upset.

He was right; my upset meant I would not rest until Roger Hanover was charged and in jail permanently. But tonight, there was no time for those thoughts; tonight was all about Enid.

"Come with me, darling." I helped her to her feet. "She's not in pain now, come on. Let's get you ready for bed. You can sleep with me tonight. You shouldn't be alone. I'll get you a sleeping draught."

Cole waited until I got her settled and the draught had done its work.

She went limp in my arms, and I went out to say good night to Cole.

His face was white. "Are you alright?"

I shook my head because I didn't trust myself to

speak. Unprofessional tears filled my eyes. I didn't have to be a professional with Cole.

"You've seen this before?" He moved forward to brush the tears away that fell down my face.

I looked at him. "Of course, but it doesn't make it easier."

"I'm sorry. I know you did your best."

"When we lost someone, we always had brandy. Do you want a brandy with me?"

"I want everything with you," he whispered.

I pressed my forehead into his shoulder. I loved the feel of his hard arms around me.

"What about when they lived?" Cole asked as he stroked my back so gently I moved closer.

"Tea." I pulled back and my eyes met his. "Laced with brandy."

"Well, brandy it is then." He let me go to get a brandy for both of us.

Outside, Oakland slept while Cole put more wood on the fire and then joined me on the settee. He opened his arms so I could curl into him. I took a big swallow as he pulled a blanket over us. He kissed my forehead as I settled in against him, shoulder hard under my cheek, arms rock hard around me. I let out a sigh I didn't know I was holding. I marveled at how my body instinctively calmed down when tucked in against him. As if on some level, my soul knew it was safe here with him.

The brandy unlocked more sadness.

"I did my best," I murmured.

"Of course, you did," he said softly as he took a sip.

We sat in silence. I watched the flames in the grate as tension eased out of me. His left hand moved against my scalp, and I sighed into his shoulder. He pulled pins out of my hair until the weight of it spilled down around us. It felt good, those pins out and his fingertips moving against my scalp. Calm fell over me; the whole world fell away. I felt him take my drink away from me.

"Time for you to be in bed. You're exhausted." His voice was low in my ear.

I didn't want him to go, and he didn't want to.

He moved, so I had to sit up.

"I have to go. I've stayed too long as it is." He got up and went to the door. "Try to get some sleep."

"I will." I stretched and got up to follow him to the door.

"Good night, Shannon."

I stood at the door as he pulled on his coat and boots. "Cole."

"Yes?"

"It's getting harder to say goodnight and..."

Cole smiled at me. "That's why the letter and the hand asked in courtship."

I nodded. "I want you to stay."

"Me too." Cole kissed me gently, reverently. "Good night, Shannon."

He disappeared into the blackness of the night.

I sighed as I locked the door behind him. I pressed my fingertips to my lips and stood still to remember the feeling of his lips on mine. The desire that sprung to life at his touch.

I put the thoughts aside as I crawled out of my dress and into bed with Enid.

Chapter Thirty

After Dr. Davies signed the death certificate first thing the next morning, the undertaker took Martha's body. I settled Enid with more sedative. Cole came to walk me to the council chambers. Cold air bit every bit of exposed skin. Frost clung to every branch creating a white frozen world. Pretty in its own way. We walked briskly to the council chamber. Nerves made my palms sweat in my mitts.

"You look like you address the council every day. You're as cool as a cucumber." Cole grabbed me as I slid across ice.

"Thank you," I said as he helped me find my footing on snow. "Don't let this calm exterior fool you. I am feeling nervous. Sometimes, I just pretend to have it all under control."

I had done my best to try to console Enid. Losing a patient hurts. Losing a patient who was a defenceless victim angered me. I was sick for Enid and devastated that Martha's life was cut short. I wanted this council meeting done and over with. At this point, I was tired of the fight.

"Well, you do a good job." He stopped me and turned me to face him. "Whatever happens in there, you are a success to me."

I nodded and smiled at him. "Thanks."

"I'm really, really proud of you." He squeezed my

hand in support.

"Thank you," I said softly. "That means a lot to me."

When we reached the town office, there were approximately one hundred and twenty women standing in front of the building. The news that the land-owning women could participate had spread like wild fire. I felt stunned and overwhelmed all at once. This was an outpouring of support I hadn't expected. They said nothing, but I nodded to them and I looked at Cole. Ada Bennett started to clap, and then Mrs. Holt, and then Mrs. Rood. Finally, one hundred and twenty women were clapping. The sound hit me straight in my heart. My eyes welled with tears.

"Thank you!" they called out to me and clapped and cheered.

Even though I hadn't spoken on their behalf yet, they showed their confidence in me. I was humbled.

Familiar faces dotted the crowd; Cole's mother and father were there along with Hannah and Nathan. I hadn't expected *any* men to be on our side. John and Ada Bennett and their daughters, along with Lady Harper and Priscilla, stood together holding onto each other. Matt Hartwell stood by Priscilla. All smiling their love and support to me. Cole squeezed my hand as I wiped the tears from my eyes.

The mayor came out to see what all the commotion was about. The women quieted when he opened the door. I waited as he looked around at all these women and went a little pale. I raised my chin, and he motioned me inside. The women followed.

The council hadn't taken their seats. With this mob of women, they quickly gathered around the table and began proceedings. There wasn't enough room for all the women of the town, so the oldest women sat and the younger ones stood. They lined each side of the room and spilled out into the hall.

Ada came up and sat right down beside me where I was seated in the row reserved for delegates.

"How are you feeling?" I asked in a whisper.

"I am on the mend. You?"

"I am on the mend, too."

"Good." She patted my hand.

With so many women present, there was little room for the disgruntled subscribers and their supporters to find seats. As men, they grudgingly gave their seats to the women and stood in the corner at the back. The mayor and council had some other items on the agenda, but they made haste to get to this thorny subject. First, they heard from those in opposition. Mrs. Daindridge and Mrs. Carr had been right. A man named Chester Manning was the biggest voice in the group. He reiterated what he'd said in the paper.

Finally, it was my turn. I stood and faced the council from the little podium they had for delegates and smoothed out my speech.

"I am here to speak on behalf of the Women's Christian Temperance Union. As you are already aware, the W.C.T.U. worked tirelessly to put this cottage hospital together. They did it for the sake of the community. If the community would prefer to elect a group to manage it, due to the fact that taxpayer money will be used in the financing, let it be known, they whole heartedly agree.

"I would like to mention though, they are yielding in this regard because the sole goal was a hospital, and regardless of who runs it, they are happy to see it up and running.

"The list of land-owning women who wish to be considered is as follows. Ladies, please stand as I call your names.

"Mrs. Holt, Mrs. Bennett, Mrs. Daindridge, Mrs. Rood, Mrs. Carr, Mrs. Royce, Mrs. Moore, Mrs. Curr, Mrs. Allen, Mrs. Madox."

Those ten women stood and joined me at the platform. The entire one hundred and twenty women in attendance burst in to applause. The disgruntled men looked at each other. Their lips thinned in fury.

"Thank you, everyone!"

The applause and cheering finally died down and my eyes flicked over Chester Manning; his eyes narrowed at me.

It really seemed to boil down to the few men with Chester at the back of the room that were actually in opposition.

It wasn't the entire town, just a few men. Maybe that would change things.

"I hope you can find a group that will be able to work as tenaciously on this hospital as these dedicated women have. I hope that whoever is elected to run it will remember the hands that cleaned, sewed, and purchased what was necessary to make this project come to fruition. I would also appeal to all of you to give these women the dignity and respect that is due to them. Articles calling these women irrational or irresponsible need to cease. The article said three quarters of the town was against the women running the hospital, and yet clearly we do not have three quarters of the community here to protest. I would expect the council to address those unfortunate and unfounded comments in a letter of your own."

The councilmen wrote on their notepads.

"In the spirit of community, please be advised the W.C.T.U will continue to support the hospital wherever necessary and in whatever capacity they can. According to Provincial Law, we would like to remind land-owning women that their vote is welcome."

"That cannot be right," protested the knot of men in the corner.

Mr. Holt had a lawyer come forward and address the townsfolk. I stepped aside and gave him the floor.

He simply read the law to all those in attendance. The men murmured, and the women were silent.

"As you heard from the lawyer," Mr. Holt said firmly, "there is no reason why some board members couldn't be W.C.T.U. members. We wish you all the best in the upcoming election."

The room erupted in protest and cheers. I turned to see these women beaming at me. It felt good to see them so empowered.

This was the first time they had seen women able to be on any sort of board of directors. The cheering increased.

"On behalf of the W.C.T.U., we would like to thank you for your attention to this matter. We look forward to supporting the council where we can in the future." I had to yell over the cheering women.

The group of men in the corner wanted the women completely removed from running the hospital. They stood up to object, but they had no legal basis to do so.

The land-owning women among us had some

power. Finally.

Furiously, the men filed out ahead of us. Cole kept a close eye on them, taking out a notepad and jotting down names in case there was any trouble.

Once the crowd thinned and those of us who could, casted our votes, Cole collected me to take me back to Hillcrest. The W.C.T.U. called an emergency meeting to celebrate even though likely these women would not be voted in. They were on the list of candidates, and the Enid situation needed a resolution.

Chapter Thirty-One

Lady Harper asked me to be at Hillcrest before the W.C.T.U. assembled to discuss our recent win and what to do with Enid. She stood by the fireplace as the flames burned brightly. Jaffrey floated around with tea cups and assortments of tiny sandwiches and dainties. Out the window, the black branches of the trees swayed against the grey of the sky. I missed the sun.

"Well, this Martha and Enid situation is a bit of a disaster, isn't it?" Lady Harper asked as she arranged her skirts when she sat down. My attention snapped back to her.

"It is very unfortunate when women find themselves in circumstances such as these," I said, a little confused.

"It's unfortunate that you got involved." Lady Harper pursed her lips as she picked up her tea cup. "You should be careful who you treat, Shannon. This is all very unpleasant. Really, this should have been left to Dr. Davies."

"Lady Harper, I'm confused. Isn't this exactly what the W.C.T.U. is all about? Aren't you actively trying to assist women who are vulnerable?" I asked.

Her tea cup froze midway between saucer and mouth, clearly offended. "Cole will not allow you to be involved in *drinking establishments* in the future." Her frown warned me she was serious about this. "You should understand that right now. We are upstanding citizens. We cannot fraternize with bar maids."

"Attending a woman who is dying is not fraternizing!" I crossed my arms.

She shook her head. "Cole will not allow this. You are courting, and what you do impacts him."

"This is my job, Lady Harper. I have been called into drinking establishments my whole life. Any man who interferes in how I carry out my profession will not be part of my life."

She sighed; my world would be utterly foreign to her. "You were in danger, and Cole won't put up with that."

"He was right there with me half an hour after I got there."

"Has he spoken to you about this?"

"He was upset that I was at the saloon and I didn't wait for him to render protection. He said I should have taken someone."

"That's all he was concerned about?" Her eyebrow lifted in surprise. "I'm surprised he doesn't care a little more about your reputation is all I'm saying."

"I was doing the right thing." I tried and failed to keep the anger out of my voice.

"I'm just letting you know from one married woman to a single woman, you are *too* independent and it will cause problems between you."

You didn't mind my independence while I was championing women's rights at that council meeting! Too independent, indeed!

I bristled.

"These women were being held against their will." I spoke through gritted teeth.

"Shannon, no one knows how these girls get into these positions," Lady Harper said lightly.

"They are in these positions because they are forced into them."

"How can we be sure they are forced?" She pursed her lips.

"No one chooses this!" I looked at her as if I had never seen her before.

"They could walk away at any time." She shrugged.

"They disagree. I saw what Mr. Hanover did to Enid before the men stepped in. I stitched her up. They didn't feel like they had a choice. We need a decision on how to assist Enid so she doesn't starve to death." I stood up and moved away from the fire, hot with anger. I tried to cool down.

Lady Harper rolled her eyes. "Bad things happen to people who make bad decisions."

"Lady Harper, a lot of people are choosing between bad and worse. Women like Enid and Martha are the most vulnerable of society. A society that doesn't even consider them people under the law! We have to advocate for those who can't advocate for themselves." I held my hands out like I was supplicating her to be reasonable.

"You are getting upset, maybe we should just leave this…" She waved her hand at me, as if dismissing me.

Don't you dare dismiss me.

"Lady Harper. We're living in the real world here! Your maid fed you ergot of rye to causing you to miscarry your babies. You didn't choose that. There is domestic abuse in this village! Emily didn't choose to have a husband who beat her. Two women were held against their will in a drinking establishment. They owed Roger money! He took advantage of them. Cole is now getting Enid's testimony to put him away. We have to ensure that their voices are heard. That has to be the focus of those of us who are privileged. You must see that?"

"You are overwrought," she said, flustered. "Have some tea."

"Tea isn't going to fix this."

"Tea is all I've got," Lady Harper's gaze locked with mine.

I sat back down. How could she, who had so much, be so unsympathetic to those who had so little? How could she, with the power behind her, ignore the weak?

Til's words came rushing back to me. I finally understood what she was saying. 'Spoiled rich women don't get their hands dirty. They don't advocate change. They are the obstacle to women like us.'

Lady Harper sat there, in a gown that would have fed and clothed Enid for five years. She wasn't going to budge in her opinions or her convictions.

Til's voice whispered to me from a jail cell in England.

You can't make a strong woman out of a weak one.

"Martha's life was cut short." My teeth were gritted with frustration. "She was a victim. Enid was afraid to ask for help because she was terrified of Roger Hanover. If Martha had medical assistance earlier, she might have lived."

She paled at that.

I get it now, Til... you didn't back down because you couldn't. Those with the titles, the money, all the power, they cling to their illusions that everything is fine. That people create their own misery. How they wrap that delusion around themselves! They cling to it so they can sleep at night when they turn a blind eye. *You were right!* If the women married to men with all the power don't start advocating, where will we be? We can't back down. We must speak for those who cannot speak for themselves.

"Let's protest the actual problem here. People don't need to be categorized into *classes*. Everyone needs a voice. Everyone. No one should have to suffer abuse." I couldn't keep the harshness out of my voice. I'd been there, in the tenements. Martha was just in a different type of tenement.

Enid would not suffer a speck of disrespect from this spoiled child in front of me. I wouldn't have it.

Lord Harper walked into the room, and Lady Harper collapsed into tears.

My respect for her shriveled and died.

Merciful heavens, stop crying. You have nothing to cry about. Oh no! I am turning into Til!

"What is going on in here?" Lord Harper went to Lady Harper's side. "What is this?"

I should back down, but so help me. I can't.

"We've had a disagreement," I said tightly.

"My wife is sobbing." Lord Harper rounded on me. "What kind of disagreement?"

"We had a disagreement about whether I should have treated Martha or left that to Dr. Davies. Lady Harper is concerned my reputation could be compromised, having attended a bar maid." I couldn't keep the ice out of my voice. "We also disagreed about how Enid and Martha came to be here. Perhaps Lady Harper didn't know the events surrounding Enid's situation."

"Why on earth would Lady Harper know of such a vulgar thing?" His face flushed with anger.

"The W.C.T.U. is going to decide if funding for Enid is in order. If they think that Martha and Enid chose this life, if they don't realize they were *forced* — you see how that could alter their perception. It could influence the choice they make." My heart pounded with indignation.

Enid's wellbeing is more important than protecting your wife from unpleasantness.

"My wife is inconsolable, so whatever this is, an apology is in order." Lord Harper brushed everything I had just said about Martha and Enid aside.

How could he put his wife's comfort above this obvious tragedy?

In his mind, I was serving class and therefore in the wrong. I would apologize, and he would forgive me, and Lady Harper would accept the apology. That's how it worked. Fury crawled up my throat and choked any apology I could insincerely give.

His eyes narrowed as I took a minute to gather my thoughts.

I'll apologize on my terms.

Lady Harper was trying to dry her eyes. I was trying not to roll mine. Finally, as the clock clicked on the mantle, I cleared my throat.

"I'm from a different world than you," I started tentatively.

How do you convey the hopelessness of a tenement, the abyss of suffering poverty opens as it sweeps through cities, leaving broken women, defeated men, and devastated families in its path? How do I get this across to you unless you've been there?

I straightened up. "When I see a woman oppressed in such a way, I know what it feels like. To be stripped of dignity, of worth like that. I have to stop it whatever way I can. I should not have come to you with this matter."

She looked up at me and met my eyes.

"I should have brought this matter to your husband."

This should offend you. Oh, Lady Harper, that was the biggest insult I could blast you with. You aren't insulted. You don't realize you have a voice, too.

"Perhaps in the future that would be best." Lord Harper spoke for her.

Of course, he spoke for her, he didn't catch the insult either.

"You lost a patient, you have been overwrought." Lord Harper was determined this unpleasantness would be smoothed away and his wife's dignity saved at all costs. He saw the look in my eye. I was not backing down because Lady Harper was crying and in hysterics.

The only thing I am saying is that I brought the problem to a child, not a woman.

"I didn't mean to upset you." I spoke the truth. I wanted her to join me in my outrage. To see Enid, the *truth* about Enid, to ensure Enid would not suffer any further. I wanted her to band with me to stop the oppression of women in all forms, for all time.

"In the future, you will address your concerns to me." Lord Harper looked down at me, and I bristled at the reprimand. "It's settled then." Lord Harper leaned forward to kiss Lady Harper's forehead and gave me one last warning look. "I'll leave you to your tea with the

W.C.T.U."

We couldn't be at each other's throats when the W.C.T.U. entered.

Lady Harper dried her eyes.

"I'm glad we can put that unpleasantness behind us, the ladies are here, I can hear them," she said, delicately blowing her nose. She was gently changing the subject. She moved to the mirror and took a deep breath.

We will put it behind us, but I will never forget that you dismissed the suffering of a woman and tried to blame her. You and your kind will not advocate for change. I am sad for you.

I put those thoughts aside we received the W.C.T.U. in the parlour.

Jaffrey buzzed around making sure everyone had tea. He handed me a cup and gave me a smile of encouragement. Jaffrey was always so taciturn; it took me off guard. He must have overheard me speak to Lady Harper. My heart warmed to him. One servant to another, he was prepared to stick by me.

As I sipped tea, I looked over the women and their grim faces. This was new territory for them.

It is one thing to say you want to help your fellow man, or in this case woman. It's another thing altogether to do it. As I sat in that meeting and watched these women struggle with the judgments they felt in their own hearts, I wondered how they would handle this. They deliberated and again, Ada came to their aid. Lady Harper might be their social superior, but Ada was like a mother to everyone. Even Lady Harper sat up and listened when she spoke.

"This is not a difficult situation to deal with."

She raised her hand to the objections. "There are chapters of W.C.T.U working hard with immigrants to integrate them into Canadian society. What's the difference? Enid needs to be able to read and write, and we can help her find a place in a factory or as a maid."

"She cannot be in a school house with our children, certainly not in contact with our young men." Mrs. Carr tried but failed to take the self-righteousness out of her voice.

"No." Ada shook her head sadly. "No, Enid would not feel comfortable there. After what she has experienced, she would not feel comfortable in the main stream school system."

I marveled at her. She deliberately misunderstood such a cruel and judgmental attitude.

I needed to take a page from her book.

I looked at Ada and wanted to applaud how she could uphold Enid's dignity and Mrs. Carr's dignity as well. While I bristled, Ada smoothed things over beautifully. The other ladies breathed a sigh of relief.

"Shannon," Lady Harper said to me. "I want to propose something to the Union. Could you and I step out for a moment so I can run it by you first?"

Now what?

I followed her into the kitchen. Jaffrey, unsure how to act with the mistress in his territory, fled out the back door for wood.

"Do you think you could help Enid get ready for a job in the few months you have left? You are already in my employ."

Kind of you not to say servant.

"We would not need to hire a teacher. This way, you can evaluate her and place her in a suitable job."

Lady Harper's mask of civility was firmly in place.

She was frosty with me, but this was a brilliant solution. It would allow me to assist Enid, and no one was out any money. Enid would maintain a shred of dignity. It would also take care of our pesky chaperone situation.

"It might come as a surprise to you, but this is not the first woman in a bad spot that we have assisted." Her face frozen into the mask of a dignified lady. She was referring to Priscilla.

"Priscilla told me of how you helped her, which was very kind of you." I extended praise like an olive branch, trying to bridge the gap between us. I still had to work for her afterall. "I think that is a great suggestion."

"Good. We'll settle her there for now and figure out where she should find work later."

"Of course."

The W.C.T.U. breathed a sigh of relief and thought this was the best solution for all involved. Enid, they all agreed, needed to heal before being moved on. She also needed to be on site so that she could testify against Roger Hanover. We were all thrilled that he had been arrested and his saloon temporarily closed.

Once all that was decided, we shared tea and scones before everyone left by three thirty so they could have supper ready. I made my way to the carriage house to make Enid and me some tea, but Cole was waiting for me at my front door so we could speak privately and Enid would not overhear.

"What did they decide?"

"She'll stay with me. I'll make sure she is employable, and after the trial they will find her work in a domestic setting. Not here."

He motioned that I should follow him to the woodpile. He picked up the axe and started chopping, making it look completely effortless.

"Are you sure you are up for this?" He centered a piece of wood on the block.

"It's going to be fine. I am up for it or I would have said no."

"I am beginning to think that Lady Harper asks too much of you, Shannon. I'm worried you're getting worn thin."

"It's just a couple of months." I shrugged.

"Will you tell her if it is too much?"

"Of course."

"That means you won't." He split the wood, and it scattered.

"Cole, it's all about getting the job done. I know what it feels like to be hurt and require a safe place to heal. I will do what I can."

He centered another piece of wood.

"When does Thomas Wheaton's trial start?"

"I am not sure. Lord Harper said a letter would be sent, so I'm waiting to hear back."

When he had enough kindling, he put the axe down and stood in front of me. I tilted my head up to look at him.

"I don't want you to take on too much. You are still healing, too." He traced his fingertips over my cheekbone. "Please don't let yourself get worn out. I worry about you."

"I can't say no to Enid. She's no trouble. She's healing, I'm healing, we'll heal together."

"Roger Hanover tried to blame all their injuries on

a bar fight that got out of control." Cole turned from me and started stacking the wood in the leather wood carrier.

"So, what did you do?" I helped him gather kindling.

"I detailed all the injuries, from your notes. Of course, he denied forcing anyone to work off a debt and screamed that we couldn't prove anything. That's when I laid the notes down on the table and said you would testify against him. The fight went out of him. Not a court in the land will let him off."

"Why not say Dr. Davies would testify? Why use me? Don't you have a better chance with a male doctor?" I wrapped my arms around my waist because the icy air chilled me.

"When I saw what we were up against, the lies he would tell... I realized Enid needs a voice. I like Dr. Davies. I respect him. But, if I was Enid and I needed an advocate, I would pick you. Every day I would pick you." His words made me catch my breath.

My spirit soared. I felt hope and happiness bloom in me.

"Don't you think you're a little biased?" I smiled at him even though my teeth chattered with cold.

"I see how you've been treated by some of these men, it's not right. So, maybe this gives you a little dignity, too." Cole shrugged and picked up the kindling. "Maybe. Let's get inside, you're cold."

"So, what does that mean for Roger? What is the sentencing do you think?"

"I'm not sure." He couldn't hide the disgust he felt. "Profiting off a woman's suffering and vulnerability, if I was in charge we'd hang him and not think twice. I will never forgive myself for not taking a closer look at what was going on there. I should have intervened long before you did." He struggled with his own guilt.

We went back into the carriage house and put the wood in the wood bin and then he turned to me. I led him into the pantry so Enid would not overhear our conversation.

He opened his arms to me, and I went into them willingly. He hugged me hard.

"I'd say the W.C.T.U. owes you one. If you hadn't helped Martha, who knows how long she and her sister would have suffered. I meant what I said. I'm really proud of you," he whispered against my ear. His breath against my neck made me lean in closer.

"I had a bit of an altercation with Lady Harper. I was really upset. She said something about how you would not allow me to attend a drinking establishment to assist a bar maid in the future."

"Well, that's true enough." He nodded in agreement. "This going to saloons would have to stop for sure."

I looked at him sharply, and he burst out laughing.

"You are so easy to tease, Shannon! I'm joking."

"I'm not laughing," I said icily.

"Shannon, I just told you I'm proud of you. Please, I was joking."

"Well, she was pretty certain you would forbid it, and I was furious at that suggestion. She doesn't know you or me, if that's what she thinks! Then she went so far as to say, 'no one knows how these women get into these positions,' which just infuriated me further. I couldn't hold my tongue, and anyway we're civil, but how can she be like that? Narrow minded, elitist—"

"She has seen nothing of what you have seen. She has lived a life detached from poverty and suffering."

"It's a little more than that though." I moved closer to him, which made him smile. "It's almost like she feels people are in their positions in life because they've done something wrong or they somehow weren't smart. She feels superior to them because she is wealthy. I was upset anyway because I could have so easily been in the same situation as Enid and Martha. My mother protected me in the slums, but when she died my father was a useless drunk. If Til hadn't taken me when she did, I could have easily been in the exact same situation or worse."

"Please don't say it. I can't stand to think of it." He pulled me closer.

"Well, I may be forbidding you to apprehend dangerous criminals in the future," I said primly in my best self-righteous voice as I pulled back to look at him. "If this relationship progresses, we can't have you placed in such compromising situations."

"You are going to have to let that go. She's not the worst."

"Ada Bennett wouldn't have said such a thing."

"You cannot compare Mrs. Bennett and Lady Harper. Shannon, please, you are funny. It's like comparing apples and oranges." He hooted with laughter again.

He was right; I laughed with him.

"Speaking of danger, how many men did it take to arrest Roger Hanover?" I laid my head on his shoulder to hear his steady heartbeat and to change the subject.

"Four of us went, and it took all four of us," he said ruefully. "He put up a fight, went crazy. Then, of course, we had to wade through all the lies."

"Did you get hurt? Did he hit you?" I pulled back further from his embrace to carefully scrutinize his face. When I checked his hands, his knuckles were raw. I traced my fingertips over them.

"Nah," he said. "I'm fine."

We could not be in that pantry all day, so finally I pulled away from him and grabbed some tea and cake. I set the table for tea while he put more wood on the wood stove, and Enid joined us.

"What was decided today?" she asked. "What will I do now?" Her pale face made her bruises stand out.

"You'll stay with me until you are well enough to work. There is no hurry, Enid. You are welcome here in my home."

"Thank you." She placed her hands over her face. Cole looked at me helplessly. I moved to her and held her while she broke down.

How could he easily apprehend a dangerous criminal, but the sight of a woman crying clearly had him so uncomfortable he looked like he was going to bolt out the window?

"We're going to get things sorted out, Enid. You just need to heal now. Come on, lie down now and get some rest. You have nothing to worry about. Roger is in custody. That chapter is closed. You are safe now."

Once she was settled in her bed, I came back out to share tea with Cole.

"In your memoirs, you need to take credit for the hope you just saw flash in that girl's eyes right before she burst into tears," Cole said as he cut some lazy daisy cake.

"Thank you." I put my hand on his. "I couldn't have

done it without you though."

"I know." He grinned. "We're a great team. I've told you that all along. You get into battles with horrible men oppressing women, which terrifies me, then you save the women. Just before the really bad guys can get a hold of you, I step in to fight and prosecute them. We're a match made in heaven."

"When you put it that way, it's hard to argue with that logic."

"So, all the bad guys are put away." He stretched and yawned. "We can take it easy for a while. I need another piece of that cake, and we're running low. Maybe if you have some spare time, you might be inclined to do a little baking?"

"Cole, stop oppressing me. I'm not going to be chained to a cook stove," I warned him. "Plus, I couldn't bake a cake if my life depended on it. Priscilla keeps dropping these off."

He laughed at that and I laughed, too. I tried to stop laughing and couldn't.

"One of us is going to have to learn to bake because when we go back to England, that's a long way for Priscilla to be dropping off these amazing lazy daisy cakes."

"What do you mean when we go back?" My breath caught.

"You have to go back to school, right?"

"Yes." My eyes searched his to see if he was joking.

"So, if you have to go back, now that we're courting, I was planning to go back with you. Malcolm sent a letter back."

I dropped my fork.

Chapter Thirty-Two

"I wanted to be with you when I read it." Cole grinned as he sipped his tea.

"Oh my goodness. This is like a nightmare I can't wake up from!" I groaned.

"Come on. Let's read it together." He laughed at me.

"Let me take some tea to Enid."

"You are stalling. Enid is fine. Let's get to this."

"Alright," I said grudgingly.

Cole placed the unopened letter on the table. He motioned me to come over to him, and he pulled me down onto his lap. "Whatever this letter says, we are going to somehow make this work."

"I am not sure I even want to know what's in it." I bit my lip in fear.

"I'll read it then." He opened it and his eyes skimmed the page. Finally, he cleared his throat, and I thought he was re-reading a section. I got nervous.

"How bad is it?"

"You shouldn't read it," he agreed. "It tells me all that I need to know."

"Of course, I'm going to read it."

"Are you sure you want to?" His eyes clouded with concern.

"Now I have to! Hand it over."

He held it out of my reach. "Ask nicely…"

I kissed him, and his reaction was lightning fast. He pulled me closer, but I pushed him away.

"Now you're stalling... hand it to me... please." I took it from him.

Dear Mr. McDougall,

Thank you for your recent correspondence. It relieves us both to hear that Shannon has recovered from her trial and is flourishing there. I understand from Lord Harper that you are a most honourable gentleman. I appreciate how you have worked hard and tirelessly to keep Shannon safe from all harm.

I defer to Lord Harper's council in this regard as he knows you personally. I have received a telegram from him, and he shouts your praises.

Have you given any thought of Shannon's education? The only concern I can see is that she is to finish her education that was so unfortunately cut short. A man who takes the time to consider another man's opinion is certainly serious in his intent. I wish to make this clear. Are you actually able to see yourself content with a woman who will be first committed to her studies and then to her profession? I am certain you have given that much thought, but I wish to state this concern. I am doing so in the most polite way possible. Know that Shannon's Aunt Til will state these concerns with the most *forthright* objection.

Shannon herself has been through a most heinous of ordeals. She has been violated most heinously. Some women find they are unable to participate in all aspects of married life after such an attack. So, I feel it is my duty to be completely straightforward in this regard. Do you believe she has recovered in mind and body to a sufficient extent? I leave that to her to answer. Women, I'm sure you will agree, are difficult to understand in the best of circumstances. Shannon has had to endure more than most. I ask that you would be most delicate in your pursuing her, if she in fact is in agreement.

I appreciate your concern and the respect you have shown in this matter. No matter what the outcome of this situation, we will remember this kindness.

With warm regards,
Malcolm

I read through it twice and just sat there staring at it.

"What are you thinking about?" he asked gently.

"I hadn't given any thought to that paragraph. Maybe I can't..." To my horror, tears filled my eyes. Shame churned in my stomach, making me feel hot and cold. I felt my neck tighten with anxiety.

"Shannon, you do not need to worry about that." His deep, gentle voice brought me back to the present, out of that gutter...

"Well, I wasn't worried until you made this courtship such a complete formal investigation!" I wiped away my tears.

"I'll stop. I'm stopping. I heard from Malcolm, he asked us to consider some things, now we can. I'm not worried about anything that he put in the letter."

"You aren't?" I tried to blink the tears back but instead they fell down my face.

Cole pulled his sleeve down and very gently wiped my tears away. "Not at all," he said with such confidence that I felt confident, too.

"But, what if I can't?" I whispered as shame shivered through me.

"It's you and me, Shann. It's different with us. It is going to be totally fine."

"What if it is not fine?" I pressed my hand to my heart.

He leaned forward and kissed me. A proper kiss. The kind of kiss that took my breath away. I leaned into him. The world fell away until Enid entered the kitchen and apologised and ran right back out. We jumped apart like guilty school children.

"Did you want to stop that kiss?" His voice was ragged against my ear.

"No." I was breathless.

"That's how I know there is going to be *no* problem."

Looking into his eyes, I knew with every fiber of my being, I had been talking tough about going back to England, going back to school. Could I really have walked away from him? Right now, this minute, with this kiss, my heart demanded that we stay together. Make it work. We could overcome anything life threw at us, *including Til.*

He fished around in his breast pocket again.

"I have some correspondence for you as well," he said. "Lord Harper sent your mail with me."

"I'm afraid to look." I took a deep breath.

I opened the top envelope, a summons to court. April 1, 1905 in the matter of Thomas E. Wheaton. Aggravated assault and battery, involuntary manslaughter. I skimmed over the page. I was to give my statement and a copy of my transcript from the London School of Medicine for Women. Cole was reading his summons as well.

"Copy of my transcript?"

"That's what they want. Sounds like they are going to try to shred your credibility." His voice was low and grim.

"Cole, women doctors are used to being discredited. I am not fully trained. I would expect this kind of grand standing. That's nothing new."

"April 1, they are taking their time with this," he commented.

"So, will we just go in on the first then?" I asked as I spied the third letter. My heart shrivelled as I noticed Til's handwriting.

The pit of my stomach clenched with nervousness. She had sent this letter from jail.

"I should go. I think Enid needs you," Cole said quietly.

"No," I said as I hesitated to open the note. "Don't leave me here to read this note alone. I'm scared to death."

"We heard from Malcolm all is good."

"There was nothing to fear from Malcolm!" I ripped open the envelope.

"It's going to be alright," he promised.

"This is a letter from Til. It won't be alright in this life or the next."

Til's letter ripped through my heart like a well-aimed bullet.

Dear Shannon,

I apologize for taking so long to send you a proper letter. First, I am so sorry that you were attacked so brutally. I am sick about it. I hope that you are recovered.

Second, Malcolm replied with his concerns to the man who is interested in you. It must be serious if he is writing. No one wrote to me, which I find infuriating. I expect you did not write, as you knew exactly what my reply would be.

The disappointment I feel that you would find a man at this critical time in your life and career, I cannot even explain my utmost despair. I urge you to re-think what this means for you. You will have to say no to school and your career. What point would there be in coming back to England?

As for you, come home to England if you intend to go to school or stay there if you intend to get married.

You cannot do both. You are no use to me or this crusade if you are married.

You will have no rights under the law. None. He can and will forbid you to work. Your full potential will be stifled.

I urge you to think with your head, not your heart.

I need to know in advance if I should cancel

your studies. I urge you to remember Katherine Elias when you make this decision. You are young. There is time for men later. Much later.

Make the right choice.

Til

Typical Til. I put my hand over my heart. 'You cannot do both. You cannot choose a man and keep me in your life. It's me or him.' *Why does everyone have to sacrifice everything for you, Til? You demand too much!*

The coldness of this letter, the first time she had written to me since I'd been put on that ship and sent away. I couldn't believe it. My hands shook.

Katherine Elias.

I closed my eyes. Mercy, she knew exactly what to say.

Chapter Thirty-Three

In a cramped tenement, Katherine Elias had moaned in pain on the floor. She was the first patient I assisted with Til. Someone, not a doctor clearly, had used implements to procure a miscarriage. There was blood everywhere. Even at fifteen years old, I knew we were too late.

The blood rushing in my head couldn't drown out her husband's cries and pleas for her to live. He was on his knees beside her. Immediately, Til dropped to her knees on the other side. I hesitated until Til pointed at me to kneel at Katherine's head.

Helplessness swept through me and made me weak with fear. No wonder Til drove herself hard to be at the top of her field. Even with all her education, we couldn't fix this. Horror replaced helplessness as the full weight of the situation slammed into me. I knelt and took Katherine's fever-soaked head in my lap. All I could do was wait for instruction and try not to let my hands tremble. Katherine was not much older than me. The cervix and uterus — both had been perforated. The sounds of her agony were still fresh in my ears all these years later.

Til automatically slid a chloroform mask over her nose and mouth and administered enough to give her relief. Impatiently, she handed the bottle to me. I nearly dropped it. Til frowned.

Oh mercy, don't drop this bottle!

"You need to concentrate," Til snapped.

I dragged my eyes up to meet Til's. Tears formed from fear, and Til's lips thinned with impatience.

"Focus on her. She's been in pain far too long. We're going to make her comfortable, count back from sixty, and give her two more drops. She doesn't need to be right out, just out of the worst of the pain."

My fear of disappointing Til paled in comparison to the terror I felt at the scene unfolding in front of me. My body shook, but I started counting. Fifty-nine, fifty-eight...

I held her and the bottle of chloroform. Til moved to spread Katherine's legs apart. Bile rose in my throat.

Forty-eight, forty-seven...

I couldn't watch. I closed my eyes as I fought to get myself under control. Tears of helplessness pooled in my eyes; we were losing her.

Thirty-five, thirty-four...

All this was just to keep her comfortable while she died.

Til cursed under her breath.

All her knowledge and education did nothing if the masses weren't educated.

Ten... nine...

"Three drops this time, she is stirring from the pain."

I complied immediately.

Til was a machine; her cool detachment was necessary. Nothing would be accomplished if she were trembling in fear and gutted with disappointment beside me.

I helplessly stroked Katherine's matted, fever-soaked hair, trying to lend some comfort to ease the pain and suffering. We watched her die. My heart broke.

Birth control would have saved her life and prevented all this.

Til finally closed Katherine's legs, pulled her skirt down, and routinely took her pulse.

"Time of death. 8:58 p.m. October 4, 1894."

Katherine's husband collapsed on top of her and in his grief, he pulled her up out of my arms and wept into her chest.

"This is not your fault." I put my hand on his shaking shoulder.

He was inconsolable. Til got up and started packing her tools.

You could take a minute to comfort this man.

When she was packed, she finally turned to him and crouched down to speak to him. He looked at her and tried to blink the tears away.

"Who did this?" Her teeth were clenched. "I need an address. I need to shut this down."

He got up and took the address off the table. His hands trembled as he handed it to her.

"I'm sorry for your loss," Til said quietly. His naked anguish was hard to face.

"We can prevent pregnancy now, but it's illegal to advertise it. Once a woman is pregnant, there is nothing I can do, but you can prevent another pregnancy if you should ever need to. You know where to find me. Send your friends."

She handed him a card, and he took it.

That awful night, that moment when I left Katherine Elias dead on the floor of the tenement, I took my stand beside Til in her fight to make contraception available to the poorest masses, not just the rich. If we had been warriors on a shield wall, that night I would have overlapped my shield with hers. She was hard. She needed to be.

The understanding that knowledge beat out helplessness stayed in my head as I enrolled in school to be a doctor. The memory of Katherine Elias spurred me on to continue, even when things were impossible. At fifteen years old, I went from assisting Til to being an active participant in the birth control movement. I knew how to fit diaphragms, how to explain how the sponges worked. We worked hard to get this education to as many women as we could. Unfortunately, the upper class could afford this knowledge and education. It was the so-called lower classes that needed it the most. We had to be careful to package it as feminine hygiene. The society for the suppression of vice hounded us. Watched every move. Til finally printed the diagrams with a printer she trusted and here we were. She had been betrayed and now she was in prison. All the more reason to go back and fight. I wouldn't stand down, it wasn't in me.

Which brought me back to the choice. England and the fight for women, or stay here and get married. I had big decisions ahead of me. I needed a clear head.

For the first time in my life, I bristled at a command from Til. 'Drop Cole, come home, and get to school.' Those demands left out what I wanted.

Til asked too much. From my place in Oakland, I could see she'd *always* asked too much. From the day I took my stand beside her I was never her equal. She expected me to defer to her, and I did. Always.

If I traded in Til for Cole, would he expect that,

too? Defer to him in all things?

Her line 'you can't ask a weak woman to be a strong one' was about to be tipped upside down.

You can't ask a strong woman to be a weak one, Til. I'll come back with Cole, on my terms. Both of you are going to have to learn how to live with that.

I straightened my shoulders and looked at Cole. Time to have a conversation with Cole's parents, especially his mother. Since he was so kind as to ask Malcolm for permission, I thought I better be honourable, too.

Chapter Thirty-Four

Cole left to return to his work, and the memory of Katherine Elias haunted me as I made my way up the frozen, narrow path to Hillcrest to perform Lady Harper's weekly examination. I couldn't shake her out of my thoughts as I let myself in the front door. The manor was very quiet; I could hear a clock tick on the mantelpiece. This was such a dark day; I yearned for some sunshine as I waited in the drawing room for Jaffrey to let Lady Harper know I was here to attend her. I felt apprehensive about meeting with her after our altercation.

She swept into the room and looked at me coolly.

"Lady Harper, you look well. I thought we should do your weekly examination."

"Certainly." Her tone was frosty.

Time to settle this.

"Lady Harper, I hope we have the sort of relationship where we can agree to disagree." I addressed the issue between us because physical examinations were personal and awkward enough without tension in the air between doctor and patient. "I meant you no offense."

Her face softened. "Of course we do. I realize we are from very different backgrounds. I meant you no offense either. How is Enid settling in?" I followed her up the stairs to their master bedroom.

"She is well. She is healing and very bright. I am

thinking of offering her to come home with me. We need nurses for the clinic. She has an empathy you can't train. She has been through so much."

"That sounds like a wonderful idea," Lady Harper agreed.

After I was assured she was healthy and happy, I asked if she could spare Jaffrey to take me to Cole's parents. Lady Harper agreed, and Jaffrey and I were quickly dispatched to the McDougall farm.

I needed an objective opinion. No one knew Cole better than his mother.

Mrs. McDougall opened the door with a big smile and welcomed me in.

"What brings you out to us?" She took my coat and settled me at her table where she was rolling cookie dough.

"I was hoping for a little visit."

"Is Jaffrey not coming in?"

"I was hoping to speak to you privately."

She turned concerned eyes toward me.

"First, I didn't ever properly thank you for coming to help me after the attack. I appreciated your kindness. I lost my mother early in life and since I've come here, I've been overwhelmed with the compassion and care a mother would give a daughter. Between you and Ada Bennett, you've helped me to heal. Not just physically."

"Oh heavens." She waved the compliment away. "I was happy to help. Let me get this squared away, and I'll put tea on for you."

She put the cookies in to bake and put the kettle on for tea in two swift movements. Her home was spotless. Even though the day was gloomy, her presence made the kitchen feel bright and happy. Mrs. McDougall already had bread rising by the stove. I breathed in the fresh smell of yeast and felt comfort settle over me in a kitchen used to sharing food, companionship, and love. I went to look at tiny, little baby James sleeping peacefully in his cot.

"He's so beautiful, Mrs. McDougall. I just can't get over how perfect he is."

"We think so." She smiled broadly as she set out tea cups for us.

We settled back down at her scrubbed table.

"You said you had a few things to discuss. Please, how can I help?"

"I need an objective opinion." I fidgeted with the letter from Til. "You know Cole better than anyone, and I need your advice."

"I'll see if I can help."

I handed her the letter from Til.

"This is a pretty stiff ultimatum." Mrs. McDougall refolded it carefully.

Her face fell as she realized the decision in front of me. She knew Cole; she knew he would never let me go back to England alone.

"She's a dictator," I said ruefully. "She has an outrageous distrust of men."

"Something happened to her?" Like Ada, Mrs. McDougall was a kind soul who tried to look beyond the action to the motive, to understand the heart of the person.

"Apparently. She's never talked about it," I said. "Anyway, I don't know how to explain her. I'm here to ask you about Cole."

Her lips trembled a bit as she handed the letter

back to me. "She seems very certain." Mrs. McDougall poured my tea first and then her own.

I shrugged. "Til is a machine. She sees where she wants her life and she moves confidently in that direction. Anyone in her way is considered an obstacle and subsequently destroyed. Unfortunately, she's decided where she wants my life to go, and anyone in my way will ultimately have to deal with Til, and... well... can Cole do this, do you think? Deal with Til. Will he even want to?"

She sipped her tea as she thought.

"Has Cole spoken to you about going to England?" I sensed that this was news to her.

"We thought that was the direction he was headed." She looked up, her eyes bright with unshed tears. I had confirmed it. "He's a grown man, Miss Stone. He'll decide and then tell us."

"Mrs. McDougall, nothing has been confirmed. I just wanted to speak to you. You're his mother. He spoke to the men in my life, all two of them, asking permission to court me. I thought maybe I should extend the same courtesy."

"Thank you." She patted my hand.

"This is the telegram I want to send back." I handed it to her. It detailed that Cole and I would return. I would resume school as promised. Cole would maintain his courtship of me so that they could meet him. "I'm afraid that if I send it, the minute she is out of jail, she will actually hop on a boat and be here in a little over a month. I don't think I can inflict Til on this little village. It wouldn't hold up!"

She read my telegram and took a deep breath.

"Would Cole want a wife with a profession?" I

asked her finally. I forced my shaking voice to be firm and forthright, even though I dreaded the answer.

"Oh, my dear, that is a question for him to answer." She folded a tea towel, carefully smoothing down the folds.

"I'm asking you." I sat up straighter and braced myself for the answer.

"I have no idea. None of us have met a woman doctor." She sipped her tea.

"Doesn't it concern you? He's with a woman so vastly different from his first wife." I was prying, and she was not comfortable.

"He chose her when he was young. He is older now. It's different." She put the tea towel to the side and clasped her hands in front of her.

"Would we expect your blessing if we were to be married?"

"Oh mercy." She pressed her fingers to her lips. "You're speaking of marriage?"

"We are courting, and he is coming to England, so I would expect if Til doesn't scare him off, marriage is certainly in the works."

"This Til, whoever she is, won't scare him off. Cole knows his own mind and his own heart. If he chooses you, we would be happy."

It hurt her to say it. This was one of the most selfless things I'd seen anyone do.

"Oh, thank goodness. I was certain you were going to ask me to leave and not come back." I breathed a sigh of relief. "Can I ask why?"

She looked at me and smiled.

"Because you are a hard worker." She fiddled with the tea towel again. "I can tell by how you look at him, you will make him happy. Life isn't perfect. There is a certain amount of risk in a relationship. He wants you happy, and if being a doctor is what it takes, you need to discuss that with him. He's a grown man and he has to do what he thinks is right for his life and for you."

We were silent as she poured more tea.

"What do you want, Shannon?" she asked me, and I could tell she really wanted to know.

"I want to make Til happy. I want to make Cole happy..."

"What will make you happy?"

"No one has ever asked me that." I looked out the window as I thought about that question.

"Someone should." It was her turn to tilt her head and wait for an answer.

I brought my attention back to her. "When I'm working, I feel like healing and helping women is a gift. The kind of gift I can't refuse. My aunt dragged me into this world of healing, and it was terrifying, but as I learned, I grew to love it. To be able to bring babies into this world and heal people, I can't give that up. The things I have seen, Mrs. McDougall. I don't even know how to describe the horror I have seen and tried to heal. As professionals, we have the power to bring healing and relieve suffering for the poor masses. It is important because we were raised there in those tenements. It brings hope to not just women, but men, too. It's my passion in life."

She looked at me to continue. I hadn't talked about the work I had left for a long time. It felt good.

"The sheer amount of education needed to bring birth control to women — it seems impossible. Til is working with the Malthusian league to make birth control available, but it's a battle. It's like being in the trenches. She wants me there, with her."

"So, you need a fellow soldier that will keep you safe. It pains me to say this, because I love my son so much, but he is that man." There were tears in her eyes. "I've seen your work here, my dear. I've seen all of it. Cole told us you saved Mary Varsdon's life. You made sure Enid was safe from Roger Hanover. You delivered my beautiful grandson into this world. If I had to pick any woman on this planet for Cole, I would pick you. You are going to do great things, and he will keep you safe while you do it."

Her tears moved me to tears. She pulled out two lacy handkerchiefs, but I moved around the table and we hugged each other.

"If you said you couldn't lose him, I would stop this," I promised as she held onto me.

"Oh, my dear, he won't be his full potential as a man without you. You won't be your full potential as a woman without him. That's how it works. You find the person that brings out your best and cheers you on to greater things in your life. It's a long life, dear. Who knows where you will end up? My son is happy. You make him happy. Maybe you'll bring your crusade back here? At any rate, my son is smiling and happy again, and I thought we would lose him to despair."

"A big part of me is scared to go home to England, after what happened." My voice sounded weak in my own ears.

"It won't happen again," she said firmly. "Cole will not let anything happen to you. You are in good hands. Don't base decisions on fear, use logic. You, not Til, are the only one who has to live with this decision."

"You are wise." I sipped the tea in her warm, happy kitchen.

She smiled at me through her tears.

Mr. McDougall came banging in the kitchen. Cole's mother immediately wiped at her eyes so he wouldn't see her crying. I tried to quickly dash mine away, too, but he noticed everything.

"Miss Stone, is everything alright?" He looked from his wife to me and then back to his wife.

He was so much like Cole, only thicker. They were the same gigantic height with heavy shoulders. Mr. McDougall's eyes were kind and they raked over me, looking for damage.

"Everything is fine, I think," I said quickly.

"It seems that Cole has been pursuing Shannon, and things are getting serious." Mrs. McDougall dashed at more tears that were falling.

"Is that a bad thing? Are you upset about something? Did something happen?" Mr. McDougall was completely perplexed.

"Can I just hand you the letter? I don't know how else to put this." I felt sick with anxiety as I handed him Til's ultimatum.

He read it swiftly while Mrs. McDougall brought him a giant mug of tea. He'd crush a tea cup, so a mug was fitting.

"This Til seems like a bit of a, um..." he searched for a delicate word.

"Tyrant," I answered for him. "It's alright. She raised me, and I have no illusions about her."

"You and Cole have some big decisions to make." He took a sip of tea.

"But he went to all the trouble to speak to Lord

Harper and Malcolm, my uncle, so I thought you should be involved, too. Maybe you want me to just go." I got up and paced around the kitchen; my stomach was churning with fear that this couple would plead with me to get to England and not look back. "Maybe you can see that I would make him miserable with all my education and work. It's dangerous work. Maybe you can't bear to lose him."

Mr. McDougall laughed heartily and reached across the table to hold his wife's hand in his. I felt my anxiety start to dissipate.

"Tell you to leave!" he hooted. "Cole's a grown man. He'll do what he wants, and he'll suffer the consequences."

"Do you think he'll suffer with me?" My face was pale. My hands trembled, so I wrung them in front of me.

"Very likely. Sit down, girl," he commanded, and I sat immediately. "Can you give up this doctoring? Could you be happy to stop and be a proper wife to him?'

My heart sunk to my feet. I knew right down to the ground. A happy, clean kitchen wasn't enough. There was too much of Til in me. I needed more than this. Making a warm, beautiful home for Cole, or any man, was not in my future. It could be part of it, but not the only focus. I thought I was so different from Til. Here I was faced with the biggest decision in my life. I felt more like her every day.

"No," I whispered. I cleared my throat and then spoke louder, "No. I can't stop. I have to finish school. I have to go back to my work."

"You're sure about that?" His eyes were steady on

mine.

"It's the only thing I'm sure about." I held his gaze.

Mrs. McDougall took her cookies out of the oven and placed them on a plate in front of us. The nerves in my stomach made me decline the cookies.

He took a cookie; his nerves seemed to be rock steady.

"Then it's up to Cole. Personally, he's gone on you. I wasn't sure until I saw him escort you to that meeting with the council. I knew right then you were going back and taking him with you. You didn't realize that?" he asked his wife and took more tea.

She was trying not to cry.

"Look, he's been like a wet week since his wife died. She was a sweet thing. It was very sad, but he needs to move on. Better he's happy in England keeping you alive than moping around here."

"So, you're alright with this?" I asked cautiously.

"Listen. He went to the men in your family, that is customary. He's making sure he shows them that respect. Cole's a grown man, and he knows his own mind."

I let out a long sigh of relief.

"There is one thing I'd like to discuss with you, if I might." He handed the plate of cookies to me and I declined once again. My stomach was still doing back flips. Their approval mattered.

"Alright," I straightened up. He was intimidating even though he was kind.

"You're one of those new-fangled suffragettes?" he asked as he took another cookie. Mrs. McDougall got up to fill his mug.

"I am, yes." I lifted my chin and I saw a look of respect in his eye. "I think that was pretty clear at the council meeting."

"Yes, we were blinded by all the legal finagling when common sense says that board needs those women running it. Anyway, that's a discussion for another day. Cole is going to be as nervous as an old woman with you in and out of danger. Will you let him do his job?"

"What job, exactly?" I asked, genuinely confused.

"I heard you went into that drinking establishment without him." His eyes were stern.

I let out a sigh and sat back against my chair. "Are you going to lecture me, too? I have heard nothing else from him."

"He spoke to you about that?" His eyebrows were arched.

"At length," I answered dryly.

"Can you handle it? Cole hovering around you when you're trying to work?"

"I'm learning to handle it." I took a sip of tea that was starting to cool.

"He doesn't have any say right now, you're not his wife, but he will *never* let you go into a situation alone if you're married," he warned me.

"He's right, dear. Cole would never allow that." Mrs. McDougall refilled my tea cup.

"He's made that abundantly clear," I assured them.

"So, what are you suffragettes really after anyway?"

Now that we were all clear that Cole was serious and coming back with me, Mr. McDougall changed the subject. He leaned back in his chair and looked at me coolly.

"We want to rule the world," I said so dead pan he

burst out laughing.

"You don't rule the world already?" he boomed. "The way I see it, women get away with everything while we do the heavy lifting."

I rolled my eyes at him and finally took a cookie. "Ten minutes in a tenement, Mr. McDougall, you'd be crying like a baby and signing a petition."

"Mayor Holt is still smarting from that dressing down he suffered from you. The way I hear it, the men in this community are forming our own group. How to deal with pushy women. Your meetings have run late, and men are worried their suppers won't be on time."

He was playing with me, baiting me.

"The Malthusians, and my aunt Til want birth control to be available to the poor." I ignored the bait and responded honestly. "They believe it is the only way to end poverty, I agree with them."

"Oh?" Mrs. McDougall ignored her husband and leaned in to listen.

"I grew up in a tenement, my father drank every dime, and I watched my mother die in childbirth."

Mr. McDougall's eyes went hard, and Mrs. McDougall's softened as I spoke.

"My protesting about making sure girls in my position in life, who don't have tyrant aunts, have what they need to make decisions that will allow them to have healthy families, and some freedom."

His mouth thinned at what I was saying.

"I think equal pay for the same job is necessary, wouldn't you? I think access to contraception is the most pressing social issue of the day. Until people see it, they don't care about it."

His eyes held mine.

"I'll give you that, very valid points. I hear you suffragettes protest. Cole will have a fit," he said honestly.

"I don't have time to protest at home. He can relax. I'm in school and at work."

"But you would," he countered. "You'd get involved with all that protesting, wouldn't you? If the council hadn't let three women on that board, you'd be in a sandwich board right now."

"Three women out of sixteen board members does not seem equal to me, Mr. McDougall," I retorted. "If they hadn't allowed *any* woman on the board, I would have protested, absolutely, rallied every woman in the land. You could count on it. If Cole wanted to come along, he could. There is a lot of heavy lifting in a protest."

He laughed right out loud. "He's going to have his hands full with you."

I smiled at him.

"And I dare say, he's up to the challenge." Mr. McDougall smiled broadly. "Listen, girl, this is a conversation you need to have with him. We'll wish you well, whatever you both decide."

I let out a long breath.

"But you'll come for supper soon so we can formally welcome you to our family?" Mrs. McDougall asked kindly.

"I would love that. Thank you so much."

I stood to leave, and Mr. McDougall stood up. I held my hand out, and he smiled as he pulled me into a bear hug that lifted me a foot off the floor. "We had seven sons, but I always *really* wanted a daughter. You'll do. Cole will get past that tyrant Til, you have nothing to worry about. I'm proud of your work here. There's been some grumbling from some of the men. Don't listen to any of that. Your work is important. I'm happy Cole will be there to keep you alive."

Mrs. McDougall came around the table and held her arms out to me. "You're going to make him very happy, and he will make you happy, too," she said as she hugged me hard against her. "Thank you, my dear, for coming out here and speaking to us. I will treasure that."

Little James squawked from the cot, and they both went to him as I pulled on my outdoor clothes. Mr. McDougall held his grandson as Mrs. McDougall rushed to bring him a bottle.

"Who needs kids when we have grandkids, right?" He smiled at his wife.

"You're a terrible old codger," she said, taking little James from big James.

"Good day." I couldn't help but grin at them as I let myself out. I found myself smiling as I went to join Jaffrey and go home.

***

Feeling emboldened from my meeting with the McDougall's, I sent a telegram back.

Til:

Thank you for recent correspondence. Eagerly waiting to hear of your release.

I am romantically involved and plan to remain so.

Will write with details of our return to England soon.

Do not cancel my schooling; I will be enrolled for September 6. I look forward to getting back to work with you, Til. I miss you and I love you.

Love to you both.
Shannon

This would hit Til hard, but with an ocean and a continent between us, I felt confident sending it.

I can't be under your thumb, Til, and I will not trade your thumb for Cole's. I need to live my life, take my chances. It's my life. I have to live it.

Chapter Thirty-Five

I was just settled in for tea at the carriage house when there was a timid knock at the door. To my surprise, when I opened the door, there stood Emily Wheaton.

"Come in." I opened the door wide and gestured for her to enter. "Are you alone, Mrs. Wheaton?"

"Yes. I only have a few minutes. I was hoping we could talk." Nervously she scurried into my carriage house.

Her eyes darted to mine and then looked away.

Emily Wheaton was a poor, tiny, beaten woman, thinner than she had been previously. I wondered how that was possible. Her head bowed slightly as if she didn't have the strength to lift it.

"Tea?" I asked as I reached for a coat she refused to take off.

"No, there is no time for that. If Carl... I have to get back."

"How can I help you, Mrs. Wheaton?" I motioned for her to sit at my table; she remained standing.

"I am here to ask you to drop the charges. Please drop the charges against Tom." Her eyes focused on the floor. She couldn't meet my gaze.

I poured her some tea anyway, to give myself a minute to think about what to say. She stood awkwardly at the door, so I tried to hand it to her. She lifted her hand to decline.

"He doesn't mean it," she pleaded. "He is always so kind the next day. He feels terrible about what he did to you. I went to see him, and he is devastated. I am begging you, please drop the charges. If you drop the charges, and I already have dropped the charges, he can get out, he can come home."

"Mrs. Wheaton." I put the teacup down and reached out to put my hand on her shoulder. She flinched and stepped away from me. "Do you remember, the night he beat you so badly you lost your baby? That night he beat me so badly, I lost my baby, too. Two innocent lives were taken at his hand that night. How can I possibly drop those charges?" I kept my voice very soft, very gentle to diffuse the anger in her.

"They'll know the truth about you. Pregnant and not married," she hissed.

Stunned, I moved away from her. She looked up from the floor finally; her eyes flashed with challenge and her face flushed red. "Everyone will know what you are."

"Mrs. Wheaton, I am innocent." I took a step back from the anger I saw flashing across her face.

She wasn't listening.

I took another step back. "I think you should leave, Emily. I think you are upset and I think it's time for you to go."

"If you testify, you will rip my family apart!" Her hands were clenched into fists at her sides.

"No," I said. "I was attacked and made pregnant by that violation. My son died because your husband hurt me. I will testify to all of it. There is no reason for me to feel ashamed. I don't care who knows what happened to me."

Her eyes changed from anger to panic.

"You don't understand. If he can't come home, what will happen to *me*?" Her voice was high with mounting fear.

"If he can't come home, you are safe." The reasoning was lost on her.

She jumped when she heard the pounding at the door. Emily Wheaton wasn't safe anywhere.

"I have to go." She turned away from me.

"You need to think about rebuilding your life." I tried to reason with her as she scrambled to the door. "Stay here. Let the constable deal with them."

"He has to get out of jail. I love him. I love him!" Her whole body trembled.

I knew love now. Cole would protect me at the risk of his own life. He wouldn't raise a hand to me. What Emily thought was love, was not.

The pounding started again and her hands shook in fear.

"I'm sorry that he hurt you, and I am upset that he hurt me. This is in the hands of the law. Even if I chose not to testify, the court is going to proceed. Your baby died. This is the consequence for beating a woman until she miscarries. He knew you were pregnant. According to the law of Canada, this is murder Emily."

"You could drop the charges. It would lessen the sentence," she made one final plea.

"It wouldn't. It's the same death sentence with one baby dead or two." I went to the window. I didn't dare open my door to the Wheatons. Thankfully, I saw the door to the barracks open and Cole came across the street. Cole walked up to the Wheatons and put himself between my front door and the men.

I let my breath out slowly. This was escalating. Two against one. Cole stood there, arms at his side. He spoke forcefully to the men, but I noticed with relief he didn't look the least bit worried.

Emily burst into tears as she turned to open the door and scurried out of the house past Cole. She didn't look up as she followed Carl and Wade to their horses.

I stepped aside so Cole could enter. He locked the door behind him.

"What on earth was that about?" He looked me over, checking for damage.

I bristled at his tone. "She came here, uninvited, insisting that I drop the charges," I said coolly.

He took my arms. "Are you alright?"

"I'm fine. She's a beaten wife. I couldn't reason with her. I can't help her, Cole. There must be something we can do... I can't think of anything though."

He sighed. "I know." He kissed my forehead and held me close. "You will need to be very careful. They are not going to stop at this," Cole warned me. "I want your word. You *will* be careful."

"Emily is not going to do anything," I assured him.

"It's not Emily that I'm worried about." His face was grim.

Chapter Thirty-Six

I had every intention of staying safe, but when Mrs. Carr sent for me the next night after supper, I didn't think. I just grabbed my doctor bag and followed Mr. Carr. "This is Dr. Davies' jurisdiction. Is he busy?"

"Dr. Davies is in Winnipeg. Storm stayed apparently."

"This winter is a nightmare. It seems like it never ends," I grumbled as I trudged through snow beside him.

Together we walked the eight blocks to his home.

Simple tonsillitis. The best solution was nitrate of silver brushed on her tonsils, which I did. I showed Mr. Carr how to do it, and after treating her fever, I packed up to go home. I detailed what to give her for her throat.

"I'll get my coat and walk you back," he offered.

I saw the weariness in his eyes. He looked like he was coming down with something himself. I pressed my hand to his forehead. Sure enough, low grade fever.

"No, you need to get to bed, too. You're coming down with a fever." I treated him with quinine and told him I would let myself out.

It's only eight blocks, I told myself sternly. I was quickly making my way back home when I heard footsteps behind me. The hair on the back of my neck stood up. My entire body tensed. Someone was behind me. Intentionally, I dropped my bag so it fell open.

"Shoot," I cursed loudly as I picked up my implements and put them back in the bag. My fingers curled around my surgical scissors. The longest ones I could find. I quickly slipped them into my right pocket.

As soon as I put my bag back together, I kept the scissors in my hand and started running. I heard my own breathing ragged from fear. The footsteps were getting closer.

"Help me!" I screamed into the still and silent night around me. My bag was heavy, but I kept running and screaming. A block away I saw a light flick on.

"Help me!" I screamed as loud as I could. A dog barked in answer.

Two men immediately blocked my path. Four blocks from home and Cole. They wouldn't let me get closer to safety.

I recognized the Wheaton brothers within moments. I screamed so loud, so long, more dogs started barking. More lights clicked on.

The biggest brother lunged at me. I hurled my bag at him, but he deflected it easily. Carl Wheaton didn't break his stride; he grabbed me with both hands and slammed me into a tree. I struggled to breathe. The bark bit into the back of my neck.

"It's hard to testify when you are dead." The smell of whiskey on his breath washed over me.

The other brother saw a posse of men in their bedclothes holding lanterns coming toward us. A few of them had rifles.

I turned and watched as Carl grabbed his brother and fled into the night.

I dropped to my knees in relief. Now that the danger was over, my whole body shook from shock.

Holt and Cole were by my side as the rest of them men yelled for horses to be saddled so they could go after them.

"Shannon, are you hurt? Let me look at you." He ran his hands over me.

"We'll go for them," Holt said to Cole. "You'll need to get a statement from Miss Stone."

"We'll go tonight and drag them back here, I'll help Matt arrest them," Holt commanded him.

"Saddle King for me, Matt, I'm coming, too," Cole ignored Holt's decision as he roared at Matt.

"Your blood is up, man. We don't need you killing them," Holt protested.

Cole looked at Holt. He could barely speak his jaw was clenched so hard. "I'll settle Shannon at her carriage house then I'll ride with you."

"No, you won't," Holt said firmly. "That's an order. Look after your woman. We'll go and you will tend to her."

"I'm alright," I said through teeth that clattered together from trembling. I tried to get up, but my knees were too weak from fear. I hated my own weakness as I sunk back down into the snow.

Cole turned his attention back to me. I was not alright.

"Take King though. He's fast." Cole came to me, scooped me up off the ground and carried me the last few blocks to my carriage house.

He sat me down on the table. Matthew came behind us with my doctor's bag.

"Go easy on her, Cole. She's in shock," Matt said as he let himself out.

Cole stoked the fires and put water on to boil.

Enid came out of her room; her eyes were wide when she saw me. "What happened?" she asked rubbing sleep from her eyes.

"The Wheatons," I said. "It's alright, please just go back to bed, Enid." It hurt to talk.

"Are you sure?" Her brow furrowed in concern.

"I'm sure. Please, just go back to bed. I'll be alright."

She left us alone and shut the door to her bedroom behind her.

Finally, Cole turned to me, his arms crossed and his stance wide.

"I... I can't handle a lecture right now... just please don't look at me like that... Cole... please, I can't..." I shook from fear and shock.

His face softened in sympathy as he watched me try to peel my fingers off the scissors I hadn't used. My hand cramped around them from terror.

"It's alright." He came to me and spoke soothingly into my ear. "It's going to be fine. Just breathe in and out. Just focus on your breathing."

I gave up on the scissors as he ran his hands up and down my arms.

"It's going to be just fine." Cole pressed my face into his shoulder and held me as I wept.

I sobbed against him.

"Shannon, you're alright." His hands moved up and down my back. Slowly, the shuddering stopped. Eventually my sobbing stopped as well.

"You're alright, you are safe now, it's all over now." His deep voice soothed me.

I took a deep breath, held it for a few seconds, and then let it slowly out. If my screaming hadn't brought the men out of their beds, what would the Wheatons have done to me? The thought of Carl Wheaton's hands on my neck made me shake.

"I'm just going to take your coat off." He carefully unbuttoned my coat. The scissors were still in my hand. "I can take those scissors, if you want?"

Now that I was calmer, I pulled my stiff, fingers away from the steel. Wordlessly, I handed the scissors to him.

"I'm sorry." I laid my hand against the hardness of his cheek to get his attention. "Sorry you had to stay back. I wish you were going after them. I can't believe they followed me. I thought I was safe. You wanted to go..."

"Shannon, he's right, I would have killed them. I might yet." He took my coat off and ran his hands over me, checking for damage. "Are you hurt anywhere else, or just your face?"

"My throat, too," I croaked.

"Let me see." He undid the buttons of my dress. My eyes were wide as he spread the material to survey the damage. His eyes darkened in anger; his teeth clenched with fury. "You are badly bruised, Shann. Your face and throat, but that's all. They didn't..." His eyes searched mine for the truth.

I started crying again. "No, just face and throat."

"Shhhh." He reached for me and he held me so hard and close that I started to calm down. "It's going to be alright."

He looked at my lip in the light of the lamp then went to the cook stove and brought a bowl of hot water and a cloth over to me.

"There's carbolic acid in my bag." He brought me

the bag because he didn't know where to find it. My hands shook as I made the solution. Cole very carefully cleaned my lip. He winced when I hissed in pain.

When he was done cleaning up my face, he rubbed salve onto my bruised neck. He picked me up off the table and brought me to the settee so we could watch the fire together.

I pulled away and watched his face cloud with confusion. "Listen, I should have said this when you found me. You've been so good, cleaning me up, and keeping me safe. We can't be together. We can't have anything to do with each other after this night."

"What? What are you talking about?" He moved to hold me and I pushed him away.

"Everything I touch turns to horror! It follows me! I can't bring this into your life..."

"Shannon, you are overwrought. This is not your fault," he protested.

"No, it's over. I'm saying no. This constant trauma keeps finding me. I hate this! I need to take all my trauma out of your life and go away and never see or hear from you again, I've decided."

"Oh, Shannon," Cole said so piteously that I cried even harder.

He got up and poured us both a drink. A real one. This was not a situation for tea.

I lay there sobbing, face down on the settee with a pillow over my head.

He sat beside me and stroked my back.

"Shannon, we need to talk. Please, honey, just sit up and let's talk about this."

"I don't want to hear it," I wailed.

"Alright, that's enough, come on. Sit up." His patience was finally wearing thin; I could hear it in his voice.

"No, not yet."

"Shannon."

"Just go."

"Shannon. Please sit up."

"I'm staying like this for the rest of my life," I wept piteously.

Cole sighed. "Shannon. I'm not leaving you this upset. Shannon, are you listening?"

I sat up then and wiped my tears, put the pillow down on my lap, and kept a careful distance.

"I've said it once, I'll say it again. It is not your job to protect me. It's my job to protect you. All this trauma is being done *to* you. You have not brought anything but happiness to me."

"You're a terrible liar," I accused him.

"Happiness and sheer terror." He smiled, and it broke the tension. "Take a sip of that." Cole handed me my drink.

I did. It was strong, and I coughed a bit.

"Take another belt of that," he commanded me.

"Stop being so bossy," I growled.

"There she is, the Shannon we all know and love." He smiled as he gathered me up and dragged me to him.

I arranged myself against him and rested my head against his shoulder. His hand smoothed my hair down so it didn't tickle his nose. He kissed my forehead.

"Shannon Stone, I want you to listen closely to what I have to say. You do not bring horror into anyone's life. You saved Ivy. You saved Enid. The W.C.T.U. has a voice in how the hospital is run because of you. Three members on the board are W.C.T.U. and that's because you are a lion in negotiations. They would have backed down, but you wouldn't hear of it. You stopped me from doing anything to John Marsden until you could investigate. You put my professional reputation first in that instance. You are the most honourable person I know," Cole said sincerely.

"It's what anyone would do. It's the right thing to do," I disagreed.

"No, not everyone would, because no one else stepped to the plate. You did it. You did all of it. You're like a soft, delicate, beautiful wrecking ball."

"Is that supposed to be a compliment?" I pulled back so I could study his face in the light of the fire.

"Wrecking balls get things done." He smiled as he sipped his drink. "You are so gorgeous. Do you know what you look like? Right now?"

"Don't take this conversation off course. I'm not done."

"You're done." He traced my collar bone with his fingertips, trying to erase the bruising there.

"The minute he touched me, I felt so much terror. I thought, maybe I was sort of healed from the whole thing, you know, that attack in England, but I'm not. These predators find me. Men like that find me" —my voice caught— "it's like they know I'm an easy target... am I?" I hated the weakness in my voice. I dragged air past my tortured throat deep into my lungs to try to calm down.

"Shannon." Cole's voice was so soft, so gentle. He took my empty glass away and cradled my face in his hands. "You're a target because you are doing the right thing."

I blinked at the intensity of his gaze.

"You *consistently* do the right thing. It doesn't matter what kind of bully you are facing! You are amazing. I've never known a woman like you. I love you, Shannon, your strength, your integrity, it's intoxicating."

My heart and spirit soared at his words. If hope were a flower, I felt its petals unfurl in me at his words. Maybe I was equal to the challenges we would face in the future. Fresh tears fell from my eyes.

"Hey, I didn't say that to make you cry." He ran his hands down my arms. "Shannon, there is no need to cry."

"I'm not crying."

"You're a terrible liar," he repeated back to me.

"I didn't know you felt that way." I dried my tears on my sleeve.

"Shannon, you're like a secret weapon. No one expects you to stand up to all this corruption, and there you are exposing it with all you've got."

"I am crying a lot for a secret weapon." I wiped my eyes.

"Well, every weapon has a flaw." He grinned.

He pulled me into his embrace, we held onto each other. It was bliss; I felt my heart rate slow to normal. My breathing became slow and steady. He was like a drug smoothing all the pain away. I relaxed against him. Hours later, I jolted awake.

"Cole." I shook him and he jumped.

"What... what's wrong..." He scrubbed at his face with one hand because I was lying on the other one.

"You have to go. It's going to be sunrise soon. We fell asleep—" My voice had a tinge of panic.

He chuckled at that as he scooped me up and carried me to bed.

My heart flip flopped as he set me down.

"Do you need a hand with that corset?" he asked hopefully.

Gracious! I am going to swoon!

"No, I'm fine." I stammered. He stood close, he kissed me softly. "It's a corset designed for a single woman. You better get out of here."

"Pity." He kissed me on the forehead and took a step back. "When that lip heals, watch out."

"You have to go," I commanded and giggled at the same time.

He groaned as he tore himself away and snuck out under the cover of night.

Chapter Thirty-Seven

The next morning, I made my way up to Hillcrest, and Jaffrey let me in. Lord and Lady Harper were sharing a cup of tea in the drawing room, and I marveled at the time they had for relaxing. *What would it be like to be able to sit and enjoy a cup of tea with one's husband?* I had no time and no husband. I was feeling weary, my lip puffy and aching; I seemed to be battered more than healthy.

Lord Harper stood at my entry. "Dear lord," he exclaimed at my fresh bruising and split lip. He looked me over. "I heard about the Wheatons and I heard they have already been sent to Brandon."

Lady Harper paled. Lord Harper cleared his throat with disapproval. I didn't care.

"Shannon," Lady Harper valiantly shifted the conversation, "we have a tea planned with the entire W.C.T.U. this afternoon. They would like to present you with a gift. We are going to celebrate the three women who have been elected in to run the cottage hospital."

"Of course, what time?"

"Two. We'll wrap up by three. Everyone likes supper on the table by five-thirty. That should be plenty of time to celebrate our big win."

She was thrilled; I tried to muster up energy to match, or at least pretend.

"Are you all in order for tomorrow?" Lord Harper asked as Jaffrey moved forward to pour me some tea.

"I am," I said more confidently than I felt inside. Tomorrow I would face Thomas Wheaton in court. I was still healing. Part of me wanted to shut the world away and sit down with a good book and some tea and give this fight to someone else. There was no sense thinking like this; I had to see this through to the end.

"Do you need anything?" Lord Harper asked. "Money, more clothes, anything at all?"

"I have what I need, thank you. I'm just tired."

"Of course," Lord Harper agreed, and we finished sipping our tea companionably. "Once this Wheaton situation is behind us, you'll have time to rest."

"Well, I'll leave you both. This came for you today." Lord Harper finished his tea and pulled a letter out of his desk.

"Thank you." I tucked the letter into my doctor's bag, not ready for any more letters just yet.

Lady Harper and I went to her room where I did a thorough examination.

"I would say this little one will be with us in around nine weeks." I smiled at her as she adjusted her clothes. I went to wash my hands at the wash basin Jaffrey had refilled with fresh water before we started.

"I am getting really excited. Do you think it will be a boy or a girl?"

"I wish we could know that." I smiled at her again.

Lady Harper ran her hands over the mound of her belly.

"I've never been happier than I am right now. I was always a little scared to be pregnant, but I had no idea I would feel this complete."

"I'm happy for you, Lady Harper." Her happy, pregnant glow magnified my feelings of being beaten, empty, and exhausted. I shook it off; no need to feel sorry for myself.

"Lord Harper has said more than once, if you hadn't come, I don't know, I shudder to think, Biddy would have gotten rid of this baby too. I hate the thought of it. I think about the other babies sometimes." She had tears in her eyes as she said it.

"Lady Harper, this baby is going to be beautiful and healthy and strong. You are still very young. You will fill this house yet. I'm just glad that it *was* Biddy and nothing wrong with you."

"You're right. I need to focus all my energy on this little person."

I repacked my instruments in the bag.

"So, now all the Wheaton men are in custody. Where is Emily?"

"I'm not sure. Cole will be dealing with that today." The sadness of the situation dragged at me.

"I'm glad that the trial is tomorrow, Shannon, it will be good to put it all behind you."

"Yes," I agreed and turned to face her before I left. "You know where to find me if you need me. I'm going to go over my notes and get ready for tomorrow."

"Remember, two p.m. We have lots to celebrate. Please let Enid know she is welcome to come, too," Lady Harper said as she got up.

"That's very kind of you." My eyes met hers, and I felt respect rekindle for her.

"Of course." She straightened her gown. "I'll see you both at two?"

"You will."

***

I found Enid in the carriage house packing a small

bag.

"I wanted to mention," Enid said shyly. "I was asked by Mrs. Bennett to come out to sit with Ivy. The family is going to a piano recital, and Ivy has been sick with a flu. She's not well enough to travel. Will you be alright on your own tonight?"

"Of course, Enid. That's good of you."

"I like Mrs. Bennett. I was happy to help."

"We have a celebratory tea to get to at two p.m. Are you up for that?" I asked as I took out my notes for trial.

"Me, too?"

"Of course, you too. Why not you?"

"Well, because I..."

"Enid. I'm not W.C.T.U. either" —I deliberately misunderstood her— "but they let me in. Don't worry about it. It's going to be great. This is a big win for them."

Enid smiled.

The W.C.T.U. welcomed Enid with open arms. We sat down to a feast of baked goods and tea. Lady Harper stood and clinked her teaspoon against the cup. We all gave her our attention.

"We would like to congratulate the following three W.C.T.U. members on their recent election to the board of directors of the Oakland Cottage Hospital. Please stand Mrs. Holt, Mrs. Bennett, and Mrs. Carr."

The three ladies stood by Lady Harper and took a little bow.

"We couldn't have done it without the lobbying of one of our group, not a full-fledged member, but an honourary member just the same. Please join us, Miss Stone."

I stood, and the cheering was so loud it made tears come to my eyes. Mrs. Bennett motioned me to join them as we stood together. They hugged me hard.

"Speech!" Priscilla called out, and I scowled at her.

"I think we've all heard enough out of me for a while!" I called back to her.

The uproar of cheering and clapping made me smile. My lip ached, but I ignored it.

"We would like to present you with a little gift from us to you." Lady Harper went to the sideboard and brought out a little box.

"Oh, you didn't have to do that!" I put my hand over my heart; I was so touched at this thoughtfulness.

"Oh, we really did. We wouldn't have had a chance without you stepping in."

I opened the box. It was a little watch that you pinned to your lapel. Every nurse in the land had one, but I didn't own one. Mrs. Bennett pinned it to me. This one was solid gold. She smiled at me, and I felt tears gather in my eyes.

The cheering died down, and I turned to address the room.

"Thank you all for this lovely gift. I will cherish this always and when I'm timing contractions, I will think of you all fondly."

They cheered, and I cleared my throat to continue. "I was only your advocate. Your hard work and determination brought this project together. You trusted me to handle the negotiations, and I appreciate that very much. I would have been dead in the water without that research. Whoever slipped the legalities to me, you won the fight. I just presented it. You should be very proud of your accomplishment. Well done, ladies!"

After the cheering was over, we settled down to tea. As the afternoon wrapped up, there were lots of hugs.

Mrs. Rood slid up to me as I sat. "I'm glad the research helped. I'll let my sister in law know she saved the day. Cora is Canada's first female lawyer. She works in Toronto," she whispered in my ear as she hugged me.

"Mrs. Rood!" I exclaimed. "I never would have guessed!"

She smiled sweetly and let go of me. "I'm not making a speech, so no need to bring that to everyone's attention."

The ladies finished their tea promptly at three. Relieved, I wanted my bed and a book. A quiet night at home was exactly what I needed before facing the trial tomorrow. Enid was leaving with the Bennetts. After a nap and bath, I sat in my most comfortable and ugly nightgown, the kind that would give Cole nightmares if he saw it, the kind women wore who had no access to contraception. I rubbed the salve on my lip to speed the healing.

Pulling a comb through my wet hair, I scrutinized myself in the mirror. The same face that used to look back at me in England looked back at me here. My skin, where it wasn't bruised, looked pale. I smoothed my fingertips over my eyebrows. My eyes were different. Leaning into the mirror, I looked hard at myself. Where I had seen such tremendous suffering in women I had treated before, I had not experienced violence like them. Now I had, and it had changed me, dulling whatever sparkle had survived the death of my mother and the stringent training from Til. What could bring it back? Winning battles? Having babies? The love of a good man? I wasn't sure.

There was a gentle tap at the door; I quickly put on an equally ugly robe.

I went to the door and peeked out the window to see Cole standing there.

I felt a panic that he would see me in this terrible outfit. I rolled my eyes at myself. He'd seen me in worse conditions, and he was still here!

"Brace yourself," I warned him after I opened the door. "I'm hideous."

"That is awful," he agreed.

Both of us burst out laughing.

I tried to stop, but couldn't. He came toward me and kissed me. That stopped my laughing, as it did his.

I wanted to put my arms around him. I wanted a lot of things, and none of them proper. He stepped away.

Cole settled across from me on the settee, and I saw his eyes flick over me. I really wished I had a nicer nightgown. I made a mental note to go to 'Hope in Oakland' and let Priscilla outfit me.

"Are you ready for tomorrow?"

"I am," I said.

"I was thinking if we left by seven, we would be at court in good time. Is that alright for you?"

"Sure."

"Everything else alright? Are you nervous?"

"Yes. I am very nervous," I said. "I still worry about your reputation once I testify that I actually was pregnant. There are always those who think the worst..."

"Shannon, don't even worry about it for a second." Cole commanded.

"You're right. It's just hard to talk about." I nodded.

"You've been through a lot. It's all going to be just fine."

"Before you go, I have another letter. I think I know what it is about. It's Malcolm's handwriting..."

"Do you want me to stay while you read it?"

"Yes," I whispered.

We settled on the settee, drinks in hand because news from England was never good. I carefully opened the letter.

Dear Shannon,

I hope and trust you are well.

Tomorrow the trial starts. We have a strong legal team and argument prepared. I am confident Til will be acquitted of these charges.

I am forwarding you a clipping you may be interested in.

We love you very much,
Malcolm

The clipping showed a man who was arrested on charges of rape. Malcolm had tracked him down; he would stand trial.

"Are you alright?" Cole reached for me as I trembled in shock.

Wordlessly, I handed him the newspaper clipping. He took it and read it swiftly. His eyes met mine.

"He's being brought to trial. Does this make it better?"

"I don't think anything will make it better." I

curled up against the arm of the settee, far from him. My arms wrapped around my knees to protect myself from the memories that washed through me.

How can anything make this better?

"He can't hurt any other women," Cole pointed out, and I read through the letter again.

"Do you want to know the worst thing about men?" I hissed. "They have to find the logical solution to everything. You're the worst. Why didn't Malcolm just kill him? Why have him arrested?"

"Because then he would be no better than a criminal. Shannon, that's vigilante talk."

"Sometimes I don't want to listen to reason. Stop being so reasonable."

"Someone has to be reasonable!" he protested.

I turned further away from him. He waited for me to calm down.

"It looks like Til's case will be open and shut." Cole offered a bridge between us.

I walked across it. "I hope so. Til is guilty of lots of things, but promotion of vice is the least of them."

Cole put more wood on the fire.

"This tarnishes her, though. Thankfully, Til won't care and she will rise to the top again. She always does." I rubbed my eyes.

"Women are complicated." He leaned forward and put his empty glass down on the floor.

"You're only learning this now?" My eyebrow arched at him.

"Well, I'm slow. I'll admit it. I was the one who so falsely believed that this village was crime free." He went to the cupboard and pulled out a blanket. Carefully he wrapped it around me. This simple act pulled down the walls I was carefully building. He made no move to pull me to him. He settled back down and waited for me to come to him.

I warmed to him. "We cleaned up a lot of crime here. Where is Emily?"

"She's out at the Wheaton homestead alone."

"What will happen?"

"She is safe. She has some decisions to make. The brothers will eventually get out. I'm not sure what to say about that. I'm just glad Ivy is safe with the Bennetts. Try to get a good night's sleep. Tomorrow is a big day. Try not to worry."

"I'm glad you checked on Emily. I was worried about her," I said.

He smiled sadly. "I can check on her morning, noon, and night, but I can't get through to her to abandon this whole Wheaton situation and get her daughter back. It's infuriating. Don't worry about Emily, just get a good rest. You're tired." He stood up, stretched, and left without touching me.

After re-reading my testimony for tomorrow and crawling into my warm bed, I was just about asleep when I felt the cold, honed edge of a knife at my throat.

"You ruined everything!" she hissed in my ear.

Chapter Thirty-Eight

I strained to see and fully wake up. The room was pitch black. I lay still and tried not to swallow because I was certain that this was it. My number was up. This incurable was going to kill me and not think twice.

"I begged you." She was so furious that there were little bits of her spit falling on my face.

Motionless with terror, I had no idea what she was capable of. Slowly, I inched my hand toward the bed warmer I'd been too tired to put away.

"This is not going to fix anything," I whispered.

"Shut up!" she screamed in my face. As she lifted the knife over her head to stab me, I wrapped my hand around the bed warmer and crushed it into her temple.

It grazed her, took her off balance, but didn't knock her out. I leaped up and scrambled out of the blankets.

She rounded the bed, the knife held high, looking like she knew what to do with it.

"You ruined me! You ruined my life! I tried to make you understand!" She lunged for me again.

With all my strength, I hit her with the bed warmer again. She staggered.

Suddenly, her hand shot out and stabbed me in the shoulder. I roared in pain. I hit her once more and she was still.

The pain in my shoulder ripped through me, and

I forced myself to look at the knife. Heat washed over me, made me sweat as the pain swept through me. It was high enough to do some damage, but nothing life threatening.

I ran into the street where my knees gave out. I called to Cole. I wanted to drag myself to the barracks, but I had no strength. Barely enough to scream.

"Help me!" The night's stillness absorbed it. Not even an echo sounded.

"Somebody, please, help me!" My head bowed as I knelt on all fours in the street.

I started shrieking at the top of my lungs, endlessly. A light appeared in Cole's window, even as he ran to me, boots and coat over his nightclothes, I couldn't stop.

Lord Harper and Jaffrey came from the other direction. The men stood there. They had never seen a woman stabbed in the street before. They didn't know what to do.

"Shannon," Cole said as he sunk to his knees in front of me. His eyes widened in horror as he saw the knife in my shoulder and the blood down the front of my gown.

Normally, he would have taken me by the shoulders and shaken me. The knife made that impossible.

He took my face between his hands.

"Shannon, what happened, Shannon?" His eyes were wide with fear, and he looked at me with such empathy and love that it made the flood of pain stop.

"She's still inside." My voice was so hoarse I could barely croak.

"Who, darling? Who is inside?" He forced his voice to be gentle.

"Oh no, it's Biddy. She must have escaped!" Lord Harper turned and ran into the carriage house.

"Jaffrey, go for Dr. Davies," Cole commanded without taking his eyes from mine.

Lord Harper came right back out. He was aghast. He knew violence, of course, but women fighting women —one unconscious on the floor and one with a knife in her shoulder. Madness.

"Who is it?" Cole growled at Lord Harper.

"Emily Wheaton," Lord Harper said, sounding bewildered.

"Take her to prison," Cole ordered him as if he were any other man in the village. Lord Harper nodded and dragged Emily out of the carriage house with a hard hand on her upper arm.

"When I've taken care of Shannon, I will be back to formally arrest her." Cole picked me up and laid me down on my table.

Dr. Davies was used to being interrupted in the middle of the night. He was in my kitchen in record time, surveying the damage.

"Shannon, I'm going to give you something for the pain."

"I have to testify... no drugs," I said through gritted teeth.

"I'm not doing this without some pain relief. Come on, be reasonable." He looked at me resolutely.

"Just a little bit, maybe." I gave in.

After giving me a shot of morphine, he looked at Cole.

"Hold her down while I pull this out."

"Sorry." Cole murmured to me as he pressed my upper body down and Dr. Davies pulled out the knife. I couldn't stifle a scream from the pain. Cole's face went white.

Dr. Davies applied pressure to my wound. "We're just going to get this stitched up, and you'll be right as rain."

Dr. Davies kept the situation calm and under control. His voice was soft; his hands were gentle.

"Cole," I croaked from the table.

He stroked my face. "Don't worry about anything. I'll send a telegram and let them know why you can't testify."

"I'm testifying."

"Shannon, you are too overwrought." Cole's patience snapped.

"No. I am doing it. I want this done, and I want it over with."

"It can wait a day." Cole wanted to yell at me, but I was bleeding all over the table. I could see it stole his thunder.

"I am testifying today as arranged, or she wins. I won't have it."

Cole's eyes swept over my body. His face went from white to green. "Shannon!" Cole pulled his hands through his hair when he saw the extent of the damage.

"Few stitches and she'll be right as rain." Dr. Davies gave Cole a hard look.

"Knock her out. She has chloroform in her bag," Cole directed Dr. Davies. "I can't watch this."

"No! No chloroform. Come on, stitch me up. Let's get this done," I growled at them both.

"If you don't calm down, you can't be in here. I'll call in Jaffrey," Dr. Davies warned Cole.

"Let him fix you and let me cancel this trial today,"

Cole begged me, forehead creased with concern.

"I want it done and over with," I said through clenched teeth. "Can you have me done by seven?" I asked Dr. Davies.

He checked his watch. "It's four-thirty. You'll be done in lots of time."

"I'll hold her down. You chloroform her," Cole suggested to Dr. Davies.

"Don't you dare. Chloroform makes me feel sick and weak. Just some more morphine," I shouted at them.

"Alright," Cole conceded because I was on the verge of a breakdown and he knew it. "Do I hold her down?"

"Just hold her hand," Dr. Davies said as he gathered his supplies.

Cole took my hand and kissed it as Dr. Davies got to work.

Dr. Davies dusted everything liberally with boracic acid powder before closing the skin with sutures. I gritted my teeth and stayed silent through the grueling ordeal.

"Almost done here." His calm voice kept the horror of the situation from escalating. "We're going to be all finished right away. This morphine will have worn off before you take the stand. Come on, no need for heroics with me."

I focused on the mantel piece on top of the fireplace. The morphine raced through my veins and made the room fall away.

"That's it," Dr. Davies placed his last stitch in my shoulder then poured antiseptic over the whole thing. The sting caused my eyes to fill with tears. He dressed the wound on my shoulder. "Take a deep breath, Shannon, don't forget to breathe. I'm almost done. Cole's right. It's too much to testify today. That court will wait for you."

"Do you want to help her to the settee?" Dr. Davies asked Cole.

"I need a pail first," I said.

As soon as Cole helped me sit up, I vomited in the basin that Dr. Davies had used to clean my shoulder.

Dr. Davies took that basin and brought me a new one while Cole helped me sit up on the table.

I was hot with mortification, but both men took this in stride. Dr. Davies handed me a towel to clean my mouth off, and once I had cleaned up, Cole very gently picked me up off the table and laid me down on the settee like I was made of spun glass.

"What time is it?"

"Six," Cole said tightly.

"I need Priscilla to help me dress and I need tea. Could you cook me an egg? It will help settle my stomach."

Dr. Davies came to me at the settee. "Good idea. Good luck today, Shannon. While I'm here, I meant to say how much I appreciate you filling in for me. My wife and I have been in Winnipeg so much this winter, the extra pair of hands were welcome."

"Of course, I was happy to help," I rasped then closed my eyes as the room started to spin around me.

"Take it easy today." He let himself out.

Priscilla returned with Cole, sleepy, but efficient. She made breakfast, and once I drank the hot tea, it soothed my throat. We ate, then she dressed me for trial. I was weak, but with a big breakfast of eggs and toast and tea, I felt human.

She finished twisting my hair up and pinning it securely. "There you are. All ready for trial."

Somehow, she made me look beautiful even though I was a beaten, bloody mess.

"Maybe you should make my hair more severe. This looks too soft, too feminine."

"You're a beautiful woman, Shannon, and you are going into a room full of men. Beautiful women get attention. You want to be heard."

"It shouldn't matter." I gritted my teeth again as the tension made my wounds ache.

"It shouldn't, but it does. Go in there and testify for all the women who have suffered at the hand of a husband. I wish I could do it. I would love to stand in that witness box and expose that monster. If only to protect Ivy," she said bitterly.

"I'll do my best," I promised. My eyes met hers. I wasn't just standing up for myself, my unborn son, and Ivy today. I was standing up for every victim that hadn't had a voice in court. Every battle we won would set precedence for the future.

"Of course you will." She hugged me very gently. "You might just see me there."

I had half an hour of lying on my settee while Cole brought the carriage to the house. He came in and looked to Priscilla.

"Can you talk some sense into her? This is going to kill her," Cole demanded.

"We are tougher than you think. She is strong. She's determined." Priscilla shrugged as Cole came to me on the settee. He was a blend of frustrated and sympathetic.

"We'll go straight there." He went to lift me, but I stopped him.

"I can walk," I said.

He helped me into the carriage.

"What time is it?" I asked, still lightheaded.

"Seven on the dot." Anger made his movements jerky.

I couldn't fault him.

"Emily is in custody." He lifted me straight up into the carriage. "She is in the prison cell. Priscilla will have a tribe of women over to your house to get things in order before you get home tonight."

"Thanks."

He was quiet for a moment.

"I'm sorry." I tried to soothe his anger by offering an apology.

"You have nothing to be sorry about, Shannon." He swung himself up beside me in the carriage.

"I have to testify today." I put my hand on his arm.

"It's fine. I understand wanting this whole thing to be over with. I want it over with, too."

We were quiet then. I was wishing we were in a cutter. They were easier to sleep in.

"You never should have been alone last night." Cole shook his head. "Once the Wheaton brothers were put away, I never even dreamed that tiny, mousy Emily would be capable of such a thing."

"It took me by surprise, too." I shuddered. "Such rage, such venom in her. When she came to beg me not to testify, I dismissed her as just being emotionally upset. I had no idea she was capable of murder. She wanted to kill me."

"I should have been there. I'm so sorry."

"How would you know that Emily would snap and try to kill me? Let's not start blaming ourselves for the actions of incurables!"

"Don't think about it," he said grimly. "Just focus on what you have to do today."

I drew in a shuddering breath.

He stopped the horses and turned to look at me then took my hands in his.

"Whatever happens in there today, you just tell the truth and tell it all. Don't hold anything back."

"I won't. It's going to be ugly though, isn't it?"

"I'm going to be right there. I am going to testify right after you. Between the two of us, he's not getting out. He can't hurt anyone anymore. We have Ivy to think about." Cole looked at me with iron determination.

I shivered and winced from the pain from my wounds.

We kept moving toward Brandon, toward a trial I felt too weak to participate in, toward giving testimony that would cause a man to be incarcerated for life. My shoulder throbbed.

"How is the pain?" Cole shot me a look of sympathy.

"Barely tolerable."

"I made a little bed in the back. Do you want to lie down?"

"Oh, yes, please. I am having a hard time sitting up."

He stopped the team and helped me settle into the bed.

I grabbed his hand as he was getting up.

"Thank you." I felt tears start to form in my eyes.

"Shannon, please don't cry. We have a long day ahead of us." He tucked me in against the raw, early spring day.

"I appreciate your kindness."

"I'm a kind person. This isn't new to you." Cole traced his fingertips down the side of my face. "Get some sleep. It's a long day."

Chapter Thirty-Nine

I had never been a witness at a trial before, and with a fresh stab wound, it wasn't the best of ideas. Nausea and exhaustion wore at me before I even started. All my preparations prior to the proceedings didn't seem like enough. Facing this jury was nerve wracking.

After being sworn in, I settled into the witness box. I felt the hardness of the chair against my back and looked out at a full courtroom. The lawyer for the prosecution, Mr. Evans, started his line of questioning.

"What led to you treating Emily Wheaton?"

"I had been assisting a neighbour with pneumonia. The hired man brought Emily to my neighbour's house. I have worked as a midwife in this area since November of last year. I am becoming a doctor, so I recognized right away that she was miscarrying her baby." I shifted on the hard chair. My shoulder throbbed.

"What do you believe caused her to miscarry?" Mr. Evans asked.

"She had sustained a brutal beating," I replied.

"Objection. Opinion," Mr. Daniels, the defence, called.

"Could you identify the marks that you believe led to the miscarriage?" asked Mr. Evans.

"Objection, she has no formal degree in medicine."

"Your honour, we have a copy of her transcript from the University of Medicine in London. Miss Stone has completed two years of medical training," Mr. Evan's said.

"Approach," the judge said.

The document was produced, and the judge allowed me to make a statement regarding the beating.

"I have documented where she sustained injury. There was bruising around her abdomen and lower back. The bruising at her abdomen was of utmost concern, of course. I assisted her as she miscarried a five-month-old fetus."

"So based on your professional medical opinion, it was the beating, the assault on her abdomen, that ended the pregnancy?'

"A woman who sustains bruising and contusions of that degree on her abdomen cannot sustain a pregnancy," I answered firmly.

"What happened next?"

"Thomas Wheaton came to find his wife. According to the hired man, he had been passed out drunk. It was Shane Lawrence, the Bennett's hired man, who assisted Emily to the Bennett residence. At approximately one a.m. Thomas Wheaton broke down the door screaming for Emily."

"What did you do then?"

"I intercepted him before he could do any further damage."

"Objection, she is not a mind reader," shouted Mr. Daniels the defence attorney.

"Did you believe that Thomas would do further damage to Emily?'

"I know, without a doubt, that if I hadn't intervened, he would have beaten her further. He was furious, screaming, and shouting. As it was, he hit her once before I could get between them."

"What happened when you intervened?"

"He attacked me instead of her. He hit me so hard, I lost consciousness. Ada Bennett said I landed on my stomach. I was unconscious when the police arrived on the scene."

"What happened next?"

"I miscarried my son that night as a result of the attack."

"I'm sorry to have to ask you to recount such a gruesome experience. Your witness."

"How long have you been married?" Mr. Daniels asked. He was looking at the jury not me.

"Objection! Relevance." Mr. Evans called out.

"I'll allow it," the judge said.

"I am not married." I wished my voice were firmer. I took a deep breath.

"So, pregnant and no husband. That puts you in a predicament," he sneered.

My eyes linked with Cole's again, and I could feel his fury all the way across the room. I dragged my attention back to the lawyer. My hands gripped the hard armrests until my knuckles were white.

"Is there a question here?" the prosecution shouted.

My confidence faltered a bit. My eyes scanned the crowd. Who was that in the back that just stood up? I squinted. Priscilla. Beautiful Priscilla Charbonneau stood up and walked toward me until we could look each other straight in the eye.

What on earth is Priscilla doing here? Is she here to remind me that my unborn child had more rights in this court room than I did?

Her look said, 'don't back down. Do not let them see a weakness, and emotion is weakness.' Seeing her pink striped dress in this sea of black bolstered me. I sipped the water again.

"A woman who is four months pregnant, no marriage. What kind of woman are we dealing with here, Your Honour?" His accusatory tone made me physically sick.

I took another sip of water, as if that glass had all the answers, and waited for the judge.

"Who is the father of your baby?"

My eyes met Cole's.

"Answer the question, Miss Stone." The judge looked at me with ice in his gaze.

I stood up.

I will not allow you to humiliate me.

I gripped the polished oak railing of the witness box so I wouldn't sway. My knuckles whitened as I tried to stay upright. Everyone appeared on edge when I stood. I liked that. I said nothing, just waited for every eye to be riveted to me. The judge looked at me warily. They thought I would break down in hysterics; the jury murmured as they looked at each other and then back to me.

I wasn't going to be embarrassed or ashamed of the brutal actions that I had endured. I was going to stand up to this, not just for me, but for future women who would someday sit in this box.

"Four months pregnant," Mr. Daniels said in an accusatory tone. "Are you, in fact, a woman of loose morals?"

"Objection!"

"Overruled. Please answer the question."

"In September of last year, I was raped and made pregnant by that attack." I sat down before I collapsed.

"Where were you at the time? Brothel? Drinking establishment?"

Cole's face flashed with rage as the defence tried to sully my reputation.

None of your business...

"I was running from a clinic that had been set on fire."

"So, you were assaulted and got pregnant. Where are the legal documents to show you pressed charges?"

"Those documents are available in London. I can get you in touch with the prosecutor on that case if you wish."

"Your lawyer produced documentation to verify your education. It's odd he didn't bother to have that documentation here as well."

"Perhaps he was under the impression, as I was, that we are here to find Mr. Wheaton guilty or innocent," I boomed at him with the last of my strength. "Not me. I am not on trial here. We are not here to judge how I got pregnant, the jury is here to judge whether Thomas Wheaton is responsible for procuring miscarriage due to assault. I am not on trial!"

"Redirect, your Honor."

"Proceed."

"You were attacked in England. Why are you in Canada?"

"Objection!" the prosecution yelled.

"Maybe you were sent here to avoid the scandal of being pregnant *without a husband.*"

"Well, we don't have to worry about that scandal now do we?" I couldn't keep the contempt from my tone. "Mr. Wheaton killed two children that night. I guess I don't have to worry about any further scandals."

Mr. Daniels went pale. I could tell just looking at him, he had expected me to try to defend my honour, not attack Thomas Wheaton's actions. "No further questions for this witness." The way he said it made me sound like trash. Like he couldn't be bothered with me because I wasn't worth it.

"Redirect your honour," the prosecution asked.

"Proceed."

"Prior to that attack in England, were you, in fact, a virgin?"

"It is *monstrous* that my virtue is suddenly to be tried as well as this *animal*."

I let the disgust hang there. When I was confident that every eye in the jury box was riveted to me I spoke. The jury didn't care, I could tell. Women who were pregnant out of wedlock better have a good reason. "I will answer, though, because I have nothing to hide from *any* of you. I was a virgin before my innocence was stolen from me."

Cole paced at the back of the room, and I could tell the leash holding him back was strained. Fury burned through me like a fever. Physically and emotionally I couldn't take much more; I felt sweat trickle down my back.

Hold it together, Cole... don't give them the satisfaction...

"You have never worked in an environment of prostitution?"

"Oh, absolutely! I'm no stranger to prostitution—" The crowd murmured, and I shifted in my seat. Moving my arm slightly to stop it from aching, I was grateful for the hard back of the chair that was the only thing holding me up. The jury whispered. The judge slammed his gavel down.

"Silence in this court." The judge looked at me derisively.

This was it. This is where I had the court's full attention, not just the jury.

"I am a midwife and I have completed two years of training to be a doctor. I have had many opportunities to attend to prostitutes. I have seen far too many miscarriages brought about by beatings — that's how I recognized it so easily. Ten years, I worked with women who had been beaten and persecuted by men *exactly* like Mr. Wheaton over there." My head felt fuzzy, and my peripheral vision was black. If he didn't wrap this up, I was going to be in trouble.

"What are your future plans when the woman you are assisting has her baby?"

"I will return to England to finish my training as a doctor."

"Thank you," Mr. Evans said simply.

"I'm calling for a ten-minute recess," the judge said.

I stood up to leave the stand. A murmur raced through the crowd. I held the railing and looked in horror as blood soaked through my dress at my shoulder. A stitch or two must have been pulled out. Not strong enough to stand up, I slumped over the railing from the loss of blood.

The prosecution rushed to assist me. Cole scrambled through the crowd and pushed everyone out of the way. I slid back down into the chair, knocking the glass of water to the floor where it smashed into a million pieces. The jury looked at me concerned. Cole picked me up and carried me out of the courtroom.

"Come with me," Mr. Evans said to both of us. He took us to a little room off the hallway.

"I'm so sorry," I said to Mr. Evans as Cole put me on a bench.

"No, never think that. You did well!"

"But, when he accused me of being a woman of loose morals... that was terrible."

"Made him look like he was grasping. You did an excellent job, and I can't thank you enough. I was worried he would get you to lose your composure. You kept it together like a champ. Your testimony has put Thomas away for life. Two babies dead at his hands. You were great. I was going to say we should meet for supper after today, but you're bleeding. I think you need medical attention."

"I think I pulled some stitches out." My vision was swimming. I tried to focus on Cole; he looked far away even though he was right beside me.

"Thank you again." He patted my hand and left us to get back to the courtroom.

"Cole," I whispered as the lawyer walked away from us. "Cole..."

"Yes?"

"I can't... I can't handle any more. This is it. I'm done."

"It's all going to be alright now."

That's when the world went black.

Chapter Forty

I woke up in a dimly lit room. The events from yesterday rushed through my mind as I blinked and tried to figure out where I was.

Cole slept in a chair in the corner of the room. I struggled to sit up; burning pain sliced through my shoulder. A nurse walked by, and I wanted to call out to her but I hated to wake up Cole.

Cole came awake quickly as he heard me rustling around.

"How long have I been sleeping?" I asked.

"Twelve hours," the nurse said.

"I'm still tired."

"I hear you've been through a lot. Your husband requested a full physical for you. He wanted to be sure that you had healed properly from the miscarriage. He filled us in on what you have been through."

"Thanks," I said as she helped me back into bed.

I met Cole's gaze as that word husband... *my husband*... hung in the room between us. The term husband shot a jolt of delight straight through my heart. I knew he had told them we were married because I wouldn't suffer any harsh judgements being unwed and suffering a miscarriage. My heart warmed to him further.

"Hey." Cole stretched and sat on the edge of my bed.

"Hey." I took his hand.

"You're like Rip Van Winkle. How are you feeling?" He stroked stray hair back from my face.

"Better."

"Still tired, though?"

"Yes."

"Do you feel up to talking? Or would you rather go back to sleep?"

"I'm alright. Is there any news from the trial?"

"Thomas Wheaton has been convicted of aggravated assault, manslaughter for the two babies. This is a felony conviction. He's in prison for life Shannon. I have to go back home to process Emily. I just wanted to be sure you were alright before I left."

"I am just so tired."

"I know, so you are staying here for a couple of days. No arguments."

"I think that's a good idea." I struggled to keep my eyes open. "Thanks for bringing me here. I really just need to sleep, I think."

"Sleep well." He tucked me in. "You're safe here, and I'll be back tomorrow." With that, he was gone.

A few days later, Doctor White, whom I had met when I had brought Mary Varsdon in, entered the room. I breathed a sigh of relief. I worried about which doctor would examine me. He closed the door and pulled up a chair.

"Sometimes, it helps if a patient tells a doctor the whole story. If you want to, you can tell me everything and it will go no further," he said kindly.

I did. I told him everything I had been through, and it was healing to tell a professional all the sordid details. He was sympathetic and he said he was going to run some tests. He mercifully kept me drugged just enough so I slept and healed. He did a full examination to be sure everything was as it should be. Doctor White didn't have to say, 'check for venereal diseases and subsequent scarring.' We both knew what he was looking for. A nurse was in the room for the exam; she held my hand as he thoroughly examined me. My eyes filled with tears at the intrusion. Finally, when he was done he pulled the dressing off my shoulder to check for infection.

"Your man wants to take you home. I told him you are not ready yet. You need to be in full fighting form before I let you out." Dr. Davies prodded the wound a bit.

"I'm not ready yet, and I don't want visitors. I just want to sleep." I slid my eyes shut.

Four sleep-filled days later, he stopped administering pain and sleep medication, and gave me a clean bill of health. My shoulder was on the mend.

I dressed, and a nurse helped me with my hair. Dr. White came to the doorway as she finished up.

"There is no evidence of venereal disease as you are aware, but sometimes it helps to hear it. You are fully recovered from the miscarriage. There is no reason why you couldn't carry a child in the future if you want to."

I let out a long breath I didn't realize I had been holding.

"When you finish your training, I would love to have a woman on staff for female patients. In cases of rape, a woman should have a woman doctor to do a pelvic examination. I'm sorry that was very uncomfortable for you. If you find yourself back here after your training, I would hire you in a second." Dr. White smiled his encouragement at me.

"I appreciate that offer." My heart warmed. It felt good to have validation from a professional.

When Cole came to pick me up, we smiled at each other. I felt happiness spread through me as he looked at me. I took his arm as we walked through the hospital halls and got into the carriage. Cole navigated down city streets as women went about their daily life. It was clothes hanging day, every street we passed had lines of clothes hanging to dry in the weak spring sunshine. The road to Oakland was frozen; the ruts in the mud told me there had been some warm weather while I was recovering.

"So, clean bill of health." Cole's eyes were warm with love.

"Clean and shiny." I smiled up at him, relief winged through me. "How did you know?"

"The nurse told me as soon as I got here, she thinks I'm your husband remember?"

"I will never forget." I settled the lap robe tighter around me.

"I have some mail for you, which I'm terrified to give to you. Every time there is a letter from England, all craziness ensues." Cole grinned at me as he handed me a letter.

"I don't feel like opening it. It's from Malcolm?" I asked. "It looks like his handwriting."

"Yes, it's from Malcolm."

"Not now." I groaned. "I will open this all later. I'm not up to anymore letters for a day or two."

"Do you want to lie down?"

"No, I'm alright. I feel better. It's such a beautiful day."

"Listen, we need to decide on a present for Priscilla and Matt's wedding."

"Well, I actually already handled that present. I don't know if I should say." I couldn't keep the grin suppressed.

He shot a look at me. "Not something I'll have to arrest you for?"

"It's not something ladies talk about."

"It *is* something I have to arrest you for!" He smiled at that. "Don't tell me. I don't want to be guilty by association."

"Let's just say, if they don't want to have a baby right away, they can wait until they are ready, while still enjoying the rights of a married couple."

"Did you put my name on the card?" He circled my wrist with his thumb and forefinger.

"It didn't come with a card. I thought you could handle that. What are you doing with my wrist?" I tried to pull my arm away.

"Checking to see what size of handcuffs you need for all this criminal behaviour. Promoting birth control! We don't allow women that kind of latitude here in Canada, Miss Stone. Here I've been keeping company with a dangerous criminal. It shocks my sensibilities!"

"In my professional opinion, a baby at this time would be detrimental to Priscilla's health. Under Canadian law I am permitted to make that call. Well, I will be when I am licensed. You have no proof. Priscilla won't testify against me. She loves me too much. Anyway, maybe you could pick up a card." I grinned as I tried to pull my wrist away. He didn't let me; instead he pressed his lips against the inside of my wrist. My breath caught and my heart pounded.

"What would that card look like?" he asked as he casually let go of my wrist.

Thankfully, I was sitting because I would have pooled at his feet if I had been standing. "I have no idea what that card might look like." I pressed a hand to my heart to try to stop it from beating out of my chest.

"What would it say? Please enjoy our gift of birth control. From Cole and Shannon, currently waiting to get approval from Til before taking any further steps, so no need of said birth control." Cole rolled his eyes at me.

"Oh Cole, we'll never get approval from Til. She'll have you strung up six seconds off the boat."

For some reason, we found that hilarious. We laughed together most of the way home.

Chapter Forty-One

Cole hovered around me like a nervous old woman, making sure I was warm enough, but not too warm. Jaffrey drifted in and out with my favourite foods. Mrs. Bennett came to sit with me for an afternoon to see for herself that I was alright. Priscilla dropped off two lazy daisy cakes. One for me, and one for Cole. Mrs. Daindridge and Mrs. Carr brought butter tarts. Mrs. Holt stopped by to be sure I had everything I needed. Such an outpouring of support helped my heart heal more every day.

Finally, I received a telegram. Til had been acquitted.

She was released from prison like a shotgun blast. She sent telegrams and letters in rapid succession. We felt the effects even in Oakland, Manitoba, Canada.

Every day, more plans. If I thought Til would slink out of prison and take it easy, I was wrong.

The telegram I read was straight to the point.

Shannon:

Released from prison.

You are attending classes at the university starting Sept. 6.

New clinic has been purchased and I am in process of staffing.

You are to return to England before July 30.

Under no circumstances are you to remain romantically involved.

Til

I sat and looked at the frozen, thawing, ugly landscape around me. The telegram felt like a bullet. A bit high handed! If I wanted to be romantically involved, who was she to stop me? Honestly! What happened to the women's rights she so adamantly fought for? If I couldn't, at twenty-four years of age, decide to be romantically involved, what rights did I actually have? I fumed and banged around my cottage a bit. I spied my doctor's bag and set to work. Once all my implements were cleaned, I double-checked all my midwifery medications, and tucked the letter away.

Priscilla wanted me for a final fitting, so I set out for her shop.

I *loved* Priscilla's shop. The sun streamed in the windows and lit up her work area. She brought out my bridesmaid dress, and I slipped it on so she could check it one last time.

She looked me over critically.

"A little nip here," she murmured as she pinned the waist of my dress in a little tighter.

When she was satisfied, I looked at myself in the mirror; I was happy with the fit of the dress. I put my dress back on and felt that letter from Malcolm Cole had given me after the trial. In all the time it took me to heal after the trial, along with the wedding preparations for Priscilla, I had forgotten to open it.

I slipped out to the bank of the river to read the

letter from Malcolm. My hands shook as I opened it. I was afraid of more abuse from England.

Dear Shannon,

I trust this letter finds you in good health. You have not requested any money from us. Please do not hesitate to ask for any funds you require.

It has come to my attention that you have received a letter from your Aunt Til. I understand that this letter was at the very least threatening in nature. I understand she has demanded that you are to break off your relationship with Mr. McDougall and resume your studies here.

Til had absolutely no right and no business sending a letter asking that of you. If you choose to pursue a relationship with this man, that is entirely up to you. You are a twenty-four-year-old woman who has been through much more than the average young woman.

I have only one request, and I have sent this request to your young man. Please do not get engaged to marry until we have met him. Til will hate him, but I would like to see how he handles himself in a variety of ways. You can tell a lot about a man by how he handles alcohol, money, and his temper.

If he chooses to return to England with you, that is great. If he is amenable to marriage while you resume your studies and assist Til in rebuilding her clinic, that is a decision for the two of you to make. If you are two people working toward a common goal and already support each other, embrace it. Try not to let Til's fears become your fears.

I have always considered you as my own daughter, Shannon. Always. Children may be born into a family, but some are found. I have loved watching you grow into such an extraordinary and hard-working woman. I have been blessed to have you in my life, to encourage you to reach your full potential.

Not all men are bad or dangerous. It seems to me that this Cole McDougall is a man ready to protect you and assist you in reaching your goals in life. If this man is willing to put up with an almost-doctor who is determined to resume her studies, and a full-fledged suffragette, then by all means, let him join the ranks.

So, my darling girl, I look forward to seeing you in a few months. I can't wait to see for myself how you are doing. I will be here to support you in helping Til see reason. I will stand beside you.

As I mentioned before, putting you on that boat with so many grievous injuries, my darling Shannon, that was the worst thing I have ever done. I want to see you and be assured that you are truly well.

With warmest regards,
Uncle Malcolm

I read the letter three times and burst into tears all three times. Finally, I wiped my tears and folded the letter carefully. I breathed in and out, letting my lungs fill with spring air, and went back to my cottage and got down to work.

There was a note on my door. 'Sorry Shannon, I looked high and low. I couldn't find an appropriate card for Matt and Priscilla.' I laughed right out loud as I entered the carriage house.

Cole continued to be busy with his duties and helping at his parent's farm. Finally, the winter released its icy grip; seeding season was upon us. I watched in amazement as the earth woke. The smell of spring on the air was unmistakable. Standing in my south-facing window, I watched the ice go out of the river. I closed my eyes as the sun soaked into my face.

Every day, Lady Harper and I played cards on her south veranda. She was too big to do much else. I had very little to do—just finish up with her pregnancy and head home. The last six weeks floated by on spring breezes and showers.

Chapter Forty-Two

The day of Matt and Priscilla's wedding dawned bright and beautiful. I was thrilled for her. I went over before the wedding to make sure she knew how to use her gift, and Matt hugged me three times. He blushed with every hug.

"I am having a hard time leaving here, leaving everyone," I confessed as I helped to make sure her veil was perfectly placed on her dark curls.

"Maybe you could stay? Why not?"

"Til," I said succinctly.

"It's your life, Shannon. It is absolutely your life, and you have to live it."

"I know." I adjusted her veil. "This is your day, Priscilla. You are just so beautiful, you take my breath away!"

She was. She'd worked hard on her dress — a stunning creation of tulle and satin. Extravagant. The spiteful would judge her, but when Matt laid eyes on her, I was certain he would weep. Her dark hair was piled high, and she glowed with happiness. I tucked apple blossoms in her hair to accent her veil.

The Bennetts had offered to host the wedding in their apple orchard. The grass had been clipped down, and the apple trees were in full bloom. Their pink and white flowers had a strong scent we could smell throughout the house.

"You are going to be so happy." We watched Matt at the altar with Cole right beside him. "It's time, my friend."

She took a deep breath.

As maid of honour, I was the last down the aisle before the bride. I wished I could take my eyes off Cole, but I couldn't. My eyes locked with his, like I was walking down that aisle toward him. It felt right.

He came to my side for the second dance.

"You are so beautiful, Shannon." He took me into his arms.

His eyes flicked over me. I felt a little self-conscious about my shoulder. I had to have the gown readjusted to cover the wound, but Priscilla had done a beautiful job. The gown was the colour of a pink tulip. Delicate after those heavy wool dresses all winter. The soft pink, almost white, of the apple blossoms in my maid of honour bouquet were a pretty contrast to the pink of my dress. I still couldn't lift my left arm, so I placed my right hand on his shoulder and he held my left hand in his. I couldn't stop myself from linking his fingers with mine.

His eyes searched mine. A slow waltz started for which I was grateful, because my shoulder wasn't up to much else.

"Can we take a little break?" I asked after two dances, during which I worked hard to build my courage.

"Of course."

I picked up my wrap, and he helped me pull it around my shoulders. We wandered out into the orchard. I caught Mrs. McDougall's eye as we left. She smiled at me, and I smiled back.

When we were out of earshot, we stood and watched the river from the top of the hill. He stopped walking and turned to kiss me. When we surfaced, he rummaged in the breast pocket of his coat jacket.

"What is it?" I asked.

He handed me an envelope.

"I was going to ask if you would mind me escorting you back to England?"

I wept with joy when I read his name and mine on two tickets to England. I threw myself at him. We were going home together. The inquisition and hands asked in courtship, it was all worth it; the kiss that followed was one full of intent.

Later, much later, we joined the dancers once again. After a few more songs, the band announced that it was time for supper. After we ate, Cole danced his way through the bridal party, and then finally he asked Priscilla to dance. My eyes followed him just as Matt's eyes followed Priscilla. Matt finally shuffled over and asked if I would dance with him.

"Sure!" I put down my punch. "But careful of this war wound!"

"I cannot thank you enough." He smiled as he led me through the dance.

"It's nothing," I replied. "I am happy to be able to help."

"We'll miss you," Matt said. "Cole will miss you, too. Are you sure you wouldn't re-evaluate? Stay here, keep righting wrongs?"

"I wish it were that simple. I will remember you all fondly." I wasn't ready for everyone to know our plans. I wasn't sure if Cole had told his family yet. It was our news, but his people. I would let him take the lead on this.

When the dance came to a close, Matt gave a little bow and returned to his beautiful bride.

I looked across the dance floor. I saw Lady Harper wince in pain and realized my night was just getting started.

Chapter Forty-Three

I moved quickly to her side.

"Lady Harper, are you alright?"

"I think it's time to go," she breathed as she leaned against me.

Cole materialized at my side.

"Would you find Lord Harper?" I kept my voice calm. "We're going to have to cut our night short." I smiled up at him.

Cole cut across the dance floor. He found Lord Harper and then left to get the carriage. The fear in Lord Harper's eyes was evident.

"Everything is going to be just fine," I said to the Harpers. "Let's get home so we can have a little privacy. You're going to meet your baby!"

She gripped my arm, and I had to stop myself from crying out.

"Lord Harper, can you help her to walk?"

He stepped in, and when the contraction eased, we moved toward the waiting carriage. Ada noticed us sneaking out the back and came to meet us.

"Would you stop by tomorrow morning to check on us?" I asked Ada.

"I'll stop by to be the first one to give the new miss or mister a welcome gift," she said encouragingly. "You'll have that baby in your arms shortly, Lady Harper!"

She squeezed my hand.

"Send Cole for me if you need my extra hands," she said quietly in my ear.

Then we were off. Cole drove because Lord Harper was clearly terrified.

This was going to be a long night. First babies typically took their time. I knew this, but everyone else in the carriage seemed to sense it. When we got to the house, I helped Lady Harper change into a nightgown. I got the bed ready and then asked Cole to send Enid to me. I was going to need at least one other pair of hands. My shoulder was throbbing already, and we had barely begun.

Enid showed up with my doctor's bag and everything I would need.

"Lady Harper," I said. "Let's get walking to get things moving. Enid, I can't hold her up, so you'll have to do it. Slowly, just walk around the room."

They alternated between walking and resting for hours until I could tell the pains were getting more intense. Lady Harper was crying now, but we had only just begun. She lay down so I could look to see that she was dilating. We were half way there. I listened to the baby's heartbeat. All was in order.

"The baby is in the right spot. Your body is opening up to deliver. Everything is moving exactly as it should."

Right then, a contraction hit her hard, and she curled to her side and threw up.

"Oh, I'm so sorry!"

"No problem." I rubbed her back. "The pain makes you vomit. That's totally normal."

Enid helped Lady Harper off the bed and continued to walk with her. I changed the sheets. She stopped for another contraction. Jaffrey dragged water up the steps like a soldier so we could fill the bathtub with warm water.

When the pains intensified and the pressure of the baby's head against the cervix became intense, she could no longer stand up. Enid and I helped her into the tub of water.

"Oh"— she breathed deeply in relief— "that is so much better!"

"Lady Harper, let's move you so that your legs are apart and you are holding onto the side of the tub. That will open up that pelvis a bit and use gravity to help that baby keep coming." I helped her to move into position. "Enid, you look after her head. I'm going to rub her back."

Every time a contraction hit, I pressed as hard as I could into her back.

"Jaffrey," I shouted as I heard him drop off more hot water, "go for Ada. We need another pair of hands."

I couldn't leave her to keep getting more water, and propriety dictated that no men should be in this room with us.

The contractions were intensifying as they should, but they were terrifying for a new mom.

"I can't do this," Lady Harper hissed at me as she doubled over in pain.

"Oh, my dear, you can do it. We're going to do it together."

"Lean back in the tub so I can have a look," I said to Lady Harper, who did not want to move, but we helped her lean back. After a quick examination, it was clear to me she was dilating, but not in stage two yet. I brought out chloroform to take the edge off the pain.

"Enid, tell Lord Harper that Jaffrey is getting tired. We need lots of hot water—two pails per half hour."

While she left to follow my instructions, I helped Lady Harper settle back into position. After placing the chloroform mask over her mouth and nose, I administered the lightest dose.

"Oh, oh thank goodness," she said as she breathed in the chloroform.

"I can't give you very much, but it should take the edge off those pains." I put more water in the tub to keep it hot.

Lady Harper's face relaxed between contractions as the heat of the water in the tub and the chloroform soothed her. I had never used a tub before, only hot towels. The tenements in England didn't lend themselves to such luxury. With a butler at our disposal though, we had all the hot water we needed, so I thought since she relaxed better in the tub, no need to move her. I would have to tell Til the tub worked miracles. She would roll her eyes at me and say chloroform worked miracles, never mind bathtubs and hot water.

There was a tap at the door and in walked Ada.

"Oh, Ada! Thank goodness," I said when I finally looked up.

"The boys downstairs are wearing a hole in the carpet." She laughed.

I laughed with her and kept administering the chloroform.

"Where do you need me?" Ada asked as she rolled up her sleeves.

"I need to take another look. Would you administer this?"

"What is this?" Ada asked as she took over the bottle and mask.

"Pain relief. It's a very mild dose of chloroform. We use it to take the edge off the pain. We have found it actually tends to speed things up because instead of fighting the pain, the woman can relax with the contractions."

"Brilliant! I've never seen chloroform used in childbirth. I'm so glad to learn this!"

"If men gave birth, it would be on every shelf in the land. Before I go, I'll leave you a bottle and the dosage."

A very long ten hours later she was dilated enough to start to push.

We lessened the chloroform so she could feel what was going on. It took three of us to drag her out of the tub and place her on her side on the bed. Enid immediately wrapped a hot towel around her lower back and abdomen. I found myself more and more impressed with her. She was quick, efficient, and instinctively knew where I needed her. Ada pushed against Lady Harper's back through the hot towel with every contraction. They were so close together now. I told Enid to keep those hot towels coming.

Lady Harper pushed when I told her to push.

"We need to hold her up a bit. Enid, get behind her."

Enid crawled onto the bed and supported Lady Harper at an angle that allowed the baby's head to put more pressure on the cervix. Ada kept putting hard pressure on her lower back and wrapping her in hot towels. I kept reminding her to push harder.

We worked like a team of soldiers in the trenches. When the head was out and a little girl slithered into the world, we all burst into tears. Lady Harper lay shaking from shock. I clamped the cord as the baby screamed, cried, and fought the world with her tiny fists then placed the tiny girl on Lady Harper's chest and told Enid she could get off the bed.

I had assisted with so many births, and yet the miracle of it always took my breath away and moved me to tears.

This baby girl was healthy and perfect. Lady Harper wept as she kissed her daughter and held her as the placenta delivered. Both Ada and I carefully checked it.

"Let's get this baby cleaned up," I said to Lady Harper, who was loathe to let her go.

Ada cleaned up the little one, and I cleaned up Lady Harper. Once Lady Harper was dressed in a fresh nightgown, the bed was re-made, and the baby brought back to her, Ada opened Lady Harper's nightgown and placed the little girl at her breast.

"I find that this calms the baby and the new mom down." She put a soft blanket around the new baby. "It's tradition in our family that the grandma wraps the new baby in a blanket she made. You do not have any family here, Lady Harper, but I think of you as one of my own, so I made this for the new little miss."

I blinked back tears at the kindness and generosity of Ada Bennett. How was I going to leave this woman? She was naturally a mother to everyone.

"Enid." I tried to clear out the emotion clogging my throat. "Can you go and fetch Lord Harper? He'll be frantic."

Lord Harper came up the stairs two at a time then wept when he saw his wife and new daughter. We withdrew from the room to give them privacy.

"I have a meal prepared," Jaffrey said to us.

"Jaffrey, you were a trooper. Thank you so much for your hard work."

"What time is it?" Enid asked as she rubbed her neck.

"It is six-fifteen," Jaffrey said as we sat down to eat dinner.

We'd only had snatches of food, and so we lit into the meal like we'd never seen food. Jaffrey poured us tea, but he'd snuck some brandy into mine.

"Jaffrey, please join us. Grab a sherry, or whatever it is you drink. We need to celebrate."

The thought of joining us was clearly foreign to him, but I insisted. We were all serving class really, and we had been through a tremendous ordeal. I was used to it, but Enid and Jaffrey were not. He was awkward, but he did it.

"Enid, you are a natural nurse. I have never seen anyone who naturally knew what to do in a birthing room. You should think about coming back to England with me and going to school."

Jaffrey looked at Enid's face and slipped out of the room.

"Oh... I don't know. I don't think I could do that," she stuttered.

"Why not, dear?" Mrs. Bennett reached across to take her hand.

"I don't think you can leave your past behind..." Enid looked from Mrs. Bennett to me.

I stood up and moved my chair closer to her. "You were a victim of a crime. You can take that terrible experience and use it. You'll learn about birth control and how to help women protect themselves. Knowledge is power, Enid. The more you learn, the less helpless you feel."

"She's right." Ada sipped her tea. "You need to build something positive out of the mess you came through, and you can do it."

Hope shimmered in Enid's eyes. Ada squeezed her hand before she let it go.

I poured her some tea as she looked up at me. "What is the expression? A life well lived is the best revenge."

"I'll think about it," she promised.

"Please think about it. All expenses paid, school, everything. We need nurses like you that will have compassion. You are a natural. Also, Cole is coming back to England with me, and we'll need a chaperone. You'd be doing me a huge favor."

Ada smiled broadly. "I knew he'd do the right thing. You got a good one there."

Lord Harper came back down, eyes red and beaming with pride.

Jaffrey returned to serving.

After the meal, I went up to check on Lady Harper and the baby again. The little one was latched on and eating her own supper.

I handed Lady Harper a cup of tea with white willow bark and a hefty dose of laudanum to ease the pain as best as we could. I asked Jaffrey to bring up a hot water bottle.

"We did it." She sipped the tea.

"You did it, and she is perfect, Lady Harper," I said softly, so the baby wouldn't stir.

"I keep wondering what would have happened if

you hadn't come to us. I keep wondering how many babies Biddy killed. I don't know how to thank you for saving this one."

"I needed a place to heal, and you gave me that." I sat down on the chair next to the bed. "You sent Cole to protect me, and it turns out I needed him, too. I will never forget your kindness to me. I am thankful that you are my friend."

"It will be hard for you to leave Cole." Lady Harper shifted her daughter in her arms.

"Oh, he's coming back to England with me." My eyes shone as I said it, and she smiled at that.

"I kept thinking you should stay here," she confessed as she traced her fingertip across the baby's cheek. "Give up on all this doctor craziness. But from that first drop of chloroform and the way you just knew exactly what to do every step of the way, I know you can't stop. It would be selfish if anyone asked that of you. Womankind needs women like you at the helm. Women like you are going to change the world. You will overthrow this entire society. Thank heavens for that. When this little one is grown, she will benefit from everything you and your kind have accomplished."

"We won't overthrow the world." I chuckled and picked up a pillow and placed in on my lap. "We will alleviate suffering where we can and try to get birth control to the masses. I've seen too much to quit. It's a big fight ahead of us."

"Then you'll need Cole by your side. I'm certain Cole's been put in this world to make sure you can accomplish whatever you set out to do."

"I hope I can help him accomplish whatever he

sets out to do, too. My time here was healing for me. And I appreciate your vote of confidence."

"When you first came here, I think you needed those votes of confidence, but you have changed."

"Oh?"

"You have. You aren't worried about the opinions of people so much anymore."

"Thank you, Lady Harper. It's time we all went to bed and had a good sleep. I'll be in to check on you first thing in the morning. Good night, Lady Harper, and good night to you, little one."

As I dressed to leave Hillcrest, Lord Harper stopped me.

"Shannon, Cole asked me not to tell you because he knew you would be exhausted, but I know you'll be upset if I don't. Cole's father has passed away, he had a heart attack."

"No. When?" Panic made my heart race as my world fell apart. Again.

"Last night. He will be furious with me, but I couldn't keep that from you."

"You are right. I must go to him. Where are they?"

"At the farm. Dr. Davies and the undertaker are there with them."

I called Jaffrey to get the carriage. I restocked my doctor bag, and together we flew across the prairie to the McDougall farm.

Chapter Forty-Four

Jaffrey helped me out of the carriage, and I sent him home. He'd been up all night, too. I gripped my doctor bag before I knocked on the door. There was no answer, so I let myself in. Cole was stone faced holding his mother. Nathan and Hannah held each other as Dr. Davies assisted the undertaker as he removed Mr. McDougall's body from the master bedroom.

I stepped aside as they carried him down the hall and out to the carriage. Quietly, I stayed in the hall, outside the kitchen, to give the family space. At first I was just numb, so exhausted I couldn't even grasp the magnitude of this.

Mrs. McDougall was sobbing in Cole's arms. I peeked in as Dr. Davies went back to the kitchen.

"Shannon." Cole's face was haggard. "What are you doing here?"

"I came as soon as I heard. I am so sorry Cole."

"Thank you." He sounded defeated.

Dr. Davies came back in with sleeping draughts for everyone, including me. He lined them up on the sideboard.

"Is there anything I can do?" I asked Dr. Davies lamely.

"See that the family gets this to help them sleep." He picked up his bag.

I knew that feeling, to come up against death and

be defeated.

"I'm so sorry." He went to the door.

Cole moved forward to shake his hand, so I took his place holding his mother, who was clearly in shock.

"Mrs. McDougall, let's help you into bed." Time to return some small measure of the kindness this woman had shown me.

I helped Mrs. McDougall get undressed and re-dressed into a warm nightgown. She wept by the fire-place in her room as I remade her bed with fresh sheets. I pulled a bed warmer through the bed, and tucked her in.

"Thank you for coming," she murmured as she lay in her bed.

"Of course." I pulled another blanket up over her. "Please drink this. It will let you sleep."

I gave her the sleeping draught and then held her while she cried. Cole stood at the door frame hovering over both of us. The sleeping draught took over, and I held her until she slept. Tenderly, I pulled the covers around her, and Cole put more wood on her fire. He left her room, and I checked one last time to be sure Mrs. McDougall was truly asleep. I couldn't imagine losing a husband and then going to sleep alone.

Hannah and Nathan had left for their own home. Cole was stacking dishes and tidying up the kitchen. I stood there and watched him fill the sink with hot water.

I went to him and ran my right hand up his back and then put both arms around his waist. I laid my head against the wall of his back. "Leave the dishes. Let me do them." My arms tightened around him.

"You shouldn't be here, Shannon. You must be exhausted." Grief made his voice raw.

"I am, but I couldn't leave you to deal with this on your own. I was so worried about you."

His eyes were red from crying, and I could tell he did not want to cry in front of me.

"He wasn't even sick, Shannon. Not in the slightest. He was having a great time dancing at Matt and Priscilla's wedding. No warning, just boom. A massive heart attack."

"It's not fair." I rubbed my hand up and down the hard wall of his back.

He pulled away from me and put his hands over his face.

I put my right hand on his shoulder. I still couldn't lift my left, so it hung uselessly at my side.

"I should take you home. It's late." He let his hands drop.

"Oh, Cole, I'm not going home."

"You have to," he said hoarsely as his eyes searched mine.

"No, I don't have to do anything. You were with me the night my son died, so I will stay with you tonight, the night you lost your father."

His eyes widened.

"If you say anything about my reputation being ruined, I will beat you with a stick. This is not negotiable."

"Shannon." His voice was a warning.

"Cole. We are facing this together. You don't always get to be the hero. Sometimes it's my turn."

I poured us both a drink and I put the sleeping draught in his and half of one in mine.

"Come on." I led him to his old room.

He started a fire, and I sipped my drink. This was a strong sleeping aid. Dr. Davies wasn't messing around. I felt it swim through my veins. My mind was numb from exhaustion and grief, so I turned off my brain and let my heart lead the way.

Cole sat by the fire and looked at the flames. I went to him and knelt in front of him. He held his arms out and I went into them.

He held me so tight it was hard to breathe.

I knew right then this was the right move, to be here to try to share all this pain.

I moved forward to kiss him. I shocked even myself. Right then, so help me, I was ready to give him anything to make him feel better. I kissed him with everything I had to offer; I felt him respond. It was like lighting a fire.

"Shannon, we can't. We cannot."

"I know," I said with such naked disappointment he smiled sadly.

"I can't go to England with you now." He stroked hair back from my face. "Someone has to put the crop in and take it off. It's too much for Nathan. He can't find a hired man at this late stage. I can't follow you until after harvest. I'm not doing this, any of this, with you, Shannon. We can't."

I moved toward him again and he held his hands up.

"I love you," he said gruffly as his eyes filled with tears. "I love you with everything I am. We'll wait. I'll follow you in six months."

"I'll stay." I heard the pleading in my voice. "I can stay and help."

"No," he said. "You are going to school."

"We can't talk about this?"

"I promised Malcolm and Til. I told them I was coming back with you, that we would start our life there. Our life together. Malcolm asked me to respect his wishes and not do this, even get engaged, until he could meet me. He sounds like a most reasonable man. He's been working to find me work…"

"You did all this without telling me?"

"Shannon, I wanted to be sure I could make it all work before I talked to you about it. My job is to take care of you, Shannon. It's my job to provide for you, not the other way around. I wasn't going to show up in England with no job and no prospects. Malcolm has been most helpful."

"We're a team, though. You should have told me you were working on all this," I said with more than a little disappointment.

"We're a team, but I do the heavy lifting." He smiled and then he scrubbed his hands over his face. "I can barely even see straight I am so tired, and you must be even more so."

I sipped more of my drink and decided to drop the subject. Cole had just lost his father; he needed support not a fight. He sipped more of his drink.

He took my face in his hands.

"I promise we'll talk about this tomorrow. I am so exhausted I can't even see you. No more tears tonight. I'm tired of crying, and I hate watching you cry. Come on. Time for bed. You're tired. I'm tired. We'll talk in the morning."

The spare room I was to stay in was ice cold. He made a fire while I put my doctor's bag on the dresser. I pulled pins out of my hair and let it fall. His eyes flicked over me and his jaw clenched.

"You are not playing fair." He stood up and crossed the room to stand in front of me.

"I'm not playing at all. My shoulder can't manage this corset. Enid helps me at home."

"Lucky Enid," Cole growled as he unlaced it. The feeling of his hands against my back was so intimate I was certain he would waver. He didn't. He rifled around in the bureau and picked up a set of flannel pajamas, men's pajamas, and heavy wool socks.

Wonderful. More ugly pajamas. *Wool socks!* There would be no scandalous behaviour in these!

"Was it a girl or a boy?" he whispered.

"Hmm?" I had a hard time concentrating as the sleeping draught hit me.

"Harper's baby. Did she have a girl or a boy?"

"Baby girl." I yawned and stretched the tension out of my neck.

"Oh no," he groaned as he turned me to face him and held the pajamas between us like an ugly barrier. "Another woman in this community. That's all we need!"

I grinned at him until he kissed me very gently on the lips.

"Thank you for being here tonight. It means a lot to me. I love you." He cradled my face in his hands before he kissed me again.

"I'm not leaving for England without you."

"We'll see," he said so sadly I felt sick.

After I dragged on the pajamas that were six sizes too big for me, I went to sleep secure in the knowledge that as hard as this was, he truly cared about my education. He cared about me enough to meet Malcolm's requirements.

In the morning, I woke up to him stoking the fire in my room. I sat up, and he turned to me.

"Don't get up yet." He came to the bed and tucked me back in. "Let the room warm up first. It's too cold."

"I should check on your mother."

"I just stoked the fire in her room, and she's still fast asleep."

"How are you?" I made room for him to sit on the bed. He sat against the headboard, and I curled up in his arms. "I love this," I sighed happily.

"Me, too." He tucked us both in. "I am fine."

"You are not fine." I made myself comfortable against him. "That's why you should let me stay here. I can help get this crop in, look after your mother. You can't do all this on your own, Cole. It's not fair to ask me to leave next week when this tragedy has struck your family. You wouldn't leave me. My school will be there next year. I can just postpone another year."

"It's different. I'm a man."

I sat up indignantly. "What is that supposed to mean?"

"Listen, I know you want to help. I love you for offering, but let's look at the big picture, please."

I shifted away further so I could face him.

"What is our goal?" he asked firmly.

"We want to be together."

"We love each other, and I've been in love like this before. We're on the verge of engagement, correct?"

Oh no, he sounds like a constable; there will be no emotional thinking in this decision!

"I think so." My heart banged so loud in my chest I'm sure he could hear it.

He reached forward to trace my eyebrow with his fingertips.

"When you go home, how much time do you think you'll be putting into school and work?"

"Honestly, I'm afraid to think about it."

"The crop has to go in, and Nathan cannot do it alone."

I opened my mouth to interrupt.

"Please, just listen. If you stay here to help, and I appreciate that offer, Shannon, I do. My heart wants you to stay here, but for us as a couple, it will put your education behind another whole year, won't it?"

Tears filled my eyes as I realized that he was right. Staying here meant another whole year lost. It pushed everything back. If we wanted to have children, my schooling had to be finished to start the next step of our lives.

"I have to put this crop in. We might find someone who can take it off, and I can come sooner. Hannah will look after my mother, and it would help us *as a team* if you got your schooling finished sooner rather than later. You also are supposed to be on site to help Til re-build her clinic, right?"

"I don't want to say right..." I felt my face crumble.

"This is impossible." He was frustrated. I was heartbroken.

"Three men took a year of your studies away from you. I won't steal another year. I won't do it. I'll try to find someone for harvest, or you have my word, I will be on the first ship after harvest. Til and Malcolm want you back. They want to be sure you are alright. I promise I will follow you."

I moved away from him, and the flannel pajama

top slid down over my shoulder.

"Seducing me is not going to work," he said firmly.

"If I were seducing you, I would not be wearing this!" We both started to laugh.

"Just so you know, Miss Stone, you could very easily seduce me wearing that," he growled, and I smiled.

"Oh?"

"Don't test me, woman." He pulled the top back into place. "I am using every shred of will power to meet Til and Malcolm's conditions and protect your honour. You are killing me."

"I just want to say something." I let the pajama top slide down my shoulder again, and his eyes smoldered.

"Remember after I helped Mary Varsdon, you admitted you originally wanted me to quit and just be normal. But, you changed your mind. A little piece of me always wondered if you truly changed your mind about my education and my job." His eyes flicked away from my bare shoulder to my eyes.

"Sorry, what was that you were saying?"

We laughed together.

"I'm trying to tell you I didn't realize until last night how dedicated you are to me reaching my goal of being a doctor, and I will remember this forever. You are selfless, Cole. I love you for that. I promise you, right now, I will return the favour."

He moved to me and pulled me back into his arms.

"But leaving you is going to break my heart." I clung to him as hard as I could.

"I'll be right behind you," he promised.

Chapter Forty-Five

My last week in Canada passed in a whirlwind of activity. I had to swear affidavits for Emily and the Wheaton brothers' trials. I also had to give statements for the upcoming Hanover trial. The lawyers had requested that I go to Brandon to meet with them. Both Cole and Lord Harper stepped in and asked them to come to me. My shoulder was healing, but it was a slow process.

Enid was busy packing with me. She beamed with excitement to be facing a new life in a new land.

Ada and John Bennett formally adopted Ivy Wheaton. She was a nervous child of four who followed Ada all over her beautiful farm. I visited there two days before I left. As I stepped out of the carriage, I drank in the sight of the Bennett's farm, how the river curved behind the house and the trees swayed in the breeze. The apple blossoms had dropped and created a pink carpet in the orchard. Ada's geese honked at me as I made my way to the front door.

Ada let me in with a smile and then returned to her kitchen counter. Once her bread was carefully placed into bread pans, she slashed the tops of them. I watched her put a light cotton tea towel over the pans. She piled our tea and scones on a tray, and we sat on her veranda overlooking fields that were just sprouting.

We sipped together companionably while Ivy played with her orange cat.

"I love knowing you are raising her, Ada." I sipped my tea in the warm June sunshine.

"Well, we already love her to bits. I loved Emily. That whole situation was just so tragic. I wanted to help her so badly. But, I can make sure Ivy has a better life, and for a mother, that's the best gift."

We were quiet for a time as we watched the sun filter through the leaves of the lilac bush that flanked her veranda.

"I don't know how I will leave you, Ada." My eyes immediately filled with tears.

"Oh, my dear, there is no need to cry. I'm not going anywhere. You can write. You can come back."

"It won't be the same." My voice caught; I could already feel the loss of her, and I wasn't even gone.

Ada put her teacup down and turned to me. Her work-hardened hands held mine. She looked into my eyes.

"I want you to listen to me. You are not the same girl that came here. You are a strong, powerful woman. You will do great things. You healed here, and you are going home stronger. I will forever be here, on the sidelines cheering on every victory, Shannon. You have a gift."

"Why does everyone keep saying this about me? I'm a disaster!"

"Oh, my dear." She chuckled as she put her hand on my shaking shoulder. "You are certainly not!"

"I don't know how you can say that," I moaned. "I tried so hard to do it all, like Til would. Right all the wrongs."

"You don't have to do it like Til does it. You're you. You did it your way. You dealt with a domestic abuse situation that needed to be dealt with. You exposed badness while helping the victims retain their dignity. You got a hospital up and running. You saw potential in Enid. All that, and you even found time to find a man who loves you with every fiber of his being. Not to mention delivering babies with a smile. That's a lot for six months, Shannon. I'll be watching to see what you accomplish in the next five minutes!"

"No wonder I'm tired!" I smiled at her.

"Well, you've got a long boat ride home to rest."

I handed her a little package.

She opened it and smiled.

"A gift from one midwife to another," I said. "Ergot of rye, only to be used if labour slows, and only if the baby is in the perfect position and the mother is fully dilated. It will also stop a hemorrhage. I will leave you this chloroform. The dosages for both are on the instruction sheet. You might have to play with the dosage of the chloroform, depending on the size of the woman. I also replaced your mustard because I used all of it when I treated your pneumonia."

"I already replaced it, dear."

We laughed about that.

"Well, next time you're making mustard plasters in the middle of the night, you can think of me."

"I will think of you often." Ada Bennett held my gaze and I knew she told me the truth. We were friends. We put down our tea so we could hug each other tightly.

Eventually, I had to leave. She and Ivy waved at me from the veranda. It was hard to walk away from her, so hard to walk away from her beautiful farm. I waved and fought back tears. I let my eyes sweep over the farm one last time, drank in its simple beauty, and forced myself to leave.

My heart ached at the thought of leaving Cole here. All I could think of was what could happen in six months to change his mind.

Emotionally, hugging everyone and saying good-bye was taking a toll. By the time Cole and Matt came to pick up Enid and me, I was an exhausted wreck.

We didn't say one word the entire ride to Brandon. I was sick with heartbreak. I had no idea how to walk away from this.

He carried my bags and stood on the platform with me until the last minute.

"I will follow you," he vowed.

I wiped at my tears, and he held me against him as long as he could. I walked onto that train sobbing and cursing Til, cursing Malcolm, and cursing heart attacks and life in general.

We'd battled domestic abuse, violence against women, and accusations from men. He had been there every step of the way. Protecting me and loving me. This was beyond anything I had ever felt for another person. Leaving him broke me.

I watched as the train pulled away. What if he didn't come and meet me in England? What if he changed his mind? I watched until I couldn't see him anymore and felt my heart shatter and splinter.

Chapter Forty-Six

We took two weeks to reach the coast; we missed the boat by twenty-four hours. While waiting for the next boat, Enid studied and so did I. When Enid got sick, we missed the next boat. We ended up being stuck in Saint John, New Brunswick for a month. I sent telegrams to Til, and she replied she was thrilled I had come to my senses. I wandered around Loyalist cemeteries from the 1700s because it was the only place that fit my mood.

The day we could finally board the boat to go to England I was numb.

The first day at sea, Enid was still weak from the flu that she had battled on land. The seasickness wasn't helping. I dosed her with everything I had, and when she was sleeping, I snuck up on deck. Looking for a peaceful place to think, a place to let my heart heal.

When I stepped through the door to the deck, the brilliance of the sunrise struck me. I walked to the railing, so enraptured with the sunrise, I didn't see anyone or anything else. I just let the light soak into my eyes, into my soul. I took a deep breath of salty sea air and felt confidence rise in me. My heart ached for Cole, but I could do this. School, work, and Til's crusade were waiting for me, and I was ready to work.

"Excuse me, miss," a deep voice said behind me.

Every hair follicle on my body stood up. It

couldn't possibly be!

"I was wondering if you would appreciate an escort home to England? I understand that you have a knack for finding trouble."

I turned, and when I saw Cole, I flew at him and he caught me. We kissed, we cried, we held onto each other like our lives depended on it. Our happiness did. We both knew it.

"How? How did you get here?" I cried.

"It's such a long story. Let me look at you." Cole ran his hands over my face, over my shoulder that had recovered. We kissed with intent. He almost devoured me, I had to hold on or I'd pool at his feet.

"Can you stand up?" he cradled my face in his hands as he kissed me again.

"No. Don't let me go. I'll collapse."

"I am going to make you very happy, Shannon Stone," Cole vowed.

"I will make you very happy, too." I dragged his face down to mine and kissed him harder.

"How are you here?" I grabbed the front of his shirt in case he disappeared.

"The W.C.T.U. marshaled their powers and made it happen."

"What does that mean?" I asked wildly.

"When Dad died, there was a flurry of letters and telegrams sent to my brother, George, in Alberta. He had recently fallen on some hard luck the family had no knowledge of and didn't want to impose on us, but he was desperate to get a job. Ada Bennett, my mother, and Nathan contacted him and sent him the fare to come back to Oakland. They were a terrible force to reckon with. Mr. Holt had found a replacement for my job five minutes after you lobbied for the W.C.T.U. to be on the board of directors for the hospital. He said if I let you go, I'd be a fool. The entire community pulled together to make this happen, Shannon. I listened to more lectures in two weeks than I can even count. They all told me I was a complete idiot. A week after you left, I was on a train right behind you. My question is how are you so late getting on this boat? What happened to you?"

"We arrived twenty-four hours after the boat left. So that meant we had to wait a week. Then the day before we were to board, Enid got so sick she couldn't travel. I was afraid for her life, actually. She had to be hospitalized for a few days. So, we had to wait for the next boat."

"She's well?"

"Yes, Enid is fine. She's excited."

"Well, here we are." His mouth curved into another smile before he bent down to kiss me again.

He very gently stroked my face where his stubble had abraded it. "Sorry, I'll shave."

"Never mind that." I shook my head.

"You didn't think I was going to actually let you go back to face Til on your own, did you? We have some unfinished business... I understand there's a document I get to sign to make sure I have no rights over you as a professional when we finally marry. I've seen the documents by the way; Malcolm sent them to me so I could peruse them before I showed up. Is there anything more romantic than signing documents before getting married? What does one wear to a document signing? Do you light candles? Have champagne? Documents or not, Shannon Stone, I can't wait to marry you. I am going to make you a very happy woman." He put his arms around me and lifted me so he didn't have to bend over to kiss me.

"We aren't allowed to get engaged, Cole. Malcolm was most clear about that," I reprimanded him primly.

Regretfully, he put me back down on my feet.

"Well, love of my life, Malcolm isn't here now, is he? And I think you and I can have a few secrets. Let's be reckless." He pulled a ring box out of the breast pocket of his jacket, and as he knelt in front of me, my heart soared.

"Shannon Matilda Stone, would you do me the great honour of being my wife? To have and to hold, while still maintaining your rights and freedoms. To love and to cherish, while using every form of contraception we can get our hands on. For as long as we both shall live?"

"I will!" I laughed and cried at the same time.

"Wait! I'm not done! I promise to sign any documents Malcolm insists on. I promise to be charming to your aunt. I promise to love you, honour you, cherish you, and protect you with every bone in my body. I promise to spend my life making sure every dream comes true if it is in my power to do it. The ones you have now and the ones we will have together."

"Can I say yes now?"

"Not yet, I'm not finished. If we have a daughter—" He paused, my breath caught at those words.

I put my hand over my mouth, the thought of a daughter with him hit me hard. I would love to see him raise a little girl.

"I promise to do my part to make sure she has what she needs to follow in her mother's footsteps."

"Stop, I am going to cry," I begged as tears filled my

eyes.

"I can't stop. It all has to be said." He had tears in his eyes, too. "If we have a son, I will try my best to teach him how to handle life with a suffragette. I am so proud of you and I can't wait to see where this life together leads us."

"Now?" I demanded, "Can I say yes now?"

"Now."

"Yes! A thousand times, yes."

He got up, slid a diamond on my hand, and kissed me again. I didn't even look at the ring because it didn't matter; he was kissing me with everything he had, and I was kissing him back.

This was absolutely a kiss with intent.

When we finally broke apart there was a crowd watching, so Cole held up my left hand like I was a prize fighter.

"We just got engaged!" he shouted.

The entire deck of people cheered.

Finally, the fanfare died down, and we stood at the railing of the ship. His arms firmly around me, we watched that glorious sunrise together. The sun glinted off the diamond on my left hand. It felt so good to lean my head back against his shoulder, to breathe in his scent and the scent of the salt water. As the sun rose, it had so much strength. Like the world was being reborn. For a minute, we could just imagine that we were suspended. Separated from the past and future, we were just here. In this moment.

My spirit soared in this beautiful sunrise. Cole's arms tight around me, I knew, right here, right now, my life would no longer be defined by that one sordid night — the night they came for Til.

The dawning sun shimmered around us; it was finally the next morning, full of hope and promise.

The End

Don't miss out on book three of this series: Taking Til. Find out what Til does when Shannon shows up in England with Cole...

Book One in this series: Hope in Oakland is Priscilla's story.

The Lemon Sugar series is a work in progress, follow me on facebook to stay up to date. First book should be released in the fall of 2020.

Thank you for reading my books.

About The Author

Rebekah Lee Jenkins

After working twenty five years as a hairstylist, Rebekah wanted a new challenge. Writing women's historical fiction was a natural progression after working so closely with women for so many years. Rebekah writes about true Manitoba and Canadian events from the turn of the century. Rebekah published The Night They Came For Til in 2017, Hope in Oakland in 2018, and Taking Til in 2019. In the Company of Men of the Lemon Sugar series is due to be released in the fall of 2020.

You are welcome to read more of her work and contact her on her website: https://rebekahleejenkins.wordpress.com or follow her at RebekahLeeJenkinsAuthor on facebook.

Made in the USA
Middletown, DE
20 July 2020